ZHASOU PURE

ZHASOU PURE

Stephen Geez

Fresh Ink Group
Roanoke

ZHASOU PURE

Fresh Ink Group
An Imprint of:
The Fresh Ink Group, LLC
PO Box 525
Roanoke, TX 76262
Email: info@FreshInkGroup.com
www.FreshInkGroup.com

Version 1.0	1995
Version 2.0	2011
Version 2.1	2016

Book design by Ann E. Stewart

Cover design by Stephen Geez

Cover art by Anik

Cataloging-in-Publication Recommendations: Science Fiction; Otherworld (Sci-Fi); Aliens (Sci-Fi); Racial Prejudice (Sci-Fi); Future Fiction (Sci-Fi); Business Fiction (Sci-Fi); Political Fiction (Sci-Fi); Romance (Sci-Fi); Childhood (Sci-Fi); Life Values (Sci-Fi); Grief (Sci-Fi)

Library of Congress Control Number: 2011927461

ISBN-13: 978-1-936442-04-1

For Kent D. Casey,
and friendship,
even when worlds apart

Acknowledgements

Thanks to the following other-worldly citizens:

Team Leader: Ann E. Stewart, Managing Director,
The Fresh Ink Group, LLC

Production Team: Tom Stockbridge, Anik, Patsy LaFave

Content Team: Lucas Cale, Beem Weeks, Mark Allen North,
Steve Morse

Support Team: Kent D. Casey, Todd Tessin,
Marshall Shearer MD, Mary Watson, Susan
Stewart, Jean Buchanan, Lendia Buchanan,
Vicky Riner, Dillard Greenwell

Member Team: All of *you* who subscribe to the newsletter up-
dates, free stories, and more at
www.FreshInkGroup.com . It keeps us going
when you buy our books and spread the good
word.

CHAPTER 1

What's the best way to kill my own children?

Sullrob was having trouble sleeping again. This whole business about terminating his kids was starting to keep him awake nights. It wasn't so much whether or not to kill them, but what would be the *best* way to do it that troubled him. It's not like he *wanted* to put them to death, but . . . well, sometimes a Seeliot must do what he must do.

Sullrob kicked the coarse sheet off and lay there bathed in the pink light of twin moons shining through open windows. The faint purple hue of his mottled skin looked even patchier than normal in the crater-splayed light. The highlights in his silky, blond hair shone brightly in the small dressing mirror. It was another one of those hot, humid spells so common in this region of Seelius, another lonely night without the wife he lost to the plague not two turns before. His job, his meager savings, this austere home on the outskirts of Tessila, a recent-model groundcar, and, of course, his two children were all he had left.

He swung his legs over and sat on the side of the bed for a few minutes, his face buried in his hands. He missed Sullruff. Some nights, even after all these years, just picturing her face was almost all he could stand. Deciding he was thirsty, he shook off the flood of memories and padded quietly to the food-storage area at the end of the living room, then poured a drink of cool water. This area, a modest bathroom with automatic flushing features—a modern addition not yet very common on Seelius—and three bedrooms made up the entire house.

He carefully removed a carved, wooden box from the larder and opened it, releasing the fragrance of the piquant Zhasou seasoning, a common food and drink spice also used as the focus of the Seelius Celebration of Life. Following the old tradition, he took the tiniest pinch between his thumb and middle finger and sprinkled a few grains into his mug. He whispered the first level of Celebration, took a sip, then repeated the process for each of the other five levels. He finished the drink and, using the remainder of the pinch, touched his left shoulder, then his right, then his forehead. Finally, he blew the last grains toward the bedrooms of his sleeping children.

He refilled the mug with clear water, then carried it over to the low table that held his dead wife's family's Chronicle of Celebration, a record of the ancient rituals, the teachings, and her family history for more than a score of generations. Sulruff's kin had followed the old ways, keeping the record for each new generation, starting a new book for each child at his birth, a personal log into which he or she would copy the stories of their ancestors—and learn and discuss them—before reaching the age of ascension. He thought again how his wife had been such an unusual mix of tradition and irreverence. She was first to suggest giving their children their own names rather than derivations of the family prefix, yet she scrupulously had each of them go through all of the ceremonies of the Celebration as they reached the proper ages. On Seelius, people tended either to embrace the old ways or eschew them entirely—Sullruff had somehow managed to do both.

He sipped his mug and opened the book to the first page, whispering the first five levels, pausing at *Memory*. He turned to the back of the book where the life histories of Sullruff's parents had been dutifully recorded, up to and including their deaths. It sometimes bothered him that neither of his children had updated their own Chronicles of Celebration with the facts of their mother's death. He decided, as he had so many times before, that they probably would when they were ready, in their own time, on their own terms. Sullruff sometimes got a little frustrated that her youngsters didn't take the Chronicles just a bit more seriously, but she understood the distractions of youth and was too busy loving them and worrying over them to fret about little things.

How can I kill my own kids?

He closed the book and took another sip from his mug. He noticed through the window that there was a light burning across the field in the house of Pirlhoff, a beautiful young Seeliot woman who had moved back to care for her aging grandfather after her parents and brother succumbed to the plague. She was up at night more and more often tending to her elder; there would be a funeral soon and then young Pirlhoff would be without any family.

He sat the mug down and eased quietly to his little girl's room, peeking in. Yantanna looked so small and peaceful, cuddled up with the little fuzzy weenshugger that hummed quietly in its sleep. The little girl had just celebrated her fifth birthday the week before—she was slightly older than seven Consortium years based on the original Earth calendar—and had received the little purple humming furball for her present. It had set Sullrob back half a tenth-turn's pay, but the little girl's delight, the sparkle in her beautiful eyes, the dimpled smile on her beatific face, and their inseparability ever since had made it worthwhile.

Do I kill the weenshugger, too?

Since Seeliots' modesty is focused more on their ideas than their bodies, there was no door to close as he left his little girl to her dreams. Next he paused outside his son's room and peeked in. Stava's had been a difficult birth for Sullruff, but they had been rewarded with the most beautiful baby any proud parents could ever want. Now at eight turns old—almost twelve Consortium years—he was, in Sullrob's opinion, the most handsome boy in all of Tessila. He had passed the one-meter mark the year before, proving he would be a tall, slender Seeliot someday. He had the faintest purple tint to his skin, blond-white hair, and sparkling violet eyes—not to mention that adorable face that, with the right smile and affectation, could disarm all women and most girls, plus soften the ire of even the sternest man. Sullrob secretly suspected that Stava practiced that look of innocence in front of the recently installed bathroom mirror; he was convinced he'd been teaching Yantanna his little tricks, too.

It had been a hard couple of turns since they lost Sullruff—since the plague had taken so many of their friends and neighbors all in less than a half-turn. Already a close family, the three had pulled together, supporting each other, making sure whomever was having a bad day knew he was not alone. The sadness and emptiness that comes from loving someone who is no longer there had been eclipsed by fear of the plague until they were finally reassured that, with the Consortium's new medicine, disease could never again steal in from the night and take away people they loved. Sure, his new job piloting for the Consortium had finally given the family economic security, but a growing fear of the fundamentalist government was beginning to scare them nearly as much. At least for Sullruff, they had the fifth level of Celebration.

Stava breathed softly in the moonlight, curled up under his coarse sheet, his new adolescent-style haircut pointing every direction but where it should. Sullrob knew it would probably be sometime during the next turn that his only son would be old enough to begin ascension, the physical changes that would make him a young man with all the privileges and responsibilities. That's *if* he lived that long.

It would be only a matter of time until Sullrob would be forced to kill his children. He knew that; he had known it for a while. It would be better to do it on his own terms, to be prepared, to make the right decisions in advance—before they were made *for* him. Tears started to form in his eyes; one trickled down his mottled cheek. He wiped his face with a speckled hand.

Finally, with one last peek at each of his children—the most beautiful little girl and the handsomest boy in all of Tessila—he stole quietly back to his own cot and buried his face in his pillow, trying not to feel so scared. It would be another night of fitful sleep, his troubled thoughts weighing heavily on his soul. There were so many important decisions to make, and he didn't know how much time he would have to make them.

What's the best way to kill my own children?

*   *   *

Brog Pawligan passed up the second round of ales. That was Brog, all right, the orbiter's consummate single dad. One quickie with the fellers at the end of a shift, then off to check on his kids—even though they'd probably be asleep by the time he got back to quarters.

"He oughta pack them brats off to somewhere ground-side and let 'em a-live with relatives," one loader commented after Brog had said his good-byes. "Ain't adoin' 'em no good adraggin' 'em from one orbiter to the next—and it's akeepin' him from a-livin' his *own* life, too."

"I seen 'im apass up many chances t'climb up in some woman so's he could arush home to them kids. I botzed him once fer asnubbin' a sister I set 'im up with an' he ajus' tol' me she'da made a lousy wife and a worse mother."

Several other loaders and a pilot in the group laughed. Ain't no kinda man worries about kids so much he passes up a chance to climb up a good woman.

"He's aslowin' down, though," the first one observed. "He used t'slide out ever' few months, a-chasin' more and bigger money jobs, but I seen 'im apass up three or four in the year he's been here. These Caskentia runs don't apay half o' what he could amake if he'd ajump out to one o' them new ore gigs—he's agot the seniority t'get way up the list."

"I think he's ajus' tired o' jerkin' them kids along ever'where they's a new gig."

"Mus' be. Ain't the money akeepin' 'im 'ere."

They ordered another round of ales and focused their attentions on a group of women loaders sauntering in after a late shift. Brog Pawligan watched and listened from the back of the canteen, satisfied that the conversation—the speculation—hadn't dwelled too long on him after his departure. He stole quietly out and took a tube to one of the inner habitat levels, his daily four-minute commute toward his home and family.

During the ride, he thought about the conversation he'd overheard. Actually, he *was* tired of jerking his kids from one orbiter station to the next. Yes, looking out for his family *was* a higher priority than climbing up the nearest pretty thing. Actually, though they wouldn't suspect, it *was* the money keeping him at Seelius Orbiter-two for so long. Oh, he tried to convince himself sometimes that he was just doing the right and noble thing, helping those who needed his help, but if push came to shove, his family counted most. His little plan would help him retire to a nice comfortable ground-side home where his teenage daughter, Selta, and his son, little ten-year-old Jowda, could make friends and *keep* them, could plant flowers or catch critters, could carve their names in some tree that would be there for them to show their own kids someday. But if he thought for even a minute that his plan was putting them at risk . . . well, that wouldn't be worth it. But in the meantime, as long as everything continued to run smoothly, then it was a fine plan indeed.

He exited the tube and walked the curved, steel corridor until he was outside his own unit. He paused for a moment, greeting several neighbors who wandered by, wondering if Selta would be up this late—again. He didn't like it when she waited up, but he never had the heart to get mad at her for it. Little Jowda had been trying to do the same more and more often, but the boy never quite lasted long enough.

Brog ran his fingers through his curly, brown hair and rested his brawny, two-meter-plus frame against the wall, deciding yet again that he needed more exercise than his pilot's job usually allowed. He touched the plate that caused the rectangular, blue door to slide aside. He stepped into the privacy foyer and waited for the outer door to close before the inner door opened into the living area.

"Hi, Daddy!" Selta greeted him—quietly so as not to wake Jowda sprawled on the couch beside her.

Every time he saw her, she looked more the pretty young woman her mother had been. He noticed that, this night, her dark-brown hair was delicately waved. Her deep-hazel eyes with little swirls of gold reflected the flickering image from the vid-screen. Wearing a ruffled, faint-orange nightgown, she was curled up watching silly shows, gently stroking the sandy-brown hair of her sleeping little brother. Brog kissed her lightly on the head and gave her the look, the one that says she really ought to be in bed by now.

"I wasn't up awaiting for you, Daddy. Jowda was, though. He awanted to acomplain again about the bullies in the school 'dule. They keep apicking on him for not agetting his face marked like all the boys is adoin'."

Brog shook his head. They'd been through this many times before. It would take months for those silly tattoos to wear off completely—and sometimes they left scars. Jowda always tried so hard to fit in, to be like the other boys—whichever boys were around each new place the family moved. Brog hoped maybe a good, permanent home ground-side would help his son develop more of his own identity and not look so hard to others for acceptance. He gathered all twenty-six kilos of the boy in his arms and carried him into his bedroom, then tucked him in.

"G'night, Dad," Jowda whispered before curling up and snoozing.

"G'night, son." He kissed him on the cheek, dimmed the lights, and pressed the door-plate on his way out.

"I know, Daddy, I'm agoing!" Selta called from the kitchenette, putting away the snacks Jowda had dragged out earlier. She kissed Brog on the cheek, admonished him for trying to tuck her in, then disappeared into her room. Brog selected an ale from the refrigerator and took it to the couch. He kicked his boots into the corner and sat back, lost in thought.

No, he wasn't putting his kids at risk. Yes, he was doing the right thing. A new home and a new life would be the reward. Maybe Selta could meet a higher class of boy for a change—and Jowda wouldn't have to pal around with those figure-faces in the 'dule. And maybe Brog could be home more—spend more time with those kids.

He'd do *anything* for his kids.

*   *   *

"In the matter of the family of Smidkar," the orator announced.

A hush fell over the chamber. More than sixty lookers-on had crowded into the sparse, concrete and wood room to watch the proceedings. Manacled in a long box behind a rail off to the side waited the extended family of the young carpenter from the outskirts of Tessila.

Smidkar fidgeted nervously in the corner seat. Next to him sat his oldest boy, a tow-headed lad with light-purple skin, not much older than four turns—or about six Consortium years. Next to him sat the junior boy, a full turn younger than his older brother. Next was their mother, Smidloof, a rather plain woman whose light-purple skin was streaked with brown. She ran her fingers nervously through her near-white hair. The next two places on the bench were occupied by Smidkar's brothers, one a farmer, the other a loader. Thereafter followed his father and two uncles, the latter seated by age.

In Seeliot society, carrying out civic responsibilities fell first upon the man. In his absence—or unwillingness—it fell to his brothers, his sons if they had reached ascension, then his father, his uncles, cousins . . . however deeply into the lineage it was necessary to delve.

"What must we know?" asked the elder of the panel of three.

"In previous action," explained the orator, sing-songing from the booklet spread on the ancient, wooden table in front of him, "the family of Smidkar was found to be genetically contaminated!" There was a gasp from the audience even though this was not new information. "Smidkar himself was tested and found to be pure, but his wife, Smidloof, was found to carry the genes of invaders and determined to be a threat to our peoples and our culture. It was ordered that she be purged on this date." A murmur spread through the room.

"Quiet!" ordered the elder, casting a stern glare across the audience.

"It was further determined," the orator continued, "that the children of Smidkar—Smidrob and Smidlok—met the conditions of 'reason to suspect' and therefore were ordered to be tested for genetic contamination. The results are ready for consideration by the Panel of Extirpation."

A hush fell over the room. Smidkar tugged at the manacles on his wrists and ankles, his head darting wildly from side to side. His wife sat stoically, tears creeping down her cheeks. The boys were scared and confused, watching the proceedings with big, violet eyes, occasionally squirming and tugging at their own tiny manacles.

"So the results shall be read; so they shall be true," the elder sing-songed.

"In the matter of the genetic purity of Smidlok, the youngest child of Smidkar, he has been found to be a true and pure heir of Seelius."

"Quiet!" the elder ordered, hushing the sudden buzz and chatter from the crowd. Smidloof started to sob audibly. Smidkar stared straight ahead. Maybe, at least, his children would be spared.

"In the matter of the genetic purity of Smidrob, the eldest child of Smidkar, he has been found to possess the same genetic contamination as his mother, Smidloof."

The audience roared, many jumping to their feet.

"Purge the impure!"

"Seelius for true Seeliots!"

"Protect us from contamination!"

"But he's just a child—"

The one or two voices of compassion were shouted down by those driven by hatred and fear. Though many other-worlders believed that Seelius' peoples traced their ancestry to early human colonization, most Seeliots were convinced theirs was a pure and superior race. They resented being woefully contaminated by cross-breeding with human traders who, only a few centuries before, had rediscovered the planet nestled among a cluster of small suns along a rarely traveled belt beyond the early trading routes.

What started as a purge of bastard babies thrown into the fires had, through the last several hundred turns, evolved into a near-religious quest to re-establish racial purity, a mission further exacerbated by the recent acquisition of technologies for testing genetic material. The most recent swing toward a more fundamentalist society was caused by the ascension of the new governor, next in line as heir to the post in the rigid patriarchy established during the trader purge centuries before. His cabinet ruled from a platform of religious fear, focusing its efforts on saving Seelius for Seeliots.

Despite such fierce protectiveness of the planet's culture and fear of contamination from human ideas and lifestyles, the recent plague had forced the governor into a tentative alliance with a trading company member of the Consortium. Ancient medicines, crystals grown from the sap of the Seelius Jurnama plant, were highly valued by humans on other worlds. Several turns were required to grow the complex crystalline structures that could both prevent and cure disease—but it broke down if not ingested soon after fully forming. A Consortium pharmaceutical cooperative could grow the same structures in just a matter of weeks, using plants harvested from Seelius, by processing them in the vacuum of space. When the Seelius plague suddenly increased the planet's need for medicine, a deal allowed Jurnama shipments to go out in exchange for an adequate supply of the crystals.

Only four Seeliots trained to pilot the transports that lifted the harvested plants to the Orbiter-two so they could be transferred to human cargo ships. No humans were allowed to travel to Seelius; the Seeliot pilots were carefully warned not to allow any human culture to be brought back and influence the local citizens. This regular—though guarded—contact with outsiders had increased the paranoia about cultural contamination and was often used as justification for the severe methods of spying on citizens and, eventually, testing them genetically and purging those not perceived as *true* Seeliots.

All of the economics, politics, and religion that worked together to make people feel justified in the kind of proceedings happening to Smidkar's family proved too complicated for young Smidrob to understand. This hostile crowd of people, local merchants and neighbors, were spewing hatred toward him. Suddenly very afraid, he started to cry, squirming and straining against his manacles.

"Quiet!" the elder ordered. As the noise faded and Seeliots returned to their seats, he continued, "Smidkar of Tessila, you have been ordered to purge your wife, the impure Smidloof, for the benefit of all Seelius. You are herewith ordered to purge your son, the impure Smidrob, for the benefit of all Seelius. Have you chosen a method?"

Smidkar sat rigid, staring blankly at his lap. There was an uncomfortable pause, the audience awaiting his response.

Finally, the elder shook his head sadly and intoned, "Smidkar has failed to take responsibility for his community and to Seelius. He is no longer worthy to walk among us. It falls to his brother, or each successive male relative, to fulfill his obligations to us all. Smidfalk of Tessila, do you accept your responsibility?"

The oldest brother sat there in a daze, but he slowly nodded assent. A man sitting at a low table beside the massive desk where the elders loomed slowly opened a carved, wooden box. He removed a tray covered with thorns.

"The right of decision has been waived by Smidkar," the elder continued. "It is ordered that the cleansing occur immediately, and that it be through the administration of Dosir thorns."

Two uniformed men unlocked the manacles on the oldest brother, watching him carefully as he stepped behind the benches where his relatives sat. The man with the tray walked over and let himself into the box, standing adjacent to Smidkar. The older brother stood behind Smidkar and, taking a thorn from the tray, paused to control his trembling. Suddenly, he plunged the thorn into the condemned man's neck. Smidloof and the boys watched in horror as Smidkar convulsed several times, then stiffened before collapsing and gasping out his last breath.

The audience remained quiet; the two boys cried. The older brother stepped behind Smidloof and, taking another thorn from the tray, quickly plunged it into her neck. It took her longer to die—her convulsions were more violent, her gasping fading more slowly. Finally, her life was over. The boys wailed in fear at the sight of their dead mother slumped over beside them.

Taking another thorn from the tray, the oldest stepped behind Smidrob. The boy started screaming, jerking at his manacles, sobbing uncontrollably.

"Please, little one," the uncle whispered in his ear. "It will be easier if you hold still." Suddenly, he plunged the thorn into the little boy's neck. The youngster convulsed only once, gasped for a few seconds, then slumped forward into a position identical to his dead mother's.

"Your family has done what is best for Seelius," the elder intoned. "You have earned the respect and sympathy of us all. You are released; these proceedings are adjourned." The three elders rose and shuffled through a door in the back of the room. The two officers unlocked the manacles on the rest of Smidkar's male relatives. The last to be freed was little Smidlok. Several older Smid women rushed over and scooped him up, cradling him in their arms.

"All is okay, little one. You will be happy with us."

The Smid men started considering how, among themselves, they could carry three dead relatives all the way back across the village for burial. The Smid women hurried the child out of the crowded room, trying to stay ahead of the mob. They tried not to look back at Smidkar, Smidloof, and little Smidrob, glass-eyed and stiff there in the box, their chains holding them upright. Tiny Smidlok, still sobbing, tried desperately to reach out to his mother, his father, his big brother. Everybody seemed to understand what had happened but him.

"Mommy!" he screamed as he was carried into the blinding glare of Seelius day.

CHAPTER 2

"Hey, Pawli-gunner!" one boy shouted. "What's *that* thing for?"

"What are those?" another asked, wide-eyed.

Three boys about Jowda's age gathered behind the rail in the load-zone of one of the launch bays. They were ostensibly there to see off their friend as he left for three days' vacation on Caskentia, but their real motive was to discern if Jowda had been lying about *really* going ground-side and *really* going someplace where he could play in a *real* lake with a beach and a *real* waterfall.

Jowda made it a point to show off his new life-jacket and pair of water-skis his father had just bought from a trader merchant. He carried his sister's life-jacket, too, an uncharacteristic act of chivalry that freed up more space in her clothing bag and gave the little brother more water-gear to show off in front of however many friends came under this pretense to bid farewell.

"These are *life*-jackets so we adon't adrown in the *really* deep deep water," Jowda shouted back, trying to sound casual about the whole thing. "These is water skis for azoomin' across the surface behind a boat or aridin' over the waterfalls."

Brog stood nearby, filling out his pilot's manifest, overhearing the conversation but knowing better than to correct Jowda's exaggeration about skiing over waterfalls while his son's friends were hanging around trying not to act too envious.

"Jowda!" Brog called.

The boy winced inwardly. *Please adon't embarrass me. Please adon't embarrass me.*

"Did you bring gloves for tree-climbing?"

"Sure did, Dad!" the boy beamed, patting his bag in confirmation.

Brog had overheard him bragging earlier about planning to climb the highest tree on Caskentia; he knew his son would appreciate some peer-audible corroboration. Truth be told, Brog never *intentionally* embarrassed Jowda in front of his friends. The occasional accidental gaffe was enough, though, to traumatize even the most socially secure orbiter-brat—especially one only ten years old. Brog wasn't sure which was better, his son's oversensitivity to peer approval or his daughter's shyness, her avoidance of all but one girl close to her age, her preference to have her only friend visit quarters rather than hang out where the other teens gathered.

"Personal effects," Brog wrote for the last four cases. Both of his children had already been counseled not to show curiosity or undue concern about them. They knew Dad had some business to transact during this recreational respite, but they weren't sure of its nature—nor did they care. Selta worried about how she would look in her new swimsuit. Jowda looked forward to scoping out new friends, understanding that all newcomers to a strange land are every bit as cool as their bluster until the natives eventually cut them down to size.

It was a smooth, uneventful flight of just over two hours, plus another hour spent landing and docking, clearing basic spaceport requirements, and storing the shuttle Brog had signed out—a perquisite of flying for Tradeworlds Transport.

The trio took a rented aircar for a thirty-minute flight way out past the outskirts of the suburbs, past the edge of the control grid so that Brog had to take over the manual controls and finish the trip to the private resort out in one of the hundred-lakes regions.

It offered a spectacular setting—low hills rolling among connected or independent spring-fed lakes, a few rocky ridges and overlooks, scenic trails, sparse development for recreation, and lush vegetation streaked with the Caskentia-characteristic swatches of blue and pink sand. One of the more popular resorts featured giant dunes of the fabled sand, surrounding and overlooking crystal-clear lakes, all walking distance from hundreds of spectacular waterfalls stair-stepping the streams that wove down from the red mountains along the eastern ridge. For a planet with a population of only several-hundred thousand permanent inhabitants, vast tracts of beautiful terrain waited to be explored.

Both children had their faces pressed against the windows. Forgotten were all their social cares; this was just too phenomenal to comprehend. They had been down ground-side on a half-dozen planets with their father before, but this vision proved unparalleled. Jowda snapped several dimension-stills for showing off to his friends back on the orbiter.

Brog wished he could afford to bring his kids to places like this every week. Luckily, the tab for this vacation was being picked up by the man he came here to meet.

Now, if all goes well . . .

*   *   *

A few dozen Seeliots from the village of Tessila waited in the meeting hall. It was not a regularly scheduled Celebration of Life; oftentimes individuals or small groups came together for informal Celebrations of their own. The group, including Sullrob and his children, was made up of neighbors and a few nearby farmers, people whose long days working under the sun or unusual schedules as loaders or, in Sullrob's case, as a pilot prevented them from attending most of the regular events. All had found they shared some common opinions, though not usually expressed to outsiders, and they had started to formulate some common goals.

This particular evening, the group was missing four of its regulars: Smidkar and his family.

Sullrob, Stava, and little Yantanna stood around awkwardly for a few minutes. Usually, this time would have been spent laughing and sharing stories, touching each other's foreheads and shoulders, and passing along tidbits of news to neighbors and friends. The mood this time was somber and subdued. Several people stood by, staring blankly, shock and outrage carved into their features.

That was how Stava looked last night . . .

It had been a rough night trying to explain Smidkar's death—and the deaths of Smidloof and little Smidrob—to his children. It took a while for Yantanna to understand that her little schoolmate, playmate, and friend—as well as his parents—were gone forever, just like the mother she could barely remember, to become part of the Celebration of Life. Once she seemed to understand, she was inconsolable, spending most of the evening alternating between fear and grief, sobbing for long periods until she eventually cried out.

Stava had stared blankly, much like some of these people in the meeting hall. Both mad and frustrated, he had betrayed his true feelings only twice. First, after being told what happened, he quietly intoned, "But there was *nothing* wrong with them." Later, after Sullrob had prodded him numerous times to talk out his feelings, with anger tinged in his voice, he simply said, "It is *wrong*—and no Celebration can *ever* make it right."

Sullrob agreed. So did all of the people awkwardly standing around, waiting for somebody to take the initiative and begin the Celebration. Finally, he decided it would be his turn to take the lead. He stepped to the front and removed a ceremonial carved box from a cabinet, placing it on a table purposefully made low enough for children to reach. He opened it to reveal a large cache of the plentiful Zhasou seasoning that was both a staple in Seeliot diets and the focus of their Celebrations.

Taking his little sister by the hand, Stava led her to the box and waited while she took a pinch between thumb and middle finger. Then he took his own pinch and stepped back to allow the others to come forward for their own. While this was going on, one of the adolescent girls stooped in the corner filling mugs from the well-water bucket. Each person took one of the mugs in his free hand, then found a place in the room to sit or stand, waiting patiently for the Celebration to begin. As the person to open the Zhasou, Sullrob automatically expected to lead this evening.

"With Zhasou, we Celebrate all *life*, from the biggest creatures in the forests, to *life* so small we cannot see. Plants and animals and people—" He paused and added a line he and many of the others had inserted only recently. "*All* people, including Seeliots and humans and Tijartians and others we do not know. We Celebrate *life*."

With that, everybody sprinkled a few grains into their mugs and took a drink.

"We Celebrate *family*, our husbands and wives, our sons and daughters, our mothers and fathers, and all *family* close and far, wherever they live, whoever they are. We Celebrate our *families* and our love for them. We Celebrate that our *families* love us."

Everybody repeated the process of adding some grains and taking a sip. Depending on how the spice was refined, it could be sweet or tart, strong or mild. This particular blend proved faintly sweet with a tangy flavor, just the way children liked to mix in their drinks. People set down their mugs and hugged all of the members of their families who were present.

"We Celebrate our *friends*. We Celebrate the *friends* who can be here with us tonight; we Celebrate those who cannot. We Celebrate *friend*ship near and *friend*ship far. We are blessed to have *friends* and for this we Celebrate."

Again the sprinkling and sip; then people started moving around the room to touch the shoulders and foreheads of their friends. The mood of the group finally started to lighten just slightly, but not very much.

"We Celebrate *community*. We honor the *community* where we live and work; we Celebrate our fellow citizens. For without them, we would have no *community*. We are lucky to have each other and this fine place for our families to live, and for this we Celebrate."

The wording was a bit different during every Celebration—especially depending on who did the recitation. Precision did not matter; only the intent. After another round of sprinkles and sips, the room grew very quiet. Some people looked down. One woman wiped her face, tears starting to form in her eyes.

More quietly than before, Sullrob continued, "We Celebrate *memory*. We Celebrate the people we have lost. They touched our lives and will forever be a part of us, a part of our *memories*, and we are better for them." He paused for a moment, then finished, "I Celebrate the *memory* of my wife, Sullruff. I Celebrate the *memory* of my brother, Sullkar. I Celebrate the *memory* of my mother, Sullnona. I Celebrate the *memory* of my father, Sullnorm." He sprinkled some grains and took a long drink.

Stava cleared his throat and announced, "I Celebrate the *memory* of my mother, Sullhoff. I Celebrate the *memory* of my uncle, Sullkar." He sprinkled some grains, took a short drink and, whispering, coached his little sister.

"I Cel'brate Mommy," she offered shyly, sprinkling and drinking.

The ritual of honoring lost people moved around the room until everyone had recalled the ones they loved. Everybody there knew all the others' names; they had heard them so many times before. These Celebrations had sparked many conversations afterward or at other times when somebody asked about a person who had been Celebrated. It was, Sullrob decided, a wonderful way to honor people, to remember them, to share memories, to keep their loved ones a part of their everyday lives.

Once all the memories were shared, the group fell quiet again. Sullrob continued, "We Celebrate our*selves*."

In unison, the group recited, "I Celebrate my*self*."

"Of the *self*, we Celebrate *preservation*," Sullrob continued.

"*Preservation*," everybody recited, touching their left shoulders with the pinch of spice.

"We Celebrate *obligation*."

"*Obligation*," they repeated, touching their right shoulders.

"We Celebrate *integrity*."

"*Integrity*," they agreed, all touching their foreheads.

Then all together, the entire group repeated, "We Celebrate our*selves*."

The group fell quiet. Normally, this would be a time to finish the spice and water, then break up and laugh and share stories and circulate, for the children to run off and play, for snacks to be produced and passed around, for the older folks to settle into comfortable chairs, for the adolescents to pair off and sneak away to quiet corners under the watchful but not too-intrusive eyes of the adults. But tonight was different. Everybody looked expectantly toward Sullrob.

Clearing his throat, he continued, "We Celebrate the *family* of Smidkar. We Celebrate his *life* and the lives of Smidloof and Smidrob. We Celebrate little Smidlok who has been taken to another village to live with relatives. We have lost good friends and neighbors." Everybody waited. Careful not to say anything that would cause "reason to suspect," he finished, "We Celebrate Smidkar and his *family* and commit them to our *memories*."

He sprinkled the rest of his spice and finished the drink in one draft. Everybody in the room followed suit.

Knowing it was time for some serious discussion, the adults all glanced around to make sure no interlopers had wandered in, then sent the youngsters off to play outside with stern warnings not to interrupt the grown-ups while they talked. Stava, already understanding what was about to happen, led his little sister toward the door. Sullrob heard her ask her big brother, "Is my friend Smidrob part of my *memory* now?"

"Yes, Yantanna. Celebrate him always."

Once the youngsters were gone and the big doors closed, the small group gathered around Sullrob, everybody brimming with questions.

"Has he learned anything yet?"

"What if somebody finds out?"

"Are you *sure* we can trust this Pawligan?"

Sullrob quieted everybody down. "Everything went just fine. He took it to Caskentia with him today—he took a short vacation with his family there. All we can do is wait and see the response."

"What if we can't trust him?"

"What if we can't trust each other?" Sullrob lobbed back. "Look," he said more quietly, "I trust Brog Pawligan. He's a family man and he understands what we need. He has *integrity*. If this works out, it will benefit *his* family as much or more as all of ours. As far as somebody finding out, we all understood that if word gets out, it could mean 'reason to suspect'—or worse." He looked around from face to face. "We all know that for most, if not all of us, that could be *very* bad. As long as we keep this just among ourselves, we know we can trust each other."

The group murmured, several faces still showing some apprehension, but all looked reasonably satisfied.

"We will wait for Brog Pawligan," one man announced.

"Yes, we will trust each other and we will wait," Pirlhoff agreed, adjusting the coarse blanket over her wheelchair-bound grandfather.

"Even if he fails," Sullrob concluded, "we will Celebrate Brog Pawligan for trying to help us and because he is a good man—because he is my *friend*."

The Zhasou was put away and the group wandered out to join their children in play, hope in their eyes, determination on their faces.

*   *   *

Brog Pawligan hadn't realized how expensive it would be for him to rent an auto-boat for pulling young Jowda around on his water skis. It was worth it, though. The boy had already forgotten his disappointment over discovering he couldn't ski a waterfall, concentrating instead on just getting better at staying *up* on the smooth flat surface reflecting colored sand and upside-down red mountains. Every time the boy went down amid a frenzy of giggly splashes, the miniature auto-boat circled around to stop beside him and patiently await instructions.

Brog noticed that Selta had tired of swimming and was working her way around the shore, exploring, watching for strange little creatures and pretty fish, pausing here and there to kick up splashes of cool, clear water as if to reassure herself that it was all real—that places like this exist and she really was here enjoying this one.

He checked his watch and decided getting ready early wouldn't be such a bad idea. Climbing out of his beach lounger, he noticed the jiggle of his slight paunch and decided he definitely needed to start exercising more. Countless hours reclined in his air-cushioned pilot's seat weren't doing much for a physique, now in its mid-thirties, that had been dozens of kilos trimmer in its youth. Using his thumbnail, he picked open a small patch on his upper chest, then clumsily peeled off his sunscreen. He repeated the process for his hairy, white legs, then crumpled the film until it was no bigger than a pea, dropping it in his pocket. He waved to his daughter, pointed at the small largely unoccupied chalet where they shared a suite, and gestured toward Jowda trying to one-ski without catching a snootful of water. She waved back and gave him the okay sign; she was now charged with the unenviable responsibility of keeping the little brat unbruised and unbroken for just a few hours more.

Back inside the suite, Brog took a fast shower—he still couldn't get used to the idea of virtually unlimited, unrecycled water—and dressed in a casual jumpsuit, combing his thick, curly-brown hair into a side-part. He leaned close to the mirror and confirmed several new white streaks just over his ears. He walked out on the veranda and relaxed while he waited, noticing that Jowda had tired of skiing and convinced his big sister to climb with him up to one of the waterfalls. They sure were having fun. What a wonderful, beautiful place. If only he had some way to make a living in such a deserted location . . .

"Mr. Pawligan?" An older man, tall and lanky, dressed in a conservative pull-down streaked with shades of dark blue, walked out onto the veranda.

"Yes!" He stood and greeted the man, shaking his hand.

"I'm Pfivvel—Dow Pfivvel. I believe you were expecting me—?"

"Yes! Good to meet you, Mr. Pfivvel."

"Please, call me Dow."

"And me, Brog," Pawligan insisted.

He led his guest inside to the suite, poured some drinks and offered seats on low couches in the overlook room.

"I would like to offer you some snacks—but not until we start our discussion," Brog explained.

The man smiled and nodded, then took a sip from his glass and, surprised, looked questioningly to Brog. "Water?"

"Ah yes, forgive me. It needs something, doesn't it?" Brog opened a small thimble box on the beverage table and, using a miniature spoon, carefully scooped a few grains of sparkling purple spice into each of their glasses.

Pfivvel watched in fascination as each of the grains started to sink, leaving brilliant purple and blue and pink trails that sparkled and exploded like fireworks. The show lasted for a full minute before the glass settled into a fairly consistent purple color that swirled with shades of blue whenever disturbed. Brog took a sip from his glass and, smiling, held it up as if to toast his guest.

Pfivvel sniffed his own glass and, tentatively, took a sip. He registered surprise, then pleasure. Taking another sip, he allowed a wide smile to creep into his face. "Why, this is phenomenal! I've *never* tasted anything even *remotely* like this! Is this what I'm here to see?"

"One version of it," Brog explained. "This is the *sweet* mix for candies and drinks and other treats for kids. The versions for seasoning fruits and vegetables, for enhancing the taste of protein supplements, for sniffing to enjoy the aroma and flavor all day without having to eat—these are but a few of the others I have available for you to try."

"You *definitely* have my interest, Mr.—uh, Brog," the visitor allowed, sitting back and drinking the rest of the swirling concoction, smiling again. "This is quite powerful for such a minuscule quantity, too—I love it!"

"I have more than forty kilos here—encompassing six of the more popular versions of the spice—ready for sale. I think you will understand why I went to so much effort insisting that you, personally, be the one to meet with me. See, this is exclusive. Nobody—*nobody* in the Consortium has this stuff or has access to it. I thought you might want to figure out how to package and market this—which of your companies, like the gourmet foods division, would handle it—and how much secrecy would surround it. I couldn't chance having too many people involved."

"Smart thinking. But what is it? Where's it from? How do I know I've got exclusive?"

"It is Zhasou, from the planet Seelius."

Pfivvel sat back and laced his fingers across his stomach, smiling knowingly. His grandfather had built the diversified mega-corporation by specializing in exotic, elusive, sometimes illegal foodstuffs. "And this is all there is?"

"You know, Dow, I think you could make a fortune on just this little bit—but there could be more—lots more—on a regular basis . . . for the right price and under the right terms," he added.

Over the next hour, Pfivvel was like a little kid in a candy shop, testing and tasting various concoctions, always surprised, always smiling. He finally agreed to buy most of the supply on hand, paying with fully charged cash wafers. It was an outrageously high price—enough for Brog to consider early retirement and private schools for his kids. A deal was hammered out for a *minimum* of fifty similar shipments with exclusive rights for Pfivvel's company over the course of one year.

Nothing got finalized, though, because the price Brog demanded was about double as high as Pfivvel was willing to offer. Brog pointed out that he had another appointment to go to. Both agreed to think over their price demands and meet again the next day. Pfivvel loaded his booty into a portable gyro-bag and, pumping Brog's hand vigorously, left to call an emergency meeting of his key product and marketing people. Brog wanted him to worry that being so obstinate about the price might cost him that one-year exclusive deal dangling before his eyes, tickling his palate, soothing his stomach, and arousing his pocketbook.

Brog used his watch to signal the watches of his children, alerting them to come and get ready for their trek. Once everybody scrubbed and dressed, they loaded into the aircar and sailed out toward the mountains in the distance. Eventually sighting a small building adjacent to a primitive road, they landed and greeted a real-estate agent, a young Tijartian woman who didn't look much older than Selta. She looked every bit as human as anybody else, but the thick, stiff spikes of black hair and light-gray skin common to all Tijartians gave her away.

Joining them in the aircar with her little briefcase, she directed them eastward, farther away from the city, over a series of higher and higher ridges until the area opened into a tremendous valley fully twenty kilometers long. A gentle river flowed through it, threading a series of four spectacular lakes, each narrowing to stairstep waterfalls. There were lush, green meadows, stands of sturdy forest here and there, swatches of blue and pink sand sparkling in the sunlight, and rocky overlooks along the side toward the mountains. Jowda was enthralled by one mountain stream in particular, flowing from the highest rock ridge, cascading down dozens of spectacular falls culminating in one giant forty-meter drop into a crystal-clear pool that followed its own stairsteps down to the largest lake. Noting no development, no trails, not a soul in sight, Brog realized he was holding his breath.

The aircar settled into the sand, letting Jowda burst out to head toward the nearest falls. Selta had trouble keeping up with him. Using the portable transceiver in her briefcase, the Tijartian established a link with the seller and negotiations began.

Little more than thirty minutes later, terms were settled. Brog would make a wafer-cash down-payment using his proceeds from the Zhasou sale. The purchase price, approximately twenty times the down payment, would be financed by the seller for two Consortium years using the property as collateral. The deed was executed and recorded, listing as joint owners: Brog Pawligan, Jowda Pawligan, Selta Pawligan, Sullrob of Seelius, Stava of Seelius, Yantanna of Seelius, Pirlhoff of Seelius, and approximately thirty more names.

The children were summoned and a very pleased agent was air-driven to her small, portable office in the woods. By the time the Pawligan family got back to their suite, they found Dow Pfivvel waiting with a contract. It seemed he would be willing to meet Brog's demands—for exclusivity, mind you, of *two* Consortium years. Brog signed the paper and bid his enthusiastic new customer good-day.

Ushering his kids out onto the veranda for a snack, Brog watched their fascination and surprise as they tasted Zhasou water and Zhasou cookies.

"Hey, Dad!" Jowda wondered, "Can we ago back to that valley with the big waterfall some time?"

"Yes, son, I believe we can. I just bought it."

*   *   *

Three old men stepped from their official groundcar and entered the back of the community hall. There would be no public ceremony from the Panel of Extirpation twice within the same week in Tessila. They came here to vote on pending cases. Though the proceedings would be private, they still followed the proscribed Zhasou ceremony.

"We don't get enough cooperation from the people of Tessila," one remarked, removing his jacket to put on the ceremonial frock.

"Never has one turned in another for suspicion," agreed the other.

The elder pulled absently at his nose, snorting several times before deciding, "We need to be careful here; I do not think we have full citizen support."

Once everything was prepared, they consumed some Zhasou and unsealed the communications chest just arrived from the Governor's Chair.

"It is another family to be placed under 'reason to suspect' based on the Chronicles of the Powloff Family. The contaminated lineage has been traced to a woman who once lived near here—Linruff, who married and became Sullruff. She is deceased, but her husband and two children still live."

"The Governor requests a determination of 'reason to suspect' to have the children tested?"

"Yes," the elder responded, signing the document that put the order into effect.

"Why don't we delay it another tenth-turn?" asked one. "There is much unrest here already; another ceremony this soon might inflame passions."

"There is already much talk about the misfortune of that young Smid child," the other concurred. "Smidlok, I think was his name."

"We shall delay one tenth-turn," the elder decreed. Then, adding as an afterthought, "Survivor siblings risk carrying contaminating resentment into another generation, so I think we should declare both Sull children contaminated—even if only one is found to be impure."

CHAPTER 3

Young Jowda enjoyed the envy of the orbiter brats once word spread that his father had bought a family vacation package at the resort where he'd learned to water-ski. That meant a year's worth of weekends overlooking the clear water and blue and pink sands. Maybe, every now and then when Dad wasn't going to be too busy, a friend might come along.

Four times during the next week, two loaders—both stout men from the village of Tessila—casually loaded disguised boxes of Zhasou when the transport ship piloted by Sullrob prepared for a run to Seelius Orbiter-two. Each time, during the flight, Sullrob transferred the containers to collapsible travel luggage. Upon arriving at the docking bay, he'd wait patiently for the loaders to empty the cargo, then carry his bags into the terminal like any other vacationer. Allowed several hours between flights to relax, freshen up, or nap, he was careful never to be gone unnecessarily long. He would meet Brog Pawligan for a drink or snack in any one of the pre-selected shops in the outer levels, then would take a small bag containing empty collapsibles when he departed, leaving the spice-filled bags for Pawligan to carry back to his quarters.

The next vacation to Caskentia, complete with loads of luggage and gear and provisions, put the group's finances four times ahead of the payment schedule. The children played in the lake or the woods or on the beach or near the waterfalls, getting to know several other youngsters whose families had bought similar packages, stretching their ground-side dispositions in a world they decided they could get used to *very* quickly indeed.

Brog took several trips out to the valley with contractors until he was satisfied with a design and bid for building a small, expandable habitat with power center, water treatment, and septic system. Paying with fully charged credit wafers in advance lubricated the process of getting a good deal. Owing to an abundance of materials, modern construction methods, and a buyers' market, the work would take only a few weeks to be completed.

Brog opened an account near the spaceport, depositing most of the leftover wafers for emergency use or, when the account grew too fat, paying down the valley mortgage.

After his first day back at work, Brog stopped by and visited the pharmacy of an old friend—a man he'd known in the housing unit back at university. They had a private meeting in the back, during which several fully charged credit wafers were exchanged. Brog left with a list of questions, returning two nights later with the answers. Several more wafers were exchanged and Brog left, a look of satisfaction on his face.

It proved both easier and cheaper than he expected.

*   *   *

Sullrob had trouble sleeping again. He got up and padded to the larder, then tried to relax with a mug of water, a pinch of Zhasou, and memories of his wife.

Sitting there in the pink twin-moonlight, he noticed lights in Pirlhoff's grandfather's house again. After a few minutes, the young woman came outside, looked toward the moons for a moment, then sat on a low bench and buried her face in her hands.

Something is wrong . . . He put on his most comfortable foot-wraps and headed into the warm night.

She was crying. When it came time to wake grandfather for his medicine, he wouldn't rouse. His days of needing medicine would be no more. Sullrob held her in his arms until she was ready to go inside and sip a mug of Zhasou to the old man's memory.

Her tears dried, relieved that Sullrob had come so soon to help, she selected a nice spot near the corner of the garden. Sullrob took two shovels from the shed and, together, they dug her grandfather's grave. Pirlhoff took a seat on the bench, her eyes toward the moons, and talked quietly about the man she so loved—the Gsudonk rides he took her on as a little girl, sitting in his lap and pretending to drive his tractor, the tears in the old man's eyes at her graduation, laboring until his back ached and his hands grew calloused while helping build her the small home where she lived during university, assisting him with Zhasou when, together, sometimes late at night, they remembered grandmother together in ways only the two of them could share.

Sullrob carried the old man to the open grave, placed him carefully in the bottom, and covered him with dirt. There would be a ceremony to Celebrate his *life* the following night, but burials were always fast and simple. Memories were not for the death or the corpse, they weren't to be focused on crypts or markers, they were of *life*, and grandfather would be a part of the living garden.

Sullrob went back and sat beside her on the bench. There in the light of the twin moons, she swept her longish, blond-streaked brown hair away from her face, revealing tear-stained cheeks. Her dark violet eyes, almost obsidian, shined in the soft light. She looked so small and helpless that Sullrob was lost for words of comfort.

"Everybody knows I planned to go back across the water again whenever grandfather died," she whispered.

Sullrob nodded. Her grandfather's health had failed quickly. Moving in to help care for him was not expected to last as long as it had.

"It is time for me to make the trip. Nobody will question where I have gone."

Sullrob understood. "Wouldn't you like to have some time to grieve, though? I mean, isn't this sudden?"

"It is not sudden; it is simply *now*." She tried to fight back more tears, her hoarse whisper continuing, "My memories of grandfather's house are of *it* as part of *him*. I don't want to stay another night. Not without him."

Sullrob held her in his arms for a few more minutes, then went inside and helped pack her few meager possessions. She selected some mementos of the old man's, then closed the door forever. The house and its contents would be sold later. He guided her back to his home, helping her with her footing across the meadow in the fading light of the setting moons, then mixed her a mug of Zhasou.

After a while, he made a palette in Stava's room for little Yantanna, carrying her in without waking her, and offered the little girl's bed to Pirlhoff. Exhausted from so many late nights tending to the old man, Pirlhoff fell asleep in no time. Sullrob sat in the lingering glow of pink moonlight for a few minutes more, then decided he needed to get to sleep.

I just don't know how I could do it. There's just no way I could kill my own children.

*   *   *

"'Ey, Sullrob! Good jump?"

"Like a pinch o' Zhasou!" he confirmed to the Seelius Orbiter-two loaders. Stepping from the pilot's compartment, he turned and handed out a beautiful young woman, purple-skinned like any Seeliot, with longish blond-streaked brown hair. "This is my sister, Pirlhoff, come along for the ride."

Pirlhoff stretched her sore muscles and graciously touched the shoulders of each loader. She was cramped from spending hours curled up inside the crate waiting for lift-off. The loaders ground-side, knowing she was in there, were extra careful with handling, but it seemed like *forever* before Sullrob let her out.

"They's aloosenin' up down there, eh?" one asked.

Sullrob nudged him with an elbow, offering a conspiratorial smile. "Little bit, Frawk. Just a bit. Still, though, *some* people might not like me showing the orbiter to my sis, so we're bein', um, *discreet* about it."

The loaders smiled. "Enjoy yer visit, ma'am."

"Watch fer them aflirtin' spacers," the other warned good-naturedly. "Yer bro's a pop'lar feller and yer a *purty* lass!"

Sullrob clasped each of their shoulders, then hoisted several heavy bags and led Pirlhoff, carrying two smaller satchels, straight to the nearest tube. After several minutes' ride, they exited and stepped into a near-deserted trinket shop where he was greeted by a large, slightly paunchy, curly-headed spacer casually browsing the displays.

"This is Brog Pawligan," Sullrob quietly introduced. "This is my friend, Pirlhoff."

They touched each other's shoulders and, after hesitating a moment, their foreheads. Pirlhoff sighed relief. She'd been very nervous all day.

So this is Brog Pawligan!

Brog took one of Sullrob's heavier bags; Sullrob took one of Pirlhoff's lighter ones—the case containing his wife's Chronicle and Pirlhoff's personal mementos—and the threesome slipped back into the nearby tube. When the door opened into the habitat ring where Brog and his children lived, he peered out to be sure nobody was around.

"It's clear. Sullrob, I'll meet you in the Dropsey in a half-hour."

Sullrob and Pirlhoff faced each other for a moment, tentatively touching each other's foreheads.

"Let's go," Brog hissed.

She followed him around to the blue door while Sullrob took the tube back out to an outer level.

"Wazoo! She's apurple!" Jowda exclaimed. "She looks alike that pilot guy y'took us t'see!" he added, circling the nervous woman like a cat scoping its prey.

Brog was carrying the bags into his bedroom. "Jowda! Be nice. She's our guest!"

Normally shy, Selta stepped forward and hesitantly offered her hand. "Hi! I'ma Selta. Don' amind Jowda. He's ajust a brat."

Pirlhoff smiled and touched each of Selta's shoulders. The young girl hesitated, then did the same to Pirlhoff. Both broke into wide smiles.

"Jus' alook at her *hair*!" Jowda continued. "Didja do that—or does it jus' agrow thataway?"

Brog came into the room again and, catching Jowda by surprise, grabbed him around his chest and lifted him, legs akimbo, off the ground. "Just say the word, Pirlhoff, and the pest goes into the trash 'cycler," he joshed.

"Dad! Aput me down!"

"No," Pirlhoff smiled back. "I kinda like the little feller. He reminds me of the Seeliot boys in my village."

Brog dropped the brat; he wouldn't have been able to hold him much longer anyway.

"Don' you be acallin' *me* no stinky Seeliot!" the boy announced. "I'm anot a purple-face!"

"Don't you *ever* say something like that again!" Brog ordered, lightly rapping his son on the back of the head.

"Ouch! Okay, I won't *asay* it, then," he spit out before tromping back to his bedroom.

"I'm sorry," Brog apologized. "Selta was being polite when she only called him a brat."

Jowda stuck his head out and announced, "An' if she's asleepin' in *my* room, she better not be amessin' with any o' *my* things!" He disappeared quickly to avoid another rap.

"Daddy, I aknow you was agonna give her Jowda's room while she astayed with us, but, if she awants, um, well, she could astay with me," Selta offered shyly.

Before Brog could reply, Pirlhoff smiled and agreed, "I would like that very much. Thank you, Selta."

Brog shrugged. "Whatever you ladies want. Pirlhoff, you're our guest and, for the next few weeks, a member of my family—" He mock-grimaced toward Jowda's room, adding, "—for what it's worth."

"You have a wonderful family," Pirlhoff offered as Selta took her by the hand and led her to the bedroom.

"I'll ashow you where everything is. Daddy arented a porta-bed—it's in his room for Jowda right now. We'll amove it into mine."

"I've got to meet Sullrob and take my flight," Brog called out. "I'll see you all tonight. Jowda, you try to be nice for a change!"

*   *   *

Out in the merchant's level, Sullrob walked toward the Dropsey, a small beverage place frequented by pilots and loaders.

"'Ey, Sullrob!"

"'Ows it agoin', Sullrob?"

"Sullrob! Aflyin' high, ol' man?"

He greeted everybody politely, wishing he didn't attract so much attention every time he was on the orbiter. It beat the alternative, though, like it used to be his first few months, treated as an alien, an outsider, something unpleasant and best avoided. Familiarity is always stronger than prejudice, though, and example guides. Thus, people like Brog Pawligan who saw beyond the purple skin and made an effort to befriend the newcomer showed others that, with a little effort, getting to know people was the best way to get past appearances. Still, Sullrob had a legitimate reason to be there; Pirlhoff did not. The stowaway refugee would need to be kept hidden at Pawligan's to avoid too many questions, weaving too many lies, attracting too much attention. He took a seat at a corner table and was joined by Brog soon after.

"I'm sorry about such short notice," Sullrob began, "especially before the habitat is ready."

"Hey, we can make this work," Brog assured him. "Besides, I think Pirlhoff and my daughter are really going to hit it off."

"I'm glad you understand."

"I brought some dimension-stills for you to see. Maybe you should just look at them here, but not take them back home."

The valley looked much more beautiful than anyplace he'd seen on Seelius. His home-world offered little more than large tracts of flat land, hundreds of kilometers across, separated by narrow bands of ocean. "It's glorious," Sullrob whispered.

"With the habitat ready in less than two weeks, we can start planning to move the others—one at a time, mind you, maybe every week or two."

"We can't thank you enough for what you're doing, you know."

Brog waved him off. "I'm getting *plenty* out of this win-win. Don't thank *me*; thank *you* for the opportunity. Say, when are we gonna get your kids moved?"

"They will have to be the last ones," Sullrob explained. "I need to be the pilot until everybody's moved. If my kids disappear, that'll just arouse suspicion."

Brog nodded. "Yeah, I guess you're right."

"Besides, I love 'em too much. I couldn't stand to give 'em up for so long."

*   *   *

They burst in just after little Yantanna had fallen asleep. Stava was studying his lessons in his bedroom. Sullrob was heating a snack for himself and his son.

"Freeze," the lieutenant announced. Six officers in all, festooned with ceremonial frocks, they carried stingers. Several weapons pointed at Sullrob standing frozen in the faint light of the corner lamp.

Four officers fanned out, weapons drawn, to locate the children and anybody else who might be in the house.

"Dad, what—?" Stava had started to come out of his room when a stinger was placed against his head. "Dad!"

Two others entered the little girl's room and roused her from her sleep. One led her by the hand into the living area while the other started to search the premises. Sullrob was manacled, wrists and ankles, without resistance. Stava was manacled next. The boy, a hint of tears in his eyes, remained stoic, his gaze fixed on his father. They had discussed this possibility many times. Still, though, neither had truly prepared for the real thing.

At the sight of her family being chained, the little girl started to cry. She tried to go to Sullrob, but was restrained. She cried harder.

"It's okay, little one," Sullrob soothed. "Hush now. It'll be okay."

He wished he had coached *her*, too. He had hoped this would never happen and didn't want to scare her unnecessarily. Now that reality had descended like a guillotine, he regretted not warning her in advance. They put tiny manacles on her wrists, but left her ankles free. All three were led to a groundcar and placed inside. Sullrob whispered to his little girl as the driver pulled away.

His face pressed against the glass, Stava watched as two more officers entered and started carrying out the family's meager possessions, opening them in the yard and spilling the contents in a frenzied search. His dad had been right. Good or bad, justifiable or not, pleasant or painful, his dad was always right.

But this is wrong!

*   *   *

The first few days sharing quarters with Pirlhoff had been tentative, but successful. Brog was the gracious host, trying to make her feel welcome. Selta spent a lot of time with her, talking about girl stuff, telling about the various orbiters where she had grown up, asking about Seelius.

Jowda never used the term "purple-face" again, but he made no secret of the fact that he regarded this interloper as unforgivingly different. Still, though, she was very nice and helpful and cooked a gazillion times better than Dad and, well, really wasn't so bad after all.

Keeping Pirlhoff hidden, afraid to take her out or have her seen by others, proved very awkward and just a bit unsettling. Jowda didn't want his friends to know they had a purple-face, but he also tired of having to keep her secret. Selta seemed to relish having her so close, like the mother the little girl had lost all those years before.

Late one night, in the bedroom they shared, they were experimenting with make-up to see if Pirlhoff could look enough like a human spacer to go out without detection. To Selta's surprise, her new roommate suddenly asked, "Tell me about your mother?"

Selta paused, looking down at her nightgown. "She's adead."

"When did it happen?"

"Six years ago, awhen I was eight. That awould be four turns ago to you," she added, remembering how Pirlhoff had explained the calendar difference to her that afternoon. "Jowda was ajust a little one. He only 'members jus' a bit 'bout her."

"How did it happen?" Pirlhoff whispered.

"Cancer."

"What is that?"

"It's a cell disease that amostly can be acured, but sometimes not. She agot it real bad."

"I'll bet she loved you very much."

Selta's eyes started to glisten with tears. She nodded slowly, whispering back, "I aloved her very much."

"Tell me about her, if you want," Pirlhoff prodded, putting her arm around the girl.

Selta opened a drawer and dug out dimension-stills of her mother. She talked for a while, telling little stories, snatches of memories, impressions embellished over time. Pirlhoff listened patiently, eventually sharing her experiences caring for her own grandfather before leaving her home-world to come hide in an orbiter in search of a better life. They laughed and cried and hugged and teased, forgetting about the make-up, just enjoying their time together. Eventually, much later than normal, they heard the outer door open to admit Brog.

"Daddy! You're alate!" Selta called, coming out of the bedroom, Pirlhoff behind her, worried at the look on Brog's face.

"What's awrong, Daddy?"

"It's Sullrob. He wasn't on the ship. Somebody else was piloting."

"Oh no!" Pirlhoff gasped. "Did he say—?"

"Yes. Sullrob and his family were taken under something called 'reason to suspect.' His kids will be genetically tested for possible 'contamination.'"

Selta burst into tears. She and Pirlhoff had talked about the Panel of Extirpation. Sullrob had been tested before his pilot's training, but the children were still vulnerable. In fact, Pirlhoff had brought their mother's Chronicle with her because it contained something incriminating that could endanger them if found. "What'll happen if they're not apure?"

Brog shook his head and collapsed on the low divan. Without looking at his daughter, he quietly mumbled, "They'll be killed."

*   *   *

"In the matter of the family of Sullrob," the orator announced.

A hush fell over the chamber. The room was packed. Manacled in the long box, behind the rail, sat Sullrob, Stava, and little Yantanna. There were no other living relatives to seat beyond the little girl. If Sullrob was ordered to fulfill his community obligation and refused, the Panel of Extirpation would have to appoint a man from the village to carry out the orders.

Sullrob watched his children carefully. Little Yantanna fidgeted, nervous and uncomfortable, not sure what was going on. Stava stared straight at the panel, hatred in his eyes, sitting very still.

"What must we know?"asked the elder of the panel of three.

"In previous action," the orator sing-songed, reading from his booklet, "the mother of the children of Sullrob was named with 'reason to suspect' for genetic contamination, based on the Chronicles of Yowloff. The children were ordered to be tested for genetic purity."

There came no other sound in the room except faint rustlings, fidgets, heavy breaths.

"The youngest child is named Yantanna," the orator continued. "The elder is

Stava. There is no explanation why their names do not conform to traditional Seeliot society," he added, glaring over at Sullrob.

A slight murmur passed through the crowd.

"Quiet!" the elder intoned. "There is no law against this, though I wonder why
a true and loyal citizen would commit such an insult." Then to the orator, he directed, "You may proceed."

"The results are ready for consideration by the Panel of Extirpation."

Sullrob pulled quietly at his manacles. Yantanna started to whimper. Stava's
gaze never left the Panel.

"So the results shall be read; so they shall be true," the elder sing-songed.

"In the matter of the purity of Yantanna, the youngest child of Sullrob, she has
been found to possess genetic contamination!"

The audience gasped. Their worst fears were confirmed.

"Quiet!"

"In the matter of the purity of Stava, the eldest child of Sullrob, he has been
found to possess genetic contamination!"

Another gasp, murmurs and whispers.

"Quiet!"

Tears formed in Sullrob's eyes, but he said nothing. *How can I kill my own children?*

"Sullrob of Tessila," the elder intoned, "you are herewith ordered to purge your
daughter, the impure Yantanna, and your son, the impure Stava, for the benefit of
all Seelius. Have you chosen a method?"

How can I kill my own children?

All eyes were on Sullrob. Slowly he raised his head and, without looking at the
little ones, addressed the elder.

"I choose for them—for them to drink Zhasou," he stammered, "into which I
will mix—will put powdered Tsalook root."

"Very well, then. Who among us has powder from the Tsalook root?"

A man in the back stood and offered, "I live just across the square. I have
some."

"Fetch it at once, for the good of all Seelius."

The man returned within minutes. Sullrob's manacles removed, he was led by
stinger-pointing officers to the Zhasou table. They watched carefully as the sad father, his hands shaking, poured two drinks, added Tsalook powder, and sprinkled
in sweet Zhasou spice. Still trembling, he carried the two mugs to his children,
handing one to each.

"Please, drink it fast," he whispered. "And remember how much I love you."

Wide-eyed and scared, the little girl gulped hers down. Stava looked up at his
father for the first time, then gazed into his mug. Looking back at his father, his
expression changed from hatred to fear. Tears crept down his cheeks as, without a

sound, he lifted the mug and gulped its contents.

Yantanna's head lolled, her eyes drooping. She dropped her mug, shattering it on the floor, then slumped back as if falling asleep. Stava set his mug on the rail, fighting against the effects, trying to remain upright, finally succumbing to the powerful potion. He reached for his little sister, gathering her in his arms before collapsing sideways. Then he lay very still, one protective hand, even in death, on the little girl.

People in the audience were weeping. Sullrob buried his face in his hands and sobbed. Several neighbors came forward to touch him on the shoulders.

The orator walked over and felt for a pulse on each child. Satisfied, he nodded his head to the Panel. The three old men nodded back and filed out of the room.

Two villagers gathered up the children; several more took Sullrob by the arms to lead him back to his home.

Stava and Yantanna were laid out in the living room of Sullrob's house. Numbly, he and several friends started to dig two graves at the corner of his garden. The sun burned hot; it was too bright. Tears obscured Sullrob's vision, making it hard for him to see where he was digging. It was hard to hold the shovel in his trembling hands.

How could I kill my own children?

CHAPTER 4

Governor Plekwag, heir to the Chair of all Seelius, was growing frustrated. Things were moving too slowly; he needed a way to be more thorough. Ling Bozathorne wasn't giving him any slack at all. Sealed inside his chamber, free from interruptions by staff, he winced at the harsh visage on the portable view-screen TradComm had given him. He didn't fully understand how the equipment worked—was always annoyed by the seconds of delay inevitable in any live conversation between Seelius and Casronia, the planet second only to distant Earth as a center of government and corporate power.

"But we've already purged more than two-*hundred* people," he protested, waiting for a response. He perched on the front of his desk, directly in front of the view-screen so Ling Bozathorne could see him. At well over a meter and a half, he was tall for a Seeliot. He tugged at the robe hanging on his lanky frame and ran his fingers through his short, all-white hair. It sure took a long time to get a response on these inter-planet conversations.

"It's not enough!" Bozathorne thundered, causing Plekwag to wince. Even on a view-screen, he was intimidated by humans' height—usually a good third-meter taller—and the massive beefy frame of Bozathorne in particular. "You've been paid handsomely, and expect to receive even more precious metals as part of our contract—"

"Unofficially," Plekwag reminded him, but the delay meant Ling wouldn't know yet that he was interrupted. It bothered him that the president of TradCo never seemed to differentiate the official contract between his company and Seelius to trade plants for medicine, and the unofficial agreement that benefited only Plekwag. He wished he'd be more discreet.

"—Which stipulates that *you* will eradicate every cross-breed on your planet— within two turns! You are almost out of time and you're not even close to your goal."

"Look, we're moving steady," Plekwag protested. "We've got just about everybody on the planet against the impure. We've got 'em turning each other in. I have secret police conducting investigations. We have Panels of Extirpation in more than two-hundred regions covering every city and village. We've stretched 'reason to suspect' to its limit. Still, though, we go too fast. There is backlash in many of the outer regions. We've had to start eliminating whole families when only one was contaminated, just to keep down dissension." He paused and studied the impatient expression on the fat Casronian. Bozathorne was mostly balding, stubble-chinned—or stubble-jowled, sweating and, Plekwag conjectured, probably stinking, too. Watching him listen to the response, he could tell Bozathorne was not pleased.

"*Burn* yer damned 'reason to suspect.' Why don't you just test every citizen and get it over with? I can send you more of the technology. I can even send you people to help."

"I've explained this before. We tried random tests right after the plague—even lied and said it was to test for dormant plague infection—but people were too against it. They were willing to force me out of the Chair—to break a succession that goes back hundreds of turns. 'Reason to suspect' has been a part of our law as long as anyone can remember. We're barely getting away with pushing it as far as we *have* been."

He watched Ling again, waiting for the message to cross space. He was glad he'd decided that avoiding participation in—or, worse yet, joining—the Consortium would be smart. A little planet like Seelius, so *unsophisticated*, would be fodder for a powerful man like Ling Bozathorne, chieftain of a conglomerate that covered dozens of planets and encompassed companies like TradCo Pharmaceutical, the crystal growers, and Tradeworlds Transport, T-rad Comestibles, Tee-gize Energies, plus TradComm Communications. Sure, trading with these companies, if Seelius had anything to offer, might upgrade life—or downgrade it if fears of the superstitious were to be believed—but the power to rule was Plekwag's birthright. Joining the Consortium would make him just a tiny weenshugger in a big burrow . . .

Bozathorne was taking longer than usual to respond. He looked somehow conciliatory as he offered, "Look, I understand your little problems. I might even be willing to *extend* your timetable, maybe *increase* your, um, bestowment . . . *if*—" He leaned forward menacingly. "*If* you were doing a better job getting us the family records. *Why* have nearly half the names on the list you provided us not included a family Chronicle for sending to me with a shipment?"

"Well, not everybody keeps one."

Looking mad, Bozathorne spat back, "You *lie*! When we made our agreement, you told me that only a few citizens didn't update their Chronicles, but that *every* family had at least one from generations past when *every* citizen kept one. I told you I don't *care* if they're updated or not—but *I want every Chronicle from any family that is cross-bred with human traders!*"

"We get every one we can! That's how we establish a lot of 'reasons to suspect'—we trace family histories. But, well, sometimes they hide them from us—have others take them for safekeeping. We even suspect they destroy them if they believe they contain evidence of past contamination. That's one of the reasons I can't push too much too fast. If *everybody* thinks they are going to be tested—to have their Chronicles taken, then they'll destroy them. They'll rise up and resist. I could lose my *power!*" he whined.

Ling Bozathorne still looked mad. "You could lose your *life* if you don't start meeting the terms of our agreement," Ling offered casually. "I understand your infant son is still at least seven turns from puberty—from the age of ascension—and, therefore, one of your rivals would be able to step in until that time and then Challenge your boy someday."

Plekwag shuddered at the thought. Mounting a Challenge required sharp wits and a cunning intellect. So far, little Plekmerk seemed to have talent for little more than drooling, throwing things, and resisting toilet training. Shifting his attention back to the underlying subject—satisfying the guy who'd been making him singularly rich—he probed, "You know, if you'd give us more of an idea what you're looking for, maybe we could, um, well, if we knew, maybe we could be more focused in our—"

That was enough time for Bozathorne to hear the beginning of the message and react. "I'm looking for *every* bit of family history on *anybody* who's been contaminated on your world. You just step up your pace. Destroy *every* person who's mixed-breed and get me *all* records. I don't care what it takes. Remember your deadline. It wouldn't be hard for me to arrange to put somebody more accommodating into your job."

"Um," Plekwag stammered, fidgeting nervously with the bangles on his hot, stuffy robe, tugging at the collar. "Um, okay. I'll see how we can pick it up some." He didn't doubt the validity of Bozathorne's threat.

Bozathorne watched him intently, listening to his promise. "I will check at this time in a tenth-turn. Have some good news for me—" He scratched the back of his neck, then started to pick some crud from under his nails. "—Or I'll have some *bad* news for you." He reached toward the view-screen and the picture disappeared.

Plekwag angrily yanked at his robe, trying to pull it off over his head. He wound up tangled in it, cursing under his breath. Calming himself enough to extricate his lanky frame from the jumbled mass, he tossed it into the corner, pressed the wired button on his desk, and ordered, "Send in Stewrik."

After a moment, a very short, stubby, muscular man—darker purple than most Seeliots with pure white hair—clomped in and closed the door behind himself. "Didn't go well?"

"He's steamed that we're not further ahead. He, um, threatened me. What can we do?"

"I've been thinking. Let's start faking some Chronicles. Let's start targeting a few people in every village—even if we have to make up the 'reason to suspect.'"

"Even if we kill *more* innocent people?" Plekwag wondered, shuddering.

"He don't know the difference. He wants more bodies and more Chronicles. If we start pickin' 'em at random, we'll accidentally get more real contaminants."

"Okay, do it. Right away. He wants results in a tenth-turn."

"Then let's give him some."

Plekwag walked around and collapsed in the chair behind his desk, mumbling more to himself than Stewrik, "Maybe we'll find whatever he's after—before it's too late."

*   *   *

Brog hoped the make-up experiment had worked out okay. It would be Pirlhoff's call; if she felt confident, then a late dinner in an out-of-the-way cafe would be a chance to get her out, show her around the Orbiter-two, help ease her profound sense of captivity and isolation.

She was beautiful! Standing there shyly, still a bit unsure but determined to make it work, waiting for his reaction. She had even colored her hair a chestnut brown. How could being a different color make such a difference in appearance?

"You look great!" Brog pronounced. "You could go anywhere incognito!" Realizing he had complimented only the cover-up, he hastily added, "Of course, you're *very* beautiful anyway, no matter what color you choose to be."

She smiled shyly. Brog tried not to seem the least bit fazed by the unexpected turn of events with Sullrob. Sure, he was worried about his Seeliot friend and the man's family, but he didn't want her to think he might get cold feet about having her hidden in his quarters.

"Thank you. You're quite a handsome guy yourself, for a peach-face!" she joked.

"I need to spend some time on Seelius to get one of them purple tans, I guess. So, the kids are asleep?"

She smiled, whispering in his ear, "Jowda's a goner, but Selta's *pretending* to be so she can listen and see what you think of the make-up." Louder she offered, "Yeah, I think so. They're both in bed."

"Good!" he exaggerated slightly loud. "I'm sure glad Selta helped with your make-up. She's a wonderful daughter—so helpful, such a sweet girl. I sure am lucky to have her!"

They both smiled.

"Do you still want to go out?" she wondered.

"Just give me a minute to freshen up."

He came out of the bathroom, slipped into Jowda's room to stroke his hair a few times, then into Selta's room to kiss her on the cheek and whisper, "Thanks, sweetie."

Over a dinner of seafoods completely foreign to the Seeliot—delicacies she absolutely loved—they scrupulously avoided their pending decisions, talking instead about his job and the day-to-day exploits of the children. She was actually becoming quite the "nanny," helping the teenage girl feel good about herself, to gain confidence and poise, and keeping just enough tether on the brat to help him survive until his eleventh birthday—without him feeling like she was *completely* running his life. The more Brog listened, the more he realized she truly cared about both of his kids. He'd seen it right away between her and Selta, but was surprised at how much she had taken to the boy.

"He's like so many Seeliot boys," she explained, "testing his boundaries, not satisfied they're firm when he finds them, too busy worrying about what everybody else thinks. He keeps trying to make me mad at him; he's not yet convinced that I really do like him just the way he is."

Brog gazed absently into the corridor. He remembered his dying wife's admonitions about raising their children without her. She had told him, "Selta never thinks she's good enough. Try to find ways to remind her she is. Little Jowda already thinks he's the center of the galaxy, but don't ever let on that he's not."

Pirlhoff really did seem to like Jowda just the way he was—she wouldn't let on that he's *not* the center of everything. What a contrast with all the women Brog had dated—they'd all considered his son a little hellion who needed to be kept on a short leash. He preferred Pirlhoff's approach. She'd put him on a long bungee cord . . .

They fell quiet for a few minutes. Finally, looking into his eyes like she was searching, she softly offered, "You know, now I'm the only one. If Sullrob can't smuggle any more of my friends or neighbors off the planet, then I'm the only Seeliot in the entire Consortium—and a disguised one at that." She looked sad, worried, lonely.

"We'll find a way to help others escape," he assured her.

"How?"

"Well, I don't know, but we'll find a way."

"In the meantime, where will *I* go? Where will I live?"

"Why, the habitat will be ready on Caskentia—"

"But you can't make the payments," she interrupted. "Without Zhasou shipments, we'll lose the land and the habitat with it."

"We may need to scale back, go with a smaller piece of land for a while. There's things we can do."

She looked down at her lap, slowly shaking her head. "But I'll still be the only one—the stranger in a strange land—the purple-face in a world where I don't fit in, where I'll have no one . . ."

Brog was lost for words. Everything he started to say wouldn't help, so he said nothing.

Looking up, her eyes glistening, she whispered, "And I can never go back. Oh, I wish I had never come. What were we thinking?"

"You were thinking of making a better life for yourself. And you *will*. Don't let a few setbacks throw you off course," he announced, his voice rising with his determination and resolve. "It may take some time; it may be a different plan, but we'll find a way to make it work."

She looked hopeful. The tears she'd been holding back were welling in her eyes, a single drop drawing a line through her heavy make-up. "You really think so?"

"Have no doubt." Then, softening his voice again, he reached across and touched her left shoulder, then her right, and finally her forehead, offering, "And you'll *never* be alone. I'm your friend. Selta's your friend."

"She's such a sweet girl—"

"And there's no way Jowda's gonna let you get away. You're the only adult he thinks he's got fooled!"

*   *   *

"I am ready to resume my job."

"But Sullrob, you are in mourning," the shipments' supervisor pointed out, surprised that his pilot had returned to work so soon—or even at all.

"I gave up my job teaching in the school. I went through the training to become a pilot. This is now my job. I have debts and responsibilities. I will grieve my children in my own time and my own way . . . until I can learn to Celebrate their lives and Celebrate my *memories* of them. For now, I must work. I have responsibilities."

"Y'want I should put Jarbuk back on loading?"

"Yes. He is still my back-up. I am ready to return to work."

The supervisor sat back in his chair and scrutinized Sullrob carefully. The Seeliot pilot stood obstinately in front of him, determination on his face. Finally, the boss seemed to understand. What else could the man do? Sit in his house and feel his pain—or throw himself back into his work? He'd already lost his wife to the plague; now he was without *any* family at all. He had nobody else.

"Okay, you can go back on the runs starting in three days." He softened his tone and leaned forward. "Listen, Sullrob, I can only imagine how hard all this has been on you." He looked around to make sure nobody could hear. "It just doesn't seem right. But you *are* entitled to go back to your work—you've not been found guilty of anything wrong." He got up and walked around the dispatch counter and clasped his best pilot on the shoulder. "You take it easy, though. If you need a day or even a few days, hey, just let me know. I'll have Jarbuk fill in—he'll be thrilled—but don't feel like you're going to lose your spot if you, you know, need some time."

"Thank you. I appreciate your . . . your *understanding*," Sullrob offered with forced sincerity. "I will be here in three days."

He turned and left, the supervisor watching him as he walked out and stepped into his groundcar.

Sullrob stopped at the community hall where his friends and collaborators were gathered waiting for him. He entered the building and was surrounded by people touching his shoulders and forehead, nobody saying a word. Finally, once the greetings were complete, everybody waited patiently.

"I will fly again, starting in three days."

The tension that hung so thickly seemed to be carried off in a gust of wind. Everybody sighed with relief.

"That is good, Sullrob. It is now more important than ever that we continue our plan," one man pointed out.

A woman stepped forward and, sadly, reported, "I am very worried. Some people I know in Waverla were taken under 'reason to suspect' just today. I am hearing that purges are increasing and the circumstances are becoming more and more questionable."

Sullrob agreed. "I don't want to risk anything important on my first flight, though, just in case there is suspicion of me. I will fill my bags with unimportant possessions."

Everybody agreed. Getting caught in the next few days would be the worst possible timing and could bring very grave consequences.

"Sullrob," another man brought up, "I think we should gather our Chronicles and pack them so you can take them with you as soon as you feel it is safe. Chronicles are being seized; the information they contain is being used against people."

"Yes," a woman agreed. "I do not even understand all of the early entries in mine. I am scared of how something might be used against me or my children."

There was a murmur of growing agreement as people considered the idea. Finally, Sullrob asked, "How many would like to send Chronicles for safekeeping?"

Looking around the room, he noticed many nodding vigorously, the others also agreeing after considering for a moment. It was unanimous.

One man offered, "I suggest you take one in each shipment—so they are not all together at one time."

"Yes, that is wise," Sullrob agreed. "Let us decide in which order. Who is most concerned about what information theirs might contain?"

There were at least three that directly traced lineage back to a trader. Contaminants—people who could never be true Seeliots because their genes had been soiled with the seed of filthy humans. Seeliots living a lie in a world that would not accept them—a world where their lives and the lives of their families were in danger. People who might die simply for who they were . . .

Like what happened to Sullrob's children.

*   *   *

During the trip down to Caskentia, Brog Pawligan insisted that Pirlhoff remove the make-up. "This is going to be your home soon. You need to be who you are.

For now, it is smart to be discreet on the orbiter—at least until after all the shipments are done or unless the politics change."

"You think people will be more accepting of my—my *differences* there?"

"It's a very cosmopolitan planet, only recently developed, with people from all over. There are many Tijartians and nobody gives them a second glance. Besides, where we're going is mostly tourists and vacationers. People expect to see something unusual when they travel—plus the locals *always* learn to be hospitable to paying customers."

Selta didn't understand why anybody would care; Jowda was not so optimistic. He'd spent the past week terrified that his friends would find out they were hiding a purple-face—worse yet, *living* with one. If she was going to go out in public looking like *that*, then Jowda would keep his distance. He liked his weekends at the resort—wanted to bring friends along on future trips. He'd even made a few tentative friendships down there with other boys whose families had weekend packages. He didn't understand why they just didn't leave her locked in their quarters until the habitat was ready; then they could move her and be done with it. Still, though, she *was* pretty cool and it wouldn't be nice to make her miss out on such a great place. Maybe it would go okay after all. It better.

What a surprise! Pirlhoff was treated like royalty. She was the *first* Seeliot anybody had ever seen! The staff and the locals were *very* concerned with her happiness. They knew that if Seeliots were to begin traveling, then Caskentia would be the closest and most logical recreation destination.

The families with boys Jowda liked to hang with were thrilled with the idea of meeting somebody from a different culture, from a different race—exposing their children to yet another part of the vast and diverse galaxy. Far from being ostracized for showing up with a purple-face, Jowda was envied, instantly made more popular.

Pirlhoff took it all in stride, trying to be low-key, not overly encouraging the staff, finding private time to spend with Selta, putting on good public appearances with Jowda for his friends.

Since traveling with a purple-face turned out to be sort of cool, Jowda caught himself wondering once or twice how it might feel to *be* one.

*   *   *

Later their first day there, Brog and Pirlhoff met with Dow Pfivvel to discuss the interruption in shipments. While the children played at the lake, the threesome sat on the veranda sharing sweet Zhasou tea, Pfivvel very pleased with the opportunity to meet Pirlhoff. He'd heard about Seeliots, slightly shorter than humans, light-purple skin, hair that tended toward blond or white, but human-like every other way. He decided the conjecture that Seeliots were descended from early Earth settlers must be true; they were too similar. Plus, if there had been interbreeding during the trader expansion centuries before, then they must be genetically compatible.

"I understand that your contract does not *require* you to make deliveries—in fact, you did warn me that if something went wrong, the shipments could be interrupted or permanently cut off. But remember, my company *is* guaranteed exclusivity. If *any* Zhasou is being shipped, then I'm entitled to it at our agreed-upon price."

"Yes, that was—still is—our agreement," Brog concurred.

"Please believe us," Pirlhoff assured him, "that no shipments have come through this past week."

Pfivvel regarded them both, his demeanor friendly, but his business instinct alert. "I assume by now you would have expected me to see if Zhasou could be replicated. The answer is no, not really. Well, my people say they *could* come very close, but the cost would be too prohibitive. It has been a big hit, especially on the world we targeted first, where most of our shipments have gone. It's a good example of supply and demand and you are the exclusive supplier, so, well, if it's the *price* that's causing the hold-up, then maybe we could talk about a *small* increase if, you know, it would help loosen up the situation—"

"I wouldn't think of it, sir!" Brog protested. "I, like Pirlhoff and all of my friends on Seelius, am a man of my word. You and I made an agreement on behalf of *your* company and *my* group; it is an agreement to be honored. No, sir, though we have had our shipments interrupted, we are still *way* ahead of schedule for meeting the minimum of fifty that we anticipated."

Pfivvel sat back, both surprised and satisfied.

Brog smiled and, with a sidelong nudge, added, "But don't think we might not look for an increase *after* we have satisfied the terms of our original agreement."

Pfivvel smiled. "I can respect that. So—okay then. When can we expect the shipments to resume?"

"I cannot promise anything at present," Brog explained. "It would not be wise for you to count on any supply unless and until it has been delivered. I *will* say that we are confident it can be worked out soon. Believe me, it is even more important to us—to all of the people involved—to solve the problem as soon as possible."

"I will count on you," Pfivvel offered, holding his Zhasou mug up as if to toast, "and wish you luck for all our sakes."

*   *   *

Actually, getting to know Sullrob's replacement, winning his confidence, and bribing him to risk his life was the only plan they had. After what happened to Sullrob, that might be quite a challenge—a risky one at that. He and Pirlhoff had considered many ways to approach it, realizing that being exposed could put Sullrob—if he was still alive—at further risk along with the others involved in the plan.

The next day, the Pawligans took Pirlhoff out to see the valley and the partially built habitat. The young Seeliot woman found the view from the air breathtaking. She'd never seen mountains or even hills. And waterfalls were something to be found in the fountains of town squares, not flowing down through a lush valley, connecting beautiful fresh-water spring-fed lakes.

"Let's show her the *big big* waterfall, Dad!" Jowda begged.

Before landing near the surprisingly large, beautiful Seelius-styled chalet being built into the side of the gentle slope overlooking the largest lake, Brog steered the craft toward the higher end of the valley. He set down not far from the pool under the giant falls. Everybody got out to admire the view, Jowda running off seemingly every direction at once.

Brog looked over and noticed that Pirlhoff was transfixed, tears in her eyes.

"This will be your new home—and *my* family's home someday," Brog whispered just loud enough to be heard over the roar of the water.

She nodded, overwhelmed with all she saw. "My friends and neighbors deserve to see this, to share this, too."

Brog put his arm around her, holding her tightly. "Don't worry. We'll find a way." He gazed at the cascading water again, noticing a rainbow in the spray. "Hey! We should name it. What are we gonna call this little town—this little colony of Seeliots?"

Pirlhoff thought for a minute, then asked, "What would *you* like to call it?"

"Me? Aw, I don't care about those kinds of things. Like decorating our quarters—my wife made those decisions. What *she* liked, *I* liked. No, it's up to you. What would *you* like to call your new home?"

She looked up at him with glistening eyes, smiling. "You have chosen a beautiful place for us, Brog Pawligan. This will be our own community called . . . Seelosia."

*   *   *

It proved a long, painful flight for Sullrob. It was the first time he'd been left alone with his thoughts—except for late at night sitting in the pink light of twin moons—to ponder what he'd been through with the Panel, having to face killing his own children, being so close to death himself. The unwavering trust of Stava that his father was doing the right thing . . .   Even little Yantanna had believed, right up until the last moment, that her daddy was only doing what *had* to be done, for the greater good of all.

Sure, they had talked about fleeing, hiding aboard one of the first transports, taking the risk that no others could escape after it became obvious Sullrob's children had disappeared. It was a calculated risk, waiting as long as possible, hoping to move everybody else first, then to help his own family escape last. It was a gamble that had kept him awake for several tenth-turns while the plan was developed, while Brog Pawligan was approached and did his part to set up the deal, while the shipments of Zhasou had begun. It was a gamble that had gone wrong. Sullrob had so hoped it would not come to this, but it had—and nothing he could do would change that now.

Sullrob knew he would spend many tenth-turns to come fulfilling his pledge, helping his friends, smuggling spice, illegally helping others escape, so that he could come home every night to an empty house, missing his family more than he could stand, his beautiful little girl, and the boy who had been the handsomest in all of Tessila.

Lost in his thoughts, he simply went through the motions as he approached and docked at the Seelius Orbiter-two. Once the pressure was equalized, the gates were opened and clearances received. He picked up several bags loaded only with one family's Chronicles and some of his meager possessions, personal items that had been prized by his children. As the door opened, he stepped into the loading bay.

"It'sa Sullrob!"

"It'sa th'baby-killer," the other loader snarled.

"Whatchoo doin' ashowin' yer purple face back *here*?"

Sullrob was confused, standing there awkwardly, not sure what to say.

"What? Y'think we'd not aknow?"

"When y'didn't ashow up, th'other pilot said you was abusy killin' yer l'il boy and l'il girl."

"Yeah, an' th'other pilot said 'twas atrue!"

They started to get up in his face, menacing, their anger growing. Sullrob quickly stepped around them and exited the docking bay.

"Aget outchere! Don' aneed no baby-killers *here!*" one loader shouted.

"Don' alet me acatch ya alone in th'tube!" the other warned.

Sullrob took a tube to one of the outer commerce levels, hoping to find Brog Pawligan as soon as possible. As he walked down the corridor, he noticed that several people stopped and glared at him, some whispering to each other, one woman pointing him out for her children then hurrying her brood away before he came too near.

Entering the canteen, he was disappointed not to see Brog there yet. He regretted leaving early, arriving a full half-hour sooner than expected. There were only about twenty or so patrons inside, but all stopped talking and stared at him.

A man in the back raised his voice. "Y'got no bi'ness acomin' back here—" He spit on the floor. "—Seeliot scum."

"Not w'the blood o' yo' babies on y'hands," a ledger-woman hissed.

The bartender caught Sullrob's eye, raising his eyebrows. He nodded his head toward the door, a bit of friendly advice from a man who preferred that violence happen outside his establishment. Sullrob backed out and disappeared into a cross-corridor. He decided against going toward Brog Pawligan's quarters. His friend might be permanently disadvantaged by having a pariah seen entering his home—his children's home. He would have to watch for Pawligan; no alternative meeting place had been arranged. Knowing his friend had just returned from a long weekend on Caskentia, not sure if Pirlhoff had gone with his family or was still hiding in his quarters, he wasn't sure if Brog even knew of the rumors spreading through the orbiter. This was going to be an unplanned problem he sure hoped Brog could figure out how to solve.

Click—a stinger had been activated behind him. "Whatchoo adoin' baby-killer?" a voice taunted.

Sullrob started to turn and look, but another voice growled, "Don't aturn around, purple-face."

Sullrob remained frozen, hearing another stinger click on.

"How'd you akill yer kids, *Seeliot?*"

"Yeah, didja ahold 'em down an' amake 'em astruggle while y'cut their throats?"

"Aheard he apoisoned 'em," a third voice coming up from behind added quietly. "Aheard he amixed 'em poison an' awatched while he amade 'em drink it."

Sullrob felt something touch the back of his neck.

"Then *this* is fer akillin' them kids!"

CHAPTER 5

"It's very different than that on *my* world," Pirlhoff explained. "There are none of those—what you called—corporations. We raise much of our own food and trade with our neighbors. To earn money—to have a job—many of us work for our government. There are jobs as makers and growers and helpers and teachers and builders and movers—oh, I expect many similar kinds of jobs as you have here and in the worlds you've visited. But it's the government that builds factories or sets up supply routes or opens schools."

Jowda was propped up in his bed with a pillow, elbows on his legs, holding his sleepy head up with hands under his chin. Pirlhoff sat on the side of the bed, Selta on a cushion beside her on the floor. Pirlhoff's attempts to tuck the boy in for the night had been stretched each night into longer and longer sessions of "twenty questions" as curiosity about Seelius gradually replaced contempt.

"Well, who agets the profits?" Jowda wondered.

"The government uses the extra money for hospitals and roads and things that benefit everyone, plus to help care for those who are too sick or old or hurt to take care of themselves. When I moved back home to take care of my grandfather, I had to give up my job working in a transparent, so the government gave us some money to buy what we needed while I stayed there."

"Awhat's a transparent?" Selta wondered.

"It's a big place made of transparency where we grow plants for food or Zhasou or medicine or to have pretty flowers. That way we can control the climate inside so the weather doesn't harm our crops."

"A *glass*house is awhat they is," Jowda decided. "We aseen 'em on Tijartia Orbiter-ten awhere we used t'live!"

Selta added, "They agrew plants t'use in th'medicine modules."

"Awhat's the kids alike?" Jowda prodded.

Pirlhoff smiled and tousled his hair—a 'do combed into a dozen little curly spikes just like all the other boys on the orbiter had been doing for the past few days. "Why, just like you and your sister." She thought for a moment, then added, "I can think of one *big* difference, though. On Seelius, once they are past puberty, they are considered adults. They have reached what we call the age of ascension; they have become citizens of Seelius. They can get married or take jobs or sign contracts or own houses and land. They can join village councils or vote at the meetings."

"Really?" Selta gasped, her eyes wide. "You mean *I* could get married right now on your planet—or, or, or—"

"Yes—if you *wanted* to . . . when you're ready. Your family would be responsible for you while you live in their home. When you move out, you are responsible for yourself. When you marry, you are responsible for each other. When you have a family, you are responsible for them as long as they live with you. If your parents or brothers or sisters need your help, you do not *have* to take care of them, but you will lose the respect of your friends and neighbors if you do not. The government will help, but you are expected to contribute."

"Selta could get amarried!" Jowda repeated, stuck on the idea that his sister could move away any time she wanted on that strange planet he'd been geostatically circling for two years but had never seen. "I'd astill have to await a few more years, though," he pointed out, lost in thought. "Know how I aknow?"

Pirlhoff smiled, poking him in the chest and making him giggle. "How?"

"'Cause when Dad agets *real* mad, he asays—" He tried to adopt Brog's lecturing demeanor, careful to drop the patois used by children and workers on the Orbiter. "He asays, 'Jowda, when you reach puberty in a few more years, I'm gonna lock you in the closet and not let you out 'til yer old enough to kick out fer good!'" Jowda grinned and leaned forward to whisper in Pirlhoff's ear, "He awouldn't really, though."

"Don't abet on it," Selta countered.

Pirlhoff teased, "Well *I'd* let you out . . . every now and then to go to the *bathroom*, at least."

"Ha!"

"I hope you have a chance to meet some children from *my* world. I think you would like them very much." She looked away, as if into the past—or the future when, she hoped, she would be surrounded by her own people. "Yes," she mused quietly, "I think you would like them a lot. You are much more alike than you are different."

"Awhat about lessons?" Jowda asked.

"Yeah," Selta joined in. "Do they astop their lessons when they areach th'age of 'scension?"

"Well, that's different than what I know about here. I don't know about Consortium planets, but you two do your *own* lessons, by yourselves, with comp-pads and comp-tutors. You only go be with other students and your teacher for assembly—"

"Not every aweek, either," Selta interrupted.

"On Seelius, children go to 'school' every *day* with adults called 'teachers' who help them with their lessons and give them homework to do at night. We don't have comp-pads and comp-tutors."

"Ev'ry *day*?" Jowda gasped.

"That's right—except holidays or when the village has Celebrations or other important events."

"Awhat kinda Cel'brations?" Selta asked.

Pirlhoff explained the Seeliot Celebration of Life, fetching some mugs of water and sweet Zhasou to show them how to go through all six levels. She finished by patiently explaining the *self* concepts of integrity, obligation, and preservation. For Jowda, she kept what actually were very complicated concepts—with nuances as varied as every Seeliot and applications that have been important throughout history—by comparing them to honesty, looking out for others, and taking care of yourself. "At first, since you two and your wonderful father took care of me, helping me escape and find a new life on a new world, I would be obligated to look out for all of you, too. But that has changed."

Selta looked uneasy. "Achanged?"

"Yes," Pirlhoff explained, reaching out and stroking the young girl's hair. "You have moved up in the levels. Now that I *love* you, all of you are my *friends*."

Selta smiled; Jowda seemed embarrassed but secretly pleased. They went through the recitation and sprinkled Zhasou for all six levels. At *self*, they took turns touching each other's shoulders, then Pirlhoff set the mugs aside and handed Selta up beside her onto the bed. She touched the girl's forehead, a gesture Selta tentatively returned. They touched like that for a moment, then Pirlhoff suddenly swept her into her arms and gave her a big hug and kiss on the forehead. Selta stood up to make room for Pirlhoff to repeat the gesture with her little brother.

Jowda looked even more embarrassed, his cheeks turning rose, but he didn't resist. They touched each other's foreheads for at least a half-minute, almost teasingly, with Jowda looking very serious, before the purple-face with the funny hair gathered him into her arms and hugged him tightly, kissing him and hugging harder. He held on much tighter than she expected, burying his face against her neck and shoulder, not offering to let go when she tested by slightly easing her grip. So she held on, and kept holding, gently rocking, finally whispering, "I *do* love you, Jowda," in his ear.

As if she understood, Selta quietly slipped out of the room. Still, Jowda held on. She could feel him trembling, his tears against her neck; he was crying, trying to keep quiet, not to betray the emotions that both surprised and overwhelmed. He kept his face buried, too embarrassed to let her see. So she just held tightly, stroking his silly boy-spiked hair, feeling his heartbeat competing with her own. Finally, he stopped trembling and relaxed his grip. Keeping his head turned so she couldn't see his face, he let go and rolled over onto his side. She pulled the covers up and tucked him in, touching his forehead one last time. She lowered the lights—he didn't like it *completely* dark, and went to the door. Surprised that she was starting to get used to the concept of privacy doors, she started to close it behind her. At the last moment, she whispered into the soft glow of the little human boy's room, "Good night, Jowda."

"G'night, Pirlhoff."

She found Selta already crawled into her own bed, a hint of tears in her teenage-girl eyes. "We didn't do much of this *hugging* back on my world," she pointed out, "but I sure do like it." She hugged Selta for several minutes, finally tucking her in for what had to be the earliest the girl had gone to bed since Pirlhoff had moved so unexpectedly into their home and into their lives.

Pirlhoff started into the living area just in time to see Brog Pawligan rush in, a worried expression on his face.

"Have you seen or heard from him?" he asked. "Sullrob, I mean. He flew in today, but I can't find him!"

"No! I've not heard anything! Oh, I hope he's all right—"

The communicator buzzed, snatched up by Brog almost instantly. He listened for a moment, then answered, "I'll be right there," before terminating.

"What? What is it?"

"The Orbiter Police have him. Something about criminal charges. I'll be back as soon as I can."

He touched Pirlhoff's shoulder, hoping to reassure the panic-stricken woman, then hurried out.

Pirlhoff stood there staring at the closed doorway for a moment, then felt a hand in hers.

"That's okay," Selta assured her. "We'll await together; I awasn't very sleepy."

*   *   *

"Motion for immediate consideration," Sullrob's attorney began. It had taken nearly forty-five minutes for Brog Pawligan to find an attorney so late at night. He didn't know if this one would be any good or not, but his fee sure was high.

"Any objection?" the judge asked. His young, well-scrubbed face appeared on the view-screen in the court section of the police office located in the commerce level.

"Time for investigation; standard twenty-four hours requested," the prosecutor objected.

"Grounds for immediate consideration?" the judge asked.

"247.85—Undue hardship," the attorney replied. "445.06—Dismissal factors in evidence; 121.64—Stipulate to immediate explanation."

"Proceed."

"Read the charges," the attorney requested.

Sullrob sat in a comfortable chair, restrained by a faintly glowing force-field.

Brog Pawligan sat to the side in one of the spectator seats. Several loaders and movers sat nearby watching curiously.

The prosecutor read from his comp-pad. "DDF.324—Murder with intent, two counts. DDK.488—Physical assault, intent to murder. DJM.421—Possession of unmetered stinger."

The attorney cleared his throat. "Will accept sanction for three of three on immediate consideration rationales." The lawyer had warned Sullrob that he could face penalties for pressing immediate consideration if none of his reasons were found to be valid.

"Proceed," ordered the judge.

"Undue hardship is caused by further delay. The defendant is a citizen of the planet Seelius. He is here to deliver cargo to a company with membership in the Consortium. He is due to return in another hour. A delay could jeopardize his employment and cause grave financial hardship."

"Prosecutor?"

"Hardship unproven."

"Will you prove it is not?" the judge asked, glaring toward where the young prosecutor sat fidgeting with his yawball jumpsuit. He'd been called away from a game. "Time to investigate," the prosecutor requested.

"Dispute the underlying facts?" the judge asked him.

"No," the prosecutor huffed, "Will concede."

"Stipulated," the judge allowed. Then to the attorney, he added, "Sanction waived. Motion for immediate consideration granted. Do you wish rulings on your other two reasons or do you prefer to proceed?"

"Proceed, judge," the attorney chose.

"Prosecutor?" the judge asked, giving him the opportunity to object.

"Request ruling on stipulation for immediate explanation."

"Defense objection?"

"Stipulated."

"Immediate explanation required," the judge ordered. Continuing, he began with the most serious charges. "DDK.448—Murder by intent, two counts. Plea?"

"Motion to dismiss," the attorney requested, "based on jurisdiction—other grounds possible."

"Prosecutor?"

"Request explanation," the prosecutor pushed.

"Jurisdiction, judge. The accusation is for acts that may or may not have occurred on the planet Seelius, not a member of the Consortium, self-governing."

"Prosecutor?"

The lad in the yawball suit punched his comp-pad several times, then reluctantly agreed, "Stipulated."

The judge made his voice sound more official, sing-songing, "DDF.324—Two counts, dismissed." Then he read the charge of assault, intent to murder. The attorney requested immediate dismissal; the prosecutor objected. The attorney offered 'explanation' as his grounds.

"The defendant," he explained, "was attacked by the man now claiming to be the victim. Sullrob overpowered him, taking the unmetered stinger from him and using it to hold him."

"Prosecutor?"

"Facts not proven, request trial."

"Trial granted."

"Immediate trial requested," the attorney hastily cut in. "Same grounds."

"Prosecutor?"

"Time to investigate."

The judge glared at the prosecutor, thinking for a moment. "You've had time enough. Motion granted." He read the third charge, possession of the unmetered stinger. The attorney had explained to Sullrob that stingers, a weapon similar to those used by government police on Seelius, are required by law to be metered—linked via microwaves to a central computer that monitored possession and discharges. Brog looked at the stinger on the evidence table, thinking that traders must have brought the same technology to Seelius several hundred turns before. For a planet so worried about cultural contamination, the government apparently had been amenable to overlooking this concern where usable technologies were concerned.

"Plead?" the judge asked.

"Request trial," the attorney asked.

"Prosecutor?"

"Agreed."

"Judge," the attorney interrupted, "Motion to bind charges."

"Grounds?"

"Guilt or not of assault charge will determine guilt or not of weapon charge."

"Prosecutor?"

"Disputed, judge."

"Grounds?"

"Investigation needed."

The judge glared at him again. "You've had time enough. Motion granted. Charges bound. Separate charges dismissed. New charge—DDK.448/DJM.421. Any pre-trial motions?"

The prosecutor exercised his privilege to make his motions first. "One, judge. Motion for time to investigate."

"You're wasting *my* time, sir," the judge castigated. "Will defense object if I deny motion without argument?"

"No objection."

"Motion denied. Defense motions?"

"Motion for summary dismissal."

The judge rubbed his face. "We're *never* gonna get this trial done, are we? Grounds?"

"Offer explanation," the attorney pressed.

"Go ahead."

"The defendant," the attorney began, "was assaulted by three men, one of whom was the victim holding the unmetered stinger. The men were mad about rumors that the defendant had killed his children. Mr. Sullrob kicked the so-called victim in the groin, struggling with him, and taking his stinger away. Request medical exam to confirm this injury if fact is disputed."

"Continue," the judge waved, obviously impatient.

"The other two men ran away while the defendant held the stinger on the so-called victim and called for the police to assist. If trial is to be held, the police who responded to his shouts will testify they came upon the scene to discover Mr. Sullrob pointing this weapon with no apparent intent to discharge, plus displaying an obvious desire to relinquish the weapon and turn over the man for custody. These issues will be probed." He waited for the judge's reaction.

"Prosecution dispute?"

The prosecutor punched his comp-pad, then lowered his audio screen and spoke through his communicator for a moment. Raising his audio screen, he admitted, "No dispute." It was better to lose than face sanctions for frivolous or malicious prosecution.

"Motion for summary dismissal granted. Mr. Sullrob, you are free to leave." The image of the judge winked out; the force-field blinked out.

Sullrob, Brog Pawligan, and the attorney walked out into the corridor. Once they were away from other people, the attorney presented a bill to Brog Pawligan, wished Sullrob luck, and walked away. Sullrob touched Brog on both shoulders and forehead—a gesture repeated by his friend. Sullrob leaned against the wall and visibly started to shake, breathing heavy.

"It's over, my friend," Brog assured him.

"On my planet," Sullrob explained, "the suspicion alone would be enough. I would be executed."

"That's why you're leaving," Brog reminded him.

Sullrob shook his head. "Not soon enough . . . not soon enough. One thing *did* work out lucky."

"What's that?"

"They searched my bags. All I had were some personal possessions and one family Chronicle—no Zhasou. I thought it might be smart to wait for my second trip before resuming our, um, smuggling . . . of bringing something *very* important."

Brog grinned. "Smart move, Sully. Smart move."

"All is well with Pirlhoff?"

"Yes. She's been scared for both you and the plan, but this will be good news. She loved the valley on Caskentia. She named it Seelosia."

"I like that." Sullrob smiled, closing his eyes.

"Now get out of here," Brog cautioned him. "You're already a few minutes late. I will see you tomorrow."

"Yes. Give my best to Pirlhoff and your family . . . my *friend*."

*   *   *

They did a fast touch-touchy and Sullrob headed off toward the docking bays. He was glared at by several people he passed. He heard murmurs and whispers, felt eyes on his back, contempt in the air. The loaders were aloof, simply opening the ring so he could enter, not making eye contact. As the hatch to his ship was closing, he heard one spit out a parting epithet.

"Purple-face baby-killer!"

*   *   *

"Sullrob," Buchvan called, trying not to be too loud. Sullrob stepped from his groundcar next to his house.

"Is all okay?"

"For now. Come see my family tonight. We're having a few people over. We have things to discuss."

"I'll be there as soon as I can," Sullrob confirmed. Buchvan walked on purposefully, continuing his casual evening stroll.

More than a dozen people had already crowded into the modest home when Sullrob arrived, all anxious for news of how the flight his first day back on the job had gone. Sullrob related the animosity he'd experienced, the attack, the criminal charges and trial. The group was dumbfounded.

"It is good that there are safeguards to protect innocent people from the authorities," one finally commented.

"Yes," another agreed, "we'll need to develop similar laws and procedures for ourselves when we move to our new home."

"*If* we ever get to our new home," a woman interrupted.

Everybody had gathered to discuss news that many dozens of homes in nearby Waverla had been searched by police that day—seemingly at random.

"They say there were 'reasons to suspect,' but no evidence of this is offered and the citizens are not entitled to see it," Buchvan pointed out.

Buchjeen, his wife, added, "But no people were detained—so what reasons could they possibly have?"

"I've heard they seized some family Chronicles," Buchvan continued. "This is why we are all here tonight. Of the people involved in our plan, we are the ones most concerned about what our Chronicles might say. We are worried that the police may come to Tessila next."

"And *you* have an even *bigger* problem if they randomly sweep houses," Buchjeen pointed out to Sullrob.

Sullrob pondered the situation for a moment. Finally he said, "We all grow Zhasou in our gardens. We have plenty for shipments and, especially this time of turn, can grow a lot in not much longer than a tenth-turn. We are ahead on our shipments."

Everybody nodded agreement.

Continuing, Sullrob decided, "I will clear out my house for tomorrow's run. The next day, I will take everybody's Chronicles and any valuables of concern all at once."

"In the meantime," Buchvan suggested, "we should hide our Chronicles in case the police come tomorrow."

"Let's gather them all together tonight," another man proposed, "and hide them in my crawl-space. Many of you have seen where it is; I think you would agree the police will not find it."

"Then we will resume our shipments of Zhasou and start moving people after the habitat is ready," Sullrob proposed.

"But we can't *all* leave," Buchvan argued. "We need to supply Zhasou for most of a turn—and need Sullrob to fly it."

"We need to find another way to satisfy our contract," Sullrob suggested. "While we try to find a solution, it is imperative that we hide the Chronicles tonight."

Everybody agreed, hurrying into the warm night to alert the others and gather their cherished family documents in a desperate attempt to save them . . . and to save themselves.

*   *   *

Assembly day for Orbiter School, Jowda and Selta would be attending to participate in group exercises, plus to be instructed and tested verbally. It would mean a chance to see many of the other orbiter children whose paths they crossed only in school.

Pirlhoff made a delicious breakfast for everybody. After eating, Brog rushed off to check in for some sort of staff meeting, a regular nuisance that came with the job. Selta lingered to help Pirlhoff clean up while her brother watched vid-programs in the living area.

Jowda was shocked and surprised to see an Orbiter-news account of Sullrob's trial—even more surprised to see shots of his father sitting in court carefully following the proceedings. He thought about calling in the women, but decided to watch on his own. He figured they already knew. Nobody ever told him anything. If he alerted them, they'd probably turn it off or lie about it. Best to watch and learn for himself . . .

The media account proved fairly brutal, Sullrob portrayed as a barbaric killer of his own children who was beyond the reach of Consortium law simply because of his citizenship on the obviously backward planet down below. Much to Jowda's horror, his father was identified by name and labeled as a friend of the defendant, even seen congratulating the purple-face after his acquittal. The story had changed to one about a shoplifting trial by the time the women emerged from the kitchen. He said nothing about the program—he said nothing at all.

*   *   *

When it came time to leave for assembly, Selta hugged Pirlhoff and assured her she'd be home in six hours with Jowda. Actually, she would be released in about five, but she would wait around for her little brother so she could walk the decks and ride the tubes with him. Pirlhoff tried to fuss over Jowda and hug him, but he pulled away and rushed out the door. She looked to Selta with a hurt, confused expression. The teenager just shrugged and said she'd have to get used to his moods.

Still, Pirlhoff was concerned. She *was* getting used to his moods, but this seemed somehow different. The little guy had been starting to make a lot of effort to be sure she liked him—had relished the attention and affection she lavished on him. Something was definitely wrong. When she saw the news story a while later she figured it out. She spent most of her day agonizing about how to undo the damage of that biased, incomplete report. Plus, she was committed not to reveal any secrets . . .

By the time the children were due home from school, she'd decided to confront the issue directly. She really hoped Brog could have been home, too, but apparently his meeting had run until time for him to start his pre-flight routine. Brog always started that early so he'd have time to take a break, meet Sullrob and, hopefully, transfer some cargo.

When she heard the outer door hiss open, she planted herself in the middle of the living area. As soon as the inner door opened, both children stepped inside. Jowda glared at her wide-eyed, then rushed past her and into his bedroom, slamming the door behind himself.

"Jowda! Jowda!" He obviously had no intention of responding. She realized there were other uses for those nuisance privacy doors that seemed so foreign to the way she'd lived on Seelius.

Going back to the living area, she saw Selta sitting on a couch, staring at her lap. The girl was *very* upset, but not in any hurry to talk about it. Tentative, nervous, scared and unsure of herself, Pirlhoff sat beside her. She waited a moment before speaking softly.

"I saw the news report. What happened today?"

Selta started to cry softly, still not speaking. Pirlhoff reached for her, but with no overt response from the girl, stopped short of touching.

"They aknew 'twas Daddy at that man's trial," she said quietly, sniffling and wiping her face. "They ateased us and apicked on us, asayin' t'watch out Daddy was agoin' t'kill us. Jowda agot in trouble fer apushin' down one o'the boys, then th'other boys all astarted asayin' t'watch out Jowda awas a purple-facer, too!" She wiped her eyes again and continued to blurt out her frustrations. "Th'boy that was agonna t'go with Jowda ground-side with us asaid his daddy awon't let him be 'round us anymore, either. M'friend Patsy's anot allowed t'come over anymore. Ever'body kept asayin' th'purple-faces isa barbarians an' acallin' 'em other bad names."

Finally, she seemed receptive to Pirlhoff's touch, so the Seeliot woman reached out and held her hand. Selta cried a bit harder, then seemed to calm down.

Pirlhoff softly said, "We're *not* barbarians, you know."

Selta started to nod, but turned it into a shrug. "Awhat about akillin' kids?"

"I would *never—could* never—kill anyone, much less children." Pirlhoff tried to hold her own emotions in check, to be the adult, to be the calming influence, but her own tears started to spill out in spite of herself. "I could never hurt you or your brother, you know that, don't you? Don't you?"

Selta shrugged again, then sniffling, nodded agreement. "I aknow."

"Good. I'm scared your brother is afraid of me. I love him too much to let that happen."

Looking up, she saw Jowda watching from his slightly open bedroom door, hatred and fear competing with each other on his face.

"Y'won't akill *me*, y'stinkin' purple-face!" he screamed, slamming his door and locking it again.

Still unsure what else to do, Pirlhoff started to stroke Selta's hair. Eventually, the girl calmed enough to quit crying, then leaned over and allowed the purple-face she'd learned to love hold her in her arms. After several more minutes without speaking, she whispered, "We aneed t'talk to Jowda." She stood, wiping her face with her hands—Pirlhoff started to hand her a tissue and wound up helping her dab the drying tears—and went to Jowda's door. With Pirlhoff standing tentatively behind her, she activated the emergency-open and pushed the door ajar.

"Aget out! Y'get th'stinkin' purple-face out!"

"Jowda!"

"I don't awant no astinkin' purple-faces alivin' in *my* house no more!"

The outer door hissed, immediately followed by the inner door. Brog Pawligan was home, pushing a wheeled travel-trunk in front of him. Hearing his father, Jowda burst out of the room and ran to him, practically knocking Pirlhoff over as he zoomed around her.

"Daddy! Amake her aleave! Don't awant no stinkin' purple-faces alivin' here!"

"Jowda," Brog barked, "we'll deal with this later. We don't have time right now. I need to get this open right away!"

He unfastened several locking mechanisms and retracted the binding. Finally, opening the lid, he revealed the cargo.

Two children stood up, stretching after a long, uncomfortable confinement. There was a purple boy about Jowda's size and a much younger, similar little girl.

"Stava! Yantanna!" Pirlhoff shouted.

"Pirlhoff!" they squealed, leaping from the trunk and jumping into the purple woman's arms.

CHAPTER 6

Six people, three bedrooms. Brog had some finagling to do. Six people: three purple-faces, three peach-faces. Three guys, three gals. Two boys, two girls, two adults—no that won't work. One man, three Seeliots, two humans. Jowda had never shared a room with Selta even one day in his entire life. Boys and girls don't share bedrooms. The purples and the peaches were going to have to mix.

What else? Little Yantanna was obviously still very scared. She'd been clinging to Pirlhoff—never letting her get more than a meter away all day. Better let those two stay together. What about Jowda? He'd been pouting, avoiding, ignoring, glaring and staring, snorting disgust—mad as a Caskentian hornet. He sure wouldn't cotton to moving a purple-face into *his* room. Which is precisely why Brog decided to do it.

Brog would keep his own room. The girls would squeeze three into Selta's. Jowda would share his with Stava. If it came to blows between the boys and somebody *had* to move, would it be better to penalize Jowda by taking him from his own room to share Brog's? Or moving Stava in with Brog to show *both* boys that a human guy and a Seeliot guy could get along? It just might be a long night.

After a quiet, subdued dinner with only few words spoken, everybody gathered in the living room—even Jowda over his protests—to talk about what had happened. Brog wanted to clear the air before everybody moved in together for the night—for the week or more. Little Yantanna was so exhausted that she fell asleep with her head in Pirlhoff's lap almost immediately.

Directing his attention most toward his own children and Stava, Brog explained, "My friend, Sullrob, the father of Stava and Yantanna—" He smiled as he looked at her. She was adorable, such a tiny little girl, sleeping peacefully after such a confusing week and now having to be away from her father for the first time in her short life. She'd even had to leave her weenshugger behind. It was a good thing Pirlhoff was there for her. "We've been making plans to help Sullrob and his family, plus many of his friends and neighbors, move to Caskentia. That's why we all bought that beautiful valley, so everybody could build their own homes there."

Jowda glared at his feet. He obviously didn't want to hear any of this and he sure didn't want a purple-face in *his* bedroom.

"Yes," he continued, "there are some bad people down there on Seeliot—people who want to kill families or children because they are different. There are bad humans who are the same way—we're no different. Some of *us* want to hate or hurt others for the same kinds of reasons."

He paused, studying Jowda for a moment. Yes, the brat was listening. He understood. It didn't have to change how he felt, though. He noticed that Selta and Pirlhoff were holding hands. Stava was listening very carefully. These were the first humans the Seeliot boy had ever met. He'd heard so many bad things, so Brog hoped this family didn't seem very different to him at all.

"I got a drug from the pharmacist—something not exactly legal, mind you, so it's important we not talk about it—and gave it to Sullrob. He was very scared about possibly being ordered to kill Stava and Yantanna, but he didn't want to ruin the plan and leave all his friends and neighbors stranded down there, so he took a chance. Well, he lost the gamble and was ordered to kill them. He had arranged for several friends to have the drug so they could bring it before the Panel and he could pretend to use poison. It put Stava and Yantanna into a temporary coma and slowed down their bodies so much that it looked like they were dead for a few minutes— just long enough to get them out of there and hide them back at home." To Stava, he weakly smiled, adding, "That must have been very scary."

Stava sort of grimaced, agreeing, "Yeah, even though Dad warned me not to be. Yantanna didn't know, though. We hadda be sure she wouldn't say something. We woke up with *awful* headaches, but they're gone." Quietly, he explained, "My sister's still very scared. She doesn't understand why we had to do that—why we had to hide—or why we had to leave home." Embarrassed, he added, "Now she's scared of Jowda 'cause he *hates* us."

"He doesn't know you," Brog corrected. "He's listening to bad things being said around the orbiter. For that reason, you and your sister, like Pirlhoff, need to stay in our quarters until we can move you all down to Caskentia."

"How much longer?" Stava asked.

"Probably a week and a half."

Pirlhoff explained, "That's about ten or eleven days."

"You kids need to get some rest, now. I know it's been a long day for everybody. Selta, Yantanna will stay with you and Pirlhoff. It's too late to get portable beds tonight, so she'll sleep with Pirlhoff. She'd probably want to her first night, anyway. Jowda, Stava will be staying with you."

Jowda snorted disapproval, but said nothing.

"Until we can get another bed for him tomorrow, you two will need to squeeze into one."

Jowda knew better than to start an argument over it. He would go along, but he didn't have to like it. As long as none of his friends found out . . .

Stava stood and tentatively touched Brog's shoulders. "Thank you, Brog Pawligan, for allowing us to be guests in your home. My father chooses his friends wisely."

Touching the boy's forehead, then tousling his blond-white hair, he smiled and nodded.

Stava stood in front of his pouting host and offered, "Thank you, Jowda Pawligan. I will respect your room and your things. I am not used to your ways. Please help me if I make mistakes."

Jowda rolled his eyes, then jumped up and padded toward the room, Stava following behind him.

Just before entering, Stava turned and gave a hint of smile to the adults. "Good night."

Pirlhoff gathered up Yantanna and carried her to Selta's room, the teenager not far behind. Pausing outside Jowda's door, she called, "Oh, Stava?"

"Yeah?"

"Humans are more modest than we are. You should wear shorts when you go to bed." She heard Jowda utter his first words all evening.

"You *better* wear something!"

*   *   *

Brog Pawligan visited his friend from college days, the pharmacist with his own shop on the commerce level of the orbiter, to lobby for more of the drug.

"How you doin' today, Mr. Calvin?"

Shar Calvin rubbed his fat, flat nose, peering carefully through his third set of implanted corneas to see who had entered. "Brog! How y'doin', man?"

"Spinning out of control, flying on manual," he joked.

"Listen," Shar started, peering around to make sure nobody was listening, "I'll be right with ya. I gotta wait for Todly to come back from break."

After a few minutes of browsing, Brog noticed the young assistant wander in and take over behind the counter. Following the gesture from Shar Calvin, Brog went into the back room.

"Gotta have more, Shar," Brog started.

"You're trying to get me locked up, y'know," Shar warned, lining up his oversized frame, aiming carefully, then dropping it into a large, padded chair. "Used what I already gave you?"

"Yep. It worked perfectly," Brog confirmed, leaning against a cabinet.

"Saved them kids' lives? I heard he killed 'em."

"Not only fooled everybody and saved 'em, but they're in my quarters as we speak."

Shar leaned forward, hiking up bushy, black eyebrows and peering into his friend's face. "Right now?"

"This very moment."

Shar grinned, settling back in his seat and wheezing several times. "Well good then. I've never seen a Seeliot. I'd like to meet 'em."

"Then come back to my place and have lunch with us."

"Can I bring my bag?"

"Bring it along. How much you check 'em out will be up to them."

Leaving Todly in charge, they took a tube to the habitat level. Jowda and Selta greeted Uncle Shar warmly; then everybody was introduced around. They settled down for a light lunch of sandwiches and Zhasou tea. Shar was especially delighted with the drink—not bashful about having thirds.

Afterwards, with everybody gathered in the living room, he explained he was curious about physiology. After assurances nothing would hurt, the Seeliot children allowed him to scan them with his medical instruments. He recorded various numbers and graphs, listened to their hearts and respiration, and took several samples of dead skin for examination under his microscope. Nothing hurt; most of it actually tickled.

After another round of Zhasou tea and a gentle reminder from Brog that he was due to report to the docking bay, Shar followed him into the bedroom for a private talk.

"They're as human as you or me," he pronounced. "Oh, they're shorter, a bit smaller, and have that pretty purple skin, but there's no real differences *I* can see."

"They act like us, too, in most ways," Brog allowed, "good and bad."

"We *must* be related. We speak the same language."

"Traders a few centuries back sure couldn't account for that," Brog agreed.

"Seeing that little girl and little boy, knowing I helped them escape with their lives—well, I'm gonna take the risk and get you a bottle full of that stuff. Just make sure whoever down there has to use it is very careful."

"I can arrange more payment—"

"I'll tell you what, Brog. Why don't you get me some personal stash of that spice? That'll be thanks enough."

"You got it."

"Stop by the shop tomorrow after your shift. I'll try to have it then."

On his way out, he touched shoulders with Pirlhoff, telling her how nice it was to meet her. He tousled the hair of all four children, then turning at the inner door, told them all good-bye.

"Bye, Uncle Shar," Selta and Jowda responded in unison.

"Bye," offered Stava.

Still a bit shy, little Yantanna smiled. "Bye, Unca Shar!"

*   *   *

The next quarter tenth-turn on Seelius afforded the opportunity for the Tessila group to ship out all of their family Chronicles, other valuables and potentially incriminating mementos, and enough Zhasou to make a significant dent in the mortgage on Seelosia. They got together for a Celebration of Life, toasting the successful escape of Stava and Yantanna. Sullrob reported that he still received chilly receptions from most of the citizens on the orbiter, but at least nobody had tried to threaten or assault him. They agreed Seelosia would be a place where people of all colors and sizes would be welcome. They hoped they would *all* be able to live there someday.

A supply of the death-mimic drug had been brought back by Sullrob, so it was carefully distributed with precise instructions. People were scared of being put into the same situation he had faced. Though using the drug on loved ones was a terrifying prospect, *not* having it could be worse yet.

Scattered reports and gossip from other cities and villages seemed to indicate that the government was continuing to step up its searches and arrests. The trails of evidence and what people were allowed to know came more and more under question. As the extirpations spread until most people had been touched by them somehow—a relative or friend or neighbor, somebody from the job or a local merchant, somebody with whom Zhasou had been shared—grumblings of dissent started to increase. What started as an easy target to hate—*contaminants*—began to have a familiar face. Many started to feel like maybe everybody should just be left alone. A few even dared speak that sentiment, only to be targeted themselves not long thereafter.

The village of Micuwena was swept one evening; more than a dozen people were detained and several had already been executed. One man whose entire family had been put to death was the boyhood and life-long friend of Lafave, the other pilot who flew regular runs to Orbiter-two. The next day, after flying back to Seelius, he saw Sullrob preparing to take his groundcar home for the evening. He approached and asked him to come meet his wife and little boy. He was very nervous, obviously upset about something.

Lafave was a skinny Seeliot with bright yellow hair. His wife, Lafpats, was very pretty with long white hair and reddish dots on her face and arms. They had a son, not quite as old as Yantanna, a miniature version of his father except that he had mom's spots. The boy was a bundle of curious, playful energy.

Getting right to the point, Lafave started out, "My wife's younger brother and his family in Micuwena were arrested last night. They go before the Panel of Extirpation tomorrow afternoon." Lafpats gripped her husband's arm, searching Sullrob's face for his reaction.

"They say he and his children," Lafave continued, "are *contaminated.*"

"We don't know how or why," Lafpats interjected, trying to maintain her composure, "but that means maybe I am, too . . . and—" She looked toward their son, busily trying to take apart one of his toys in the corner.

"I can't let them hurt my wife or son—can't be the one to do that—" Lafave explained.

"It's wrong, no matter *who* our ancestors might be," Lafpats added.

"You are right," Sullrob agreed. "It is wrong, no matter who somebody is."

Both Lafs were relieved. They'd been afraid Sullrob might not sympathize, especially after what he'd been through. Still, they needed help, and he was their only hope.

"The only thing I can think of is to take them somewhere else—somewhere off Seelius—maybe start a new life."

"Have you planned anything?" Sullrob asked.

The couple looked at each other, sadness in their eyes. Lafave admitted, "We don't know how. That's why we want to ask for your help. You know your way around the orbiter; you've been flying longer and you leave the launch bays when you're there. You've gotten to know people, to know how things work there—maybe even know about other places people fly. If I sneak my family aboard and take them to the orbiter, I wouldn't know what to do next."

"We know we're taking a big chance talking to you about this," Lafpats offered, "but—" She looked toward her son again and lost control of the tears she'd so bravely held back.

Sullrob knelt down in front of the couple and touched one of their shoulders each simultaneously. He assured them, "There is a way I can help, but you must be patient. More importantly, there is a way you might be able to help your brother and his family, but you must gather your relatives tonight and plan very carefully. We will ask for you to help *us*, too. First, though, I want you to take me to see your relatives right now. I must be sure you are honest with me. I cannot risk my friends and their families without being sure."

Sullrob met Lafpats' older brother's family, another terrified couple with two small children, and was convinced this was not a trap. All agreed that Lafave would begin carrying Zhasou and eventually start smuggling people for resettlement on Caskentia. He gave them some of the drug and patiently explained how to use it. An intense evening, filled with fear and many tears, turned to optimism and renewed hope.

Sullrob had one last request. "Each time you fly to the station, avoid saying things that create prejudice against Seeliots. Tell the loaders I didn't really kill my children, that it was a mistake or bad rumor or something. We have problems *here* we want to escape, but we may be facing even bigger ones out *there* in the galaxy. We need to prepare for them as best we can; we need to make sure we don't *cause* them."

Finally making his exit, he drove home to feed Yantanna's weenshugger, to sit alone in an empty house, to miss his children even more than expected, to wonder when he would finally stop worrying about their future.

*   *   *

Stava and Jowda went into the boys' bedroom to get ready for sleep. Jowda had been tolerant and reasonably friendly the past few days, but he wasn't going out of his way to make anybody feel welcome. Brog seemed relieved at that much progress. At least the gossip and hostility around the orbiter—especially the teasing of Jowda—had faded away. The children Jowda might see in the recreation areas had lost interest in the issue even faster than adults. Still, Brog kept urging his son to stay home with Stava rather than running off every chance he could. The young Seeliot didn't seem to mind. He spent his time reading his mother's Chronicle or watching programs, trying to learn about human and Consortium culture.

Jowda closed and sealed the door, then quickly changed into his sleeping shorts and t-shirt. He nonchalantly watched Stava strip completely and don similar shorts.

Wow! He's apurple everywhere! Jowda was surprised to see that, otherwise, Stava looked just like any other boy. He wasn't even sure what he'd expected, smiling at the irony in spite of his losing battle trying to maintain a bad attitude.

"Awhy ado you guys akeep atouching shoulders and heads?" he wondered.

Pulling on a similar t-shirt, Stava answered, "It's alike your handshakes and hugs. Awhen we atouch shoulders, we're asaying hi or bye or agood job or athank you or I alike you or whatever. Awhen we atouch foreheads, it's stronger, alike a hug or something. We akiss, too, just like you guys—on the cheek or on the mouth if yer boyfriends an' girlfriends." He smiled, a sneaky leer crossing his features. "Sometimes they's big wet sloppy ones like I aseen 'em adoin' in the back of assembly."

"Yuck," Jowda pronounced.

"Double yuck," Stava agreed, though it really didn't seem *that* awful to the young Seeliot nearing ascension.

Stava started to climb into bed, but Jowda stopped him. "Ashow me how."

"How to *akiss?*" Stava joshed.

"No, dooker! Ashow me th'shoulder thing!"

Stava looked pleased. Jowda didn't really need to be shown; he'd seen it dozens of times. "It's alike this." He placed three fingers on the front of Jowda's left shoulder, giving a gentle press. He repeated the same on his other shoulder. "Agood night, my friend."

Jowda repeated the gesture, using his own statement to remark, "You're okay—fer a *purple-face!* Ha!" he teased, laughing.

"Peach-face!"

"Purple-butt!"

"Pawligoof!"

They poked each other's chests several times, dissolving into giggles and wrestling on the bed. Their energy spent, they finally crawled under the sheet and lay still for a few minutes, still breathing hard.

Jowda wondered, "Ahow come y'don't atalk alike my dad and Pirlhoff alike y'did yer first day ahere?"

"I'm alearnin' from *you*."

Satisfied with the answer, Jowda remained quiet. He reached up and touched the light sensor, lowering the illumination to a faint glow.

"Awhen's yer dad acomin' t'stay—or t'move to Caskentia?"

Stava thought for a minute. "I don't aknow. Amaybe many tenth-turns or even a whole turn."

"Ahow will y'see him after y'move ground-side?"

"D'know."

"Amaybe y'can acome avisit us an' asee him when he abrings Zhasou."

"That's what I was hoping—what I was ahopin'," he corrected.

"Ahow come they akill kids on Seelius?"

Stava didn't say anything for a moment, maybe not sure of the answer himself. "Athere are Panels for adecidin' if somebody adid really bad things, and if they adid, then somebody has t'kill 'em so they wouldn't ahurt nobody else. Anow they're startin' t'do it for people who ahave human traders amixed in 'em so only true Seeliots can a-live there."

"An' you agot human amixed in you?"

"Athat's what they asaid."

"Awhat's awrong with that?"

Stava was quiet for a moment, then quietly answered, "Nothing. Nothing's awrong with it. Everybody's agot lotsa people amixed up in 'em."

Jowda was lost in his thoughts for a moment. He couldn't think of anything wrong with being mixed either. His curiosity was enjoying its first opportunity to probe the mysteries of his new friend. "Awhat's that areally big, old book you abeen areadin'?"

"It's my family Chronicle—my mother's. It's a book awith our Celebrations and a list atellin' about my grandparents and then their moms and dads and theirs and theirs all the way back a long time. Everybody agets one when they're aborn. In th'old days, we used t'write ever'thing from our mom's and dad's in our book. Now we jus' amake zip-copies and add our own stuff, or we akeep theirs after they adie and astart our own t'go with it."

"You abeen areadin' 'bout people from long time ago?"

"Yeah. I wanna t'find out how I agot human trader amixed in me."

"Is yer mom in there?" Jowda wondered.

Stava paused a moment, then quietly admitted, "Not ayet."

"Awhat ahappened to her?" Jowda wondered.

"She adied in the plague. Awhat about yours?"

"Adied o' cancer when I awas alittle. That's a sickness sometimes y'don't aget better. Don' a'member her very much. Awhen did yours adie?"

"Awhen I was almost eight turns—about two *years* ago. I a'member her a *lot.*"

"Awhat was she alike?"

Stava talked about Sullruff for a little while, telling stories, recounting the time she found a weensnake in the house, cooking Zhasou cookies, reciting the Celebration of Life . . .   The more he talked, the more his emotions washed over him. Jowda listened very quietly, occasionally prompting, letting the Seeliot boy's thoughts wander wherever they needed to go. Hearing Stava's voice crack a few times, Jowda peered over in the faint light and noticed the Seeliot boy was crying quietly. Neither said anything for a while, both fading into yawns.

"G'night, Stava," Jowda whispered.

"G'night, Jowda. Athanks." Stava reached over and touched Jowda on the forehead, then snuggled down under the cover.

Jowda wiggled down farther, too, then reached over and touched Stava's forehead, whispering one last expression of affection for his new friend.

"Purple-butt!"

CHAPTER 7

Lieutenant Stewrik found Governor Plekwag sitting in his office doodling absently. The mundane administrative work that went with the job—mostly reviewing predictable reports or signing routine documents—had been neglected with increasing frequency of late. The Seeliot ruler had been perplexed about Ling Bozathorne's threat to replace him.

"You've got less than a quarter tenth-turn 'til the next Rep-assembly," Stewrik reminded him.

"Yeah yeah yeah," Plekwag waved off sullenly.

The dark-purple, white-haired advisor pulled a chair over, dropping his short, muscular frame into it so he could face the governor across his desk. "You've got dozens of decisions to make before you address the Reps. Some are quite costly, like the requested water projects in the drylands. There's been a lot of discontent lately; you can't afford to appear derelict in your regular responsibilities."

Plekwag glanced up, creasing his brow to assume his "serious-business" look.

"That's the beauty of using the Rep-assembly each tenth-turn to distribute supplies of crystal-drug. If issues start to boil over, I just find a way to focus attention on each Rep being the hero who brings home life-saving medicine every time he travels to the capital city."

"It's getting old, 'Wag. People aren't afraid of the plague like they used to be. Too much time has gone by."

Plekwag shook his head and turned his chair sideways to stare at the electronic equipment on the console in the corner—technology furnished courtesy of TradCo and Ling Bozathorne. He stroked his hair absently, finally blurting out what was really on his mind. "I gotta figure out how he could get me replaced."

"What's the big deal? We're giving him what he wants."

"Not fast enough—and apparently not completely enough. Bozathorne's a 'shugger-eater. He'd as soon rot me as help me. He could get mad any time and feed me to the waterwogs."

"So what can we do about it?"

"Figure out his game and stop him."

Stewrik thought for a moment, flexing his muscular shoulders and stretching his arms. It was a gesture that secretly annoyed the taller governor, a lanky, weakling of a Seeliot. Every time Plekwag had started a regimen to bulk up so he could look more "masculine," he'd always lost interest after a day or two and settled for keeping his hair short and avoiding clothing that might look too feminine.

"He'd have to line up somebody he could trust to do secret deals," Stewrik pointed out. Plekwag had been cutting him in for a small percentage of the payoffs that came from satisfying the demands of their corporate, human benefactor.

"I don't see how," Plekwag pointed out, turning back to face his assistant, leaning forward and trying to look tough.

"How did he first start dealing with you—with Seelius? I thought that would've been against Consortium law."

It was a subject that Plekwag always avoided. Maybe it was time to tell the story. After all, if Stewrik was going to help strategize, he needed to know how the enemy operates. "I found a capsule in my garden one morning. It had landed sometime during the night."

"A capsule?"

"Yeah. Smaller than a half-meter across, it had a tiny thruster, navigator, and disposable power cell. It was quite burnt from its trip through the atmosphere."

"You still have this capsule?" Stewrik wondered, leaning forward eagerly.

The governor waved him off. "Destroyed. Didn't want any evidence around. Anyway, I took it inside and opened it. An ephemeral message pad offered a cure for the plague."

"That *was* illegal, then. When Seelius demanded sovereignty from the Consortium hundreds of turns ago—back when traders were starting to come here—we were promised that no contact would occur unless and until we requested it."

"That's why there was a crude transceiver in the capsule. It was a simple device that looked like maybe *we* had developed the technology ourselves so we could make contact. Basically, that was it—a message offering a cure and reminding me that I had to be the one to ask, plus instructions for using the device. It ended with what sounded like an advertising slogan: Save lives, preserve your power, call now."

"So you called?"

"What else could I do? People were dying. Our whole planet could have been wiped out."

"That's what *I* would've done," Stewrik assured. It was the truth. People were dying; everybody was terrified. Personal profit aside, something had to be done. "And Ling Bozathorne answered your call."

"Like he was sitting there waiting."

"How did *he* know whom to contact? That we had the Jurnama plants that could grow the crystals? I mean, he must've known you had something he wanted, or why else would he make the offer? He doesn't seem particularly altruistic."

"No, he's a businessman all right. Since Consortium members don't use government for commerce, to them business is *very* important. He admitted that his company rented major portions of the Orbiter-two and had been monitoring—spying—on us. He said old trader records showed we had an abundance of the plants he wanted, so they started to monitor us to figure out whom to contact and what the best approach might be. Once they discovered we were being devastated by the plague, he recognized we had common interests and very little time to lose."

"How convenient."

"Yeah, well, I figure he'd been planning it for a long time. I mean, the Consortium builds those orbiters all along their shipping channels and they certainly didn't need *our* permission to build outside our atmosphere—but why *here* and not nearby Caskentia? *That's* the only planet they ship to around here. I suppose since Ling's company rented and therefore financed most of the station, it was *his* influence that got it put closer to us than his biggest customer in the area."

"So he could spy on us and figure out how to set up a deal for the plants," Stewrik finished, sitting back and flexing some more, deep in thought. Finally, he concluded, "So you contacted him, asked for help, and cut an exclusive deal with his company."

"Which opened the door for him to send more-sophisticated communications equipment and eventually furnish the ships and train our pilots."

"I'm surprised he didn't want to use his own pilots to—"

"Oh, he did," the governor interrupted. "That's when I pointed out our aversion to contamination. Actually, he liked that better. He said it would make it harder for others to squeeze in if we kept tight control over the situation."

"That's right. He'd have to be *very* concerned about competition."

"And he made sure *I* would be, too. After all, both sides are getting rich off this. Anybody else might not be willing to make, you know, *private* arrangements."

Stewrik smiled. They were both involved in a crooked kickback deal, but Plekwag never could bring himself to admit that out loud. "I used to think the monitoring array to prevent unauthorized contact from outsiders was so we could avoid contaminating our culture, but he also wanted it so we'd know if others were contacted about business."

Plekwag managed a weak smile. "Yeah, he thought he had me fooled."

"You'd think with all his technology, he could monitor communications himself."

"Sure, on *this* side of the planet. For him to put something in space that would monitor the other side, it would be too obvious to his competition and the legal authorities. By putting sensors ground-side, one on each continent, we can do our own monitoring without it being obvious."

Stewrik was taking it all in, fitting this new information into the various hypotheses he'd likely formed on his own during the last few turns. "He's picking up the signals that come from here and monitoring at the same time we are," he guessed.

"So what?"

"Well, yeah. He's got his own interests to protect. I wouldn't expect anything less."

"No," the governor agreed. "He's protecting *all* our interests."

Stewrik walked over to the primary console and examined the small boxes like he had so many times before. The devices were a mystery to him. Finally, he pronounced, "These are his. He knows how to control them. He could shut them off or make them give us false readings without us ever knowing."

Plekwag hadn't thought about that, but didn't want to admit it. "Yeah . . . so? Why would he want to?" Too late, he realized the answer to his own question. He hated to look dumb in front of his lieutenant.

"To contact somebody else."

"I've thought of that!" the governor asserted, almost too defensively. He walked over and stood beside the shorter man, eyeing the devices suspiciously. "But he's got no way to influence our politics. In fact, he'd be playing right into people's fear of contamination. That's our excuse for purging which, for some reason, he wants just as badly as we do—if not more."

Stewrik let that subject hang awkwardly in the air, the unspoken mystery ignored. They had conjectured together on many occasions, never coming up with a satisfactory guess as to why the man cared so much about Seeliot purity—or why he wanted to get so many of their Chronicles. "So we give him what he wants and collect our cut for a nice retirement someday," Stewrik concluded.

The governor walked back and dropped into his seat. The lieutenant sat down across from him. Plekwag pulled a stack of documents over and started to sort through them.

"What do we need to do to get through this Rep-assembly without too much hassle?"

*   *   *

Pilot Lafave's wife, Lafpat, arranged for friends in Tessila to help hide her brother's family. The last-minute ruse with the drug that temporarily mimicked death had proven successful. Her friends turned out to be people who were already in on the plan with Sullrob and the others. It would only be a matter of time until they attracted undue outside attention, though, so they joined the others on the waiting list for eventual evacuation.

Lafave started smuggling the cases of Zhasou which, along with the large amounts already being brought in by Sullrob, started to pile up in the storage areas of Brog Pawligan's quarters. His weekend trips to Caskentia would not be enough to keep up with the pace being set by *two* Seeliots shipping the valuable spice.

Brog remembered that one of Jowda's friends had a mother who piloted for one of the smaller importers, supplying textiles to Caskentia. He suggested that his son invite his little friend along on the next weekender ground-side, providing an excellent opportunity to meet and become familiar with the boy's parents before broaching the possibility of them earning some extra income on the side. Their plan needed another pilot they could trust.

Young Jak Hewed was dark-skinned with jet-black, tightly curled hair. Most of his ancestry could be traced to Earth's continent of Africa—if records had survived the explosion of stellar migration that had begun several millennia before. He was slightly older than Jowda, but not quite as old as Stava. Playing together in one of the activity areas—jumping and diving and whirling in a frenetic game of centrifi-snag that involved trying to capture each other's floating "birds"—they seemed un-aware of the collage of dancing colors caused by the variations of hair, skin, and their game-vests in bright, primary hues. Excited and thrilled at the chance to rec-reate on Caskentia, young Jak gladly accepted an invitation for dinner at the Pawli-gans' to discuss the possible trip. Because his father was gone months at a time crewing for a long-distance shipping company, only his mother could join them.

Lival Hewed wasn't at all nonplussed by the colorful skin of Pirlhoff and the Sull children. Although there were other planets where the vast majority of humans were dark-skinned, she was a minority in this region of space. Her family had settled here because of her husband's job and the opportunities for newly licensed young pilots like herself. She seemed enthusiastic about getting to know others who also didn't fit the common mold. She had been raised in an orbiter, having made only brief trips ground-side to several planets, and dreamed of retiring someday and owning a small piece of land on which she and her husband could build a home. She'd taken young Jak with her to Caskentia a number of times as part of her job, but had never ventured more than a few kilometers from the launch terminal in the few hours she was allowed before having to return to Seelius Orbiter-two.

Yes, it was okay for Jak to spend the weekend ground-side with the Pawligans, Sulls, and Pirlhoff. In fact, she was thrilled with the opportunity for her son to experience something so new and unique. She and the boy's father had talked many times of making a similar trip, but their schedules made it difficult and the cost, the expense of which would dip into the savings that were earmarked for that unseen patch of land somewhere in the galaxy that awaited them, was just a little too much.

Brog knew he had the right people. Best to let the boy have some fun first, then let word spread among the Orbiter-two children that the purple-faces were good people after all. He would get to know Mrs. Hewed just a little better before making her the offer of a lifetime.

Everybody enjoyed a fine dinner at the Pawligans'. They laughed and talked and compared parenting stories and job shop-talk, then covered topics like daily life on Seelius and, eventually, got around to mentioning Seelosia, still letting her believe it was the resort. Later, well past the kids' bedtimes, she gathered up her son and, with lots of handshakes and hugs, left to ride the tube back to her own quarters.

She had decided these were good people, people she liked, people she wanted to know.

And Seelosia sounded like a fine place indeed.

*   *   *

Several boys were hanging around to watch Jowda, Jak Hewed, and the others depart for their short "vacation" on Caskentia. No effort was made to disguise the three purple-faces in the group, a decision that made Brog apprehensive. He wanted to avoid unnecessarily stirring up anti-Seeliot sentiment, but ultimately decided that exposure to the real thing—especially in the form of a pretty young woman, a polite lad, and an adorable little girl—ultimately would do more to dispel prejudice before, if left unchecked, it could grow to be a problem. He thought he heard a murmur or two; the unfamiliar boys were wide-eyed and curious, but Brog's concerns were for naught. Stava, introduced to the group as a "visiting friend," instantly achieved the first level of acceptance—*walks and talks like he fits in.*

Pirlhoff was still a bit nervous, but she busied herself fussing after the girls, reviewing their pack-lists, offering snacks from her shoulder bag. The Zhasou cookies were a hit all the way around—especially since they were shared with *all* of the children in attendance. The girls were both quiet, but at least Yantanna was no longer clinging to the older Seeliot. In fact, she'd taken to Selta and had started to emulate some of her more human mannerisms. Amid lots of blatant hints from the gathering horde of boys— "sure ahope *I* can ago with ya sometime, Jowda"—Brog managed to load the substantial amount of luggage and herd his travelers aboard the borrowed ship.

It was a fun jump with each of the kids taking turns sitting at the console and touching the off-line controllers. After reaching ground-side and renting an aircar, they stopped at a terminal for a manual wafer transaction, then visited a clothing outlet. The humans—Jak included—selected several casual outfits, but most of the purchases were for the Seeliots since what little clothing they owned had been purchased for exorbitant prices on the Orbiter-two. Some of the items would be brought back to the Pawligan household, but most would be left at the habitat in anticipation of moving in hopefully during the next jump. For Jak and the Seeliots, it was their first chance to own swimsuits. Jak had never played in open water before; the purple-faces weren't used to wearing them. Brog made one last stop before heading out toward Seelosia—setting up a credit account at a home-furnishings outlet and taking a comm-catalog along so Pirlhoff could order items for her new home.

The "family" checked into the resort, lingering long enough for a fast lunch before flying out to the valley. Brog watched the youngsters carefully for their reactions. Selta seemed more relaxed ground-side than she ever did back in space.

Jowda was the too-cool bigshot veteran of recreation trying very hard to be matter-of-fact about the whole thing. Jak Hewed was so excited he could hardly contain himself, alternating between chattering "alook at that, alook at those" and quietly gaping in wide-eyed awe. Stava and even Yantanna never stopped grinning. At first apprehensive about how much they would like their new home-world, they quickly decided it was much nicer than any place they'd seen on Seelius. The lower gravity—eight percent less than the orbiter, which was already several percent lower than Seelius—was an unexpected bonus. Stava kept trying to see how high he could jump.

Pirlhoff was enjoying herself, too. Brog was pleased to see that her apprehension from the week before seemed to be fading away. Sure, she still fussed over the children and fretted about details and arrangements, but that was how she felt most comfortable. Brog remembered that his wife used to be like that, too.

In the valley, the children tore off to explore the waterfalls while the adults looked over the habitat-in-progress. Pirlhoff stood in front for several minutes, holding her breath. For some reason, she wound up fighting back tears, overwhelmed by the magnificence of her new home. Based on Brog's crude drawings, it mimicked Seeliot architecture with arched, pointed roof-lines always angled toward one side or the other and walls of faux stone, all in earth tones. It was the size that most impressed her. She said it was as big as the governor's place. With dozens of rooms and a huge courtyard—not yet landscaped—set into the gentle slope of the hill, it overlooked the largest of the lakes with a deck-side view of some of the waterfalls.

"Plenty of space for human guests," Brog teased.

Inside, she was even more excited. At first concerned how she—even with friends and neighbors pitching in—could manage such a big place, she was awed by the many modern conveniences that made the place almost maintenance-free. Seeliots considered automatic toilets to be the height of modern luxury. Here, the robotics and sensors and auto-this and auto-that were like new toys.

Soon, the children drifted in and started to explore, annoying the members of the porta-crew that was busy installing amenities. For Stava and Yantanna, it was technology. For the humans, it was size and space—and the outdoors resplendent just outside every window, spread out below every balcony or deck, the open sky and the deep lakes and the red mountains overlooking this magnificent world.

After a time, a representative of the construction company showed up and gave them a more formal tour. The children, no longer able to resist the call of pink and blue sand and crystal clear water, changed into swimsuits and ran off to play and splash in the water—"no place deeper than your waist for now!"—while the rep sat with Brog and Pirlhoff on the big deck.

"You know," the rep offered, "I can make sure the suites of rooms at that end, plus the smaller meal area and several bathrooms are livable by tomorrow afternoon if you all want to stay here tomorrow night."

"We would need supplies," Pirlhoff pointed out to Brog.

"Let's order some from the resort tonight and have them sent in tomorrow morning then," he allowed.

Smiling, the rep produced a log of dimension-stills and lapsed into a sales pitch for extra amenities that could be added for minimal cost. Brog bit on several—the biggest ticket item being the aircar garage with full-service capability—but Pirlhoff, used to much more austere living, was not an easy sale . . . until the greenhouses were brought up. Seeing her eyes light up for the first time, the rep hurriedly contacted his office and had a full catalog downloaded within minutes. His heart started pounding when Brog uttered the words every salesman likes to hear.

"Don't even think about the cost, Pirlhoff," Brog assured. "They're all quite inexpensive. You know about these things—pick out the biggest and best one you like. Get exactly what you want."

"Well, you know, I was thinking. When some of my friends start moving in, they're going to need something to do. Seeliots aren't happy just sitting around for very long. We like to be productive. If I start a transparent—a greenhouse—then there will be jobs and responsibilities available as soon as they move in."

"Excellent!" Brog agreed.

The rep gushed for several minutes, then patched in a direct link with his company's glass-structures specialist. They had progressed past a "hobby" sale; this was starting to sound like a commercial project.

Pirlhoff, surprising the expert with her savvy of greenhouse operations, put both reps through their paces for the next hour before settling on the design and location she wanted. Brog kept quiet, enjoying the most enthusiasm he'd ever seen from his new friend. He divided his time between watching her and keeping an eye on the children at play. By the time the transaction was completed, Selta and Yantanna had wandered back in to sit with the adults. The boys were showing no sign of running out of energy, playing water games, laughing and splashing, like they'd known each other all their lives.

Once the rep was gone, Selta asked, "Awhat's a greenhouse alook like?"

Pirlhoff showed her a dimension-still of the design she'd ordered, explaining that she could use it to grow all kinds of plants. "We're going to grow a lot of our own food for everybody who lives here," she announced proudly.

"Yeah," Brog agreed, "and you can grow lots of beautiful flowers, too—many kinds you've never seen before."

"You could ahave *so* many things agrowin' in there!" Selta bubbled, her face aglow with possibilities. "It asounds alike *so* much fun!"

"Can I agrow something, too?" Yantanna asked Pirlhoff shyly. Both adults grinned at her use of orbiter patois.

"Sure sweetheart, anything you want. What would you like to grow?"

The little girl looked thoughtful for a moment, then satisfied with her choice, announced, "I want to agrow some Zhasou!"

*   *   *

"Less than a quarter tenth-turn from now, Pirlhoff will actually be living in Seelosia." Sullrob grinned.

"Here's to Seelosia!" Buchvan toasted, lifting his Zhasou mug. His wife, Buchjeen smiled and lifted hers, too.

Sullrob gave the little weenshugger one last scratch behind its ears before setting it on the floor and lifting his mug for a hearty draft. "To Seelosia!"

The Buchs had left their infant son and daughter with a friend while visiting Sull-rob for snacks, a pinch of Zhasou, and some discussion about the status of their plans. The weenshugger lingered, rubbing against Sullrob's leg, still humming quietly from the scratching.

"I see how she could get attached to her little 'shugger," Buchjeen commented. She reached down to scratch the critter's head, laughing when it jumped into her lap and snuggled close for more petting. About the size of a shoe, the Seeliot pet was covered with dark purple fur. Rather oblong, it was difficult to tell which end was which unless its eyes were open. Similar to Guinea rodents kept by many humans, weenshuggers were considerably smarter and were known for their melodic humming that started in adolescence and developed into beautiful songs by adulthood, their method of communicating not only with each other but with Seeliots. A loving owner who raised one from infancy could learn to understand the moods and ideas expressed in the nuances and variations of each song.

"After she left, Shuggy—as Yantanna calls him—alternated between hiding in her bed and searching the house for her. I swear I could hear him in there at night crying, but I'm sure he was just learning to sing."

"He sure likes attention," Buchvan remarked.

"Yeah." He smiled, watching the furball cuddle in Buchjeen's lap. "It was probably just a coincidence, but he finally stopped searching for Yantanna when I sang a little song at him that she taught me." He repeated the ditty for them; it was just a few notes and nonsensical syllables. "Wa-loo. Acca-loo-wa-joo. Acca-loo!"

The weenshugger raised his head and looked at Sullrob, his eyes shiny in the softening, pink light of evening. He looked up at Buchjeen, then rested his head in her lap and continued his humming.

"I'll bet she misses her little pet," Buchjeen pointed out, starting to scratch again. The 'shugger rolled over on his side and pointed toward his underside with a tiny front paw. Buchjeen laughed and started talking baby-talk to it, scratching his belly. "I'll betchoo miss you li'l girl, yes you do!"

"So sneak him aboard and take him to her," Buchvan suggested.

"I thought about it—especially at first when she—and the 'shugger—were both so scared. But I'm afraid he will move around and make noise—or, worse yet, start singing—and give me away."

"I'll see if I can come up with a safe container with plenty of air that will block out the sound," Buchjeen offered. "Put a little water cube in there and the little monster—" She scratched his face, laughing at the characterization. "The little beast should do just fine."

"Yantanna sure would be grateful. She sure loves that thing. It broke my heart to take her away from him."

"You had more important things on your mind," Buchvan interjected somberly. His shift in tone suggested it was time to discuss plans.

"They're in Seelosia right now, having a relaxing vacation, but checking on the progress of the habitat at the same time."

"Your children are there, too?" Buchjeen asked.

"Yes. It's the first time they will see their new home. I'll bet they like it." It would've been a sucker bet; the kids had spent so many hours studying Jowda's dimension-stills that the real place had achieved near-mythical status. "They won't be moving in until the next trip—if it's ready in time—which is why I said Pirlhoff will be living there in less than a quarter tenth-turn."

"Won't the children move in at the same time?"

"I'm not sure. I've left it to them to decide—and to Pirlhoff and Brog. They're really starting to be close to Brog's family, so a few extra weeks on the Orbiter-two could be good for strengthening those relationships while Pirlhoff starts to get the place ready. Besides, if we get you two moved in the next few quarter-tees, then there'll be adults there to deal with any problems with locals before exposing the youngsters too much."

"Problems?" Buchjeen wondered, sounding more alarmed than perhaps she intended.

Buchvan nodded, explaining, "Yes, we'll be strangers to Caskentia. We don't know their ways or their customs—don't even know *human* ways very well. The first few times we go into town and meet local people, become customers of the vendors, start to get to know our way around—there's too much chance we'll make unexpected mistakes, offend someone, stir up prejudice or no-telling-what other kinds of problems we can't even anticipate. We don't want to place the children in any danger."

Buchjeen's good humor gone, she looked distracted, lost in thought. No matter how smoothly things went, it seemed like there was always something else for worry. "We'll trust Brog to help guide us," she said softly. The other two nodded.

"I'd like to take *you* first," Sullrob directed toward Buchvan.

The Seeliot leaned back in his chair, thinking it over. He scratched his paunch—he was somewhat heavy for a Seeliot—and stroked his longish, white hair several times. Finally, he agreed. "Pirlhoff should have a man to help, especially if the locals treat men differently from women. Plus, I want to check things myself before sending our babies or my wife there."

"That's another problem," Sullrob interrupted. "Sending your babies could be even more dangerous than sending the weenshugger. Little Seeliots cry a lot louder than 'shuggers—especially if they're scared and nobody, not even their mama, is there to hold them."

Both Buchs looked stricken. This was a problem they'd probably pushed to the backs of their minds, not wanting to face the complication that maybe they couldn't take their own children, at least not 'til the youngsters were older.

"I won't go then," Buchjeen announced. She wouldn't leave her babies behind—wouldn't even consider it.

"I mentioned this to Brog. He said they have things they can give babies or children that put them to sleep for a few hours. He's going to talk to his friend who got us the poison that mimicked Tsalook without actually killing. I'm not sure what or how it works, but he told me he would look into it."

"If he can help us with our babies, then we will go. If not, we will stay," Buchvan pronounced.

"Let's assume it will work out," Sullrob interjected, regretting having broached the subject. "We should move you first, then the babies the following quarter-tee, and Buchjeen after that. Then we have that family from Micuwena—Lafpat's brother—that Normlou is hiding."

Both nodded agreement. Then Buchvan brought up another subject. "If I'm leaving Seelius that soon, there's going to be a vacancy on the Assembly right away. I'll make the next tenth-turn at the capital in three days, but we'll need a new Rep after that. I think you should take it, Sullrob. We'd have no problem getting you elected to represent Tessila. If you'll be here the longest—so you can keep piloting the ship—you might as well take the job."

Sullrob hadn't thought about that, but it made sense. He was constantly worried about what the governor might be up to. Buchvan had been good at listening between the speeches, picking up scuttlebutt, gathering information. It was critically important that the clandestine group not be caught off guard. "You're right," he agreed.

"Then come with me to the next meeting," Buchvan suggested. "You don't fly that day. I'll show you the lay, introduce you around."

The logistics were decided, then the trio relaxed with snacks and Zhasou, their heads full of plans for the future. Buchjeen didn't relax completely, though. She probably needed to get home and check on the babies. Even thinking about leaving them behind would make her yearn to pick them up and hold them close, protecting them from harsh, cruel worlds.

After they had gone, Sullrob wandered aimlessly into his bedroom to stretch out and think. The 'shugger followed him in and hopped up, snuggling into the crook of his arm and humming quietly. Sullrob pondered the world where he'd grown up, the home he'd always known, a place that had become dangerous and deadly, where the government could take people and their children away during the night . . . the kind of place he could no longer live.

And he was going into politics?

CHAPTER 8

All of the devices and machines and instruments looked kind of scary, but Brog assured Stava and Yantanna that all would be okay, reminding them that nothing would hurt. Pharmacist Shar Calvin had gone to extraordinary lengths to provide thorough physical exams for the Seeliot children before he would arrange to give over sleeping tonics to use on the babies. Closing his pharmacy for the day to conduct "inventory," he moved all of his stock and equipment to the front, setting up a portable medical lab in the back. A friend of his, a medical researcher named Orman, had traveled all the way from the research center on Diltomarius Orbiter-six to help with the exams. All he wanted for his fee was some Zhasou and permission to take confidential specimens back with him.

Brog had a case of the coveted spice and some goodies with him so, in the interest of making the children more comfortable, they all started the long session by relaxing with mugs of chilled Zhasou-ade and cookies. After a bit, "Uncle Shar" announced it was time to get started, only to be startled to see both children casually strip off all their clothing. After all, to them, that's how medical exams were conducted. The researcher hurriedly offered them frocks, joking awkwardly about cultural differences. The youngsters, still both confused and amused by human modesty, wrapped themselves in the billowy gowns and took seats on the table.

The researcher collected data and specimens, alternately hooking them to machines or scanning them, feverishly taking notes and labeling containers, all under the watchful, protective eye of Brog. Throughout the process, "Uncle Shar" kept them entertained with jokes and conversation, occasionally asking more serious questions about their diet, hygiene, treatments back home, medical histories, and other things that were reasonably easy to answer. He took notes on a pad, occasionally nibbling a Zhasou cookie.

Nothing hurt after all—in fact, sometimes it even tickled. The researcher pronounced the tonic would be safe for Seeliots to use, so Shar handed over a small case with six vials and a neatly printed card of instructions.

"Sure would like to see some Seeliot babies!" he remarked, watching Brog and his young purple friends head toward the tube.

*　　　*　　　*

Sullrob and Buchvan watched the proceedings from seats near the back of the crowded Rep-assembly chamber. There were more than two-hundred reps present, a number swelled by another fifty with guests and alternates. Governor Plekwag and his four lieutenants, including Stewrik, sat on the raised platform in the front. After a morning full of committee meetings—the important process of winnowing down requests to the ones that can garner consensus—it was time for the governor to give his responses to the last tenth-turn list and read the items on the new lists just compiled. The meeting usually lasted a few hours, followed by informal gatherings in the ceremonial room and courtyard before picking up cases of crystal-drug and heading for home.

Sullrob already understood the process—every young Seeliot learned it in school—but he was impressed to see it in action. The mesh of ideas and conflict of opinions laid the groundwork for mass negotiation in the smaller groups. Most items never made the lists. Some did as a result of persuasive argument, changed minds, newly embraced goals. Still others were traded off for support, debts collected, obligations for the future, favors for friends.

Buchvan explained that the process proved somewhat the same every tenth-turn, but this time he noticed that the more mundane items were dispatched quickly for prolonged discussion about a concern growing in many people's minds—the Panels of Extirpation and their role in purging contaminants. After much discussion, theoretical analysis, and a few personal anecdotes, it was obvious that most everybody had been touched by the increase in purges. While nobody directly condemned the goal of cleansing the race—that would be tantamount to blasphemy—all agreed that the process needed new safeguards built in.

So it was that Buchvan's committee requested that evidence of 'reason to suspect' be made public prior to all hearings, that results of genetic tests be independently verified, and that a monitor be appointed in each region to provide independent oversight of the entire process.

These were bold requests from people who had trusted their Panels process for countless generations.

*   *   *

Lots of boisterous conversation echoed throughout the chamber while everybody waited for the Zhasou ritual that would officially open the proceedings. The governor hastily looked through the requests provided by the various committees, discussing them quietly with whichever of his lieutenants was appropriate—infrastructure, manufacturing, education, or whoever had subject expertise in this informal advisory role. He showed Stewrik that virtually every committee had some form of request pertaining to the process of contamination purges.

"You know you don't have to give answers today," Stewrik whispered.

"No, but they'll be watching for my reaction—a hint of what my answers will be."

"Don't give them any."

"But I usually tell them what they can reasonably expect—or what information I need or whom I may need to consult before giving the official reply at the next assembly."

"So be generous with a lot of the other items and avoid dwelling too long on this one."

"Circuses and bread for the masses," Plekwag mumbled. "Give 'em things that make them happy and hope they'll not pay too much attention to the Dosir thorns in their shins."

"Something like that," Stewrik allowed. "Look, just tell them you need time to consider your options and consult with others. Then act like this process, something that was good enough for every generation before us, should never be tinkered with. Act like you care, but imply that these are very serious requests, not to be undertaken lightly, which may take some time to consider and implement."

"Buy some time?"

"Sure. Next tenth-turn, we'll have some new information for them, plus questions and comments and such to string it out longer. In the meantime, let's pay attention to whomever seems to be the most vocal about this."

That's how they handled it. The mood of the group started to grow combative when many of the more zealous people started to feel like their requests weren't going to be treated seriously. Several exercised their little-used option to speak during the governor's review, voicing near-heretical condemnation of the entire process, even hinting that maybe contamination was not worth paying the price of watching their friends and neighbors carted away for execution. Stewrik patiently took notes during the outbursts.

Several new names made the list.

*   *   *

Buchvan wanted to rise and speak, but Sullrob held him back.

"Why not? I'll be leaving Seelius after this meeting."

"Because you'll draw attention to Tessila. Let others handle this. We have our *own* plans for dealing with this."

"But we've got to do what we can for the others—for those who are defenseless, unable to protect themselves."

"An admirable goal, my friend—and one I agree with. But speaking now will not help. It will only place many of us in danger. I promise, if I am the new Assembly-rep from Tessila, I will help however I can."

"So be quiet for now, huh?" Buchvan asked, already convinced, but having a hard time with the idea of backing down.

"Yes. We've seen the process start here today. It will take time. It must be done carefully. I'm not even sure of the best way. There *is* one thing I'm sure of, though."

"What's that?"

"That you have a wife and two little babies at home who need you—and you're *not yet safe*."

*   *   *

"Mama!" Jak squealed. "It awas *so* ultimate!"

"Why, Mr. Pawligan! Jowda! Stava is it? Come in. Come in!"

"There awas *big* lakes 'n' waterfalls 'n' I'm alearnin' to aswim 'n' a *big* big house 'n' mountains 'n' *tall* trees—*real* trees 'n'—" He finally paused to catch his breath.

"He had fun," Brog added drolly.

"Oh Mama! It awas—"

She put a hand over his mouth, smiling at her guests. "Please, Mr. Pawligan, sit down."

"Brog. Call me Brog."

"Only if you'll remember to call me Lival."

The adults sat in the living area. The boys did too, but Jak's enthusiasm kept getting the best of him so he had to jump up and start unpacking his bag.

"I've agot d-stills!" he exclaimed. "Just await. You'll asee!"

"I'd have to agree, Brog. I'd say he liked it ground-side."

"What's not to like? It's a beautiful place with plenty of fun to be had for all."

"Alook! Just alook!" Jak squealed again, shoving a handful of dimension-stills into his mother's face.

"Jak. We have company right now—"

"Go ahead," Brog offered, amused. "I'd like to see your reaction."

She was truly awestruck. Sure, she'd seen photos like these—and even better ones of some of the galaxy's more spectacular settings. But these had shots of her son in them, laughing, playing, aglow in the sunshine, buried in pink and blue sand, posing perilously beside a giant waterfall, floating in the shallow end of a sparkling blue lake, climbing a small tree, lounging in a meadow framed by spectacular red mountains and billowy white clouds forming cartoon characters in the vivid-blue sky. She realized she was holding her breath, one hand to her mouth. "This is a spectacular resort," she whispered.

"That's not the resort. That's some property some friends and I have invested in," Brog corrected.

"You *own* this area?" She was shocked, all at once jealous and wistful.

Brog smiled. "It's not paid off yet—and it's shared with some of my friends . . . from Seelius."

"Mama! Awhen the planet aturns, the day-star amakes the sky achange *all* different colors. I *anever* aseen *nothin'* alike it!"

Lival Hewed laughed again. "Now you hush and let us *talk!*"

"Come with us," Brog offered quietly, "next weekend."

Jak's eyes grew wide. "Mama can acome, too? I can ago again?"

"Really, Mr. Pawli—Brog. It must be so expensive—"

"Nonsense. It's all paid for except food. You can cover your own meals if you like, but I'd rather you be my guest."

She tried unsuccessfully to concel her excitement. "It's *so* beautiful," she repeated. "Oh my, I don't know what to a*say*!"

"Will your husband be able to come along, too?"

She looked disappointed. "No, he's not home again for another three weeks. He sure would like a place like this, too."

"Maybe we can work out an opportunity for him to see it."

"Well, if I can delay accepting your invitation for that long—"

"No you can't," Brog interrupted. "That's a *different* invitation. We'll catch your husband on another trip. *This* invitation is for the weekend coming up. We leave the forty-third, whenever you're home and ready to go, and come back the forty-sixth."

"A*please*, Mama! I'll ateach you how to aswim!"

*   *   *

Sullrob sat in the Buch's living room talking with Buchvan and a dozen neighbors involved in the plot. Buchjeen sat off to the side monitoring two purple babies and Yantanna's 'shugger—all three of them sound asleep. She kept looking nervously at the time-monitor on the wall.

"Of course! We won't have to smuggle the Zhasou if we can just grow it on Caskentia—at Seelosia in the transparent!" one of the women remarked enthusiastically.

"It's not that easy," Buchvan corrected. "It'll take too long to get the operation up and running."

"How long would it take to build one?" one of the men wondered.

"Oh, it's not that," Sullrob explained. "The transparent will be ready to go in about a quarter tenth-turn or so, but Pirlhoff says even if we can get her several dozen plants, it'll be at least a tenth-turn before she can take cuttings, then another one and a half tenth-turns before she can get cuttings from those and again from the originals. Anyway, she said she needs most of a turn before she can build up the stock enough to start actually harvesting some for sale."

"But over the long-term, it's ideal," Buchvan concluded. "We can control the supply and have a way to generate income for our little colony from then on."

"At least we can stop this risky smuggling now and just concentrate on moving people," another man pointed out, more as a question than a statement.

"I'm afraid not yet," Sullrob disagreed. "See, we're only a third paid-off on the property, plus our expenses will go up with the transparent. We'll also need money to build homes for each family once they get moved and settled—oh, the original habitat will be good for the short-term, but everybody will want their own place eventually. Anyway, our highest priority needs to be to pay off what we have or we could risk losing it all—including the place to grow our Zhasou."

"So we keep smuggling for now," Buchvan added.

"What about the problem we're having getting the spice down to Caskentia? Aren't we still moving it up to the Orbiter-two faster than we're getting it to the customer?"

"Brog thinks he's lined up another pilot to help us," Sullrob replied. "He's taking her to Seelosia on his next trip before he brings up the subject. I think it will work out."

The faint sound of humming started to fill the room. The weenshugger had awakened. Sullrob noted that its nap had lasted not quite five hours—plenty of time to make the trip. Everybody relaxed with some Zhasou ale and watched the babies sleeping so peacefully. Not long after, one, then the other, woke up. They were quiet and relaxed, non the worse for wear. The sleeping tonic provided by Shar Calvin had performed perfectly.

"You make the next trip," Sullrob told Buchvan, "then I'll bring your babies as soon as you're settled in."

Buchjeen looked up at the two men, tears in her eyes. "It's going to work, Van. It's going to be okay."

Sullrob took another sip of his ale, also pleased with the tonic. Brog Pawligan and his friend had been a life-saver—twice—with their miracle medicines. "Yes, Buchjeen," he whispered, "you can stop worrying now. It'll be okay."

Sullrob took another long draft, thinking, *At least we won't have to make your babies look dead just to save their lives.*

*   *   *

It was quite an entourage traveling to Caskentia. The light-skinned humans included Brog Pawligan and his two children. The dark-skinned humans were Lival Hewed and her son. The purple-faces included Pirlhoff and both Sull children. By the time the air-limo flew in over the valley, the habitat and the greenhouse were both complete. The auto-maintenance garage was still under construction, but the transportation grid was already on-line. Brog no longer had to use manual controls to navigate and land.

"We'll need to buy an aircar or two," he explained, "plus some shuttle-mods for the kids to travel around the valley."

"You amean we can ago down to th'other end with the *big* big waterfall all a-by ourselves?" Jowda asked excitedly.

Brog smiled. "We'll have to have some rules," he pointed out.

Jowda and Jak rolled their eyes. "Always some arules!" they moaned in unison.

"Really, Uncle Brog," Stava asked earnestly, "you amean we can afly anywhere in the valley with auto-grid?"

"Pretty great, huh?"

"When *I'm* not using the car," Pirlhoff teased.

Lival Hewed was speechless, staring at the vast panorama, trying to take it in all at once. Brog had spoken candidly with her during the flight down, divulging a basic sketch of what was going on. To his surprise and pleasure, Lival had offered to help; he didn't even have to ask. They agreed to discuss it further later on. He wanted her to see what he had to offer before asking anything too specific.

Brog left them all there to explore the habitat and grounds, flying back to the resort to pick up the Zhasou shipment and make the delivery. By the time he returned, Pirlhoff had everybody hard at work, moving and arranging the myriad furnishings she'd had delivered during the week. She resisted unpacking most of the greenhouse supplies for the moment, concentrating instead on trying to make her new house feel like a home.

Brog was pleased to see Lival and Pirlhoff getting along famously. They were laughing and talking, comparing tales of each other's worlds, regaling themselves with comparisons of how all the children were more alike than different. Because Lival was a smallish woman about the same height as the Seeliot, with similar hairstyles and builds plus the same wide smiles, Brog was struck by how color was the only real difference he could detect between them. Shar Calvin's belief that Seeliots were descended from humans had to be true.

Brog waited until the following afternoon before broaching the subject on his mind. "We need help smuggling spice shipments from the Orbiter-two to Caskentia. I can't keep up—even bringing the enormous amounts of luggage like I have been."

"It would be easy for me to include one or two cases during my regular trips every day," Lival offered. "You'd just have to arrange a rendezvous to pick them up from the storage facility at the terminal—or let them build up until the weekend and move them yourself when you come down."

"You could bring even more if you also came here weekends with us," Brog pointed out.

She seemed both pleased and relieved, looking wistfully across the lake that reflected red mountains in its smooth surface. "I was hoping you'd say that," she said quietly. She caught a glimpse of her son and the other two boys climbing a gentle slope, exploring their new kingdom, venturing into a world both bigger and more beautiful than anything the nicest orbiter could ever offer. "I *sure was* hoping you'd say that. Sure, *I* like it here, but having a place like this to bring my son—

well . . ." She gazed again across the valley and saw Pirlhoff lowering the air-limo to pick them up. Dinner would be ready soon; she was bringing them back to wash up and eat. Brog watched with Lival as the boys were loaded, then saw Pirlhoff pick up the girls from the beach at the lower end of the lake before flying back.

"If you'll help us, you can share in all this. I mean, well, you and your family can build a home here and stay—be a part of the community. Help us until we pay off the valley and a parcel of it is yours. Help us generate more income after that and we should be able to finance your building, too."

She was overwhelmed with the possibility, not even sure how to answer.

The boys burst into the room, little Jak shouting, "Mama, adid you asee me? A-did you asee me?"

She managed a weak smile, "Yes, son, I was watching."

"Next time acan you ago with us?" he asked.

"Sure, son. Next time I can go, too. Listen, Jak, I want to talk to you about something. How about if we go for a quick walk 'fore dinner?"

The boy, surprised and confused by his mother's emotions, whispered, "Okay, Mommy."

She stood and took his hand, leading him to the door. Just before going out, she turned to Brog and nodded, "You've got a deal."

Everybody watched as the mother and son walked down to the beach. She knelt down in front of him, the two of them talking earnestly for a minute. Then Jak started to jump up and down with his characteristic excitement, throwing his arms around her and hugging until she lost her balance and tumbled with him in the pink and blue sand. Finally, they sat up, facing each other and holding hands.

"Why is she acrying?" Jowda wondered.

"She's ahappy, Jowda," Selta explained. "They're both ahappy about asomething."

"Awhat about?"

Pirlhoff tousled his hair and answered softly, "About the kind of thing that makes us *all* happy. She's found a way to make a better life for her child."

CHAPTER 9

As inviting as the new habitat was, both Brog and Pirlhoff felt reluctant to leave Stava and Yantanna ground-side in such a foreign world. Secretly, though he had confidence in her ability to deal with unexpected situations, Brog didn't like the idea of Pirlhoff being the only adult there to deal with the alien culture, either. Besides, when talk turned to the possibility of the young Seeliots being separated from their young human friends, they *all* balked. Yantanna misted up with tears and started clinging to Selta again. Stava, usually so somber and serious except when playing with Jowda, or more recently Jak, wanted to defer to Brog's and Pirlhoff's judgment. When they finally decided to bring the young Seeliots back to Orbiter-two, Stava couldn't help but betray his feelings of relief. The new home at Seelosia was a powerful Siren call, but with their new friends they were forming bonds nobody wanted to pull apart.

It was agreed that Buchvan would be smuggled up during the week; then he would help *all* of the Seeliots move ground-side during the next "vacation." At least, then, Seelosia would have two adults and the varied sensibilities of a man and a woman to grapple with assimilation.

Lival Hewed began smuggling Zhasou during her daily or twice-daily trips ground-side. Her part of the operation ran smoothly without the pretenses of "vacations" and "luggage." She could move the coveted agricultural product five times faster than Brog was managing. Lafave and Sullrob also both pushed their limits, resulting in an overall increase in volume that thrilled Dow Pfivvel and put the group, by Brog's calculations, just more than a half tenth-turn—about three weeks—away from having the valley and related debts completely paid off.

Two days before the next "vacation," Brog, already finished with his shift for the day, paced nervously in his crowded quarters waiting for Sullrob to show up. If all went smoothly, he might have another Seeliot with him. Pirlhoff had laid out trays of finger foods—including several traditional Seeliot dishes—in anticipation of celebrating the successful trip, of welcoming her neighbor and friend. Lival and Jak Hewed also were invited so, after the festivities, the next "vacation" and actual relocation of Seeliots could be planned.

Brog nearly jumped when the communicator chirped. It was Lival with exciting news. Her husband, Heilen, was home early. They'd had some maintenance problems with his freighter, so their cargo had been transferred to another ship before he returned to the terminal on Caskentia for repairs. It would be another month before he'd be ready to ship out again. Thrilled with the opportunity his wife had seized in his absence, Heilen was anxious to meet everybody involved. Brog, peering around at his modest quarters—already stacked to the rafters with cases of Zhasou—urged her to bring him over.

The communicator chirped again. It was Sullrob, in good spirits, asking for some help with his luggage. Brog hurried out and, after about ten minutes, wheeled in a large travel-case followed by the Seeliot laden with carry-bags. Sullrob dropped the bags and fell to his knees, gathering his children into his arms and holding them tightly while Brog unfastened the bigger case.

"Buchvan!" Stava squealed uncharacteristically at the sight of the Seeliot neighbor climbing gingerly from his cramped space.

"Pirlhoff!" was the new Seeliot's first reaction. "Stava! Yantanna!"

There was a fast round of touches and hugs, then Brog stepped forward and introduced himself. First, they shook hands, then they touched shoulders. "So *you're* Brog Pawligan," Buchvan pronounced. "We Celebrate you often," he added.

By the time everybody was introduced and there had been several rounds of hugs and touching, the Heweds arrived and the process started all over again. Heilen Hewed was the largest man in the group, a big, brawny fellow with very dark skin, short curly hair, and a broad nose set off by wide, thick eyebrows. When he laughed, which was often, he showed big, pearl-white teeth in perfect rows. He was very gregarious, speaking loudly, touching and grabbing people, snatching up his son to wrestle him in the air when the boy least expected it, caressing and holding his wife whenever she ventured within reach. All of the children managed to be gathered up into his big arms at one point or another. The girls always giggled. Jowda squealed and wrestled back. Stava, trying to be staid about the whole thing, wound up getting tickled until he gasped for breath.

"Yousa some abunch o' peoples yous is!" Heilen declared in classic "spacer-shipper" patois. "Alet's aferget asmugglin' an' we *all*—" he started, glaring at each of the children appraisingly, "—we's *all* gonna abee them *space pirates!*" Then he laughed again and snatched up Jak, pulling his face close to give him a menacing glare until both dissolved into giggles.

After some fast snacks, Brog quieted everybody to talk about business, reminding them all that Sullrob had to leave in an hour. Yantanna, already sitting in her father's lap, threw her arms around him and buried her face in his chest. Brog noticed that even Stava was never letting his father get more than a meter away, preferring to stand beside him with his hand on the older Seeliot's shoulder. Brog smiled when he saw Sullrob look up at the boy like he'd just noticed him. "Is that *you*, son? I hardly recognized ya; you're getting so big!" Stava smiled proudly, reaching out to touch his father's forehead.

Brog started the discussion. "Well, I have one request for starters." He looked around at the crowd stuffed into the tiny room, children on adults' laps or crammed into the open spaces on the floor. "*Please* don't bring me any more Seeliots until we start moving them to Seelosia. We're gonna knock the walls down!"

Everybody started laughing. Buchvan countered with, "Tough luck, Pawligan! I got two screaming babies in them bags!"

Brog pretended to grow faint while Pirlhoff explained to Yantanna that he was only kidding.

"But seriously," Brog continued, "if we get Buchvan and Pirlhoff and the two kids settled into the habitat this week, we can start moving the Zhasou plants so she can get the transparent running. Then we'll be ready for those screaming babies *and* the comforting arms of their mother."

"Athis See-*low*-sha asounds alike a *very* nice aplace, indeed it ado!" Heilen pronounced.

"We hope you'll come day after tomorrow with us to see it," Brog invited.

The large, dark-skinned man stood and bowed graciously. "It apleases me greatly t'cept."

The discussion shifted to all the details that needed to be taken care of groundside in order to get the place settled. Pirlhoff was still apprehensive about the rude stares and unfriendliness she'd felt in the city. Granted, everybody at the resort was nice, but she understood they were used to making a living welcoming otherworlders. Moving in meant the Seeliots, for the first time, would not have Brog Pawligan to help during trips to the nearby towns or when dealing with humans via communicator.

"There are so many cultural differences we're not used to or don't even know about," Pirlhoff pointed out.

"Maybe it would be a good idea to leave the children here—" Buchvan smiled weakly at Brog. "—with our generous host until you and I make sure things will run smoothly."

"What exactly are your concerns?" Brog wondered, starting to think Pirlhoff was being overly apprehensive.

"I don't know—that's just it," Pirlhoff answered, pulling Yantanna into her lap. "I mean, a little thing like human modesty doesn't seem that important to *me*, but if we didn't know about it and went clothes shopping, we could really create a problem trying on items right there in front of everybody."

"What do *humans* do?" Buchvan wondered.

"We use dressing rooms," Lival answered. "Though I'm not too shy myself and never did understand why other people care about that so much."

Heilen grinned. "An' she's a *fine* sight in*deed!*" he averred, reaching over to squeeze her leg, laughing again when he made her smile.

"Buying things is another example," Pirlhoff continued. "I mean, back home we always set a fair price for food and expect to pay what is asked, but everything else involves a process of bargaining. I know Brog has bargained our Zhasou deal and when he bought the valley, but I keep being surprised when he pays whatever is asked for everything else."

"That's because there is competition," he explained. "If we don't like the price, we can go to another vendor with a better price—if we can find one. It's normally considered rude to *challenge* a price. Lack of competition made the Zhasou deal and buying the valley exceptions."

"She's got a good point," Buchvan agreed. "It's not only a matter of *knowing* these things, but of getting used to them so we don't accidentally make a mistake that offends someone or turns people against us."

"That's what *I'd* be most worried about," Sullrob interjected. "Having humans turn against you—especially based on what they *think* you are—can be *very* danger-ous," he recalled, the sting of taunts, threats, and even criminal charges reminding him how easy it is to feel vulnerable or in danger.

"We're anot *all* bad," Selta spoke up defensively.

"Oh, Seeliots are alike that, too," Stava quickly pointed out. Seeing the puzzled look on the faces of the other Seeliots, he explained, "It's ahow we atreated the human traders. We alearn from our history how most Seeliots awelcomed them, but some awere against them and ahated them. They aturned others against them, too, until a few got akilled and then they was all abanned—asent away an' atold never to acome back or acontaminate our planet."

"That's right, son," Sullrob supported, still at heart the school teacher he'd been for so many years before his pilot training. "I'm glad to see you learned the real lesson there—which was that it only took a few having that kind of hatred. Then the poison spread until it was so dangerous that people's very lives were at stake."

"Athere's *another* problem fer bein' acareful 'bout," Heilen mentioned, very se-rious for the first time. He looked around the room like he was studying everybody, sizing up whom he could trust, whom he needed to watch. "Thievin'! Y'all be amovin' some *verrry* value-able cargo. I'm ahearin' 'bout the rich-man's spice at Dilltomarius. They be apayin' *any* price t'be the ones can aserve it t'they friends! Only abee matter o'time 'fore *some* Takener abee alookin' fer o'where it acomes." He looked around again, wagging a finger admonishingly. "An' they awon't abee alookin' t'*buy* yer goods." He paused for emphasis, barking out a sudden, "They a*take* it . . . an' awon't acare if *some* carrier abee agettin' hurt."

"Good point," Sullrob agreed uneasily, his eyes darting toward his children. "Buchvan and Pirlhoff won't be much used to crime—dangerous crime. What little we have, if the Panels of Extirpation find the transgressor guilty, then he pays back the victim and the community. If he's dangerous and hurts or kills, then *he* is killed for the good of all. The justice system *I* got a taste of was a lot more sophisticated— and probably *needs* to be for such complicated worlds—but I sure didn't understand how to deal with it except to have Brog help me."

Heilen pointed out, "We asure got *all* kinds o'bad ones. I aseen 'em *all* kinds."

"As a trader-shipper, he practically *is* one," Lival added half in jest, probably speaking more in truth than most suspected. Though Heilen seemed an honest man, he would be an exception for his line of business.

"Is awhy *I* ashould be agoin' ground-side wit'ya fer th'first few aweeks," Heilen concluded. "Y'got th'*big* big place fer a *big* human alike me. Awon't nobody aget over on *us* wit' *me* 'round."

Everybody looked around for reactions, then started nodding agreement.

"I'd feel a lot safer," Pirlhoff was first to say.

"It's a *great* idea," Buchvan concurred before everybody broke into a buzz of assent.

Heilen looked sheepishly at his wife, offering, "We'll ahave *our* time t'gether 'fore y'start yer runs. Then I'll acome asee y'*ever* day at th'terminal—" He paused, pulling her hand up and placing it over his heart. "Acountin' th'days 'til you acome again fer the *next* weekender."

She smiled resignedly. "I jus' get yer hide back and you run off again." She rolled her eyes to the others, advising, "Never marry a spacer-shipper!"

"Y'know I adon't alike t'sit in th'orbiter. I'll atake m'boy ground-side an' ateach him t'climb a tree!" he announced, reaching down and flipping Jak head over heals to a squeal of delight.

"I can acome, too, Daddy?"

"Don' asee why anot."

"Well, if *Jak's* agoin' . . ." Jowda started. All the children stirred, searching the adults' faces for their reactions.

"It's time *we* move, too," Stava concluded. "That we amove, too," he hastily amended, remembering to speak like an orbiter brat.

Sidestepping the speculation, Heilen pointedly asked, "Y'got th'wafers fer air-cars an' such?"

"Oh yeah," Brog answered. "Money should be no problem. I've opened accounts there, plus we have charge-wafers and there are credit lines already established. I need to go over it with one of you and, hopefully, turn it over to somebody to manage. I'm not an accountant, but I understand—" He looked inquiringly at Buchvan.

The Seeliot smiled. "You must've heard I managed a currency exchange back home."

"I was *hoping* you'd volunteer." Brog was relieved. He liked to keep his routines simple. The responsibility of managing the increasingly complicated finances of a growing community had been starting to worry him.

"So *who's* agoin' t'stay in Seelosia?" Jowda demanded.

Everybody paused awkwardly, then Pirlhoff answered. "Well . . . all of us except Sullrob will be going day after tomorrow for three days. As far as staying, Buchvan and I will be, and I guess Stava and Yantanna will be moving in. Jak and his dad will be staying for a short while for now—maybe a few weeks—"

"Acan Selta astay?" Yantanna asked meekly.

"And Jowda?" Jak asked.

Brog looked at Pirlhoff. She just smiled, her expression suggesting everybody already knew the answer.

"You'd have to keep up on your lessons," Brog admonished.

"The same also goes for *you* two," Sullrob added for his own children.

"You behave, and mind the adults," Brog warned.

"It's bonds like these that make a good community," Sullrob pointed out, feeling better about sending his loved ones into a strange new world.

"Yay!" the kids shouted in unison.

"Community?" Heilen thundered, opening his arms to encompass the entire group. "I'd asay iss be amakin's fer a *big* big fam-lee!"

*   *   *

Sullrob looked around at Brog's empty, now seemingly cavernous quarters and smiled. "Peace and quiet," he pronounced.

Brog grinned sheepishly. "Yeah, I'll admit it's been nice, but I already miss my kids and, well, Pirlhoff and yours, too. It's been, what?—three days now since I left 'em all down there? I still can't get used to it."

Sullrob pushed the cases inside while Brog unshouldered the bags. "I've been trying to get used to it for a while now. I used to lie awake at night, scared I'd have to face having them condemned. Now I just lie there feeling lonely for 'em."

"It brings back—" Brog hesitated, looking away embarrassed.

"Me, too." Sullrob offered quietly. "I didn't think I would ever get over losing my Sullruff. You know, I still don't think I ever will." He touched Brog on the forehead, then quickly turned to open the biggest cases.

"Selta's not that many years—not that many turns away from being out on her own, but . . ."

"So the time you have left with her is that much more precious. I know how you feel, friend. I just have to keep imagining getting through this and someday living with Stava and Yantanna and all my new friends and neighbors in the place with the waterfalls." Flipping open a case lid to reveal thousands of tiny cubes containing Zhasou plant cuttings, he added, "And these little darlings, hopefully, will mean I can stop smuggling sooner than expected so I can get on with being a dad again!"

"A retired, leisure-class dad." Brog grinned, poking the Seeliot where people touch shoulders.

"A *rich*, leisure-class, retired dad living the good life!"

"Here here!" Brog agreed. "You got a little time?"

"Time enough for an ale or two," Sullrob proposed.

Brog was already heading into the dining area to get some cold ones. "I got a code-pak from Pirlhoff this morning," he called out. "She says all is going well—though they're getting a little restless waiting for these cuttings." He handed Sullrob his ale and went into his room to retrieve the capsule, still talking over his shoulder. "She says Heilen's been taking them places in town, making them relax and enjoy the culture. She says they've been stared at a few times and even been treated rudely by a few, but Heilen is unabashed. He handles situations like he has all the confidence in the world," he continued, coming back in with the message, "and ignores strangers who seem uncomfortable. Pirlhoff says they're getting to know some of the local vendors and are now being greeted by name. They think it's going to be okay." He motioned the Seeliot to sit down and took a seat across from him. "There's also some personal messages in here from each of the kids." He handed over Pirlhoff's letter and notes from Stava and Yantanna, then sat back and drank his ale quietly while Sullrob read. The Seeliot handed Pirlhoff's message back, then put his children's in his pocket for later. Brog understood; he'd been choked up by his own notes from Jowda and Selta—and *his* kids had only been gone three days.

"I got some good news—at least I *hope* it's good news," Sullrob announced.

Brog leaned forward, smiling mischievously. "You got elected, didn't you?"

"I'm the new Assembly-rep for all of Tessila! I'll be going to my first session in a half-tee."

Brog held up his ale in toast. "To the purple-face politician!"

"May he not fall on his purple ass!" Sullrob toasted back, sounding rather unlike the school teacher for a change. As if the lapse in proper character reminded him, he changed the subject again. "I brought more lessons for my kids in there." He gestured toward one of the bags. "I know they overlap a lot with the human schooling they've been taking, but I want to make sure they keep up with their own culture as much as possible."

"And *I'll* insist that my kids follow *your* lessons, too, because it'll be an awful small valley we try to share someday if we don't know and understand each other."

"We have achieved consensus," Sullrob agreed jokingly. "By the way, the history pads and even some paper books that Stava wanted are in there, too."

"About the traders?"

"Yeah. He's really serious about learning what happened back then, and I think he should. Maybe he can find out some things that will benefit us all."

They finished their ales, then unpacked the rest of the luggage. They hurried through another ale each, trying to talk about anything but their families and their big plans before Sullrob announced he needed to go.

"I hate to see you leave," Brog told him. "It's too quiet here."

"Every trip back gets harder and harder for me," Sullrob agreed. "All I've got to go home to is a purple hair-ball that sings *all* the time." Just before exiting, he turned to face Brog. "But I'll be back," he added, "and one day it'll be my last trip."

"It's going to work," Brog said quietly.

They touched each other's shoulders and foreheads, then shook hands. As he was leaving, Sullrob quietly summed up, "We're not making plans of global proportion, but I've staked everything that matters to *me*."

Brog nodded soberly. "To *both* of us."

*   *   *

Breakfast at Brog's was becoming a nice routine. This was the third straight day Lival had started her morning this way. She and her paunchy pilot counterpart had been pretending to discuss plans for Seelosia, worrying about every little thing that would have to fall into place to achieve their ultimate goals, but they usually wound up talking about themselves and their families, trying to chase away the loneliness of missing their loved ones.

"It's so rare I aget to be with Heilen for several weeks in a row, I adidn't like to asee him ajumpin' ground-side," she admitted, "but I positive as aknow the feelin's o' them Seeliots. Y'sure don't asee many dark-skins out this way. Oh, they's a few on Caskentia, but I never aseen but one other family up here, and they's agone now."

"Why are you settled so far out here, then?" Brog wondered.

"Prob'ly same as you. Money's in pilotin'; the jobs is out here. Couldn't have done it without Heilen, though. He's bigger'n life—don't alet nothin' an' nobody abother 'im—" She paused and smiled, adding, "Never aseen no one a*messin'* with 'im, either!"

Brog laughed with her, enjoying how happy she was when talking about her family, and how she finally felt so at ease with Brog that she lapsed into a more casual spacer diction. He finally understood how carefully she normally chose her words, usually trying to fit in with the more-educated professionals found on orbiters.

"You think you remember 'bout takin' care o' babies?" he asked. I know *my* memory's a bit fuzzy."

Lival laughed again. "I 'member what they's best at!"

"Me, too—an' I remember many times havin' t'clean it up!"

She took another bite of grain patty, then reached over and patted Brog's hand, reassuring him, "I think we can handle some li'l purple babies fer a day or two 'til we get 'em down to their daddy. I hope Sullrob brings 'em today; I'm 'cited 'bout havin' 'em. Best way to ahave babies is to enjoy 'em fer awhile then agive 'em away!"

They both laughed some more and, realizing how late it was, hurriedly finished their meal. Lival stayed to clean up while Brog rushed out to meet Sullrob at the dock.

He paused outside the loading area and watched the big board that tracked ships and cargo, not wanting to draw attention that he was there to meet and help the Seeliot. He saw that Sullrob's ship was just docking, so he lingered in the passageway and watched for his friend to emerge. Five minutes went by, then five more and another five. It had never taken so long before; Brog felt the apprehension that always gnawed at him before every rendezvous. Finally, he saw Sullrob emerge flanked by two burly humans who were dressed more formally than typically seen on an orbiter.

The Seeliot looked worried, like leaving with those two was not of his own choice. He averted his eyes from Brog until just the right moment when he was sure the men wouldn't notice. He mouthed the words, "Babies! Babies!" and tilted his head back toward the loading areas. Then, giving a slight shrug to suggest he didn't understand what was happening, he disappeared around the corner with his escorts.

Brog felt panic, not sure whether to follow the Seeliot or try to recover his personal cargo. He decided Sullrob could fend for himself better than two packaged babies, so he strolled casually into the docking area and greeted the loaders. He noticed that Sullrob's bags and cases were in one of the storage areas, already locked behind a security field.

"Abeein' a bit early, eh Brog?" one wondered.

"Just checking the board—heard there might be some changes." He wandered over to the illuminated shipping schedule, pretending to study it. He could see the wheeled case that must hold the infants, but couldn't think of any way to get at it. Finally, noticing that the loaders were watching him, he turned to leave. Then he noticed the board display for Sullrob's return flight. He recognized the codes that meant, "Canceled; not rescheduled."

Hurrying back into the passageway, he followed the direction the two men had taken Sullrob, hoping to find them waiting to catch a tube. Unsuccessful, he rode tubes to the administrative and shipping-office levels, searching as frantically as he could without attracting attention, but nowhere could he find his purple friend or the escorts. Not sure what to do, he hurried back to his own quarters to see if there waited any kind of communication.

Lival greeted him with a big smile and open arms. "Y'got me some babies? Abring 'em on—" She took one look at Brog's face, then put her hand to her mouth. "Oh no. Asomethin's awrong!"

CHAPTER 10

The Seelosians gathered in the greenhouse. They were young and old, dark-skinned, light-skinned, purple-skinned—but they were all Seelosians. They'd talked it over the night before and decided it didn't matter where anybody was from, whose ancestors belonged to whom. They liked the idea that what counts most is who you *are*, where you are, and whom you're with. Seelosians, they were.

Pirlhoff was demonstrating how to care for the tiny Zhasou plants. She covered problems to watch for, techniques for enhancing their growth rate, and how to increase the number of shoots for future cuttings. The men were showing polite interest. The girls were enjoying themselves, looking forward to growing the spice and learning how to tend other plants, as well. Jowda was fidgeting impatiently—he wanted to get back to the maintenance garage and study the aircar equipment some more—but Jak was so excited he jumped up and down every time the Seeliot woman let him practice what he was learning about plants.

"Alearnin' to agrow abee fine indeed fer a boy t'know," Heilen whispered to Buchvan, smiling proudly. "Amaybe awill akeep 'im ground-side awhen he abee agrown!"

The demonstration was interrupted by the hum of the newly installed security grid immediately followed by the chirp of a communicator. Heilen had installed the network to keep air and ground vehicles without coded authorization away from the valley. Heilen walked over to the greenhouse's console and activated the communicator. A Tijartian woman's face filled the screen.

"It'sa th' real-estate lady!" Jowda exclaimed.

She introduced herself and requested permission to fly in. Heilen sent a temporary code to her aircar, asking her to land at the garage. She was greeted by the entire group.

After being introduced to everybody in the circle, she asked, "Your Mr. Pawligan is not here?"

"Not today," Buchvan responded. "Is there a problem with our mortgage?"

"Oh me no!" she smiled reassuringly. "It is very much opposite of a problem! I bring *good* information!"

"Well, Mr. Pawligan has turned over the financial management of our group to me," Buchvan clarified, "and there are no secrets among us, so would you like to come inside? We can discuss your good news with cold drinks."

The Tijartian gushed about the beautiful building and simple, yet elegant decoration, gratefully accepting a mug of cool Zhasou ade. She took a sip, registering surprise and pleasure, then took a longer drink. "It is *very* delicious!"

Once the proper period of politeness had lapsed, Buchvan asked, "What is the news you bring?"

The Tijartian set down her mug and unsheathed a satchel of papers. "Well, the seller has increased his listings—probably, just between us, because you are valuable customers and he wants to explore other opportunities while the timing is good." She spread the paper copy of a large-scale plat on the table. Everybody leaned forward to look.

"And which new listings might these be?" Buchvan inquired.

"Well, the owner's holdings include everything that is not blocked in pink. The valley your group purchased is here, marked in blue." A thin, blue streak of irregular width was smudged into the middle of the map.

"He or she has substantial holdings," Buchvan remarked indifferently.

"Oh, doubt it not. It was for him a long-term investment. My company is empowered to bring inquiries to his attention, but he has listed only three parcels in this region—two, now that you have purchased the valley—as attractors for potential customers. Confidentially, it was his belief that it would be many years before development in this area would make such vast tracts marketable. He has given me permission to offer you any—or *all*—" The words caught in her throat; just thinking of such a monumental sale gave her an emotional charge. "—as much of this region as you would like to purchase," she finished reverently.

Buchvan looked toward Pirlhoff and Heilen Hewed, then effected an air of nonchalance. "We already have all we need—"

"Think of the future, Mr. Buchvan," she interrupted. "You could substantially increase your holdings here for—" She leaned toward him as if sharing a secret. "—probably for only a fraction of the rate you paid for this valley." Not allowing anybody to interrupt, she continued, "For example, the next valley over toward the mountains is even nicer than this one. I think he would accept an offer of not much more than half—possibly even lower if you buy more. That's why you got such a good deal on this place—starting a community probably meant you would be poised to grow."

Buchvan looked thoughtful for a moment, still containing his enthusiasm. "As I said, we're really not very interested—"

"What would *make* you interested?" she quickly asked.

"No doubt your seller has noticed that we have been able to make substantial, regular payments, far exceeding our minimum obligation," Buchvan started.

"That's why I'm here so soon." She smiled.

"While there might be some small value—over the long-term—of owning more of the area around here, I would not want to commit our group to a monumental debt that would take substantial time to pay off."

"It would hurt nobody to make an offer that makes you comfortable," she quickly pointed out.

"So maybe we might consider a small parcel—say another valley or two—that we could pay off in a few weeks. That way, if our investment interests turn elsewhere, we'd not be over-committed."

"The bigger the parcel, the lower the price," she pointed out.

"If we could reach agreement on an *option*," Buchvan dangled, "then *maybe* we might be willing to look at everything on your plat."

The Tijartian practically gasped. She grabbed her mug for a quick sip, looking deep into it as if to discover its secret for good flavor. Based on how the conversation had started, she'd likely given up hope of selling the entire region. "What kind of option?" she finally asked.

"If the price was so attractive that we might want to take advantage," Buchvan started, "then we might agree to divide the region into twenty areas and purchase them one at a time—at a previously set price. You say your seller has no immediate plans for the area anyway. This would give him a likely sale but allow us out of the obligation if our fortunes change or our attentions turn elsewhere."

"I certainly would encourage him to accept such an offer," she allowed, visions of regular, ongoing commissions clouding her thoughts.

"If your seller is willing to negotiate under those kinds of terms, we will entertain making an offer," Buchvan summed up. "However, warn him we are thinking it would be at a rate equal to only a few percent of what we paid for this valley."

"That's awful low—" she started.

"But it's an impressively large amount when you consider the vastness of the total area," he reminded her.

"Yes, I guess it would be," she agreed. Then, smiling conspiratorially, she offered, "I will do my best to help him see the value in just such an arrangement—to see the benefits to him."

The Tijartian stayed just long enough to be polite, then left the plat with the Seelosians and hurried out to her aircar. She had a mission.

As soon as she was gone, Heilen clapped Buchvan heartily on the back, laughing broadly. "Can abee one space-shipper—th'way you asended her to ado yer werk!"

"You mean telling the seller our terms?" Pirlhoff asked.

"Amakin' her n'gotiatin' afor ya! Aplay *my* way or I awon't aplay! She'll abee aworkin' on his hide t'meet yer terms 'fore she even abee acomin' back to atalk price." He laughed again. "They'll abee a good deal soon!"

Buchvan smiled knowingly, but said nothing.

Stava interrupted, asking, "Buchvan, I know it would be a good idea to have more land someday, but why so much?"

"How else can we establish the biggest Zhasou production and export operation in the galaxy?"

*   *   *

Don't look nervous. Don't attract attention. Don't keep staring at the board. Don't look nervous.

Brog looked nervous. He kept looking at the board, hoping not to attract attention. He was waiting for the code that would signal that Lafave's ship was coming in to dock. *Stop looking at the board, Brog. Don't attract attention to yourself.*

The Tijartian ale was getting warm. Glancing around to be sure nobody saw, he quickly dumped it in the table 'cycler, then touched the symbol that ordered another one. Stop looking at the board, Brog. Don't look so nervous.

Another cold ale arrived. He took a small sip, then—*bing!*—the signal for Lafave's ship appeared. He left the nearly full drink behind, but at least he didn't look nervous as he rushed out.

Strolling with forced casualness into the loading area, he greeted Lafave. "Hey, bud! Caught me with too much time on my hands. Store your personals there with Sullrob's and I'll buy you an ale!"

Lafave was surprised and confused, but luckily he had the presence to play along. "Only if you're paying!" he agreed, touching Brog's shoulders.

They shoved his bags and cases over in front of the storage area where Sullrob's belongings were secured. Brog whispered, "Signal the controller to drop the field."

The man in the control booth hesitated, but saw nothing wrong with both Seeliots sharing a space. "What's going on?" Lafave whispered as the field was deactivated.

"Make sure nobody is watching. I want to switch cases."

Lafave made pretense of helping Brog put the cases and bags in, keeping an eye on the loaders and using his body to block sight of Brog's activities. "Clear," he whispered.

Brog pulled Sullrob's wheeled case to the side and quickly put Lafave's similar, spice-filled container precisely in its place. Just as quickly, he shoved Sullrob's outside of where the field would fall. More loudly, he announced, "Bring the one with your change of clothes and we'll fit in a game of 'snag!"

Signaling for the field to be reactivated, they casually strolled out, pushing Sullrob's case. They both glanced at the board. Brog felt relieved to see that Lafave's return flight wasn't canceled.

As they worked their way toward Brog's quarters, he explained, "Two men took him somewhere. You *saw* that his flight's canceled. I assume it was Sullrob who decided to secure his cases. That's all I know."

"Everything *I* brought is packed with Zhasou," Lafave said.

"I know. It concerns me, too. But *this* one should have two sleeping babies in it!"

Lafave caught his breath. "I hope they're okay."

They hurried into Brog's quarters, greeted by Lival.

"I was just aleavin' you a note. Gotta make my flight . . .   Oh! You agot 'em! But where's Sullrob?"

"Still don't know," Brog explained, quickly unfastening the case. "This is our other pilot and friend, Lafave. He helped get Sullrob's luggage."

They smiled weakly at each other, then vied to be first to peer into the open case.

"They're adorable!" Lival squealed. Brog carefully lifted out a sleeping purple infant and handed him to her. He lifted the other out and carried him to the crib he'd rented for Selta's room. Lival placed the boy beside his sister, then turned to see Lafave holding something in his hands.

"What is *that?*"

Brog did a double take.

Lafave stroked it several times, amused by their surprise.

"Why, it's a weenshugger."

*   *   *

Guided to a seat in the small conference room and offered a drink, Sullrob accepted a cold bubbler, asking yet again, "What's going on?"

"Ms. Clayjams will be right with you," one of the escorts finally replied. They both disappeared through a side door. Less than a minute later, a phenomenally skinny, very tall woman entered. She carried a satchel that matched her blue business suit. Sullrob guessed her old enough to be a great-grandmother, but decided he wasn't very good at pegging the ages of humans.

"I am *so* pleased to meet you, Pilot Sullrob," she gushed with forced politeness, extending a wrinkled, boney hand with extra-long painted nails his way.

Resisting the impulse to protect his wafer-pouch, he stood, politely touching her hand and then her shoulder before offering her a seat at the conference table. "Who are you?" he asked, trying not to betray his mix of anger and fear.

"Why, I'm Ms. Clayjams," she offered, sounding surprised. "I thought you knew! Oh," she mumbled as if befuddled, "they must not have explained."

"They explained nothing," Sullrob offered evenly.

"We postponed your return trip overnight so we can do some maintenance on your ship! We sent word to the launch terminal ground-side, but you must not have received the message before you departed. Oh," she continued, realizing a complication, "I hope they informed your family not to worry about you tonight."

"I have no family."

"Oh, good then! I mean, not that you have no family. Just, well, you know, that the late message—well, never mind. How *are* you today?"

"Startled and confused. I was practically abducted."

She pouted. "I *do* apologize! They really should have explained."

"I suppose I can make arrangements to stay overnight. So if you'll excuse me, I'd like to get my personal luggage and—"

"Your things are *perfectly* safe. I saw to that. We *do* have something to take care of before you go. In the meantime, here is a fully charged hundred-k wafer for you to use tonight. In fact, keep it, compliments of TradCo for use during all of your trips here. That much will buy a *lot* of ales for you and your friends." She winked.

In fact, it would practically buy a brewery. Sullrob felt suspicious of such generosity. "Thank you. *Why* is it I'm waiting?"

"For the conference. That's right; they didn't explain *anything!* It's *such* an honor, Mr. Sullrob. Our *chairman* would like to meet you." Sullrob looked indifferent. "That's *right!* Our chairman *himself!* He wants to meet the Seeliot pilot who so courageously carries the medicine that helped *save* your people."

"It won't take long?"

"Oh no, he's a *very* busy man. In fact, it's almost time. Have you ever talked through long-distance in space? Of course not," she corrected herself. "I need to warn you, there are delays while the signal goes back and forth. It'll take about six seconds each way, so you have to be patient."

As if on cue, the TradCo logo lit up an area of the wall. The light in the room dimmed everywhere except for the illumination on Sullrob.

"Standing by," Ms. Clayjams announced. Then, whispering to Sullrob, she explained, "I'll give you some privacy. Be back when you're through talking!"

As she disappeared through the side door, a fat face filled the screen. Sullrob had never seen such a large, overweight, multi-chinned man. Ling Bozathorne's skin looked greasy even on the communications monitor. The powerful human, smiling artificially, welcomed the Seeliot pilot, gushing about what a valuable service he provides for his home-world. It had obviously been scripted.

"Well, thank you, sir. I'm glad to be of service. Thank you for taking the time to meet with me," Sullrob returned, realizing the awkward expression on the fat man's face was because he was waiting for the reply to cross space.

"I sure hope you are paid handsomely for your important efforts. Please consider the wafer given to you as a small token of my company's appreciation."

"I am paid fairly," was the only reply. Ling betrayed slight disappointment when the message reached him.

It was a tedious, uncomfortable conversation for Sullrob, lasting more than thirty minutes. The fat man seemed to be feeling out Sullrob's reactions to various subjects including the possibility of relocationg someday. Catching on, Sullrob allowed himself to seem conspiratorial, somewhat greedy, surprised but interested in the notion of retiring to another world besides Seelius. After all, a single man with no obligations sure had a lot of choices to make when charting his course through life.

Sullrob grew disappointed that Bozathorne never seemed to get around to what was really on his mind. The meeting must have been a test. Sullrob hoped he passed; he was getting very curious.

"This has been a *very* nice talk, Mr. Sullrob. I hope we can meet again." So Sullrob must have passed. "If there is *anything* I can do, you just let me know."

"I do have one small request," Sullrob asked, thinking of it just in time. "Will you take some time with the ship's maintenance so I can have an extra day on the Orbiter-two?"

*   *   *

Heilen maneuvered the aircar into the maintenance garage and shut off the power. Buchvan was in town taking care of some financial business, but everybody else gathered from all directions, anxious to see if the babies had arrived.

He poked his head out, announcing, "They *both* 'em abee awet!"

He handed one infant out to Pirlhoff, the other to Selta. Everybody crowded in to see, gushing oohs and ahhs and baby talk and the silly sounds perfectly normal adults often make around babies.

"Agot asomethin' fer Yantanna!" he announced.

"Shuggy!" she squealed, carefully taking the purple furball and cradling it in her arms. "It's Shuggy!"

"Agot one more!" Heilen announced stepping out of the vehicle. Somebody else was getting out behind him.

"Daddy!" Stava exclaimed. "You came to asee Seelosia!"

*   *   *

"He's on Caskentia right now! He got a two-day layover," Brog explained.

"Good for him! Good for him!" Shar Calvin said. "Still, though," he added more seriously, "can you make sure you get this kit to him? Better yet, bring him by the pharmacy if he has time when he comes up. It's important that we get these specimens. It would *really* help our research."

"I'm sure we could work that out. What's this for? Why the hurry?"

Ignoring him, Shar asked, "Do you know the other pilot well enough to get him to use this other kit?"

"I believe so," Brog offered cautiously. "I want some answers, though."

"I can't, Brog. I just can't. Not yet. You've known me long enough; you know you can trust me. It's—well, I promise to tell you soon. I can't say anything yet until we know more. That's why we need these specimens."

Brog looked his friend over appraisingly. Shar was right; Brog could trust him. "Should I be worried?"

"I wish I had the answer. I hope not; that's all I can offer."

"Okay, Shar. I'll get what you need. I hope you're accomplishing something useful."

"You can't imagine."

CHAPTER 11

Everything ran smoothly during the next few quarter tenth-turns. The quantities of harvested Zhasou being smuggled were cut back to make room for Seeliots and more live plants. The greenhouse operation flourished through the patient efforts of Selta and Jak under Pirlhoff's watchful eye. The extra plants and faster-than-anticipated growth rate led Pirlhoff to predict marketability in three thenth-turns—or about four months.

The first Seeliots to move after the babies were Buchjeen, then the family of Lafpat's brother. Though their separation had been brief, the reunion between the babies and their mother was very emotional. After a few days of being overprotective, Buchjeen realized how much Pirlhoff and Selta loved her youngsters, how much they were continuing to look out for them. She started to feel like a part of the new community—her new family.

Still mysterious yet urgent, Shar Calvin asked for more Seeliot specimens. Sullrob took kits ground-side and collected several dozen from friends and neighbors, specifically labeling which were suspected of human contamination. The most explanation he would offer was an off-hand confirmation that all Seeliots were clearly human descendants. That had been established early; his interest lay in other matters.

The Seeliots had no significant problems with locals whenever they ventured to the nearby towns or cities. They experienced occasional misunderstandings about customs or what was expected, but people were largely helpful and understanding. Heilen Hewed stopped going along the last few days before he shipped out, giving them all a chance to gain confidence on their own. Pirlhoff still seemed the most nervous of the purple-face group, but she gradually acted less like a stranger and more like somebody who happened to be the newcomer. Once Brog passed along Shar Calvin's remark that research had already proved Seeliots were human, everybody in the group started to think only in terms of different colors—like Jak versus Jowda—rather than humans and aliens. Of course, convincing the citizens of the Consortium to think that way probably would take a long time, if ever, to accomplish.

With only one week before Heilen was scheduled to make another space-shipper run, Buchvan offered for the group to replace his lost income if he preferred to stay. The big, dark-skinned member of the Seelosian family didn't want to lose the pension he was so close to earning. He only needed a few more assignments to assure that young Jak would have his own income if he ever lost his father. Heilen promised that he would be back for visits and would settle permanently soon enough. Jak left to spend a few days on the Orbiter-two with his mother, but he promised to be back the following weekend, expressing a desire to divide his time between gound-side and the space station until his family could relocate.

During one of their trips to town, Pirlhoff allowed Yantanna to bring along Shuggy. They were stopped several times by gushing parents admiring the little creature, only to disappoint tearful children that no amount of money could purchase the little furball. Buchvan started keeping a list of interested people after a wealthy older couple offered an obscene amount of money to acquire one for each of their dozen grandchildren. He decided to ask Sullrob to ship several young female 'shuggers to Seelosia. Marketed correctly, the little hummers could be a valuable commodity. Besides, raising them would be a nice way to keep the children and some of the expected influx of new residents both busy and productive.

Pirlhoff was pleased to see Stava immersing himself in the Chronicles that had been sent for safekeeping, making charts, writing out summaries, and copiously studying the history texts his father had provided. Many evenings, she relaxed with him, talking over his work, studying his notes, acting as sound board for his ideas. She was surprised at how little she knew about what an impact traders had made on her homeworld—especially by introducing new technology—and was fascinated with the diverse personal family histories of her friends and former neighbors. The group set aside one evening for everybody to let Stava explain what he had been learning.

"There awere only eighteen traders that acame to Seelius just amore than two hundred turns ago," he explained.

"That's *all?*" Buchvan asked, surprised. "I thought there were hundreds or thousands. I thought they were overrunning us—that's why the citizens revolted and we had to purge them."

"No, athat was all. And six of them aleft after about a quarter turn. Twelve astayed to aset up for atradin'—three on each o' the four land-strips. They a-lived much separate from the Seeliots at first, but then some astarted to a-live with Seeliot families. A few got amarried an' had some kids before the purge agot 'em akilled. The history books don't atell who they were or anything, but I afound some in the Chronicles of Buchjeen and Leisdee and Zustew and—" He hesitated, looking away for a moment, then finishing, "and my mom, Sullruff."

Buchjeen put her hand to her mouth. "So it *was* a trader," she said quietly. "How can you be sure?"

"Several things agive it away. It alooks in all of these like the people awrote them after the purge so it awouldn't be so obvious. They acalled 'em *export merchandizers* in the Chronicles."

"Maybe that's how they talked back then," Pirlhoff conjectured.

"In one of the history books, that's awhat it asaid some people acalled 'em. I asearched the phrase in my cross-ref—it asaid was slang for human traders. There awere no other entries."

"That's why you missed it," Buchvan directed to his wife. To the group, he explained, "Her father told her a trader was part of her family, but she could never find a specific reference in the Chronicle."

"Another thing—" Stava continued, "the name of the export merchandizer in Buchjeen's family awas anamed Jonbagwell. That's too long to abee a true Seeliot name. People adidn't abreak name tradition then like some adoo now. I athink it awas a two-name, a human two-name like Jonbag Well or Jon Bagwell. In my mom's family, it was Samfowler—maybe Samfow Ler but prob'ly Sam Fowler. I afound other entries that amentioned Sam, but there is a gap of two generations."

Buchjeen had moved over to gaze at her sleeping children. Everybody turned to watch. Quietly, she said, "I don't care if they're contaminated—if *I* am, too. There's *nothing* wrong with them."

Buchvan moved behind her, encircling her with his arms. "They're perfect."

She turned half-way, looking up at him. Tears were forming in the corners of her eyes. "You would've been ordered to kill them—to kill me," she whispered. She buried her face in his chest, trying not to cry.

"That's the past, 'Jeen. We are safe now—*they* are safe. We got away just in time and found a better life and a better world."

She looked up at him again, this time smiling through her tears. "And friends to love. Our babies owe a debt to Sullrob that can never be repaid."

Nobody said anything for a moment. Finally, Pirlhoff offered softly. "We *can* repay that debt. We still have twenty-nine friends trapped on Seelius. We can make a home and a new life for them here, then welcome them with open arms when they arrive."

Stava walked over and touched the Buchs' foreheads. "Then we will ahave much to Celebrate."

*   *   *

It didn't seem like such a tall order, but during the long groundcar drive Sullrob started feeling almost like he wished Stava hadn't asked. Though pleased that his son had so thoroughly gone through Sullruff's family Chronicle, he doubted the missing documents to which it referred were worth all this effort. It wasn't so much the long trip to the village of Guntserille, but the memories stirred as he contemplated going back to Sullruff's long-dead parents' family home. Losing his wife to the plague was something he still thought he would never get over.

As he neared the outskirts of the village-turned city, he kept wondering how the house would look after all this time, remembering it as it was during those years he used to pick her up for their dates. In his mind, there she sat on the porch bench . . . waiting for him to arrive in his battered groundcar, only to rush to her room needing more time to get ready, not realizing he'd spied her peeking through the window . . . walking hand-in-hand with her new boyfriend in the garden . . . so nervous he got sick the first time her stern-but-loving father invited him to join the family for dinner . . . Celebrating *life* with Zhasou . . . helping bury her father in the garden . . . driving back with her to present little Stava to the boy's grandmother, then little Yantanna . . . watching the older Seeliot woman cry as she touched the faces of her grandchildren, creating images in her mind that her failing eyesight could never confirm . . . digging one last grave in the garden, then holding his young wife and mother of his children in his arms while she cried, little Stava tugging at her clothes and reassuring her that grandmother's *memory* and *life* would be Celebrated always . . .

He realized he was parked in front of the house. It looked the same, yet different in so many ways. The gardens and shrubs and trees had grown a lot. More homes had been built nearby. The walkways had been resurfaced using that new Tsalook-resin method. The ghosts of the past were gone . . .

He felt awkward approaching the house. He wished he'd contacted the current owners in advance, explaining what he wanted, asking for permission to invade their privacy and stir up so many old memories while they diligently created their own new ones. Stava was right, though; alerting them in advance would probably pique their curiosity, cause them to search on their own, jeopardize anything of value that might be hidden where the Chronicle had insisted the rest of the family records could be found.

"Hello," he offered, more nervous than he'd expected. "My name is Sullrob."

They were a young couple, probably about Buchvan's age, with a toddler clinging to his mother's leg. "And we are Trom—Tromlee, and this was my wife, Trompag. Our son is Tromdale."

"I am sorry to intrude, but this was my wife's family's home—"

"Oh!" Trompag exclaimed. "How nice. This *is* such a lovely house. Is your wife not with you?"

"She is part of my *memories*," he explained, looking down and feeling, inexplicably, somehow embarrassed.

"I'm sorry," Tromlee offered. "This must be hard for you to come here. You must have good reason . . ." He left the thought hanging, perhaps feeling it might be rude to ask so directly why Sullrob had appeared at his family's door.

"My son believes that the rest of my wife's Chronicles are in a hide-space here. I was hoping you would let me look, and take them if they are."

"Oh, please *do* come in," Trompag offered, turning to open the door and motion the stranger inside.

"I'm afraid you may not be successful," Tromlee apologized. "We've already found the hide-space behind the well-pump, and there was nothing there."

Seated in the visiting room, Tromlee served cold Zhasou for everyone, including a bottleful for young Tromdale still clinging shyly to his mother. She absently stroked the boy's blond-white hair while they talked. "Are your wife's parents a part of the garden?" Trompag wondered.

"Yes—near the back corner, close to the Tsalook shrubs."

"That's such a pretty spot," she allowed. "My mother lived with us here for a time after we married. Now we Celebrate her; she is close to the old-growth Zhasou along the far edge."

They talked for several more minutes before Sullrob explained that, according to the records, there were four hide-spaces. He asked permission to check the other three. Trompag waited while Sullrob and her husband looked behind the cabinet in the remodeled bathroom, then the enclosure that protected the master-bedroom air-vent, and finally under the flooring in the closet. There he found the box full of Chronicles, documents, and old-style photo-stills. The Troms graciously allowed Sullrob to take the box without question. They invited him to stay longer, if only for a few minutes.

Sullrob explained how his wife had grown up in the house, how he'd come there so many times himself during the turns after he reached ascension, how they had married and followed job opportunities to Tessila. Tromlee fetched some fresh mugs with cool water, then placed a box of Zhasou on the table. Together, all four went through the entire Celebration of Life, lingering for a while with their *memories*. Afterward, they went for a quiet walk through the garden.

Sullrob thanked them and left to make the long drive home. He hoped he'd found what Stava wanted. As he drove, he thought of his wife, dwelled on how much he missed his children, pondered how important it had become to build a life for his family in a world safe from Panels and racial-purity prejudice. There were a lot of records in that box, facts and dates and proofs and descriptions and mementos of real people long gone, about the family of the only woman he'd ever loved, history as it happened, leading him to a future he could never imagine.

$*$ $*$ $*$

"The meeting is called to order," Brog announced.

"Sounds *very* official," Pirlhoff teased.

"Awhy adoo *you* aget t'run the meetin's, Dad?" Jowda interrupted.

"I am acting chairman unless and until a majority calls for election of new officers. Now be quiet, shareholder Jowda Pawligan, until you are recognized by the chair."

"You aknow who I am!"

Brog gave him that quit-fooling-around look, so Jowda complied. "First on the agenda, adoption of by-laws for Seelosia, Inc. Open discussion."

Buchvan was recognized, offering, "We've been hammering on these for a while now—and spent more than a few wafers on legal and corporate experts to help us make sure they meet Consortium requirements, but I still have one last recommendation before we entertain motions to adopt." Brog expected the company's new chief financial officer to make some kind of fiscal proposal, but was surprised to hear, "It is our company's prerogative, according to Consortium law, to set our own stock-vote requirements. Our shareholders who are under the age of sixteen C-years cannot legally transfer their shares without guardian permission, but I recommend we use the Seeliot system of requiring age of ascension for them to vote."

"What exactly is that age?" Lival wondered.

"The onset of puberty," Buchvan explained.

"How is that decided?"

"The family declares it. In rare cases where it is challenged, a physician could be brought in to make the final determination, but on Seelius, it's always been accepted that when the family declares the child has begun the transition to adulthood, then it becomes official."

"So who awould aget to avote?" Jak asked. His parents were pleased to see that he felt comfortable enough to participate and ask questions.

Brog explained, "Right now, Selta is the only one among the children. Your shares, as well as Yantanna's, Jowda's, and Stava's would be voted by your guardians."

"You amean I ahave t'wait a few years 'fore I avote?" Jowda clarified.

"That's what it means."

"But Stava ashouldn't ahave t'wait. He's astarted puberty!" Jowda asserted.

It was the first time Brog had seen Stava look embarrassed. Human—non-Seeliot—culture must have been starting to affect him. Buchvan just smiled and offered, "We'll have to talk to Sullrob tomorrow and see if he's ready to declare Stava. As for today, it's not yet official." Pirlhoff reached over and tousled the young Seeliot's hair.

"I move we adopt the by-laws with the amendment that Seeliot age-of-ascension be the criterion for voting eligibility," Buchvan interjected.

"Asecond!" Heilen announced.

It passed unanimously, including the proxy Brog exercised to vote on behalf of Sullrob and the children.

The next item was issuance of stock. The board and shareholders officially approved establishment of one million common shares with certificates of ten-thousand going to each person, regardless of age, who was a member of the community.

Certificates were handed around, delighting Jowda and Jak the most. Everybody voted to provide ten-thousand-share certificates to all new members of the community arriving from Seelius.

The plat showing how portions of the valley would be divided into residential and commercial uses was presented and approved, along with the motion that each shareholder be given a parcel of residential land, selected first-come first-serve, subject to board approval.

"You amean *I* aget one, too" Jowda asked, surprised and demanding immediate clarification.

"Yep!" Brog responded. "Until you're older, you can live in *my* house—when I get around to building one. Then when I kick you out, you'll have land to build your own. That's not something you'll have to worry about for . . . at least a *few* more months."

"Afunny, Dad." Selta laughed. Everybody else grinned.

The purchase options to expand their land holdings which Buchvan and Brog had negotiated through the Tijartian agent were approved. It would be a large sum of money to pay if *all* the land was included, but it would give Seelosia, Inc. ownership of an area bigger than many cities—plenty of room to expand for many years or turns to come.

Also approved unanimously, they set up a stock-option plan that allowed shareholders to increase their holdings in lieu of dividends, or to take any portions in direct income. Enthusiastically added at the last minute, they bestowed the same stock/land package on Shar Calvin, their pharmacist friend who had helped save some of their lives with fake poison and sleep tonic.

Jowda wondered when he would be able to explore the next valley over—the first to be added to the corporation's holdings. Heilen offered to expand the trans- and security-grids right away so the kids could safely ride their air-bikes over there.

"I have a rather *modest* suggestion to make," Pirlhoff interrupted. "At first, I thought the purples would just have to get used to staying dressed all the time—the way the beiges and browns customarily do. But lately, I've noticed *everybody* has been getting more *casual*—even Jowda and Jak, whom I found sliding the water ramp with Stava yesterday. I thought all three were smiling at me— 'til I realized they were going down on their bellies!"

Everybody laughed. Brog recalled his initial embarrassment at noticing his daughter and Yantanna sunbathing on the far beach—without having to worry about tan-lines. Secretly, he was pleased to see his shy teenager so comfortable with herself.

"Later, I doctored all three boys' bruises," Pirlhoff continued, "remembering how nice it was not to have to worry about all this, um, *artificial* modesty that always makes me so nervous. Anyway, since this valley will increasingly become an area where business is conducted, why don't we ask people to practice Caskentian attitudes here everywhere except in the habitats and around the lower lake, but designate that the next valley over be fully clothing-optional? Everyone would understand that if they bring guests there, they will be responsible for warning them and ensuring that nobody is made uncomfortable by our cultural differences."

"Sometimes it *adoes* aseem silly to aworry about acovering up *all* the time," Jowda agreed.

Brog was surprised to hear his son say that; this was a big change for the boy who once hated purple-faces but now was starting to think like them. Of the group, Brog had probably most retained his modesty, but he endorsed Pirlhoff's idea along with everyone else, vowing to himself to get over there soon for a practice romp or two. *After all,* he thought, *this is our community. We should set our own standards.*

The last item of business was approval of staff hiring. Brog presented his recommendations. "I propose that I continue to act as chairman. Sullrob will be president. Buchvan will be chief financial officer. Pirlhoff will be director of agricultural production with Jak Hewed as her assistant—" The latter two were surprised and thrilled. "Heilen Hewed will be director of shipping operations with Lival Hewed in charge of pilots and schedules, and Jowda Pawligan will be apprentice to learn ships' maintenance." There were more surprised and thrilled faces. "Buchjeen will be director of pet industries—breeding 'shuggers for now—with Selta Pawligan as assistant and Yantanna in charge of product happiness. Everybody else is invited to apply for the many jobs that will be available. We will give employment preference to future residents of Seelosia. We will solicit the neighboring communities for more employees as needed. Everybody has something important to contribute; everybody should enjoy their work!"

The vote was unanimous.

*   *   *

Sullrob took the newly discovered family records to Brog Pawligan on the Orbiter-two and was surprised to see that his son had come up from ground-side for the week. It seemed his only son needed to be "declared." Noticing that the boy's voice squeaked a few times, Sullrob allowed as how he didn't need any more proof than that, but Stava insisted he go through the full ritual examination and recitation. After all, it was a tradition that would happen only once in every young Seeliot's life and Stava didn't want to be denied the full treatment. Shar Calvin was invited to stop by to join them. It took all of fifteen minutes, but Stava felt proud, his father even prouder. The foursome went out to celebrate with ales before Sullrob had to depart for his return flight. Stava went back to Brog's quarters and set to work on the box full of information.

The following day, Sullrob was approached by the same two men who had once led him to the TradCo conference room. It seemed Ms. Clayjams wanted to meet with him during his brief layover. Brog was out on a flight at the time, but Stava was waiting down the corridor to help. As they approached the boy, Sullrob glared at his son, barely shaking his head "no." Stava quickly ducked into an alcove to watch the small entourage. Sullrob casually remarked, "I hope my luggage is secure until Stava can pick it up." He saw his son nod agreement as they passed by.

Ascended barely one day, his scared son still looked very much like a vulnerable little boy.

*   *   *

Stava hurried to the loading area, relieved to see he was expected. He moved the cases to Pawligan's, opening them to discover more than sixty weenshuggers inside the biggest.

Buchjeen, with Selta and Yantanna, were already tending their first seven-'shugger litter ground-side, but this new breeding stock would kick their operation into high gear. It was a good thing because Buchvan had contacted the older couple to see if they still wanted some for their grandchildren. Not only did they, but they had contacted every pet distributor in the galaxy hoping to acquire little purple furballs without success and kept a list of those wanting to find a source of the new-wave pets. It was a *very* long list.

*   *   *

Sullrob's presence seemed somehow to thrill the tall, skinny, and very wrinkled Ms. Clayjams. He wondered why she hadn't, like so many older humans, used organ regeneration to replace her sagging skin.

"Welcome, Mr. Sullrob! Our Mr. Bozathorne would like to meet with you again!"

She left him alone for another conference with that multi-dimensional image that emanated from the wall in a unique, inter-planetary, delayed sort of way.

"Hello, Mr. Bozathorne," Sullrob greeted evenly, polite but not quite enthusiastic.

"Hope you've been enjoying your charged wafer, Mr. Sullrob," Ling offered with a wink and figurative nudge. "Just say the word if you run low—there's plenty more."

"I appreciate your generosity. I don't want to be too deeply in your debt, though—I might start to feel like I need to find a way to repay you." Sullrob was fishing. If the first meeting was a test, maybe this time the corporate giant would get to the point.

"I understand congratulations are in order! The governor mentioned that you're now an Assembly-rep! Your family must be proud."

So much for being low-key about his new role. Sullrob feigned pride, agreeing, "Yes, that's true. Our Rep had to leave the area, so I assumed responsibility for the good of the citizens of my village. But I have no family, only good friends and neighbors."

"Good for you! Good for you! I'm sure you have a lot of important issues to deal with!"

Sullrob was starting to get used to the delay in transmission; he liked the extra seconds it allowed to consider his answers. He made it a point to look relaxed and pleasant during the lags, remembering that Ling was studying him very carefully. "Yes, I hope to help my people."

"Of course, it is always good when a man can find ways to help himself at the same time he helps others, is it not?"

"That is my credo," Sullrob allowed, offering a conspiratorial smile. He wasn't going to find out what was on Bozathorne's mind unless he seemed interested in playing along.

"I understand how important it is that your people remain racially pure. That's why I helped out by furnishing the equipment that screens for genetic contamination." Sullrob felt rage rising within himself. The TradCo chairman obviously didn't know his technology nearly cost Sullrob his family—not to mention the lives of many of his friends and neighbors. "If there was enough support in the Assembly for it, I could provide equipment to screen everybody on the planet in short time."

"That sounds like a great idea, but I don't have very much influence," Sullrob countered.

"Maybe not yet, but don't underestimate yourself, Mr. Sullrob. You're a smart man. If you handle yourself well, you could go far—*maybe even all the way.*"

Sullrob grinned. "I sure like the sound of *that.* Maybe you have some ideas about how you could help me?"

"Indeed I do. But there's plenty of time for that later. Remember, a man must find ways to look out for himself first. Maybe you can help me accomplish some of *my* goals and I could help you, say, become a wealthy man—maybe relocate to another world after you've cleaned up your own home-world, to live a life of luxury and comfort. At a minimum, maybe amass some precious metals which would be very valuable on Seelius, to improve the quality of life for yourself and those you love."

"I would *like* to be a rich man," Sullrob agreed, trying to look enthusiastic over his inner repugnance. It was difficult to keep the images of executed families—especially innocent children—out of his mind.

"As do I, Mr. Sullrob. I've made it my practice to become a rich man, then to continue to grow even richer. I've done quite well, and hope I can share some of that with you."

"How can I help make you richer along with myself in the process?" Sullrob wondered, sounding very sincere.

"As you know, my company is making a handsome profit marketing Jurnama crystals as medicine—made from the Jurnama plants you ship up here on your runs. Luckily, we have found a way to do this for everybody's benefit—especially your planet's, helping cure and prevent an outbreak of that *terrible* plague—all without contaminating your culture. In fact, while even helping you with methods for purifying your race." He paused, waiting for a reaction.

Not sure what to say, Sullrob countered, "We owe you an enormous debt of gratitude."

Ling smiled magnanimously, his layers of chin pulling up on each side to form a sort of grotesque triple-grin. "Nonsense. I am repaid with profits from my Jurnama business. What I *would* like to do is find other ways to help your world and, hopefully, increase my profits other ways—without contaminating your culture, mind you. I think if you can accelerate this process of purging all the contaminated Seeliots—say, by pushing for mass screening so it can be handled more quickly— then your people won't need to be so afraid of infiltration when we introduce new ways to do business."

Not entirely understanding the logic, Sullrob played along. "That's a good point. We need to get this purge over with so we can move on—look for *new* opportunities."

Ling triple-grinned again. "I like your attitude, sir. Still, though, I'm not sure what those opportunities might be. I need a consultant—somebody like yourself— who can advise me in these matters—for generous compensation, of course."

"If we can talk without attracting attention," Sullrob clarified. "I wouldn't want to jeopardize my efforts to bring about a mass purge."

"Oh, of course! Of course! That can be arranged. I could give you a private communicator so you can talk to me directly from your home—without anybody knowing about it."

That explains how the governor communicates with TradCo—how he negotiated the deal in the first place. He must have a communicator in his home and/or office. Sullrob wondered how the first contact had been accomplished. "That would be much better than continuing to talk like this from the Orbiter-two. It could arouse suspicion."

"Yes, we can't have that. Ms. Clayjams will give you the device and explain how it works. She will be your contact here, and will arrange to have me included whenever I am available." Bozathorne hesitated for a moment, leaving Sullrob unsure if he should speak. Finally, he added, "I have another proposal I would like you to consider." Sullrob nodded, then realized Ling wouldn't see it until seconds after he had continued. "It would help us find ways to do business while preserving your culture if we better understood your people. To do this, my team would like to study family Chronicles. I hope you agree that these are priceless documents that you should be concerned about preserving for future generations. It would help if you would muster support for your governor's proposal to start a central library consisting of precisely reproduced copies of every family's records. My company would provide the reproductions at no charge. Only you and I will understand that we really want to study them to learn about Seelius, for the good of *everybody* involved. Your friends and neighbors need only understand that their most prized heirlooms will be preserved for posterity, plus returned to them in their original condition."

"An *excellent* idea!" Sullrob agreed, all the time wondering why Bozathorne would consider it so important to study mundane family histories.

By the time Sullrob left the conference room with a planetary communicator sealed inside its case, Brog had arrived on the Orbiter-two. Sullrob waved him off, pointing at the case under his arm. He nodded wordlessly asa he passed Stava, who was patiently keeping an eye on the now-empty cases near the loading area. He boarded his ship and headed for Seelius, self-conscious that someone could be listening. Stava would figure out that the man with no family had reason to pretend not to know his own son.

Harsh truths had made a man of the boy long before his ascension.

*   *   *

Stava caught up with Brog in the tube. Neither said anything until they were safe inside the Pawligan home.

Brog dropped heavily onto the couch and poked the lad in the ribs, trying to lighten the tension in the room. "Congratulations on your ascension, son!"

Stava nodded soberly, then sat closely beside the older man. "Thanks, Brog."

Brog put his arm around the boy/man, pulling him close. Stava could tell Brog was scared, too. Both hated mystery, wrinkles in the plan, not understanding what was going on.

"What was that about?" Stava asked quietly.

"I don't know. I wish I did. Your dad didn't seem too alarmed, though, so he'll handle whatever it is. He's a smart man; he'll figure out what needs to be done."

Stava nodded agreement, but wasn't convinced. The time he'd seen Seeliot officers arrest his family had shaken him up, but at least he'd been prepared and understood what was happening. This was different; he *didn't* understand and wasn't convinced his father had contingency plans. A situation he thought was under control suddenly seemed very threatening again.

After a moment, his voice squeaking from change and cracking with emotion, he said, "I wish we could get the rest of our neighbors moved and get some more plants and just be done with this. Then Dad could move to Seelosia and we'd all be together again and everything would be okay."

Brog noticed the young Seeliot wasn't effecting Jowda's and Jak's spacer patois. It sounded as unusual as when he'd first *started* to imitate the other boys. "Me too, son."

Stava started to tremble slightly, fighting back tears. "I guess I'm a man, now—with ascension and all," he whispered.

Brog put his other arm around him, holding him tightly, letting him cry. "I guess you are."

"It sure doesn't afeel like it."

CHAPTER 12

Pirlhoff grew very pleased with the greenhouse Zhasou production. Little Jak had really taken his responsibility to heart, learning and working diligently, seeming to take the success of every cutting personally. The playful little boy had a strong nurturing side, handling the little plants tenderly, fussing over them, feeling the sting of failure the rare times one withered rather than take root. He was working too hard, resisting letting her hire some helpers from the nearest town, trying to keep a protective wing over his little charges, sharing them only with Pirlhoff and his extended Seelosian family.

When all that could be done for the day was accomplished, she ordered him to go pry Jowda away from the data manuals in the maintenance garage and Stava away from his Chronicles and records so the three could have some fun. She walked outside and studied the second greenhouse being constructed farther up the slope. There would be too much work for Jak soon enough. *Why live in paradise if you don't live a little while you're there?*

She decided that would be good advice for herself to follow. With several more hours before time to leave to meet Brog at the terminal, she stopped by the habitat for a pillow, float-chair, and comm-magazine tablet, then headed for the beach to relax and read in the sunshine. She paused as she passed the 'shugger-hut, listening to the symphony of contented hums. She heard giggles from Buchjeen and the girls, then a shift in the weenshuggers' "song" that made them all sound like they were laughing in musical harmony. Enthralled by its simple beauty, she decided not to disturb them, so she headed down to lie on the beach for a while.

After so much teaching the young'ns how to work, she would prove herself an expert at how to relax.

*   *   *

Back in the habitat, Jak and Jowda paused to watch Heilen tinkering with a small electronic device, urging him to come play with them. The large dark-skin had just quit his job to work full-time at Seelosia. He wanted to get a shipping system set up, but giving his son a chance to stay ground-side and work in the greenhouse clinched the decision. Jak had passed up every other week on the Orbiter-two with his mother—actually, to see her there only whenever she wasn't off on flights. This was made easier by having his father around all the time. Seeing his mother weekends and visiting the terminal to greet her several times each week offered a good compromise.

"Can't abee aplayin' witchoo boys now—agot to ahave this aready for Brog t'give t'Sullrob." He explained how it would record conversations between the Seel-iot and Ling Bozathorne while masking the communication waves and monitoring for outside eavesdropping.

They tried Stava next, finding him in the company office pouring over his doc-uments. Stava looked like he might actually take a break and join them until Buch-van came in and asked what the newly ascended Seeliot wanted to speak to him about. Giving up, they headed down to the lake where Pirlhoff lounged.

"No outsiders around!" Jak announced.

Pirlhoff looked up from her comm-mag and smiled. "Go ahead!" she con-firmed.

They slipped out of their clothes and splashed into the shallow water, laughing and spraying, careful not to get her wet.

What is it with grown-ups that they're satisfied just to lie on the sand when they could be playing in all this cool water?

*   *   *

"I aneed some information," Stava explained to Buchvan.

The older man pulled up a chair and joined him in front of the documents. "Any way I can help!"

"Seelosia, Inc. is a Consortium company," Stava stated matter-of-factly. Buch-van nodded agreement. "Acan outsiders aget information on other Consortium companies?"

"Some, yes. There are public filings on a regular basis."

"Acan we aget information on stock ownership, acurrent an' historically?"

Buchvan allowed as how he thought it could be done. With the company's finances not yet very complicated, he'd been spending nearly all his time learning about Consortium economics and business. For a man who played with numbers and flow-charts like games, the galaxy had suddenly become a very big toy store. "Do we have a certain company in mind?"

"TradCo. The one arun by that guy acontactin' my dad."

"So you want a list of all current and past shareholders and information about how the company was founded. Anything more specific?"

"You might check on each of the traders in our Chronicles." He handed over a slip of paper with names. "I'm especially interested in awhat the one in my grand-mother's Chronicle, Samuel Fowler, ahad to do with TradCo. Also, there's the name Carlysle Fowler, too, but I adon't know if he was involved with the company or not."

"I'll get right to it!" Buchvan left Stava pouring over his documents. He went to his personal office and activated the business net. It was time to search through business files. It was time to shop for toys!

*   *   *

Sullrob felt nervous about the Rep-assembly. Paranoid, might describe it more accurately. Ever since he'd taken the communicator home, he'd felt watched, fearing unseen demons lurking in the shadows, an evil presence behind a face with three chins. At the Assembly, he didn't know what kind of spying devices the governor might have, who else might be involved, whom he could trust.

The afternoon began with the customary committee meetings. Sullrob wound up elected chairman of the third-region panel, replacing a man who, like Buchvan, inexplicably disappeared "to move away." It seemed like a substantial turnover since the last Assembly. Sullrob suspected too many people were afraid. The politics had become more acrimonious than ever before, with ideas and demands being floated that some might consider borderline traitorous.

Sullrob proved a competent chairman, leading a short version of Celebration, covering old business, disseminating information from several subcommittees, skillfully dissuading unreasonable requests for development or improvements, quickly covering and recording the projects that had merit. The group was very cooperative, trying to complete the agenda quickly, with one major issue seeming to permeate their collective minds.

Recognized by the chair, one man stood and announced, "It is sure we'll not be satisfied by the governor's answer. The purges continue; the Panels are more aggressive. If change was planned, we would see it by now!"

A barrage of shouts challenged Sullrob's ability to keep order. He rapidly recognized more than a score of shouters, letting them one-at-a-time vent their anger, make suggestions, and rage against the authority that both infuriated and alarmed them. Ultimately, consensus started to gel. The committee wanted to place on its list the demand that *all* purges cease, that contamination no longer be punishable, that 'reason to suspect' be limited to criminal accusations.

"Put in there that if we don't get the answers we want, there'll be a Challenge, there will—and the governor will be losing his *life*."

Over shouts of agreement, Sullrob pointed out, "The list of requests cannot include threats, no matter how strongly we feel about our issues. From what I remember in my history texts, that is not how to mount a Challenge."

"Tell us, Sullrob. We want to understand the Challenge."

The room grew quiet, waiting for the former teacher to deliver yet another civics lesson. "The last Challenge was mounted more than two-hundred turns ago, by the family of Plek, against Governor Mikwurt. The Challenge was successful; Mikwurt was executed and Plekjud was installed. Had it *not* been successful, Plekjud would have faced execution for mounting a *false* Challenge."

Several gasped; apparently most hadn't realized the risks involved with the ancient process of overthrowing their government. "Plekjud was an ancestor of Governor Plekwag?" somebody asked.

"Yes. The Pleks will hold the chair until there is no male heir to succeed, or the family loses a Challenge."

"How do we Challenge the governor?"

"It must come from an individual or a group naming someone as its representative. The governor must be accused of capital crimes—any crime for which punishment is execution. That would take him out of the chair, but he would still be succeeded by the eldest of any heirs who have reached ascension. To take the chair away from the entire *family*, it must be proved that the crimes are against all people, and that the *Challenger* would better serve the citizens. The evidence is heard at a Rep-assembly by all of the Panel elders and all Reps. The elders must reach four-fifths agreement by vote that the governor is guilty. The Reps must reach four-fifths agreement that the Challenger would better serve Seelius. If a Challenge is to be mounted, there must be notice given for a quarter tenth-turn, with the Challenger identified, and the crimes named."

Sullrob sat back, listening to the buzz, waiting for questions. The mood had been dampened; most wanted a change, but didn't yet see how to accomplish it.

"We have much to consider," one finally concluded, putting temporary closure on the issue.

The discussion adjourned with more than an hour until the big Assembly. Most wandered off to have lunch in local establishments. Two men approached Sullrob and asked if he would follow them to a groundcar parked nearby. They had something to show him.

"What *is* that?" Sullrob wondered, studying the damaged silica capsule covered in burn-damaged accountrements.

"We was hopin' *you* might know—" one started.

"—Seein' as how you go to the orbiter and see human things."

"We thought you might recognize it."

"Where did you find it?" Sullrob asked, keeping his voice low to avoid attracting attention from passersby.

"I found it in the old part of my garden—"

"An area he'd not used for many years," the other added.

"We were cleaning it up to plant Jurnama—"

"And there it was, half-buried—"

"Grown over."

Sullrob looked at it more closely. Obviously not of Seelius, it *had* to be human. Finally he offered, "I do not recognize it, but I know people on the Orbiter-two who may be able to help us. I would like to take it and ask their opinions. Will you two bear witness to where this was found?"

"Oh yes, if it's something that needs to be told."

"Our wives and several neighbors saw us dig it out, too."

Sullrob nodded. "Say nothing until we know more." He had them drive to where Sullrob's groundcar was parked, then clandestinely transfer the artifact to his vehicle, covering it with a small tarp.

The Rep-assembly went as predicted, with Plekwag spinning rhetoric, postponing decisions about the Panels, emphasizing what heroes each would be for taking the cases of medicinal crystals home to their villages to save lives. The crowd left displeased; Plekwag clearly felt their fury, ending the meeting and quickly making an exit. As Sullrob left the building, he noticed Stewrik watching the crowd, listening to snatches of conversation, studying faces.

Driving back toward Tessila, Sullrob felt uneasy. The mysterious capsule worried him, but the mood of the Reps was his greater concern. What had started for him as a desire just to escape with his family had thrust him into the middle of a battle to change Seeliot culture, over whom would control Seeliot government.

Somebody was going to get hurt, to get killed over this. Sullrob must remember his own goals, stay with his plan. His children and best friends were so very far away; nothing was more important than being with them again.

Nothing could *ever* be more important than that.

*   *   *

"Here's your list of shareholders," Buchvan offered, pulling up a chair next to Stava and inserting a small wafer into the data slot. A header appeared on the small screen in the desktop.

"Any of the names we asearched in the list?"

"Naw, and you'd think they would be—just about everybody else's is. There's 170,000 shareholders. This list is ordered by number of shares held, greatest to least."

"Awhat's the first one—the SFP Trust?"

"There's lots of those in there—trusts, partnerships, holding companies, investment funds, mutual funds, subsidiary holders, and the like. They're different legal definitions for shares held by an entity other than an individual."

"This one is *huge!* It's aright on top, alisted as having—awhere's the total of all shares?" He scrolled to the bottom of the list to see the number, then back to compare it with SFP's. "That's a*half* of all the stock. Awhat a big investor." Stava scanned rightward through a series of screens to see what else was listed pertaining to SFP. "Nothing else about awhom or awhat they are, except that it awas established 160 Consortium years ago and all voting is assigned to the TradCo chairman."

"That gives him majority and total control, then, even if he doesn't own shares of his own."

"Awouldn't it amean the board acouldn't afire him? And that he acould achoose his own successor?"

"I'd have to wade through their by-laws, but yes, that's probably what it means."

"That guy acontactin' my dad is *very* powerful. You'd athink he awouldn't ahave time to achit-chat with some ol' purple-face."

"He must think there's big money to be made off Seelius if your dad can help him get past the cultural prohibitions."

"You acan alearn more about the SFP Trust? I'm areal curious."

"Sure, I'll get right on it. I want to get deeper into the history, too. All I got was a pretty little presentation about how the company was founded by two people, Marlowe Bozathorne—probably an ancestor of the chairman—and Sarah Lund some 290 Consortium years ago. The rest is about its expansion, adding subsidiaries, spreading throughout the galaxy, doing wonderful things like curing disease and bringing food to settlements—all for a tidy profit, I assume."

Stava searched the list for shareholders named Lund. There were none; the family must have sold out many generations back. "Nothing about Sam Fowler?"

"No, not yet. But the shareholder and employee records only go back 160 years to when the company was reincorporated and listed in the Galaxian exchange. I've covered all the free info; now I have to make inquiries to several info-for-pay services to see what they can offer and for how much."

"Adon't aspend it *all*, Buchvan, but I asure am curious."

*   *   *

"Oh good, you got my message," Shar greeted, letting Brog Pawligan and Sullrob into his quarters. "I hope you don't mind. It's been a long day and I need to get on my juvie. Please, don't mind me—make yourselves at home. Brog, you know where to find drinks and snackies."

"What would you like?" Brog asked, heading into the kitchen area.

Sullrob watched in fascination as the pharmacist eased his heavy frame into a reclining device and placed his feet and calves into the openings of a piece of equipment. A slight hissing sound emanated, followed by symbols playing across a display screen on the side facing Shar. "I hope I'm not rude to watch," Sullrob started. "I have no idea what you're doing."

"Sit down and relax," Shar waved at him. Sullrob set aside the large case he'd brought and took a low chair several meters from the device that seemed to be eating Shar's feet. "It's a juvie. I'm in the early stages of regenerating a vital organ, so this taps into my various biological systems—through my lower legs—and starts to circulate the germi-ducers that I'll need to build up before going to hospital."

"I thought you started that months ago," Brog cut in, returning with cold ales for all three.

Shar thanked him, took a very small sip, and set his aside. "I did, but I've been putting off the last phase—been too busy."

"You've never told me how you damaged your pancreas or why you need to replace it—" He paused, but got no offer of explanation from Shar. "—but surely you can't put it off *too* long. Work is *never* more important than your health."

Shar shrugged, shifting uncomfortably in what he sometimes called his "iron maiden"—a reference he'd heard but never understood. "You never know. Right now, maybe it is." Trying to sound more upbeat, he added, "But actually I've been doing so well, I *can* afford to put it off for a while longer. So what's this device that has you so curious?" he asked, changing the subject.

Sullrob removed the silica capsule from the case, handing it over to Shar. "This was uncovered from a garden on Seelius. It looks human, but unfamiliar."

"Looks to me," Brog conjectured, "like it's been shot down through the atmosphere from here or some ship. It's heavily damaged, but it obviously had energy and propulsion cells. This over here," he pointed, "could have been some sort of simple guidance system. The inside is undamaged—obviously opened after getting through the atmosphere, but I don't recognize what it is."

Shar inspected the interior, opening several layers by manipulating some levers to reach a honeycomb labyrinth that the other two hadn't penetrated. "It's a bio-chem transport. They're common, really. It's a protective container with six levels of containment to safeguard against breach. This design is used for transporting volatile chemicals, dangerous bio-substances, and unstable medicines. Those Jurnama crystals, when grown in gravity, have to be moved in similar containers; they're too fragile. That's why we grow them up here in zero-g; that makes them so strong you can carry them around in your pocket—not to mention growing them much faster, too."

"Why would something like this be in a garden on Seelius? Could it have been an accident?"

"Oh, I don't think so. The capsule means somebody shot it down there intentionally. I'd like to send it to some people who might be able to learn more specifically what was in it. I do have a guess, though."

"So do I," Brog added.

"Medicine," they said simultaneously.

"You mean the Jurnama cure for the plague?"

"Of course. This is obviously not more than a few turns old. What else would somebody down there need—that would have to be sent with this kind of protection? I'd guess somebody ground-side had connections—had a way to get medicine in the early stages while everybody else was dying from the plague."

Sullrob jumped to his feet and clenched his fists, barely able to contain his rage. The thought that somebody had a cure while Sullruff lay dying, twisted in suffering agony, her loved ones watching helplessly . . .

"We'll get some answers, Sullrob," Shar said quietly. Brog stood, putting his arm around the Seeliot's shoulder, handing him his ale and guiding him back down to his seat.

Changing the subject again quickly, Shar offered, "I got something else that might interest you."

Sullrob stared off toward the kitchen, Brog watching him carefully. He snapped out of it, asking, "Um, what is that?"

"I assume Brog told you humans are true Seeliot progenitors—that genetic tracing has left no doubt about that."

"Yes. Besides, it's fairly obvious once you learn to look past the prejudice. Everything about us, from language to most aspects of culture, to values and family and community—we're too much the same for it to be coincidence."

"*Very* much the same," Brog added.

Shar continued, "My, um, *friends* have isolated how your genetic screening works—what's being used to check for so-called contamination."

Sullrob sat forward, very interested. "You mean how they could tell my children are impure?"

"So to speak," Shar confirmed obliquely. "It's your height!"

Sullrob looked puzzled. Brog interjected, "But there are lots of humans—um, *human* humans—who are shorter—"

"But with Seeliots," Shar explained, "it's a *separate* gene. All of the samples we checked had the normal cluster of genes that affect height. It's just that most of them *also* had something we'd never seen before—a dominant gene that overrides those and imposes the shorter stature. There's so much variation in normal height, you'd never know for sure without a genetic analysis."

"Where would this come from?" Brog wondered.

"It would have been a mutation present in the colonists who first traveled to Seelius. There probably weren't more than twenty or thirty on the ship. If it turned out to be the only ship to land there, then such a small gene pool suggests that the dominant mutation would have been present in every offspring after probably eight or ten generations of breeding, especially if monogamy wasn't strictly practiced."

"It wasn't," Sullrob pointed out. "Though it has been held out as the *ideal* throughout our recorded history, early records also show that polygamy was widely practiced until three or four hundred turns ago. After that, it was considered too primitive, too much a throwback to less-civilized times, and eschewed in favor of stricter codes of marriage between one man and one woman."

"Yeah, well, mixing it up would have been important when there were only a few of you. It would've been smart for every childbearing woman to have as many fathers in her brood as possible."

"Why wouldn't those designated as impure have this gene?" Brog asked, still not clear how so-called contaminants could be screened out.

"They *do* have it. It's just that it's been tagged recessive through the mix of trader genes."

"Tagged recessive?" Sullrob asked, not understanding. The look on Brog's face suggested he was starting to figure it out.

"That's one of our great medical advances of the last five-hundred years," Shar explained. "Young mothers-to-be are injected with inoculations that prevent birth defects and immunize against several hundred diseases. Infants are injected with a booster that mimics RNA and supports anything bound to the sites of interaction which were isolated during the first injection."

Confused again, Brog asked, "But wouldn't that only last for one generation—for whomever received the injection?"

"Yes it would—but the *marker* would still be attached to the gene after it was reproduced. That's why so many things that used to be problems have been virtually wiped out. When recessive genetic anomalies resurface generations down the line, they are already marked. Each new generation's injections become more accurate—more *effective*. Unless it's an entirely new mutation, it's got a little bull's-eye on it."

"The easier to target," Brog interrupted.

"Right! So when traders went to Seelius and started to interbreed, they would have brought their medicines with them. They would have injected their pregnant wives and the infants just after birth. They probably had some surprisingly tall Seeliots for a generation or two—however long until they were sent away or killed during the big purge. By the next generation, the dominant Seeliot gene for shorter height would have taken over again."

Sullrob smiled. "But—"

Nodding and smiling back, Shar finished, "But they had little markers on them. We found them on several samples you collected, Sullrob, mostly on those that people identified as suspected of contamination."

"There's no other way for those markers to get there?" Brog wondered.

"None," Shar confirmed.

"So my kids each have a shortness gene with a little bull's-eye on it?"

"Um, well, actually no."

"Huh?"

"Stava and Yantanna don't have the marker. *Your* kids are pure Seeliots."

CHAPTER 13

The room fell silent. Everybody watched intently, holding their breaths, afraid the slightest movement would break the spell of the moment. The little girl sat cross-legged in the middle of the floor, the adults and other children off to the side. Shuggy sat on the youngster's leg, reared up on his haunches, his head cocking from side to side, studying her intently.

After several minutes of this, he crawled closer, nuzzling under her arm, undulating as she gently stroked his purple fur. He backed off slowly, perching again on her leg, raised on his haunches to study her some more. Finally, he climbed down and waddled over to a cluster of weenshuggers—maybe fifty or sixty in all—lined up along the wall, lounging on padded nests in neat little rows. He approached several of the tiniest ones, pausing in front of each, studying, taking a moment to nuzzle, sitting back and studying some more. He moved over to some of the other smallest ones, repeated the same gestures with each, then returned to the little girl.

Little Darla Pfivvel would be celebrating her sixth birthday soon. Her grandfather, "Grandpa Dow," had brought her along to spend a day and night at Seelosia, to relax and play on the pretty blue and pink sandy beach, to see real waterfalls, to meet some nice people and make a new friend, Yantanna. "Unca Brog" had liked Yantanna's secret birthday suggestion so, with permission from Dow, everybody had gathered to watch in fascination as the pretty little girl with long auburn tresses and rosy cheeks could hardly contain her delight at the purple furballs.

Shuggy climbed into her lap again, pausing to study her some more. He turned and, looking over his shoulder, carefully eyed one of the tiny boy 'shuggers near the end. He looked back at her one last time, then waddled over to the one he'd selected. The younger 'shugger peeped a high-pitched squeal of delight and rushed over to Darla, fast as his little legs would carry him, and climbed into her lap. The little critter snuggled into the crook of her arm and started to sing a quiet lullaby.

"Grandpa Dow—look!" she exclaimed, trying not to disturb her new pet. Shuggy started to sing what sounded like a rhythmic laugh. All the other weenshuggers joined in, a cacophony of laughing songs mixed with the chuckles of people. Satisfied he'd found the perfect match for his son, Shuggy waddled over to Yantanna to be picked up and cuddled, to sing his happiness for all to hear.

Later, they toured the greenhouse operation. Jak showed his work with pride; Dow clucked his approval. They agreed that the long-term prospects of production would be more reliable than import-smuggling.

Afterward, Brog and Dow relaxed. Sitting on the balcony overlooking the lake, gazing at the reflections of red mountains and clear-blue sky rippling across the surface, watching two little girls playing games with singing furballs on the beach, Dow took a sip of his cool Zhasou-ade and remarked, "You know, Pawligan, I wasn't sure what to think of you at first." Brog just smiled and took a sip of his own. "Oh, you've got the mind of a businessman and diplomat, that's for sure, but you surprised me when you didn't try to finagle a price increase early on. I practically offered you one, thinking you were pulling a fast one—and that little speech you gave about being a man of honor—" Dow laughed, shaking his head and admitting, "Frankly, it sounded just fake enough that I still thought you were trying to pull something. I just couldn't figure out what."

"Did you ever?" Brog teased, almost rhetorically.

"Actually, I think I did. It was so obvious, I'd forgotten how to recognize it."

"Clue me in," Brog insisted, half curious, half amused.

"Good business—that's what you were up to. The kind where everybody has a profitable relationship based on trust and integrity, where you look for good, comfortable, long-term relationships rather than short ones built on deceit and sub-terfuge—the kind you can look back on someday and say you were a success and you helped others be successful and everybody benefited. *That's* the kind of busi-nessman *I've* always tried to be, but there are so few of us, I'd forgotten how to recognize one when I saw one."

"Good." Brog chuckled. "It's working. I've got you fooled!"

Pirlhoff came out with a tray of Zhasou pastries and a pitcher of ade refills, cautioning Brog, "Shhh! Don't give us away *now!*"

Dow laughed again, admitting, "I was just kidding. I know a ruthless Dilltom Weevil when I see one. You know, Pirlhoff, I'm going to have to insist that you stop waiting on us and pull over that chair—I'd offer to drag it for you if I were a gentleman—"

"If there were *any* gentlemen here—" Brog added, looking around to see if any were available.

She thrust the tray into Brog's hands and pulled her own chair over. "My mug is empty," she announced, holding it out.

"You're undoing *all* my careful training," Brog pleaded with Dow.

"It'll be undone soon enough, Brog," Dow warned. "Those differences in gen-der roles on Seelius will melt away when she's exposed to more Consortium culture. You'll just be lucky if she goes easy on *you!*"

Everybody paused to sip and look at the mountains for a moment. Brog mused, "For a businessman with heart, you certainly have been successful."

"Oh, I guess so. It pays the landlord. I've been lucky, sometimes through dog-ged determination, sometimes by being at the right place and time—like our little Zhasou arrangement—but I've missed some big ones, too."

"Oh yeah?" Pirlhoff wondered. "What do you *wish* you could have done?"

"Well, there's been a few. I once passed up an exclusive on the flavo-dots that made billions for TradCo's T-rad Comestibles. I thought they were too low-end—they really are a repugnant little product. I had too much pride in the Pfivvel name; we'd built our reputation on quality."

"Success in what you want is better than even greater success at what you don't," Brog offered sagely.

"Yeah, well, tell the landlord that. Another one is the Jurnama-crystal business. I've got a fledgling pharmaceutical subsidiary that makes a small profit competing in the juvie market. It's all very cutthroat, really, with no guarantees year-to-year who will have how much market share. I thought about getting into Jurnama crystals back when they were highly speculative, but the start-up costs were enormous and the plants were too difficult to grow on any Consortium worlds. TradCo Pharm got into it with modest success—until the deal with Seelius was struck and the supply problem was solved. Now TradCo could use its pharmaceutical profits alone to buy out my entire corporation—*if* it were for sale."

"Have they tried?" Pirlhoff wondered. She'd noticed a hint of acrimony in Dow Pfivvel's voice as he'd said it.

"Oh, yeah. Many times. It's not for sale, though—not to those Dilltom Weevils. Ling Bozathorne—he's the chairman of TradCo—he's been after my primary operation, my food division, for a long time. Once our success with Zhasou becomes well known, he'll be approaching me again, I'm sure."

"Are his offers not profitable enough?"

"Oh, they've been quite good, actually. I could retire a very wealthy man—and be *very* generous with my sons, little Darla, and however many other grandchildren they bless me with."

"Why don't you?" Brog wondered. Retiring wealthy, endowing his family, living the good life—these were all concepts he'd never dreamed of when he was younger but now thought sounded like very fine ideas, indeed.

"Well, I wonder why not every time it comes up. I usually start out thinking I like the work, take pride in my business, want to keep at it and help it grow. But the older I get, the less that excuse appeals to me. Another reason is my employees. Many of them are second-generation entire families who have been part of the Pfivvel company, people who've invested their lives in our success and who trust me to look out for them, as well. There have been instances in time of tragedy when Pfivvel, Inc. has stepped in and done right by its people. I take pride in that, and I couldn't turn all those people over to the likes of Bozathorne, not trusting that they would be looked after as well as I would."

"You inspire loyalty," Pirlhoff said softly.

"No, I try to earn it," Dow insisted regally. Realizing how passionately he'd retorted, he laughed at himself. "No, really—we've made it work and I'd hate to see somebody else break it. Another thing is the company charity work. Pfivvel is known on many worlds for using a portion of its profits to help the communities of its customers. Bozathorne would never make guarantees that our charity work would be part of the deal."

They all sipped for another moment before Brog teased, "You just like seeing your name on the company headquarters."

Dow smiled mischievously, admitting, "That's more true than you might think."

Brog raised his eyebrows. "I pegged it!"

"When my grandfather started the company, he operated from the principle that everything was done in his name. That's why he went after quality products, started the charitable work, become known as the best place to work. It has been given to me, along with the name, entrusted to my care." He gazed toward his granddaughter wading in the lake with a 'shugger perched atop her head. "I've continued to stake the integrity of my name on what the company does, and hope to pass it down the same way. If I sold out to TradCo, then *Pfivvel* would be just another registered trademark to do with as he and his marketing people see fit." He watched the girls squeal and laugh as their 'shuggers climbed down and swam lopsided circles around them, splashing in the cool, clear water. Quietly, he finished, "Yeah, I like to see the name on the building. I care what Pfivvel means, so for now, I just better be the one to keep an eye on it."

*   *   *

"SFP is the Samuel Fowler Probate Trust," Buchvan explained, pulling his chair over and inserting the chip.

Stava's eyes were big. "No akidding?"

"No akidding, akiddo. Would I akid you?"

"What exactly is it?"

"Samuel Fowler was the only child of Carlysle Fowler, who was the nephew and only heir of Sarah Lund, co-founder of TradCo. Sam Fowler owned half of TradCo back when it wasn't very big by today's standards."

"Then awhat's the trust?" Stava wondered, studying the flowchart on the screen.

"He designated an heir in his will, but after his death at a young age, the heir was never found. So the shares totaling half the company were placed in probate. Some two-thirds of a century later, when the company was reorganized, an attempt was made to turn the shares over to corporate ownership. The bank holding the trust mounted a legal battle and won. The shares were placed into a fund called SFP Trust to be held until an heir could be found—if ever. The courts *did* accept the argument that the company needed autonomous control, so it granted voting power to the chairman until the shares are claimed."

"So awhy acouldn't they afind the heir?"

"That's one of the great mysteries in the world of Consortium business. All of Fowler's records disappeared after his death—"

"Awhat adid he adie of?"

"A disease that was never identified. He was cremated—his body was burned up—right away. It will never be known. Anyway, all of the records disappeared—including his will. Testimony was taken from people attesting that Fowler claimed to have a child on one of the worlds he visited and that the child would be his heir. That was enough to get the first trust set up."

"Worlds he avisited?"

"Yeah, he was a business lead-man to new worlds, taking teams of traders and setting up deals for commerce. Once things started to run smoothly, he would move on to the next one. Somewhere along the way, he left behind this child. He moved back to Earth permanently, intending to have the child and his mother brought there to be with him, but he died before he could make that happen."

"I asure awish it awas Yantanna and me that awere his heirs."

"How do you know it's not?"

"Well, Uncle Shar already afound out we're apure Seeliot. We acan't be descended from Sam Fowler."

"Maybe Shar's wrong. Seelius was the last world Fowler visited."

"No, the Chronicles asay what ahappened while he was on Seelius. He amoved in an' a-lived with my mom's great-times-six grandmother Oralee, who awas a widow with a son anamed Orawil. At first, I awas all excited 'cause my mom awas the last descendent from Oralee, but the records asay that Sam Fowler and Oralee never agot amarried and never ahad any babies. Then he aleft and never acame back. Uncle Shar is aright. We adon't ahave any trader blood. Anybody on Seelius who adoes, it's anot from Sam Fowler."

"That's too bad," Buchvan allowed, looking disappointed. "I was going to ask you for a loan."

Stava grinned. "If I awas a rich trader, I awouldn't aloan money to no astinkin' Seeliot!"

*   *   *

"They don't need to keep taking the crystal medicine," Shar began.

"Who?"

"The Seeliots. They don't need to keep taking the medicine. The plague is gone."

Brog was shocked by the news. "You're sure?"

Shar told Todly to keep an eye on the pharmacy, then led his friend into the back room, closing the door behind him. He gestured to a seat in the corner, lowering his own frame into another. "Further tests wouldn't hurt, but I'm sure."

"I thought way back when this thing started you said all the information about the plague was confidential—research belonging to TradCo Pharm."

"It is. I got my info from several other sources—starting with the specimens provided by Sullrob's family and friends and neighbors."

Brog looked over at the box of specimen kits Shar and his friend had used. "But the medicine is well known."

"Let me start from the beginning. First of all, we've always known the plague was a virus. That's what Jurnama crystals treat. Except for insiders at TradCo Pharm, it's 'source-unknown,' and 'strain-unknown.' Everybody assumed the virus is still present in the environment down there on Seelius—or in host bodies. That's why Seeliots would need to keep taking the crystals. As soon as somebody contracted the disease, they'd be cured before any damage was done."

"Then it couldn't live in host bodies if everybody was taking the crystals," Brog countered.

"Not true. Crystals don't eradicate it, they just force it to become dormant. They're cured of the damaging effects. With most viruses that are treated this way, they become dormant for some period of time—or for good if the crystals keep suppressing them before they can regenerate. One of the reasons my friends wanted specimens was so we could isolate the virus, maybe see if cheaper methods might be more effective, maybe open up the Seeliot market for some competitive medicinal commerce.

"And you found no virus in the specimen—it's gone?" Brog hypothesized.

"Oh no, not at all. It's there in plain view. But it's been permanently suppressed by the crystals. There's nothing we can do to revive it."

"So everybody down there was eventually exposed to the virus—"

"Or nearly everybody," Shar cut in. "It's in every specimen *we've* seen."

"Those that weren't too sick got the crystals in time to suppress it."

"Permanently. It's a harmless freckle in certain cellular membranes now." Shar got up and pulled out a colored chart with lines and lots of fine print.

"Why doesn't this virus need to be suppressed on a regular basis? I mean, why did the crystals shut it down permanently?"

"That's what I'm about to show you. This line here is the only strain of viruses that are affected that way." Brog looked, but the chart didn't mean anything to him. "The virus we found in the specimens is a variant of this strain."

"So they don't need to keep taking the medicine—and there's no need to worry about it coming back now that it's been permanently suppressed?"

"Well, theoretically, no. Except there's one problem—the question of where it came from in the first place." Shar paused to be sure Brog was keeping up. "This strain of virus is not naturally occurring."

"Then—you mean?"

Shar nodded, tossing the chart on the countertop and sitting back down. "It's man-made, Brog—and the Seeliots don't have the biomedical technology to do something like that."

"Somebody *infected the entire planet?*"

Shar nodded. "There's no other explanation—especially since this is clearly a variant of the original virus created in the labs on Dilltomarius."

"But how would they—?" Brog stopped, figuring out the answer himself. "It wasn't medicine, was it?"

Shar shook his head. "'Fraid not, Brog. The capsule they found in the garden was a viral transport, plain and simple. I'm surprised I didn't recognize the containment filters when I first looked at it. The thing is, the honeycomb look is because it was on delayed release. It looks like each cell was opened one at a time, probably every week or so, over a period of about six months. It was designed to pump virus into the air attached to tiny spore-like bio-pods on a steady basis over a period of time. That's because the virus wouldn't live more than a few weeks on the tiny bio-pods without a host body. Whoever planted the virus wanted it to pack a wallop over a period of time, not infect everybody all at once. The destruct mechanism that would eliminate the capsule after the last viral release was damaged. That's why it was there to find after all this time."

"But why?"

"It's like viro-terrorism. They didn't want to kill *everybody* all at once. They wanted to kill some, make others sick, give most more time before infection would set in."

"But who would—?"

"Who would benefit from having a planetful of desperate people dying from a disease they didn't understand?"

"TradCo Pharm—the ones who sold them the cure in exchange for the highly profitable Jurnama shipments."

"The ones who conveniently knew exactly what would cure the plague the moment their help was desperately needed."

"Why a virus that shuts down once treated?"

Shar shrugged. "Easier to control—less subject to mutation or surprises—*less chance of accidentally killing off all your customers.* Take your pick."

Brog sat stunned for a moment, trying to sort it all out. Finally, he wondered, "Why go to so much trouble? Why couldn't TradCo just start a farm somewhere and grow their own Jurnama?"

"Brog, it's a *very* unique plant. The minerals it draws into its sap interact in a very odd way—something that can't be replicated except in a lab setting. It works on Seelius because of the two moons. The Seelius moons have gaseous atmospheres that filter out various rays from the nearby sun. That's why they have the legendary pink moonlight down there. It's the moonlight that catalyzes the mineral reaction in the Jurnama sap. What grows like weeds down there won't work anywhere else. Oh, they can grow the plant, but they can't get the right kind of crystals from the sap. I don't understand it much myself, but that's what my friends tell me. They know of whence they speak," he offered matter-of-factly.

"So TradCo murdered tens of thousands of innocent people on a planet that wanted only to be left alone, just to make the survivors so desperate that they would sell the valuable plants—would give a *monopoly* to TradCo. . . all for profit."

After a moment, Shar offered, "I think I should hang on to the capsule. The packet there is a set of detailed dimension-stills of it, along with a simple technical description of its purpose and how it works. Sullrob's going to have to decide what to do with this evidence."

They sat there looking at each other for several minutes. Brog was dumbfounded. Sullrob's beloved wife was murdered—the mother of Stava and Yantanna . . . and Sullrob was earning his living delivering the killers the booty that cost Sullruff her life.

CHAPTER 14

He tried to sprinkle the delicate granules of spice into his mug, but his hand was shaking. Not since the first days after his wife died had Sullrob had so much difficulty focusing on Celebrating her *memory*. Back then, he was too devastated, too confused, too scared that he might lose his children to the fatal disease—or leave them orphaned and fending for themselves at a time no friends or neighbors could help. This time it was just rage—and a burning passion for revenge. His wife had been murdered as surely as if her throat had been cut or a Dosir thorn had been thrust into her flesh. She had died slowly, in agony, in a way that had scarred those who loved her, who watched helplessly, feeling every bit of her pain. And she had died afraid—fearful for her husband, her precious little boy, her adorable little girl—that they might yet suffer as she had. For the first time, Sullrob finally had a direction to focus his outrage.

The communicator chirped again. It was chirping when he got home; it had been chirping tauntingly for more than an hour while he tried to marshal his nerve to face the man he blamed for murdering his wife. *Chirrup chirrup. Chirrup chirrup.*

He stood up and stretched, then walked into Yantanna's bedroom and sat on the side of the bed. He stared around at the walls, at so many of her personal things she'd been forced to leave behind, the toy puzzle he'd made her, the little nest in the corner where Shuggy slept whenever she was gone. He picked up her pillow and held it to his chest, sure he could smell her, feel her presence. He so wanted to be with his children again. He'd not seen Stava since the little guy's ascension, Yantanna even longer.

He walked into Stava's room, reaching out and touching his possessions, the toys and games and globe of Seelius . . . little boy things for the son who was already an official Seeliot man. Stava had passed the final days of his childhood a world away from his father, without his mother, the woman who was murdered . . .

He stretched again and walked purposefully to the communicator. He activated the recording device Buchvan had sent, then pressed the contact. Ms. Clayjams appeared on the screen almost instantly.

"Mr. Sullrob! Good to see you! I'm *so* glad you're home! I *surely* do hope you've had a *very* nice day!"

Sullrob nodded, managing a smile. "It was a good flight. I stopped to visit with friends on my way home."

"Good. Well good! Mr. Bozathorne wanted me to ask if you want some fully charged wafers deposited in a safe-box on the Orbiter-two."

"No thank you, Ms. Clayjams. Mr. Bozathorne is unduly generous. After all, I've not been able to help *him* with anything yet."

"Oh—well—I'm sure I know *nothing* of that, but you can discuss it with him *yourself!* That's right! He's available and would like to speak with you!"

"I am ready anytime," he said evenly, trying to sound a bit more enthusiastic than he could muster.

"Good. Good then! Please stand by."

The screen turned into the TradCo logo for several minutes. Sullrob realized he was breathing heavily, clenching and unclenching his fists. He knew that when that fat face appeared on the viewer, he would want to reach right through it and wrap his hands around the folds of flesh hanging on that greasy neck . . . He calmed himself again, remembering that he could never reach across space with his hands. If he ever wanted to lash out and take down the man who killed his wife, he would have to find another way. For now, that meant playing along. Just playing along.

"Mr. Sullrob! So good to see you, sir! Still fighting the good fight?"

"As always, Mr. Bozathorne. I hope business is going well for you."

"As always, Mr. Sullrob. As always!" The chairman laughed at the play on words. "Have you, uh, been making any progress on our goals?"

"Before we get into that, I want to be clear on a few things. It seems like maybe the stakes are going up; I want to be sure this will work out for me in the long run."

Ling looked very serious, no doubt hoping he hadn't underestimated the Seeliot school teacher-turned-pilot cum Assembly-rep. "Why certainly. What would you like to review?"

"What's in this for me? I mean, if I can help you crack into our business market, to help you get copies of every family's Chronicles, to purge every last impure Seeliot from the face of this planet—if I take the chance of being politically unpopular and possibly going before a Panel and facing execution, what's in it for me? Why should I take all this risk?"

Ling squirmed uncomfortably as the first words reached him. He continued to listen carefully to Sullrob's list. Finally, he looked conspiratorial, serious, ready to roll up his sleeves and square off against a worthy adversary. "Isn't what we discussed enough?"

"Well, you weren't very specific the first few times you contacted me. For example, what kind of precious metals are you offering me—to make me rich—and how much? When would I get them?"

"A thousand times your present income, Mr. Sullrob. A thousand times your annual salary in one lump sum for helping arrange to get me those Chronicles. A thousand times more every year if we can start new business there. That's in precious metals of *your* choosing if you decide to stay there. I can offer you even more if you decide to, say, emigrate."

"Tell me about that. You'll provide safe transportation to the world of my choice?"

"Any place in the Consortium you want to go. TradCo will buy you a generous portion of land, build you a fabulous house, bestow an income on you that will allow you to live *very* comfortably for the rest of your life."

"That's a very attractive offer."

"These goals are very important to my company," Ling countered, spreading his arms wide, hands open, palms up.

"I would like to work with you," Sullrob announced as if he'd been thinking it over. "For *ten*-thousand times my salary."

Ling listened to the rest of the transmission, then looked Sullrob over carefully, finally breaking into one of those repugnant triple grins, showing even rows of big, white teeth. "Done!" Then, leaning closer to the viewer, he added, "*If* you help me accomplish my goals."

"I will accomplish much," Sullrob responded.

"Good then. Tell me, what progress have you made?"

"First off, the governor is betraying you." Sullrob gazed at the screen without expression. Ling's reaction would determine what he said next.

"How?" Bozathorne appeared to be trying to contain his anger. Sullrob had guessed correctly; there was more to the relationship than made public.

"Well, the Jurnama deal is going smoothly enough, but I don't think he's trying to help you accomplish your other goals, regardless of how much friendship you've shown him."

Ling looked even madder. "I am *very* displeased when associates do not fulfill their obligations. How has he betrayed me?"

"Well, first of all, he never even mentioned your proposal to copy all the Chronicles under the pretense of setting up a central library."

"It was never brought up at the Rep-assembly?" he practically bellowed.

"Nope, not at all. In fact, I maneuvered for us to request something similar on our committee list and he quickly dismissed it." Sullrob was taking a chance that Ling didn't have knowledge of what was said at the meeting.

"Then he's a *liar!*" Ling bellowed.

"If he reported back that he advocated your proposal, then yes, he is a liar. Something else, too—he's been sending you falsified family Chronicles. The ones he's been getting from purges, after the Panels have declared executions—he's screening them and sending you only the ones he wants you to see, and then not necessarily the entire Chronicle." He hoped he'd guessed correctly what was happening with seized Chronicles.

Ling narrowed his eyes, glaring into the screen, trying to contain his fury. "You *know* this?"

"There is much talk about his double-cross of you. He has bragged to several of his lieutenants how he is taking your payments, but not delivering what you ask."

"I will *destroy* him! He has *betrayed* me! After I have made him a rich man, have saved his world from the plague and made him a hero, have guaranteed that the incompetent ass will have a chair to pass on to that little drooling bastard Plekmerk." Ling jumped to his feet and started to pace, revealing the interior of a spectacularly luxurious office. A transparent along one wall overlooked a wooded lake with tremendous fountains creating water designs in the air. Some of his energy spent, he huffed back in front of the viewer and took his seat again. "He will pay for his betrayal. He will pay dearly."

"There's another problem," Sullrob continued, effecting an air of conspiratorial concern. The act was getting easier. Seeing Ling's frustration and rage urged him on. "This is something not even the governor knows. In fact, only I and one other man knows."

"What? What!?"

"I'm good friends with a medical technician who's been studying the effects of the plague. He tells me we no longer need to take your medicine—that the plague is permanently cured."

"What? Plekwag assured me that Seelius was too primitive ever to figure that out. He promised that no research would be done, that your people were too backward to study biomedicine to that degree. The bastard *lied* to me. Nobody is supposed to find this out!"

"Luckily, I convinced my friend to keep it to himself for now. He is one of the only few who *could* figure it out. If he can be *persuaded* to remain quiet, it will probably be many years before somebody else could reveal our secret."

Ling rubbed his chins, thinking. "He can be paid off?"

"He wants to be a rich man."

"If we pay him off, we can keep this quiet?"

"I believe so."

"You negotiate on my behalf. Find out the minimum of what it will take to shut him up for good, to destroy his work and all the evidence, to discourage ever pursuing this kind of knowledge—then offer him a bit more, just to be sure he is satisfied. If you can accomplish this, another ten-thousand times will come your way. I can see now you are a smart man. You understand what needs to be done. You are looking out for *our* interests. You have anticipated our needs and shown initiative to stop this information before it caused damage." Ling turned on his fake smile again. "I only wish I had been able to work directly with you all along—better than that simpering liar Plekwag."

"I believe we understand each other. I will promise you one thing more—I will endeavor to bring him down."

"Good. Good! Just make sure nothing jeopardizes the Jurnama deal. We need the shipments to flow—even *increase* over time. We need your people to keep thinking they desperately need that medicine. After all, your friend may be wrong. They may need it again, after all."

Sullrob fought down his rage at the implied threat. He wasn't going to let on that he understood the plague had been planted all along. That was too much to reveal right now. Ling probably wouldn't admit that much, anyway. He had more than enough information without giving away that he knew more than he could explain.

"Contact me if anything changes," Sullrob offered. "In the meantime, it will help me if you continue your payments to Plekwag and don't reveal what you know of him. Give me time to work. If I need your help, I will contact Ms. Clayjams."

"Good luck, Mr. Sullrob. There is a lot riding on this. My vast resources are at your disposal."

They both nodded before the image winked out.

Sullrob paced the room for several minutes, trying to spend some of his pent-up energy. Finally, he walked into his bedroom and removed a still of his wife from the drawer, carrying it to the bed. He held it in his lap while he pondered what he'd learned. His suspicions had been correct; the governor was involved in TradCo's plan. Plekwag had helped kill Sullrob's wife.

He lifted the image in his hands, looking into the smiling face, the sparkling eyes of the only woman he'd ever loved. There would be no Celebration this night; he was too furious. He sure missed her, missed his children. He tried to focus his rage, to plan his strategy, to figure out how to bring down an entire government and one of the biggest corporations in the Consortium.

But he couldn't. Not right then. Not that night. He reached out and touched the photo, tears spilling from his eyes, blurring his vision.

He stayed up very late, a man trying desperately to cling to his *memories*.

*   *   *

During the next few quarter tenth-turns, Sullrob held many private conversations, seeking the opinions of friends and neighbors, weighing his options, considering every possible course of action other than what appeared to be inevitable. A Challenge would have to be mounted; the governor needed to be unseated. Since advance notice must be given, he decided to wait until his next trip to the capital for Rep-assembly. That would give him time to seek out the best individual to present the Challenge, to present the evidence. Besides, he needed more time to move people and plants.

His group of friends at Seelosia, Inc. discussed the status of their smuggling, sending word to Sullrob through Brog that he should make priority of helping the rest of the Seeliots in their original group escape. Though more Zhasou cuttings would hasten their timetable for producing mass shipments of the harvested spice, and though more adult weenshuggers would geometrically increase their anticipated rate of shipments of the cuddly, singing pets, time would eventually solve both of those problems. But it was starting to look like time—a very short amount of time—might permanently cut off the transportation needed for the other Seeliots to escape.

So move people he did. The numbers at Seelosia quickly swelled with wide-eyed, ecstatic purple-faces, people thrilled with and grateful for the opportunity to live in the exotic new world, to be part of an already growing community of good friends, to be presented with certificates and land deeds and opportunities in a free-enterprise system that made them instantly more wealthy than was possible back on their home world.

Shar Calvin had to be away from the Orbiter-two for a week, promising to return with a simple media presentation that explained and proved how the man-made virus had been permanently eradicated by the initial doses of Jurnama-crystal medicine, with assurances that the doses were no longer needed. Sullrob stopped taking his own medicine—to no ill effects—but insisted that his children continue until he was satisfied there would be none.

Brog arranged to meet with Shar Calvin and Sullrob as soon as the pharmacist returned to orbit. With the pharmacy in Todly's capable care, they went to the back room and studied the presentation. Sullrob was impressed, finding it easy to understand and very convincing at the least.

"Once my people understand they no longer need TradCo's medicine—and that they have been taken advantage of for Bozathorne's own profit—they will demand that the shipments stop, that the private deal between our corrupt governor and the murderous chairman be dissolved. I may not be able to choke him with my own hands—" Sullrob caught his breath; he was letting his emotions overwhelm him. "But I can at least take away the profitable deal that he went to all this effort to create."

"You can't do that," Shar said quietly. "You can't."

Brog and Sullrob were taken aback. Brog explained, "He is within days of having the last of his friends moved. All he has to do is give the evidence to trusted people at next week's Rep-assembly, then make one last run up here and abandon his ship at the docking-terminal and head for Caskentia. Let the bastard figure out how to get his own ship back. Then let him just try to land it on Seelius."

Shar stood up and paced around the room, trying to find the words. Finally, he stopped, looked at Sullrob, and said simply, "You can't stop the Jurnama shipments. You need to find another way."

"I'm listening, Shar. I owe you my life—my children's lives. If you feel this strongly—"

"Look, Sullrob. People need that medicine. It's not just somebody's profits you'd be cutting off, it's a very important cure that *many* people need." He paused, averting his eyes, adding softly, "Something that *I* need."

Sullrob nodded. Brog moved closer to the pharmacist, reaching out and putting a hand on his shoulder. "Are you sick, Shar?"

Shar waved him off, finally admitting, "Yes, but it's a *lot* of people. It's my nephew . . ."

"Little Greggo!?" Quickly explaining to Sullrob, Brog added, "Greggo is his sister's boy. He's—what? About five now?"

Shar nodded. "He just spent his fifth birthday strapped into a blood synthesizer a few weeks ago."

"What's wrong with him?" Sullrob asked.

"What else? The one major thing we've never been able to cure. He's got one of the two-thousand-plus forms of cancer. His has invaded the marrow of his growing bones."

"Brog explained to me what cancer is when he told me about his wife—" He looked at his friend apologetically, knowing how painful it can be to be reminded. "He said *most* cases are cured, but that his wife's was just too far spread."

"We don't cure it, 'Rob, we *eradicate* it. We isolate it as best we can and remove it, using organ regeneration to replace what was lost. Where it involves skeletal structures or the nervous system, it takes a longer time and is physically immobilizing. When it involves the brain, it can cause loss of functioning during regeneration, or permanent loss of memories or abilities—like replacing the memory crystals in your processors, the data is permanently lost. In the case of people like Brog's wife, Ralorna—" He looked apologetically toward Brog, "Her cancer had spread quickly through several critical systems. She lost the race between eradication and being able to regenerate fast enough to survive."

They sat down again, Shar reaching over to touch his friend's shoulder this time. Brog explained, "Yes, with Ralorna it was a race. She was *so* close. We thought she would make it. Then, in the last days, it became obvious—" His voice cracked. "I couldn't tell Selta or Jowda. They thought she was going to—" He rubbed his forehead with his hand, then shook his head and looked away.

"When it has invaded the five-year-old bones of a growing boy," Shar said quietly, "it is a similar race. The only thing is, even if he wins, you can't regenerate still-forming, still-fusing bones like that without permanent damage. Greggo is trying desperately to survive so he can be deformed and crippled for the rest of his life."

"I thought the crystals were for curing *virus*," Sullrob asked, overwhelmed with compassion for his friends but still confused.

"They're used during regeneration. Organs and vital systems don't have auto-immunity until the later stages. That's what the juvie is for—that device you saw me using last time. It provides a battery of protections and cures and preventions and enhancers and no-telling-what-all to protect the growing organs until they can protect themselves. The Jurnama medicine is used in that to protect against any of the millions of viruses all around us."

"What's wrong with you, Shar?" Brog asked.

Shar just shook his head. "What else?"

"Bad?"

"I've been winning the race."

Brog surprised Sullrob by revealing his usually private feelings about losing his wife. He said that cancer was something he had only remotely heard of—had never known anybody suffering from it—until Ralorna was diagnosed. Since then, he'd had to learn a lot about it in a short amount of time. He'd also met a lot of people who suffered its ravages and many more involved in its treatment . . . and a few who specialized in helping people be comfortable as they died from it. Medicine, for him, had always meant dealing with pesky viruses, delaying the process of aging, treatment of injuries. Before Ralorna's fatal illness, he'd never known anybody who'd gone to hospital except for broken bones or deep cuts. The memories of feeling like medicine was inexorably a race against time—a race against this merciless, ancient cluster of diseases commonly called "cancer"—were now flooding back. His friend was sick; he felt worried and helpless.

"You can't do anything that will interfere with the shipments," Brog said to Sullrob.

The Seeliot nodded his head. "I will make sure my people understand."

An awkward silence hung in the air for a long time. Brog was probably thinking of his children, and Stava and Yantanna, and little Jak . . Sullrob wanted to hold his own, to hug them, to laugh and play with them as well as Selta and Jowda . . . Surely Shar was scared for his own life but, as always, pushing those thoughts aside, Sullrob thought of Shar's sister, Sharlotte, and her little boy . . .

                    *   *   *

A million kilometers away, Sharlotte gently stroked the silky brown hair of little Greggo, trying to look brave and strong, torn apart by the very sight of his little body fully encased in that awful machine that caused him so much agony, wondering how he could muster the strength to keep fighting, watching helplessly as tears spilled over onto his face and he winced with the pain of yet another awful treatment.

"Just a few more minutes, son. It'll be over soon," she whispered.

Greggo winced again, stifling a little cry, fighting back the tears, panting several times to catch his breath. "It's okay, Mommy. Let's sing—let's sing—the song."

Her voice cracking with emotion, she continued to stroke his hair, leaning close and joining him in the little song he'd made up:

> "I'm better than a sweet cookie,
> And I'm better than a new toy,
> 'Cause I'm gonna be yer *best* friend,
> And I'm a *very* special boy!"

*   *   *

The new arrivals proved *very* pleased with their spectacular Seelosia valley, but most were too nervous to travel to nearby Caskentian cities and interact with locals. Heilen decided it was time to confront their feelings of being confined to a small area and make them start feeling more comfortable about venturing out. He was afraid they might close in on themselves, eschewing *all* "humans," creating their own isolated subculture which would ultimately cripple their offspring's ability to take advantage of all the opportunities available to Consortium citizens throughout the worlds. He insisted on taking the whole group on a tour one afternoon, so they loaded into several aircars for a dose of culture immersion.

With Brog and Lival both up-side, that left Heilen and three of the children as the only non-purples in the group. Everywhere they went—strolling the plaza, visiting a merchant mall, viewing the fountains—they attracted curious-but-polite attention. The Seeliot adults tended to draw together, hanging on tightly to their children's hands, watching furtively for signs of non-existent hostility.

It was in the park by the river that Stava, Jowda, and Jak finally managed to pry away several purple boys for a romp at the playground. Selta, holding Yantanna by the hand, convinced several protective mothers to let their little girls go with them to the doll center just up the hill. The area grew fairly crowded; it was late enough in the afternoon that many people had finished working for the day.

The boys started racing motorized miniature hookie cars, joining in with a half-dozen local lads already seriously involved in the competitive fun. Between and during races, there were lots of frank questions lacking in tact or delicate social propriety.

"Wow!" Heilen heard several times. "How'd you get so purple?"

Once everybody's curiosity was satisfied, the Seelosians were encouraged to come back any day at the same time for more playful competition.

The adults sat on benches overlooking the water, admiring the city and scenery, finally starting to relax amid the foreign crowd. They continued to attract polite attention, but the locals largely kept a short but clear distance from the unusual group. Two city men walked by several times, glaring at Heilen and the purple-faces.

Both were beiges who didn't seem to take well to people of different colors. They seated themselves just up the hill, watching the group, continuing to glare. Finally, one, then the other, started to shout out taunts.

"Musta been asomethin' they ate!"

"Ahope it ain't acatchin'!"

"Used t'be you could ago t'the park without aseein' freaks!"

Heilen thought about making paste of their faces, but knew that would only exacerbate the situation, turning the crowd against the Seeliots and confirming the newcomers' worst fears about local prejudice.

Other people stopped to watch, but nobody else joined in. A murmur went through the crowd, attracting still others until it seemed hundreds were pausing to view the unfolding drama. Once the buzz reached the play area, the boys went down to see what was happening.

*   *   *

"Awho is *that* 'shugger-eater?" Stava wondered.

 "A penis awith legs!" Jowda asserted.

"A butthole with hair," Jak corrected.

"He's my dad," one of the boys admitted, embarrassed.

After a few more minutes, the boys worked their way down toward the water about thirty meters from the group of purples. They continued to watch, growing more concerned when several others joined in the taunting.

The boy who'd admitted his father started it all whispering among themselves, climbed outside the rail hanging over the water and inched carefully along it toward the purple-faces.

Just as he reached the first Seeliots, his father noticed him and shouted, "Aget down from there! You'll adrown yerself!"

Suddenly, the boy lost his grip and tumbled into the river, disappearing below the surface. Buchvan and another Seeliot man dived without hesitation into the murky water and brought the boy up, lifting him to the other Seeliots before climbing out to stand there dripping. The father and his cohort ran down the hill; the crowd surged forward.

"He is okay; he is fine," Buchvan told the heckler as he ran up panting.

"Awhat'd I atell you?!" he shouted at the boy, rapping him in the back of the head. He turned and thanked Buchvan and the others for saving his son, apologizing sheepishly for his own behavior. "I awas just agoofing ya."

"We could never stand by while *any* child was in danger," Buchvan explained.

"Awhere you guys afrom, anyway?"

Several other locals joined in the conversation, curious about such different-looking people, eager to show that everybody was welcome on Caskentia. There was even talk of inviting the group to some kind of community function the following week.

With the attention finally off the wet boy, he turned and whispered to Stava, "How'd I adoo?"

"Aperfect!"

"Awas a good idea."

Stava smiled. "Awas all I acould athink of!"

*   *   *

Sullrob spent every spare moment traveling around the planet, talking to committee chairmen and other influential Seeliots. He presented his evidence, leaving behind a wake of fury and rage, a burning desire to oust Plekwag for his murderous traitorism, to see a new governor installed for the good of all. Most of those he visited were eager to become the successor, to take over the chair and rule the planet, pledging to restore the dignity and order on which Seeliots had prided themselves since long before the trader invasion.

He had one big problem; none that he spoke with were willing to continue the shipments of Jurnama to TradCo. They blamed Ling Bozathorne and his minions for the murders of loved ones—rightly so—and wanted to close off all outside commerce, re-establishing the planet's centuries-long isolation from the Consortium.

Several people seemed to have strong personal self-interest, a lust for power and control, notoriety and history. Others seemed more interested in the fate of the planet, wanting to take the reins to assure a safe and successful future for their families and friends. Most wanted Sullrob to turn over the evidence so they could personally mount the Challenge, to hold all the cards and emerge as the hero.

Sullrob kept the evidence to himself. He wanted to avoid involvement as much as possible, but he knew he would have to be the star witness, explaining how he'd learned the truth, how he'd trapped Ling Bozathorne. He wanted to find the one man he could trust, who would assure continued commerce for the millions of innocent citizens across the galaxy who needed the powerful medicine. He wanted to find a man who cared about little Greggo, but he could not.

Ravaged by lack of sleep, immersed in rage over his wife's murder, intimidated by the complicated political process, scared for his very future, Sullrob paced the floor late the night before Rep-assembly. He walked to the kitchen and drew a mug of cool water, pausing to get a pinch of Zhasou. He sat in the soft pink moonlight and recited the Celebration of Life. He lingered with his thoughts of Sullruff, remembering the time she had argued with a tearful Stava. The boy was pleading that something wasn't what he was *supposed* to do at school. Sullrob couldn't remember what the issue was about, but he did know what she had told him.

"Always do what is right, son. Always do what you know in your heart is right." She'd held the tearful boy in her arms, whispering, "Even if they punish you, you'll know you did what was right."

Sullrob would be the one to mount the Challenge. Only as governor could he be sure that little Greggo would receive his treatments, that a course for Seelius would be charted that both preserved its culture and helped it learn to reap the advantages of joining the other worlds in the galaxy. Besides, after effecting the changes, when issues were settled and attitudes had evolved, he could resign and retire to Seelosia to be a part of the new world he'd help create. At least, in the meantime, it would be safe to bring his children home again. Soon they would be free to travel to nearby worlds, to visit their friends, to laugh and play and splash in the cool, clear waterfalls cascading into reflections of red mountains rimmed with pink and blue sand.

You were a good mother and wife, Sullruff. You are still helping me understand. I will do the right thing.

One last time before retiring for several hours of fitful sleep, he sprinkled Zhasou into his mug and Celebrated his *memories.* Then, with a final gulp, he steeled himself to face his future.

CHAPTER 15

"Mr. Bozathorne!" Sullrob began. "I'm glad I could reach you before I had to leave."

"You put Ms. Clayjams through her paces; she pulled me from a *very* critical meeting. This is something urgent?"

"Yes. I've just learned that some important things are going to happen at today's Rep-assembly. I wanted to make sure I coordinated with you for *our* advantage."

Bozathorne's demeanor changed from annoyance to pleased and curious. "Good. Good! Go ahead."

"There are going to be Challenges to the governor's chair announced today. We can't take a chance on somebody we don't trust taking over—he may even suspend the deal you have for Jurnama."

Bozathorne was taken aback. This was an unexpected development. "Who is planning this? What do you know?"

"There are at least three guys who have evidence of corruption in the governor's conduct of business down here—awarding contracts for building projects, taking kick-backs, ordering substandard quality that endangers people while he pocketed some of the savings." He could see Bozathorne swearing to himself as the offenses were listed. "This can go bad two ways. Either somebody else will gain control—somebody who'll be afraid to dally in anything controversial or—worse yet—everybody will fail and be executed. Then if Plekwag continues to betray you, it will be much harder to get *anyone* we can trust to take the risk of Challenging him." Sullrob paused.

"That bastard! I can't believe, while *I* was making him rich beyond his wildest dreams, he was stupid enough to get tripped up over petty corruption. What can we do about this?"

"If you agree it would help us out, then *I'm* going to be the one to mount the Challenge."

"That would be great! But on what grounds? How could *you* bring down that stupid kunkle?"

"*Mine* is a sure Challenge, because I can charge him with attempted murder."

"Murder? Of whom?"

"My son."

"You have a son? I thought you had no family!"

"My wife died in the plague. My son was supposedly killed as part of the purge.

Remember I said Plekwag was lying to you—was just doing some random purges and tampering with Chronicles to pretend he was helping you out? He had a Panel claim my son was contaminated, so I faked the boy's death and hid him. If he was contaminated, I would have let him die for the good of my people, but I knew from our family histories that he was not. I believe this so strongly, I am willing to produce him before the Assembly and demand that he be retested in front everyone. When he is proven pure, Plekwag will be found guilty of his attempted murder and of the murders of many others who were also pure. It will come out that he ordered random executions rather than go to the trouble of truly investigating to find contaminants."

"If you are wrong, you will die with your son," Ling pointed out, concerned about losing the only Seeliot cohort he trusted.

"Not if the equipment you provided is true and accurate. If it falsifies results, then I could lose. If the equipment is true, I will win."

"The equipment will reveal the truth—and it cannot be tampered with. If your son is tested in front of witnesses and he is truly pure Seeliot, then the equipment will verify that for all to see."

Sullrob was relieved. He wanted to be sure it was Seeliots who were corrupt and not the testing equipment supplied by TradCo. He also wanted to keep Bozathorne apprised of his pending Challenge. Surely, Plekwag would contact Ling soon after the Assembly to inform him and ask for help—before Sullrob could get home and make his own contact. He couldn't take a chance of looking like he was conducting his own agenda. He had to play the TradCo stooge, if only in appearances. "Plekwag will probably contact you trying to find out how to falsify the results. You might lie to him, give him some false information so that he will go to the Challenge confident he will win. That way we won't risk a desperate man exposing what has been going on."

"Yes! Good thinking. He must not learn he will lose until the very last moment. I'll consult my people now and have a good way to mislead him when I'm contacted."

"I will summon Ms. Clayjams when I return home and update her on the proceedings."

"Good. You do that. And be careful. Good luck to you."

"Good luck to *us!*" Sullrob corrected. "This is the first step toward a *long* and profitable relationship between my world and your company."

As Sullrob prepared to leave, he remembered once berating Stava for telling a half-truth, only to have the youngster counter with a speech about situational ethics. *Okay, Stava, I'll concede this one. You always were good at seeing the bigger picture.*

*   *   *

"I've been Challenged! Some damn 'shugger-eater Challenged me!" Governor Plekwag paced his office, agitated, while the visi-mod dutifully transmitted his image to Ling Bozathorne's office.

Ling looked appropriately concerned, wondering, "*Who* Challenged you? On what grounds? What do you think will happen?"

"One of the new Assembly-reps—the one from Tessila!" Plekwag barked, pausing to gaze at the three-chinned image sweating its way right through his view-screen. "The grounds are *murder* and *attempted murder!* He says he's going to prove that the Panels of Extirpation, under *my* authority, have ordered executions when people weren't really contaminated." The governor paused a few seconds to catch his breath; he was starting to pant from rage and fear and the exertion of his vigorous pacing. "I don't see *how* he could win this Challenge. Your equipment has been used to screen specimens from *everybody* brought under 'reason to suspect.' Only when somebody was truly contaminated were executions ordered."

"What about the siblings who *weren't* actually proven by the testing?"

"Well, yes. *You* were the one that pushed that—you know, because like you said, the contamination doesn't always show up, but *all* children with the same parents *must* be even if only one shows the evidence."

"When did you start including the siblings?"

Plekwag rubbed his chin, looking around for the nearest chair, then pulling it over in front of the screen and dropping heavily into it. "Right after you told me this. What—probably two tenth-turns ago? We didn't start purging sibs until you explained it to me."

"Is it common knowledge that siblings, even when not proven contaminated, also have been ordered killed?"

"No! Of course not. People wouldn't stand for that. They're already starting to revolt over the ones who *are* proven contaminated."

"If Panels have ordered death to people whose only crime is to be the brother or sister of a contaminant, then I can see why some would call it murder. But how could the Assembly-rep from Tessila prove this has happened? Who else knows of this practice?"

"I can get around that. I mean, my lieutenants and the elders of each Panel were all informed of this change, but I think I can talk my way through that. It's only logical that the sibling *must* be contaminated. I'm surprised we didn't realize that until *you* pointed it out. That can be carefully explained, even understood by the ignorant and stupid. No Assembly-rep can prove they're *not* contaminated—it just doesn't make sense."

"Then you have nothing to worry about?"

Plekwag pondered for a minute. He stood, pushing the chair out of his way, and walked behind his desk to sit officiously in the big seat. "I don't think I do.

There's no way he can prove the brother or sister of a trader descendant isn't also a trader descendant. They would *have* to be."

"Is there *anything* he could use against you?"

"I don't think so. The only person who knows you've been paying me to purge contaminants—and for the Jurnama crystals—is Stewrik, but I've been paying him off. Our scientists are too stupid to discover we don't really need your medicine—or to figure out you sent the virus here in the first place. Only Stewrik knows of my plans to escape Seelius if things go badly here."

Ling Bozathorne smiled, exposing perfect artificial teeth and raising the folds under his face into another of those grotesque triple grins. "Just in case you are wrong—or your adversary has a surprise for you, let me suggest how you can protect yourself . . . how you can protect your wife and son, little—what is it? Plekmerk?"

Plekwag nodded, knitting his eyebrows curiously. "Yes, it's Plekmerk. You're right. Prepare for the worst. What else can I do?"

"First, we need to protect you from *other* ways a Challenge might hurt you or your son. Too many people know of our, um, our *arrangement*—especially your cabinet. We need to conceal the evidence. Punch code 8781 into the pad on our communication equipment, then designate a time one to two hours after the Challenge and add -400. That will destroy the equipment if you do not come back and punch in 8781 again immediately. Then some governor pro tem won't find something that might cast a long shadow on your son."

"8781?" Plekwag wrote it down. "Time and -400."

"Second, if you *are* found guilty, we need a way to save your life and help you escape."

"Yes. Yes! Good!" Plekwag liked the idea, but realized he didn't know how. "How?"

"Send all of your precious metals in the Chronicle case with the next shipment. I'll have my people pick it up so your money is waiting for you off-planet if you flee. If you win the Challenge, I'll send it all back with the next payment. The day before the Challenge, I'll send a vial of pseudo-poison instead of your payment. Give it to your male relative—your sister's son, I believe, would be next in line to carry out your punishment. Give him instructions to use it for killing you if you lose. Call it something that it looks like down there. You could even put it on a sterilized thorn. When it's administered, it will make you appear to die and look dead for about six hours—plenty of time to remove your body to your nephew's home. After you automatically revive, stay hidden there. In about two quarter tenth-turns, I'll have a private shuttle land and pick up you and anyone in your family who wants to flee. That 8781 code will wipe out the security grid, so nobody will know a small ship has penetrated your atmosphere."

"Excellent! Obviously, I want to preserve the chair for Plekmerk, but if something goes wrong, my wife and son and I—plus possibly my sister's family—will all be able to retire to another world using my precious metals to start a new life!"

Ling smiled again. "You see? All is well. Even if it goes bad, it will turn out good. You have nothing to worry about. Think nothing of this Challenge. Show confidence; go about your regular business. Don't give it another thought."

Plekwag smiled. Everything was under control. There was no reason for concern. Even if he lost the Challenge, he had a very powerful friend in the Consortium. Ling would take care of him and his family.

There was nothing to worry about.

*   *   *

Two boys, about eleven years old, plus a fourteen-year-old girl stood curiously in the loading area, watching in fascination as Brog Pawligan talked to a *purple* man! They didn't know Sullrob and, even though Brog had warned them he'd need to meet this unusual person before they left for Caskentia, they were still surprised at how different he looked. Brog had said there'd be lots of purple people where they were going.

This sounded like fun! Besides, Jowda and Jak and, for the older girl, Selta would be there—not to mention lakes *full* of water and waterfalls and mountains and trees and stuff. The kids were excited about being invited for the long weekend, but were only beginning to imagine why their parents were so thrilled with the opportunity for their young ones to experience ground-side.

Brog looked concerned, but he finally smiled, touching his purple friend on the shoulders and forehead, then shaking his hand before coming back over and ushering the three visitors aboard his borrowed ship. Each carried an overnight bag stuffed with clothes and snacks and still-cams with lots of dimension-chips to record their vacation. They also had swimsuits, hastily purchased at the last minute even though Brog had warned their families that the youngsters ground-side had pretty much gotten to where they didn't bother with them.

Though the girl was more shy than the boys, all three pestered Brog during the flight down with questions about what to expect ground-side. They watched in fascination as he docked the ship, then squealed with delight when greeted by Jowda and Jak and Selta and close to a dozen *purple* kids all enthusiastically welcoming them. Pirlhoff and Brog took turns laughing and shaking their heads at the raucous din in the air-bus during the trip to Seelosia. You'd think these kids had never seen land before. Truth be told, two of the three newcomers hadn't.

The valley was a hit, but that was no surprise. Once bedrooms were assigned and guests were situated, Heilen served a big lunch for everybody followed by a tour of the kitchen including detailed instructions that each child was to feel free to eat as much as he wanted whenever he was hungry except . . .

"These *here* isa the meal times!" He pointed at a list on the wall, then arched his eyebrows and glared suspiciously at each child, causing them all to giggle. "Adon't you abee a-eatin' yerselves fat fat fat th'last few hours 'fore a meal. We agot big big big meals planned t'please an' a-delight y'all—an' if'n you's too *full* t'eat—" He paused, glaring at each again. "Then *I* abee the one t'have t'eat it all an' I'm *already* too fat fat fat!"

Fast as he could move his arms, he poked every child in the belly, bringing more squeals and giggles. He smiled again at several whispers to Jowda and Jak, "You guys got *great* dads!" By the end of the weekend, they'd also agree that Jowda and Jak had great haircuts and ideas for games and ways to ski and a myriad of other things to imitate.

Ever the follower, Jowda had finally become the one to emulate.

*   *   *

Brog called a meeting with some of the key adults and the youngest ascended Seeliot, Stava. Peering around at Pirlhoff, Heilen and his wife, plus the Buchs, he looked serious for the first time since he'd arrived.

"I have startling news from Sullrob." He saw Stava lean forward, concerned. "Sullrob has mounted a Challenge against the governor."

Stava was shocked. Buchvan blurted, "He did *what?* Why?" The Heweds were confused.

Brog went on. "A Challenge is when somebody accuses the governor of crimes for which he can be executed."

Buchvan asked, "Did he Challenge the man or the family?"

"The family."

Buchjeen explained to the Heweds, "If it was the man, then the governor's heir would take over the job. If it's the family and the Challenge is successful, then whoever Challenges takes over the job."

"Y'mean our man Sullrob—he amight abeein' the *governor* of *all* Seelius?"

"If he wins," Buchvan confirmed.

Stava looked stricken, was barely audible as he choked out, "And if he loses . . ."

Everybody watched him for a moment, then looked to the Buchs for confirmation. Buchvan only nodded. Buchjeen stared at her lap. Stava pushed away from the conference table and paced over to the window, staring out at the mountains reflecting in the lake, at the children romping on the beach and splashing in the water, all bereft of the cares and fears of a Seeliot man so young his changing voice still sometimes squeaked his excitement.

Brog hastily added, "He assures me that absolutely *nothing* can go wrong—that he *will* be victorious."

Everybody was still watching Stava. Lival asked, "But if he becomes the governor, how can he move here?"

"Well," Brog explained, "the original plan was to spend more than a year—nearly a turn on Seelius—smuggling and setting this up. He didn't expect to be here for some time anyway. He believes he can make some important changes there—can save countless lives and help his people—then resign and come here still within the time we'd originally planned."

Everybody nodded, concern still creasing their faces. Stava, from behind, looked like he might be trembling.

Pirlhoff whispered, "Maybe we should talk about this more later."

Everybody nodded, understanding. They quietly filed out, leaving Brog and Pirlhoff and Stava, the boy-man still staring out the window. Brog went up behind the young Seeliot and put his arms around him. Pirlhoff moved beside him and reached out to stroke his blond-white hair.

Brog whispered, "How 'bout just the three of us grab some air-bikes and zip over to one of the lakes in the next valley?"

Stava nodded, wiping his face, then turned to lead them stoically out of the conference room. They stopped long enough for Pirlhoff to grab some flat-mugs and a bladder of Zhasou-ade, then flew toward the mountains, down toward the lower end of the next valley, settling into the sand beside the water. They collapsed the bikes into simple loungers and stretched out where they could take in the view. Nobody spoke for some time.

Finally, Stava asked, "Why adoes it—why does it have to be *my* dad?"

Brog quietly explained, "He tried to find somebody else to do it, Stava—*anybody* he could trust, but he couldn't. You see, there are sick people all over the galaxy who need that Jurnama medicine. Everybody he talked to wanted to cut off the supply. The governor needs to be Challenged for the good of Seelius. It needs to be done by your father for the good of *all* people everywhere."

Stava shook his head. He paused, then said, "He could just come here and be done with it, you know."

Pirlhoff asked, "Does that sound like the kind of man your father is, Stava?"

He managed a weak smile. "No."

"No," Brog agreed.

Stava sighed, rubbing his face with his hands. "I wouldn't even be here now if my father wasn't the kind of man who always adid the right thing."

"You don't doubt that you and your sister are most important to him, do you?" Brog asked.

Stava shook his head. "No."

There was silence for another minute before Brog broached the next subject.

"Um, Stava? There's more."

The young Seeliot rolled his eyes. "Isn't there always?"

"He needs your help."

"*My* help?"

Brog nodded. "The basis of his Challenge is that even pure Seeliots are being executed. He needs you there to have you tested in front of the Assembly. He wants me to take you back after this weekend, then he'll take you down to Seelius on his next flight. He says he'll bring you back up after the Challenge so I can cart yer purple hide back to Seelosia again. You'll be gone for just the week."

Stava laughed. "He acan't abecome the governor without *me* ahelpin'!" he mocked. He stood up and paced around in a circle, still goofing. "I aguess I'll a-go ahelp him then!"

"That's my guy!" Pirlhoff exclaimed.

"Good for you!" Brog agreed.

"Well, if I only agot a few more days, I abetter go aget into some fun with the *new* kids," he announced. He unfolded his air-bike and hopped aboard. "You two atake yer time. I'll asee you when you aget back." With that, he was gone, flying toward the ridge that separated the valleys.

"You think he wanted to leave us alone?" Brog asked, mockingly suspicious.

"That boy's been trying to set us up all along," she laughed. Suddenly, she stood up, peeled off her jumpsuit, and ran splashing into the water.

Brog, still getting used to the modesty thing, hesitated, then finally doffed his own and followed. Swimming to her, he explained, "I'm still not used to tromping around in front of people with all my parts hangin' out, you know."

She tweaked his cheek, then reached down to tweak another cheek, laughing. "I don't see why not. All yer parts *do* look good!"

"I *have* been losing weight and getting in better shape," he allowed.

"Don't think I haven't noticed." She kissed him on the cheek, then quickly swam to the shallows, sitting in less than a half-meter of water. Brog followed, sitting beside her and putting an arm around her, pulling her close.

"Yeah," he whispered, "I used to be a fat spacer who just didn't care. Now, with such a grand future ahead of me, I want to be healthy and live forever."

"Good for you," she whispered back. "Now if we could just get some purple in *all* yer cheeks!" She laughed, but was interrupted by a gentle kiss.

She put her arms around Brog, tentatively kissing back. He kissed her again, more passionately, holding her tight. They fell back into the water and sand, gentle ripples washing over them, and kissed yet again. They rolled onto their sides but got water in their faces, so he got on his knees, scooped her into his arms, then stood and carried her up the beach, laying her gently in the pink and blue sand. He snuggled up close to her and kissed her again, then again.

It seemed to them like they were enveloped by a rainbow. It wasn't the colors of their skin. Maybe it was the blue water or the red mountains, the lush green vegetation, the pink and blue sand, the flowers growing up the hillside in yellow and red and violet and orange and pink and . . .   Maybe it was just the clear blue sky.

They weren't looking around, just into each other's eyes. They could be anywhere in the galaxy.

Just them.

CHAPTER 16

Stava enjoyed the afternoon playing with Jowda and Jak's friends from the Orbiter-two. Part of their time was spent climbing waterfalls, waterskiing and swimming, hiking along the ridge while competing to see who could discover the most native wildflowers, building a giant sand-castle on the beach. Throughout it all, he answered lots of questions about life on Seelius, asking just as many—even when he already knew the answers—about the orbiter and the few other worlds one of them had visited. They all got along famously, affirming that boys are boys wherever they live, however they look, whatever they've experienced.

Stava was preoccupied, though. There were two pieces of unfinished business gnawing at him—going through the rest of his mother's family's files and updating the Chronicle with the circumstances of her life and death. He'd already been through all of the documents, but he wanted to read them more thoroughly, to discuss things he didn't understand with Buchvan or Brog. He'd already started making notes to update his mother's life, but each time he'd been overcome with emotion, unable to finish the project through his tears and his memories.

But a third thing preoccupied him most. He couldn't shake the thought that he needed to be prepared when he went back to Seelius, with everything worked out in advance for his father. Finally, he asked Brog and Buchvan if they could meet privately late that evening.

"My dad will probably reveal that the plague was acaused by TradCo, awon't he?" he asked, sitting at the head of the big table in the habitat conference room.

"He said he's not sure," Brog answered.

"It could be risky," Buchvan pointed out, "especially since one of his priorities is to continue the Jurnama shipments so sick people don't lose their medicine."

"He said it may have to be his trump card—his overriding weapon," Brog clarified, "especially if the murder part isn't strong enough or convincing enough."

"He's arisking his life for the good of all Seelius. I adon't want him to be afraid to use his—his *trump card*, as you called it—for aworryin' about sick people. We aneed t'help him on that."

"What do you have in mind, son?" Brog wondered.

They talked for several hours, making lists, bringing in Heilen to help. While they worked, Brog put in a contact to Dow Pfivvel on Dilltomarius. The chairman of Pfivvel, Inc. promised to put together a team and arrive on Caskentia late the following afternoon. The next morning, Stava begged off of the waterfall-climbing expedition and went to see Buchvan instead.

"Buchvan, I aknow I'll only be gone a quarter tenth-tur—I amean a week. Please hold on to my mother's family's records for me. I awant to aread them some more when I acome back. I'll akeep the Chronicle and take it with me. I awant to update it."

Buchvan carefully took two cases of records and secured them in the habitat lock-up, promising the young Seeliot he could count on their safety.

Stava packed a case with his portable comm-pad, his mother's Chronicle, and snacks and drinks, then boarded an air-bike and flew across to the far ridge and selected a spot under a towering tree to sit and write about his mother. Occasionally wiping tears from his eyes, sometimes smiling to himself at the fond memories, other times solemn and deliberate, he recorded the important events in his mother's life, paying particular attention to her husband and the two children she had loved more than life itself.

He finished with more than an hour to spare before the meeting with Dow Pfivvel, so he stripped off his frock and ran down the ridge to splash in the water for a few minutes. His excess energy spent, he climbed the hill again and packed his belongings onto the air-bike. As an afterthought, he rummaged through his satchel and produced a palm laser-cuter. He studied the trunk of the massive tree for the right spot, then carefully carved his father's name in the bark. Below that followed his mother's, then his own, and finally Yantanna's. Satisfied, he hopped on the bike and flew off in search of Jowda and the other boys. After all, he still had a little time to stir up some hijinks.

He spotted the girls first, so he flew in and landed on the beach where they were sunning themselves. He sat and talked with them for a few minutes.

Little Yantanna asked, "Is Daddy areally agonna abee the governor?"

"It sure alooks that way!"

She got up and went over to him, then sat and snuggled her head against his shoulder. He put his arm around her and held her close.

"Why adoo *you* ahave to a-go?" she wondered.

"He aneeds my help. Don't aworry. I'll abee right back."

"When will Daddy acome t'live with us?"

"Before your next birthday," he assured her. "He's got to ahelp a lot of people; then he'll acome t'stay for good."

"Okay, Stava. You apromise?"

"I apromise, Yantanna."

They hugged each other for a minute before the little girl resumed her sunning alongside the others.

Stava returned to the habitat and paced nervously in the conference room, waiting for everybody to arrive. Finally, Dow Pfivvel, three assistants, Brog, Heilen, and Buchvan filed in. Two of the assistants were women, the other a man. One of the women was dark-skinned like the Heweds.

Brog indicated which chairs people should take, leaving the head of the table open. He gestured for Stava to take that one. Stava looked at him wide-eyed, not sure why he should sit at the front.

"This is *your* meeting, son," Brog whispered. "We're here to help any way we can. Just relax and explain why we're here; then let's see where it goes."

Stava took the head chair, pulling it close, then reaching down to activate its riser mechanism until he could put his elbows on the table. One of Pfivvel's people started to chuckle, but a sharp look from Dow made him decide there was nothing funny about a little purple lad running the meeting.

"Seelosia, Inc. has a profitable deal with Pfivvel, Inc. based on mutual business interest, friendship, and trust," Stava began. He took a deep breath and, looking around at each person at the table, continued, "We would like to explore opportunities to expand that arrangement, including possibly agiving—giving the Jurnama business to your company."

The Pfivvel people knew that's why they were there, but there were still murmurs of pleasure and anticipation.

"We are pleased and honored that you have considered us first," Dow responded.

Stava smiled slightly, nodding at Dow before continuing. "As you know, the Governor of Seelius has the right to enter into such business agreements on behalf of the entire planet. We have reason to believe that my father, Sullrob, will abecome—will become the new governor before the end of the next quar—the end of the *week*."

Dow's eyes went wide, though not more so than those of his aides. "Excellent! Congratulations!" he added.

"Thank you," Stava continued, "but that is still premature. It is not accomplished yet. My father will be risking his life—and mine, I suspect—to achieve this for the good of our people and the millions throughout the galaxy who aneed—who need—Jurnama." The Pfivvel people looked concerned, but waited for him to continue. "I would like to see if we can areach—can reach agreement before I leave tomorrow so my father can make the necessary changes as soon as he assumes power."

"Your father must be a great man," one of the assistants offered.

"He is," Dow affirmed. "And so is his son."

"We have much to work out," Stava continued, pausing after the compliment only long enough to imagine his father's face. The image urged him to keep moving, get down to business. "In addition to setting a price, we will need ships and processing and distribution and many other things, plus we must consider how this may benefit the people of Seelius so my father does not meet too much resistance."

Dow nodded. His aides started to reach into the cases to retrieve comm-pads and data chips.

Stava waved them off, explaining, "Before we begin, I would alike to introduce you to one of our customs, the Zhasou Celebration of Life, something we do before all meetings to remind us what is most important."

Heilen grinned, adding, "It abee a *fine* Celebration—an' it abee atastin' good, too!"

The Celebration lasted fifteen minutes. The meeting took another four hours. Agreement was reached pending ratification by the new Governor of Seelius.

The Pfivvel contingent had already planned to stay overnight, so the group wandered out to take in the panorama of the valley, the spectacular sunset over the red mountains, the reflections in the water, packs of children roving and laughing and playing here and there.

Heilen asked the three aides, "D'you people abee ahavin' children?"

"I have two," one of the women answered.

"I have one," offered the other.

"I win!" the man announced. "I've got *four* of the little weasels!"

Heilen threw his arms wide, grinning and announcing, "The *next* time y'be acomin' back, y'be abringin' yer *whole* fam-lees! I'm abelievin' there's a 'shugger here fer *ever* one o'them little ones!"

"Why thank you!"

"That sounds *very* fun; this is such a nice place."

"What's a 'shugger?"

Heilen's eyebrows shot up as if he'd spotted a likely mark. The others chuckled as he led his new victims off to the 'shugger-hut for a serenade and petting session.

First Dow, then Brog and Buchvan took turns clasping Stava on the shoulder, thanking him for his foresight, congratulating him on doing such a fine job.

He took it good naturedly, then looked serious. "It sure is hard to a-celebrate so soon, though," he said quietly. "I'm aworried 'bout my dad."

*   *   *

"Hi, Sharlotte! I'm surprised to hear from you. I wasn't expecting your signal 'til the end of the week!"

There was a pause while the message traveled to Dilltomarius and the reply was transmitted back. "Oh Shar! I couldn't wait! It's a miracle. I just had to let you know."

"You mean?"

"Here, let Greggo tell you. He's just bursting with excitement."

Shar shifted uncomfortably in the recliner attached to the juvie. His lower legs were encased by the contraption. "Hello, Greggo?"

"Unca Shar! Guess what? I no have to use the bone thing that hurts no more!" Used to the delays whenever he talked to his uncle, the little boy waited patiently.

"You're in remission—you're all better now?"

"Yeah! Mommy says only the juvie now, but that don't hurt none."

"Good for you! Good for you, Greggo. Okay, now let me talk to your mom again. You be a good boy, Greggo!"

"Bye, Unca Shar!"

"Shar! Isn't it wonderful?"

"Double wonderful, sis. Double. Mine is going away, too. The team seems to think that by the time I get my pancreas juvied, I'll be a hundred percent."

Sharlotte wiped tears from her face. Quietly, she congratulated, "Oh Shar, good for you. Good for all of us. This is a blessing, is what it is. A real blessing. I never dreamed—but then, *you* did, didn't you?"

"I couldn't give up, sis. Oh, I'd started to resign *myself*, but when our little guy there got sick, I just had to hang on. I couldn't let—I couldn't—well . . ."

"Shar, do you know what this means?"

"Yeah. I'm only just starting to imagine."

Shar could see little Greggo peeking around from behind his mother, grinning like an imp, waving surreptitiously. "Look, Unca Shar! I can walk again!"

*   *   *

Stava, Brog, and Sullrob hurriedly pushed the large cases into Pawligan's quarters.

"I hope you got plenty of room in the transparents," Sullrob jibed. "I got nearly six hundred Zhasou cuttings here, plus Lafave will have more than that when he gets here in another hour."

"The transparents are full, Dad, but we're ahaving numbers four, five, and six abuilt right now. Pirlhoff a-says the climate on Caskentia, as long as she acontrols the soil and nutrients inside the transparents, is better even than Seelius for Zhasou!"

"Good. Good!"

They unloaded the cases, collapsed them, and readied them for Sullrob to take. Brog went out and came back with mugs of warm Zhasou tea, inviting Sullrob to relax a few minutes before hurrying back to his ship. They sipped quietly for a few minutes, not saying much of anything.

Finally, Brog asked, "Is it still day after tomorrow?"

"Yeah," Sullrob confirmed, taking another sip. "Everything remains as planned."

Brog looked toward Stava, then back at Sullrob, raising his eyebrows in silent question.

"I've got it worked out with Lafave," Sullrob answered, acknowledging the unspoken. "He'll bring the news and handle things if there's a problem. I'll explain the details to Stava during the drop ground-side."

Brog nodded, relieved. Stava looked curiously at the two men, but said nothing. Sullrob finished his tea, then stood, announcing, "I need to get back."

Hustling to his feet, Brog asked, "I'll see you tomorrow?"

"Oh yes, same schedule."

"Good. And when—?" He nodded toward Stava.

"Within a few days, depending on how tense it gets."

"When you're the governor," Brog started, "you won't be flying daily runs anymore." It was more of a statement than a question.

"No, my backup will take over. We don't know him well enough to have him smuggle, but Lafave will keep up the shipments. We can afford to cut back, now that everybody is moved and there is plenty of weenshugger stock—all we're doing is filling more and more greenhouses."

"When will I see you next?"

"Well, I'm thinking in about a week. As governor, I'll be free to travel as I see fit." Smiling conspiratorially, he added, "I think I'll need to be off-planet most weekends to deal with issues surrounding Jurnama trade."

"Speaking of that, your son has negotiated a phenomenal deal for you to ratify. I think you'll be pleased—especially since it takes the business away from the man and company that caused so many deaths on your world."

Sullrob looked admiringly at his son. The purple lad almost blushed, but wasn't quick enough to evade a fast headlock and noogie from his father. "I look forward to hearing about it. I may need to appoint Stava the official Seelius off-world business liaison!"

Stava grinned, throwing his arms wide in imitation of Heilen. "For a big big sala-ree!"

*   *   *

During the flight ground-side, Sullrob carefully reviewed his plans for the Challenge with his son. He triple repeated all the details of the elaborate escape plan he'd worked out with Lafave to smuggle the youngster back to Orbiter-two if the worst happened and Sullrob lost his life. All the assurances that it wouldn't happen weren't enough to calm the man-boy's fears, but he listened patiently, paying careful attention to exactly what he was supposed to do.

Next, Stava pulled out copies of summary documents and outlined the deal he, along with Brog, Buchvan, and Heilen had negotiated with Pfivvel, Inc. Sullrob was very impressed, pleased that he would be able to switch customers immediately upon assuming power. Listening as Stava explained the details, he praised his son's foresight and planning, the proud father. "And to think—it is only a half tenth-turn since you officially ascended. Your mother would have been proud, too . . ."

Stava hid inside a travel case as Sullrob passed through the terminal, then climbed out once the groundcar was safely underway. He kept his face pressed against the glass, staring eagerly at every detail in the home world he'd not seen for what seemed like such a long period in his short life.

At home, Stava ran to his bedroom, opening drawers, exploring everything, fingering his belongings, throwing himself on the bed to see if it still felt like he remembered. It did. It was where his mother used to tuck him in, singing a little song or telling him a story, always hugging and kissing him good-night before stealing out to leave him bathed in pink moonlight and warm feelings.

Sullrob eased in and gently lay down beside him, not saying anything. Stava snuggled close, enveloped by his father's strong arm pulling him closer. After a while, the youngster asked, "You're ascared, aren't you, Dad?"

"Yeah. A lot."

"I understand why you have to adoo it."

"Good. That's important. That's *very* important to me. I have doubts sometimes, but I know in my heart it's what I have to do."

"Don't ever adoubt it, Dad." He paused for a moment, adding, "Mom would be proud."

Sullrob nodded his head in the softening daylight, a light pink hue starting to play across his features. After a few minutes, they got up and went out for mugs of cool water and pinches of Zhasou spice. They recited the Celebration of Life, lingering on their memories of Sullruff and all the friends they so senselessly lost to the plague. Afterward, Stava unpacked his carry-bag and showed his father the Chronicle, reading aloud the parts he'd updated to include his mother's life. Sullrob listened patiently, nodding approval, occasionally wiping his eyes, several times reaching out and spontaneously grabbing his son for a hug.

The next morning, Stava woke his father with a familiar but almost-forgotten sound—somebody in the house, moving quietly in the kitchen area, making breakfast for the slumbering Seeliot. It was a meal fit for a king—or a governor at least. While they ate, Stava broached another subject on his mind.

"You know, Dad, I've athought of a project I awant to work on while you're down here abeein' the governor. It may cost some money, though, but I think it'll be worth it."

"You don't have to give up playing and having fun just because you're ascended, you know."

Stava smiled. "I ahaven't. I adon't *ever* plan to aquit aplayin'."

"Good. Well then, what's your project?"

"Ling Bozathorne owns less than one-tenth of TradCo because his ancestors asold a lot of shares. Somewhere on one of the worlds Sam Fowler visited, he got amarried and had a baby. Wherever that is, there's somebody or a bunch of people who now own half of TradCo. I want to afind them—adoo a lot of research, maybe even atravel to those worlds, afind out who can take control of the company away from that 'shugger-eater murderer that acaused the plague."

Sullrob smiled. "Okay, it'll be up to Buchvan and Brog how much you can spend—and I want you to take one or two older people with you if you travel, but I think it's a great idea. Maybe you can be the one to bring down that horrible man and stop him from ever being able to hurt people again."

"I probably awon't be able to afind out who, though. It's been acovered up for a long time."

"You won't know until you try, son. And if you can . . ."

Stava nodded, asking, "You aknow what I athink?"

Sullrob raised his eyebrows questioningly.

"I athink that's why Ling Bozathorne awanted Chronicles—to asee if he could adiscover if any heirs are on Seelius. I athink that's why he aprovided testing equipment and awanted to ahelp the purge—to akill anyone who amight abee able to claim control of TradCo."

*   *   *

Sullrob stood in the hastily erected Challenger box at the front of the Rep-assembly wearing a ceremonial frock. Governor Plekwag wore a similar frock, though his was festooned with additional gemstones befitting his station. He was standing in another box about ten meters from Sullrob. All committee meetings and other business had been canceled. The hall was packed with Reps, alternates, and special guests. Stava secretly hid in a small room at the back of the great hall. The Challenge was about to begin.

The eldest of all Panel elders stepped to the dais between the two boxes. The crowd grew quiet. "Today," he thundered, "we have a Challenge to the family of Plek from the family of Sull. Sullrob has Challenged Governor Plekwag with crimes against the peoples of Seelius. The Challenger understands the consequences if his Challenge is false. The governor understands the consequences if he is found guilty." Turning to face Sullrob, he intoned, "How say you, Challenger?"

Sullrob cleared his throat, then addressed the throng, his voice gaining strength as his confidence began to match his resolve. "I Challenge Governor Plekwag for many crimes against the peoples of Seelius."

The elder interrupted, announcing, "Each charge shall be dealt with individually. What is your first charge?"

"I charge Governor Plekwag with murder of many hundreds, possibly even thousands of innocent people, under the guise of purging contaminants, having declared people through Panels of Extirpation by his authority to be worthy of execution, with no basis in fact and no proof of contamination."

The elder turned to the governor, asking, "How do you plead?"

"Innocent! This charge is untrue and the Challenger should pay the penalty to blaspheme your esteemed leader."

The elder turned to Sullrob, "And what proofs will you offer?"

"I call the elder of the Panel for Tessila, Waverla, Micuwena, and Erinsilla."

The old man emerged from the area set aside for Panel elders, stepping vigorously to the front to stand beside the man conducting the proceedings. "I am Kentdug."

Sullrob asked, "Were you ordered by the governor to declare siblings of contaminants also to be contaminated, ordering their executions even without evidence of their own contaminations?"

Kentdug simply responded, "Yes. It is true."

The audience gasped and murmured. Several people shouted, "He is a murderer!"

The elder clapped his hands sharply, calling for order. "How do you respond, Governor Plekwag?"

"It is well known by genetic scientists throughout the Consortium that contamination does not always show up in the tests. But if a child is from contaminated lineage and another child has the same parents, then it is only logical that both children are contaminated!"

Sullrob could tell from the buzz in the crowd that the audience believed the argument. He was already losing his momentum. Looking over at the smug expression on the governor's face, he grew angry. Carefully controlling his ire and with measured determination, he pressed on. "Do you recall receiving the results of tests performed on my children, Stava and Yantanna, examined for contamination under 'reason to suspect'?"

"Yes I do."

"What were the results furnished to you by the chair of the governor?"

"Your daughter was not found to be contaminated. Your son *was*. Both were purged on this evidence." A murmur of sympathy for the Challenger swept through the crowd. He'd lost his children; now he would lose his own life in this ill-advised attempt to exact revenge on the person he blamed for their deaths.

"I demand that the testing equipment be brought here."

"So it shall be done," the elder intoned.

Stewrik hustled out and returned in a moment with the genetic testing equipment.

Facing the audience, Sullrob continued, "I had reason to believe that my children were *not* contaminated. I believed the governor to be guilty of murder. I faked the deaths of my children until I could prove this." He nodded to Lafave, who stepped out and returned with Stava. The youngster marched purposefully to the front and stood beside the elder. "Is there doubt that this is my son, Stava?"

Several people stood in the audience, shouting out, "I can vouch. I know the Sull family."

The elder seemed satisfied, ordering to Stewrik, "You will test Stava."

Stewrik took a small specimen collector and held it against the young Seeliot's arm. Then he placed it inside the machine and pressed a contact. After a moment, the results appeared on a screen. The elder stepped over to read the message. He studied it for a moment, then turned and announced, "Stava of the family Sull is shown to be true and pure Seeliot!"

Stava stole quietly to the back of the room and left with Lafave while the crowd erupted amid shouts of "Depose the murderer!"

The elder asked Plekwag, "How do you respond?"

"It was clearly an error. I do not operate the equipment myself. Somebody made a mistake reading or recording and reporting the results. You must prove this was *not* an honest error."

Sullrob felt kicked in the chest. The audience fell silent, waiting for a counter-argument that didn't exist. Clearing his throat, Sullrob announced, "I would like to proceed to the next charge, reserving the right to continue this afterward."

The elder nodded, intoning, "You may proceed."

"I accuse the governor of participating in a plot to exchange Jurnama for small quantities of worthless medicine, solely for his own personal gain, of participating in a plot that deliberately infected our peoples with an artificial plague that killed tens of thousands for the profits of men—tens of thousands of murders, including of my wife, Sullruff, and the friends and family members of every person here today who lost loved ones to the plague!"

The audience erupted with rage. Everybody had lost someone to that horrible death. They didn't need proof right then; discovering the "mistake" about Stava had already weakened their trust of the governor, smugly standing there trying to hold on to his power and his life. It took the elder several minutes to restore order. Finally he asked Plekwag, "How do you respond?"

"This is *not* true. I leave the Challenger to his proofs."

Sullrob nodded, calling one of the planet's top scientists forward. The man carried a display of dimension-stills. He explained in lay terms how the virus had been eradicated from the population and that the medicine was no longer needed. After review and acceptance of his credentials, he was followed by four more scientists who confirmed the testimony. Plekwag offered nothing to counter this evidence. Then Sullrob had the damaged silica capsule brought forward. The same men testified to its properties for carrying viruses, its design for slow release over a period of time, and its damaged destruct mechanism that had inadvertently left the evidence intact. The two men who had turned it over to Sullrob testified where and how it was discovered.

As the evidence mounted, the elder had an increasingly difficult time maintaining order. Revenge, bloodthirsty vengeance, raged through nearly every mind. The governor appeared similarly outraged.

"How do you respond?"

"I thank Rep-assemblyman Sullrob for bringing this to our attention. I did not know of this. I recommend we make appropriate sanctions against TradCo for its deceit and murder and request that Sullrob be spared from purge for this Challenge. Though I am not guilty of these crimes—and though he has offered no proofs that I am—it is good for the peoples of Seelius that he has brought this evidence forward. He deserves honor, not execution."

Plekwag managed to win the sympathies of the crowd, magnanimous pity for Sullrob, agreement that he shouldn't be executed for bringing such important information forward, but the rage against TradCo was overwhelming. "Cancel the deal!" and similar shouts started to ring through the hall.

The elder calmed the crowd, then turned to Sullrob, asking, "Have you more?"

"Yes." Then louder, "Yes! Yes I do! I have proof that Plekwag conspired with the chairman of TradCo, the perpetrator of the plague that killed your loved ones, to sell Jurnama for his own personal gain!"

"How do you respond?" the elder asked.

Plekwag spun a response that thanked Sullrob for the information but painted him as misguided and overzealous in his prosecution. Ultimately, he left his Challenger to his proofs.

Lafave carried a small console to the front and set it up beside Sullrob, then walked to the back of the hall. Sullrob announced, "I know this because the man from TradCo tried also to entice *me* to participate in his illicit dealings. I played along to collect this evidence for the good of all Seelius!"

He activated the playback on the recorder Heilen had furnished him, projecting an image against the front of the hall and filling the air with the voices of Sullrob and Ling Bozathorne. People gasped during key statements Ling had made, repeated through technology similar to what was already being developed independently on Seelius.

"A thousand times your annual salary for helping arrange to get me those Chronicles . . . a thousand times more every year if we can start new business there . . .precious metals . . . even more if you decide to, say, emigrate . . . I will *destroy* him . . .he has *betrayed* me . . . after I have made him a rich man . . . made him a hero . . . guaranteed that the incompetent ass will have a chair to pass on to that little drooling bastard Plekmerk . . . he promised that no research would be done, that your people were too backward to study biomedicine . . . nobody is supposed to find this out . . . if we pay him off, can we keep this quiet . . . shut him up for good . . . make sure nothing jeopardizes the Jurnama deal . . . need your people to keep thinking they desperately need that medicine . . ."

The fury once again directed toward Plekwag. The elder asked for his response.

"This man conspired with Sullrob. Any mention of me may have been to help this Challenger take my chair and put it in the hands of a corrupt man after his own interests to the detriment of Seelius!"

Sullrob had to admit to himself that Plekwag was good at this. The elder asked Sullrob if he had more.

"Using this equipment, I have intercepted a communication between Governor Plekwag and this Ling Bozathorne!"

The visual image and voices filled the hall again. Plekwag could be heard replying, "I don't think so. The only person who knows you've been paying me to purge contaminants and for the Jurnama deal is Stewrik, but I've been paying him off. Our scientists are too stupid to discover we don't really need your medicine—or to figure out you sent the virus here in the first place. Only Stewrik knows of my plans to escape Seelius if things go badly here."

Sullrob stopped the recording before it could reveal the plan to fake Plekwag's death. He didn't want to be responsible for one more execution. He understood Ling Bozathorne well enough to doubt he would really send a rescue ship. Even if he did, the main goal was to wrest power from a dangerous man, to take charge for the good of Seelius. Sullrob was not a vengeful man.

The tide had turned. The crowd could not be placated. Plekwag could not respond. Stewrik tried to escape, but was bodily held and roughed up until authorities could push their way through and arrest him.

The elder called for the votes. The Panel elders agreed unanimously that Plekwag was guilty of capital crimes. The Reps were unanimous in their agreement that the Plek family should lose the chair, that Sullrob would better serve the interests of the people of Seelius.

Plekwag tried to bolt from the box, but he was restrained. His nephew was called forward. With shaking hands, Plekwag's relative poured what he called Tsalook root into a mug of water and gave it to the former governor to drink. Glaring defiantly at the angry mob, Plekwag quickly downed the poison. He convulsed several times and slumped, apparently dead. A physician examined him and declared him deceased. The governor's ceremonial frock was removed and handed to Sullrob who, immodestly, removed his own and stood there with the coveted uniform draped over one arm. The nephew and several others carried Plekwag's body out of the great hall.

The crowd quieted in anticipation. Sullrob stood in the front, gazing across the great floor, his eyes falling on Stava and Lafave standing in the back. He smiled and nodded his head. Then, with a flourish, he quickly donned the frock. The crowd roared its approval, cheering its new leader.

Governor Sullrob let them carry on for a while, then held up his arms for quiet. The crowd fell silent again.

"There will be no more tests for contamination—no more purges without a real crime!"

A murmur rose, then a dull roar, and finally cheers of approval.

"The deal with TradCo for Jurnama will be canceled!"

An instant cacophony of approval roared.

"People across the galaxy need the Jurnama medicine! Seeliots are true and good! They would never take medicine from sick people! Beginning next week, a different company will furnish ships, supplying us with precious metals and medical technology for the good of all Seelius! After time, we will be compensated with other valuable commodities and information as we, with the approval of *you* Assembly-reps, see fit!"

Sullrob was relieved when the crowd approved.

"As your governor, I pledge to protect our culture—but I will travel to other worlds as your representative, learning about the Consortium, discovering new ways we can benefit for the good of us all!"

The crowd started chanting, "Celebrate the governor! Celebrate the governor!" Zhasou was distributed, mugs passed through the crowd, toasts drank to the new regime. As his last official act for the day, Sullrob led the crowd in a Celebration of Life.

*　　　*　　　*

Far away, a cache of precious metals, cleverly concealed and shipped by Plekwag, were deposited into the private account of Ling Bozathorne. He had no intention of giving them back. The communications equipment couldn't be found by the Plek nephew—the -400 had subtracted four hours from the programmed time, causing the intricate mechanism to be vaporized hours before the Rep-assembly Challenge.

All through the night and well into the next day, Plekwag's family tried in vain to revive him. Only slowly did they realize he would never wake; no ship would come from the sky to take them to a new world and a new life.

Not understanding that his father was dead, nor how lucky he was that Sullrob had not called for death to the perpetrator's heir, little Plekmerk simply drooled.

CHAPTER 17

Six more simultaneous acquisitions increased the land area of Seelosia more than ten-fold. Jowda made serious work of trying to visit every valley and meadow and lake and mountain, to see every river and waterfall, the wooded areas, the rocky crags, the blue and pink tracts of sand with gentle dunes—every place Buchvan had marked with yellow on the plat that hung in the conference room. He returned to the habitat one day, quivering with excitement, jabbering about a great river and the biggest waterfall in the entire galaxy. The next day, more than a score of Seelosians, young and old, went with him for a picnic lunch. A giant fall, more than a hundred meters across and dropping close to sixty meters from its highest point, roared so loudly they could barely talk. The water was streaked with red and pink, reflections of the rock cliffs concealed beneath the water. It was worth the trip.

Jak went with Jowda on many of his excursions, as did some of the other community children, but the young Hewed divided his time between exploration and helping Pirlhoff. In addition to all the greenhouse activity, they were landscaping the habitat courtyard plus the areas along the hill where individual families had started to build homes. The lavish courtyard floral arrangements, a mix of the most exotic from many worlds, created a botanical garden unrivaled on all of Caskentia. Pirlhoff often found Jak sitting quietly by himself, among the flowers, breathing the fragrant potpourri, gazing in wonder at the many blooms. Yantanna picked out some of her favorite flowers, visiting them every day with Shuggy, giving them names that befit their personalities.

The day after the Challenge, Pirlhoff couldn't stand the suspense of waiting to learn what had happened. She knew Brog also would be uneasy, so she booked passage on a commercial flight to the Orbiter-two to surprise him. He was thrilled and relieved to see her; spending time together would make the wait much easier for both. They had lunch at the place where they'd shared off-world seafood their first time out. This time, she didn't wear make-up to hide her beautiful violet face.

After lunch, they went down to the docking area and found seats to watch the velvet-black sky through view-windows. The light reflecting from Seelius shined so bright it obscured the stars, a beautiful sight. Pirlhoff looked longingly at her home-world for a few moments, then decided her *true* home was the other direction, in a small valley on Caskentia, in a world she had named Seelosia.

They watched several cargo ships fly in and dock before Brog recognized an independent carrier leased by TradCo, the ship similar to Sullrob's being piloted by Lafave. They rushed down to the dock and waited anxiously. After a few minutes, the causeway opened and Lafave emerged, pushing the customary cases filled with Zhasou cuttings. Spotting Brog and Pirlhoff, he smiled and shouted, "Look! It's friends of the governor!"

Lafave only had about an hour before he had to depart, but it proved long enough for a few fast ales while he related the short version of how Sullrob earned the greatest challenge of his life—leader of an entire planet with hundreds of thousands of Seeliots. He reminded them he would be bringing Stava the next day, then begged off and boarded his ship to leave.

Brog and Pirlhoff started to walk back toward the tube junction. Suddenly, spontaneously, she started to tremble and cry. Relief, joy, a flood of feelings—it all came out at once. Brog put his arms around her and held on until she dissolved into uncharacteristic giggles. He started giggling too, something that continued inexplicably all the way back to his quarters.

Deciding to go out and celebrate, they changed into nicer clothing and went dancing in the only club on the station that seemed appropriate for their ages. They enjoyed a late dinner out, then went back to quarters again, exhausted both from their merriment and the tension they'd both felt since Sullrob announced his Challenge. After catching each other yawning several times, they agreed maybe it would be a good time to retire for the night.

Two adults, three bedrooms. One human, one Seeliot. Brog's room and two kids' rooms. A man and a woman, obviously in love.

They left Jowda's and Selta's rooms undisturbed.

*   *   *

Hard as it felt to leave his father, Stava was thrilled to see Brog and —surprise!—Pirlhoff waiting outside the docking area. Lafave hadn't bothered to hide the smuggled boy-man this time; there were only several TradCo flights left before Pfivvel's ships would take over lifting Jurnama for transfer to other long-distance carriers or processing in the Orbiter-two non-grav labs.

All four went out to lunch during Lafave's layover.

"Lafave," Brog started, "what are your plans? You know you can have a job flying for Pfivvel—at higher pay, I'll bet!—continuing as you have. *Or*, you could move with your family to Seelosia and retire—or start flying as part of Heilen's network of Zhasou shipments. As for myself, I've already tendered my resignation, effective at the end of the week. I'm moving ground-side to spend more time with the people I love. When I get restless, we'll see what my interests lead me into."

Stava smiled conspiratorially at Lafave. "Gee, awhat a choice!"

Lafave grinned knowingly. "Odd you should ask. It's what the governor's son and I talked about the whole way up here. I've decided it's time to *see* Seelosia for the first time. If I like it, I think I just might become a permanent resident at the end of this week, too."

"You're not gonna like it," Pirlhoff teased. "It's dark and dirty and smelly and . . . and—we've been making up all that good stuff just to trick people into moving there!"

"That's what the little man kept trying to tell me," Lafave pointed out, reaching over to poke Stava in the belly, "but I'm not fooled. I've already seen the dimension-stills."

"Bought 'em out of a catalog," Brog insisted.

Stava exclaimed, "See, I atold you!"

"Yeah," Lafave admitted, "he tried that one on *me*, too. You know what? I don't care. *I don't care*! As long as my friends are there and I'm a free man not having to worry about purges and it doesn't matter what kind of genes I've got in me—and I can *not work so hard*, well, then, count me in. Besides, Lafpat loves the idea and what my wife loves, I love, too."

With only two and a half more round trips left in his career carrying plant-stock for TradCo, Lafave bid them farewell and departed for gound-side. They watched his ship through the view-window until it shrunk to little more than a glowing speck entering the atmosphere.

As the trio headed toward Brog's quarters, Stava kept watching the other two curiously. A gentle touch, knowing glances, occasional smiles, a fast caress—he liked what he saw. *It's about time*, he thought.

Once inside Brog's place, Stava explained, "I've got some information to pass on to Dow Pfivvel. If it's okay, I'd like to atry to areach him on comm-link now and aget it over with. Then I'll have some time to aget with some of my friends here on the orbiter—especially those two who just avisited Seelosia. After ahosting *their* trip, they owe *me* a little hospitality."

After about a half-hour delay during which Stava related some of the missing details about the Challenge—sometimes jumping up and acting out the parts of key players—Dow Pfivvel finally appeared on the view-screen.

"Stava! Brog! Pirlhoff! Good to see you! You look happy and that makes me happy—and *that* makes all my employees happy! I trust the Challenge went well?"

"Aperfect!" Stava agreed, accidentally slipping into the spacer patois he always tried so carefully to avoid when dealing with Dow on a business level. "*My* dad's a governor!" he mocked.

"Congratulations! I trust it went off as planned?"

"Not exactly," Stava explained. "It was very touchy for a while—like maybe it wouldn't awork. But in the end, Dad was anamed—*named* governor *and* Ling Boz-athorne awas exposed for the criminal he is."

"Good then. Did your father accept the contract we tentatively worked out?"

"Yes he adid," Stava chuckled. "He called me a 'shugger-eater who took advantage of you!"

"Nobody takes advantage of *me*, son, unless it's to *my* advantage." Dow paused to laugh, too, explaining to Brog and Pirlhoff, "You better watch this fellow—he'll be selling you your own shoes and making you think you got a good deal."

Looking at his feet, Brog dead-panned, "Um, he *did* give me a good deal on them."

By the time the delays in transmission let the chuckles on both ends catch up with each other, Dow wondered, "Did your dad announce the deal to the Rep-assembly?"

"They actually acheered it!" Stava confirmed. Dow looked relieved as the response reached him.

"When can we begin? What do we need to work out?"

Stava explained that there would be only three more days of shipments for TradCo, then Pfivvel could take over the following week. Sullrob had okayed for six ships to start making regular runs, with possible increases as needed depending on the reaction of the locals. "Dad's not going to tell Bozathorne until the last day. Then he's going to make the last run up here himself and leave TradCo's ship at the dock. He wants to spend the weekend at Seelosia, then go back on *your* first ship and hold some kind of ceremony welcoming Pfivvel, Inc. to Seelius."

Dow liked the idea, volunteering to be on hand for the first flight himself—a symbolic gesture of new friendship between the many worlds of the Consortium and Seelius. Stava relayed other details, including coordinates for the ground-side terminal. The conversation drifted to personal matters including yet another heartfelt thank-you for little Darla's weenshugger. "You've made grandpa a hero!" He laughed.

Brog casually mentioned, "Dow, if you can come to Seelosia this weekend—and bring anybody you want—I think it might be a fun time. There's going to be a big celebration!"

Dow perused his comm-pad for a moment, pressing a few buttons, then smiling broadly. "I gotta warn you," he pointed out, "I may just bring my sister's two grandsons and they've been *awful* jealous of Darla's 'shugger."

Afterward, Stava contacted several orbiter boys and was eagerly invited to visit their families. There was even a bit of competition as to whom would host the young Seeliot for dinner. Before heading out with a small bag of supplies and goodies, he predicted a time he would be back that night, explaining, "I'll acontact you before I acome home. No surprises during your *alone* time!" he teased.

Actually, he did contact them later, but only to say he'd been invited to sleep over. They insisted he enjoy himself, confirming he'd be back in the morning before Brog left for his daily run to Caskentia.

Having finagled to give them more private time together, Stava hoped they would notice what he could already see.

*   *   *

The next morning, Brog contacted Seelosia and had a private talk with Jowda and Selta. He asked them to bring the core crowd to the ground terminal when he arrived with Stava and Pirlhoff.

They all gathered in a ground-side passenger bay to see Brog before he had to leave to return to the orbiter. He looked at all their faces—the Hewed family, the Buchs, little Yantanna busily hugging and rehugging her returning brother, his own children smiling conspiratorially, Jowda practically dancing a jig with bottled-up excitement.

"You've all heard that Sullrob is the Governor of Seelius!"

"Hoo-ray!" Heilen whooped, throwing his arms wide and hugging everybody he could grab.

"I want you to prepare the *biggest* celebration *ever* for this weekend. When I come home, I'll have the governor *with* me!"

"Daddy!" Yantanna squealed.

"Hoo-ray!" Heilen bellowed.

"We're going to celebrate Sullrob's victory! We're going to celebrate the expansion of our community—including Jowda Falls, the biggest waterfall in the galaxy! We're going to have a Celebration of Life! We're going to have another celebration, too, right after the wedding!"

Everybody gasped, taken by surprise. There before them stood Brog, his arm protectively around Pirlhoff, her hand across her chest showing off the traditional human ring of engagement. Jowda beamed. Selta smiled with tears in her eyes.

Lival Hewed was first to regain her composure, "*That's* awhat you've abeen akeepin' secret!" she blurted at Selta. Then she rushed forward and hugged Pirlhoff.

Everybody quickly joined in, congratulating, hugging and laughing, admiring the ring. Brog hugged each of his own children several times before Pirlhoff finally managed to corner them off to the side. She wanted to be sure they liked the idea; though Brog had told her they were thrilled, she knew she'd feel better hearing it herself.

"I athink it's awonderful!" Selta assured her, adding a kiss on the cheek and touching her forehead for emphasis.

Jowda grinned his delight, wrapped up in Pirlhoff's loving arms. He whispered in her ear, "I awas ahopin' all along!"

Brog announced that Pirlhoff wouldn't be going home that night; she'd be returning to the orbiter with him until the weekend. He asked them to make all the preparations for the wedding, suggesting they'd like to hold the ceremony near one of the beautiful waterfalls.

Heilen threw his arms wide, taking in the excited crowd, announcing, "It abee time I'll ahave t'show y'all jus' how t'have a real real *real* cele-brashun!"

*   *   *

Sullrob took his groundcar from the governor's mansion out to his home in Tessila. He'd planned to sleep there the night before—especially since it was much closer to the shipping terminal, but he'd been too busy to get away. After contacting Ling Bozathorne earlier in the week to give him the good news about the Challenge, Sullrob had set an appointment to update the chairman this morning. He drew a mug of cool Zhasou-ade and activated the communicator.

"Hello, governor!" the grinning chins greeted. "Have you had a good week—a good quarter tenth-turn?"

"The best, Mr. Bozathorne. It's been a *great* week."

"Have you made progress on any of our goals?"

"Well, I *have* done a few important things. First, I've stopped the purge—no more Seeliots will be executed for being descendants of Consortium trader stock. We'll not be sending any more Chronicles off-planet either."

Ling's eyes narrowed suspiciously as the message started to reach him.

Without pause, Sullrob continued, "The good news is, we're tripling Jurnama shipments next week!" He waited for the response.

Ling's face brightened, those grins twisting up again into a display of Cheshire greed. "Good! I'll arrange to have more ships sent down. We'll need to train more pilots, unless you're willing to let some of our—"

Ling was talking, but Sullrob had already interrupted, cutting him off as the signal reached him. "I've given the business to Pfivvel, Inc. One of our pilots is docking at Orbiter-two right about now. He'll leave your ship there. I'm leaving in a few minutes with your other one. You'll find it at the station, too."

"You can't do this! I won't let you! You don't have—I'll expose you—"

"I've already exposed *you*, Ling. I've proven to the entire planet that you conspired with Plekwag, that we don't need your medicine. I've proven that you sent capsules containing virus 35976, causing the plague and murdering tens of thousands of our citizens. You're lucky that *business* is all you're losing. If you'd like to try your luck among our citizens down here, you're cordially invited to visit anytime. We'll make it a *memorable* trip—on this you can count. Maybe you can witness a purge!"

Sullrob cut off the communication, winking out the image of three enraged frowns.

*   *   *

Stava and Yantanna went back to the Orbiter-two with Brog. They wanted to be on hand to meet Sullrob after his final flight in the ship that had smuggled everything from weenshuggers to Zhasou to living Seeliots. Lafpat joined them to meet her husband. It was the first time for all of them to ride in *Seelosia-one*, the private space-to-ground ship given to the community as a gift from Pfivvel, Inc.

The small entourage greeted Lafave, then went off to start a little early celebrating in the canteen where Sullrob had been ostracized after rumors spread that he killed his own children. Brog was greeted by some of the regulars—the loaders and shippers who'd never been able to get him to drink that second ale. Attitudes had changed enough that nobody seemed to care if the group included purple-faces. In fact, several quietly commented that Brog seemed to be enamored of Pirlhoff. Agreeing that she was a beautiful young woman, he achieved envious approval from a gang that tended to talk more than walk.

Brog, Pirlhoff, and the children left the Lafs after a while to go watch for Sullrob's ship. With faces eagerly pressed against the view-window, they identified a faint glow as it escaped the Seelius atmosphere and began to grow into recognizable form. Checking the big board, Brog could see that it was due to arrive in eight more minutes. Stava produced some silly party hats from his bag, insisting that everybody don one, clutching his father's in his hand. Their excitement unparalleled, this reunion would mark the first time all were truly safe and free. There was good news to share—including an engagement—and a fantastic weekend of Celebration ahead when, for the first time, they would *all* be together.

At about three minutes to go, the ship loomed large enough to recognize. Brog had watched for that familiar sight so many times. It was hard to believe this would be the last flight.

With two minutes until arrival, Yantanna called out, "Hey, Daddy! It's Daddy! Look!"

At that moment, the sky lit with a shower of sparks, a brief fireball fed by onboard oxygen, broken pieces of a vessel drifting in every direction.

Sullrob's ship had exploded.

Pounding furiously on the glass, Stava screamed, "Daddy!"

CHAPTER 18

It started as a fairly thorough investigation. Once Pfivvel, Inc. sent a team from Dilltomarius and brought in experts from several more worlds, it became one of the most meticulous investigations in the galaxy.

But virtually all of the evidence was destroyed.

The area of space near the explosion was canvassed thoroughly, every fragment chased down and recovered. Among the tiny specks, bio-molecular samples were found and tested, genetically confirmed to be the remains of the pilot.

There was no doubt Sullrob had died. Those remains, turned over to Stava, were encased in a box smaller than a thimble.

The ship had been destroyed by an internal detonating device which caused a rupture of the power core. That rupture caused the massive explosion which incinerated the ship.

Lafave's ship was seized and searched; a similar device, controllable through radio and laser frequencies was found aboard. TradCo explained that all of its ships traveling to alien planets carried such devices so they could be destroyed if taken by unlawful owners. Any child with simple equipment could actually cause an explosion—if he knew the elaborate codes programmed into each device. Finding—and proving—all the people who actually knew those codes would be impossible.

TradCo's public-relations team portrayed the incident as a regrettable accident, an unfortunate combination of events in which somebody's use of simple equipment must have hit the near-impossible odds of sending out the precise code that led to Sullrob's death. Enough monkeys and enough typewriters had apparently created another *Hamlet*. Though a generous donation was offered to Sullrob's heirs to ease their burden, TradCo would not admit guilt. Only mutual sorrow.

Pfivvel's investigator's calculated the odds of a random transmission causing the explosion at seven billion-billion to one. This would be small solace to anybody who actually believed the "accident" assertion; it was near-proof of nefarious intent to everybody else.

But nothing could be proved. No link to Bozathorne would ever be established. A permanent memorial to Sullrob floated in space near the view-windows of the Orbiter-two, financed by TradCo, as further proof of the giant corporation's sorrow and benevolence.

Though Sullrob's daily smuggling was lost, Seelosia, Inc. had enough Zhasou crop grown beyond the cuttings stage to begin harvesting its own. A substantial amount of regular income had started to pour in; the projections for the near future were staggering. Heilen decided to spare no expense in beefing up security for the community, its people, and its exclusive agricultural business operation. He worked with the team from Pfivvel and set up ground, air, and space surveillance with interception capabilities. The community's private ship, *Seelosia-one*, was also equipped with the ultimate security precautions.

Most who were familiar with the situation blamed Bozathorne for Sullrob's death—or at least blamed *somebody* somehow involved with TradCo. Maybe the murder was committed to force a transition in power, maybe to sour the deal with Pfivvel, Inc. by sowing seeds of distrust among a peoples already wary of Consortium invasion, or maybe just simple revenge for taking away all Ling had worked for in his dealings with Seelius. Whatever the motives, one fact remained.

Sullrob was gone.

*   *   *

Human funerals, depending on the home-world and local culture, tended to be brief ceremonies. Sometimes they included religious practices; they nearly always involved one or more people speaking of the deceased. Seeliot funerals tended to be modified Celebrations of Life during which the Celebration of *memory* was expanded to focus on the person friends and family gathered to honor.

Yantanna wavered between confusion and fear and inconsolable grief. Stava barely cried right after the explosion, then steeled himself to face a harsh and unforgiving world, an uncertain future. After that, he remained stoic, driven perhaps by his refusal to let Ling Bozathorne break him down, fueled by indignant hatred.

Brog's immediate intention was to cancel the wedding. Pirlhoff agreed to honor his wishes if he really preferred a delay, but she explained how on Seelius sometimes happy occasions mixed with sad ones to provide balance. She said she had seen cases where big events were pushed up to coincide with a funeral—an opportunity to affirm that life goes on, to honor the dead along with the living.

Early the next morning, a small crowd of Seelosians and friends like Dow Pfivvel's family and Shar Calvin and people from the Orbiter-two attended a wedding ceremony near the grand waterfall named for its discoverer, Jowda, conducted by Heilen Hewed, to everybody's surprise an ordained and licensed justice.

Brog had three best men standing beside him: Jowda, Stava, and Jak. Pirlhoff boasted two maids, Selta and Yantanna. Before a low table with two mugs of water and a small box of Zhasou, everybody else faced them in a semi-circle. Similar tables were scattered among the group.

Heilen stood behind and between the bride and groom, also facing the crowd. He looked around, breaking into a broad grin and throwing his arms wide to encompass the entire group. "Abee *anyone* t'here t'day awantin' t'get amarried?"

Brog and Pirlhoff both tried not to laugh, keeping quiet while the big man behind them continued to scan the crowd.

"You? Ahow 'bout you? Any y'bodies? Gots t'have *some* amarryiners fer t'be aweddin'!"

Brog and Pirlhoff pretended to ignore the big man. The group started giggling. Confused, Yantanna blurted out, "I athought Pirlhoff and Brog awas agettin' am-arried!"

Brog looked surprised, then intrigued. What an idea! "Hey! Y'wanna marry a peach-facer like me?"

Pirlhoff seemed to think it over for a moment before agreeing. "Well, okay— but only 'cause I like them kids of yours."

"Well all right then! Let's a*doooo* it!"

"We ahave a weddin'!" Heilen bellowed.

Heilen Hewed had described conducting several dozen weddings through the years, most when he was a young shipper-apprentice. His favorites were the sim-plest: both parties agree to accept the license, they get pronounced, then they lead their friends in a raucous party.

Brog had been exposed to a variety of religious and secular ceremonies as a frequently moving "orbiter-brat." His marriage to Ralorna had been a simple comm-registration announced several days later at a reception for friends.

All of Pirlhoff's experiences had been Seeliot, a modified version of the Cele-bration with *marriage* and Zhasou for the couple added to the end. Brog liked that idea, feeling for the first time in his life like he was connecting, laying roots, becom-ing part of something bigger. Heilen promised to muddle through a sort-of-Seeliot Celebration as best he could, refusing to write down the lines.

It lasted ten times longer than most Celebrations. Sometimes he asked the *guests* to recite portions, having the youngsters repeat them, talking about what they meant, comparing and adding customs or sentiments from other cultures, often laughing, occasionally sad, lingering for a long time on *memories* . . .

"We aCelebrate our *mem-reees* of Sullrob," Heilen said quietly. Everybody seemed to hold their breaths. They could hear the roar of the waterfall, the "wooty-wooty-wooty" of a pair of circling wootbirds, the buzzy-hum of crickadids in the tall grass, the frantic wheeze of a cask-frog announcing his intentions along the shore.

Brog cleared his throat, dropping a pinch of Zhasou into his mug and announc-ing, "My first true friend has become part of my *memories*. I and my family, our whole community, owe him the happiness of our futures. Many owe him their lives and their children's lives. I Celebrate what he has done for all of us; I Celebrate my *memories* of Sullrob." He took a long draft and wiped his eyes, pulling Pirlhoff into an impromptu hug.

Yantanna started to cry, softly at first, then harder, overwhelmed with the finality of her loss and uncertainty of her future. Pirlhoff picked her up and held her. Others started to cry softly, a domino-effect of pent-up emotions desperately seeking relief. Brog cradled Selta in his arms, then opened wide to admit Jowda, too. The children barely knew Sullrob, but they knew how much he meant to their father and Pirlhoff; they understood the painful loss felt by Stava and Yantanna. The group milled around, hugging, squeezing hands, touching shoulders and foreheads. Stava accepted many touches, even allowed a few hugs, but he watched the proceedings stoically, grief in his face, but without tears, bottled up by his steely resolve.

Once Yantanna calmed, Pirlhoff, holding Brog's and the little girl's hands together, dropped a pinch in her mug and announced, "I Celebrate my *memories* of Sullrob—a great man who loved his family and his friends, who sacrificed his own happiness for the good of his people, who gave his life for a better Seelius *and* Seelosia."

The recitations moved around the group, some sticking to the script, others pausing to share stories about the man they honored. Sometimes Heilen interjected to ask questions, to draw out people's feelings, to comment or compare, sometimes just to laugh and help break the tension. Many people who had already spoken once interjected again, usually with lighter stories, personal thoughts, new *memories* sparked by the reminiscence: Sullrob's frustration during pilot's training when he crashed the simulator three times in a row, dickering the cost of Shuggy and trying to act like he would leave when the man knew all too well Sullrob's resolve to give the singing furball to his little girl, visiting nearby homes every day during the plague to help those in need even while his own family suffered its ravages, getting lost coming back from his first trip to the capital when everybody in the groundcar was too stubborn to ask directions, seeking advice from friends on the best way to kiss the teenage sweetheart who would someday be his wife, calling all his friends and neighbors to come see the proud father's newborn son—then doing it again for his little girl, calming the frightened group in the meeting hall by telling them he, too, was scared of the purges, but that he had a plan . . .

When the three boys were the only ones left who hadn't spoken, Jak quietly dropped a pinch into his own mug and recited the line, taking a sip and burying his face at his mother's breast.

Jowda wiped his eyes and looked at Stava. Finally, he took a pinch and said quietly, "I aCelebrate the *memory* of my best friend's father," then quickly took a drink and looked again toward Stava.

Unable to avoid it any longer, Stava dropped a pinch and said quietly, "I Celebrate my *memories* of a great man, somebody I love, my father—" His voice cracked, his eyes started to glisten in the sunlight, but it was quickly replaced by his practiced stoicism and he finished simply, "I Celebrate my father, Sullrob."

*   *   *

The tone for the rest of the ceremony proved markedly different. Sullrob's death had weighed heavily on them all—always would in some form throughout their lives—but Seeliots are quick to Celebrate their dead and move on. Heilen had been wise enough to understand that the wedding could never be truly Celebrated until everybody's feelings about Sullrob had been confronted. He'd never seen a funeral combined with nuptials, but it was what the group needed. He quickly took them through the rest of the Celebration rites, frequently asking for help, continuing to discuss and explain and involve the children—Jak included—as much as possible. Finally, at the end, he surprised everybody with a new category, a topic that willy-nilly would become part of every Seelosian Celebration for countless generations: he Celebrated their *diversity*.

"Abig big big peoples an' li'l peoples, people of *ev*-ree colors, afrom *all* over th'galaxy, no amatter a*how* they abee aspeakin'!" He laughed, then reached out and grabbed Jowda, hoisting him up in the crook of one arm, then gently picking up Yantanna and balancing her on his other shoulder. "Alook at us! Jus' alook! Adoo we amake *some* kinda big big fam-lee or awhat?!" He bellowed his laughter, those pearly teeth gleaming in the sunshine. Everybody started laughing, dissolving into hysterics as he rushed around the group eyeing everybody and announcing, "Alookee *here!* We agots a purple one with *white* white hairs and *big* big big ears. Alook! Ahere's a real shorty! An' there's a skinny!" He pondered Brog for a moment, then reached out and poked him in the gut, laughing as he announced, "They abee several of us *not*-skinnies!" He raced around faster and faster, grabbing and poking and patting heads, leaving the crowd in hysterics. "We agot agrowin' ones! We agot a-olden ones! We agot a-*handsome* ones!" he shouted, pointing at himself and striking a he-man pose. "We *surely* agot some apretty ones!" He grabbed his wife and lifted her off the ground swinging her around and around.

"You aput me adown you crazy-man!" She laughed.

He rushed over and grabbed Pirlhoff, twirling her until both were dizzy, shouting, "Ahere's *another* pretty one. Brog amay abee amarryin' her, but she a-belongs t'*all* of us!"

Still in a frenzy, Heilen dropped large pinches of Zhasou into Brog's and Pirlhoff's mugs and bellowed so loud that everybody grew quiet, though giggles still tittered here and there.

"We's ahere to aCelebrate a *marriage!* Pirlhoff! D'you wanna?"

"Yes!"

"Brog, d'you wanna?"

"Well, I guess so," he mocked.

"Ashall we alet 'em?" he shouted to the crowd.

"Yes!"

"Yes!"

"Yes!"

"A-yes yes yes!" Jowda mimicked Heilen.

"Then Brog Pawligan an' Pirlhoff, they abee amarried! I aCelebrate the *marriage!*"

Everybody in the crowd started shouting the same thing, taking pinches and sips, repeating it again and again. Brog and his beautiful bride stood at the front, holding hands, smiling to their friends and family.

Once the cacophony quieted down, Pirlhoff took a pinch, putting some in his mug and some in her own. He repeated the gesture. Then, together, they drank from each other's mugs and recited, "I Celebrate my *love* for you."

The crowd erupted again, people crowding around, hugging and touching and squeezing, offering congratulations, laughing, shedding tears, celebrating another milestone in the lives of people they loved.

Birds circled in the bright afternoon sky, singing, "Wooty-wooty-wooty."

*   *   *

Despite talk about honeymooning off-world or at the original Caskentia resort where Brog had first taken his children, the newlyweds decided to start their new life together in the original valley of their new community. Though it would be weeks before their new home across the ridge overlooking one of the falls would be ready, Brog's suite would do just fine in the meantime. Several people conspired to cook up a feast, leaving the food and chilled Caskentian wine—and plenty of Zhasou—in the suite to surprise the happy couple.

To give them privacy, Brog's kids moved out for the weekend. Even with plenty of available rooms, Selta opted to stay with Yantanna. Her little friend was still scared and confused, grieving for her father. Selta wanted to comfort her as much as she could.

Jowda asked Stava if he could stay with him, earnest even though his friend acted so distant, so indifferent. "If you awant." That night, after all the commotion, the boys settled into Stava's room. The young Seeliot went over to his desk and spread out some documents from his mother's family's hide-space and started to read. Jowda sat on the side of the bed and watched him curiously, not speaking. Stava continued to study for five minutes, ten, a half-hour. Jowda kept watching, waiting patiently.

Finally, Stava could stand it no longer. Without looking back, he asked, "Aren't you agoing to adoo something?"

"I am," Jowda said quietly, his voice cracking with emotion.

Surprised and curious, Stava turned to see his friend still sitting on the side of the bed, a trail of glistening tears down each cheek, still waiting patiently. "Awhat? Awhat are you adoing?"

"Athinkin' 'bout my mom."

Stava sighed, then closed the cover and walked back to sit beside his friend. "Adoo you awish your dad adidn't amarry Pirlhoff?"

"No way! Jus' a'cause my dad aloves Pirlhoff adoesn't amean he adon't still alove my mom, too."

"No, it adoesn't," Stava agreed quietly. "I'm aglad your dad and Pirlhoff alove each other."

"Me, too."

They sat quietly for a moment, then Stava noticed another tear trickling down his friend's face. "Awhat are y'thinkin' 'bout your mom?"

Jowda shrugged. "She awould've aliked it here. She used t'tell my dad she awas agonna amake him aretire and amove ground-side before me an' Selta awas agrown up."

"Then she agot her wish," Stava pointed out.

Jowda actually managed a full grin at that. "I aguess."

After another awkward pause, Stava wondered, "You still amiss your mom, huh?"

"All the time. Adon't you amiss *your* mom?"

Stava nodded, but said nothing. He crawled around Jowda and stretched out on the bed, staring at the ceiling. Jowda lay back beside him, wiping his face with his hands, lowering the lights with a voice command.

Jowda whispered, "I asure awish I aknew why everybody aliked your father so much."

Stava gritted his teeth, suddenly mad, feeling like something sacrosanct had been questioned. "He awas a good man!" he asserted.

Jowda prodded some more. "I aknow about ahelpin' people escape and abeein' the governor and those things, but awas he a *nice* man? Awould I alike him?"

"Yes you awould!" Stava retorted, his voice louder.

"Ahow d'you aknow I awould?"

"You just would!"

They stared at the ceiling for a while, then Jowda pointed out, "You adon't act like you amiss him."

"I adoo. I jus'— I— I agot too many things t'worry 'bout."

"Somethin' more important than your dad?"

"*Nothin's* more important than my— my dad!" Stava's voice cracked. He closed his eyes tight, but tears squeezed out anyway, coursing down his cheeks. "*Nothin's* more important than— my— Oh Jowda, my dad's gone." The cork popped; all of his feelings bubbled out all at once. He started crying very hard.

Jowda started to cry again, too, reaching over and touching Stava's forehead. Stava gasped, trying to catch his breath, shaken again and again by waves of grief. Finally, he reached over and touched Jowda's forehead, too. They lay there for a while, an incongruous pair of different-colored friends, their hands awkwardly on each other's heads, trying to settle down, fighting back tears yet relieved to let them flow.

When both eventually calmed down, Jowda asked again why he would've liked Sullrob. They stayed awake very late while Stava told his friend stories. Sometimes they laughed; sometimes they dissolved again into tears, occasionally touching shoulders and foreheads. Once, as if to stave off another round of crying, they inadvertently hugged each other, quickly letting go in their embarrassment, giggling at themselves for how they had acted.

They took turns yawning and drifting until the conversation finally started to peter out. Jowda had one last issue on his mind he wanted to ask before floating off to sleep.

"Stava?"

"Um, huh?"

"Awill you acome avisit every weekend after you amove to Seelius?"

"Amove to Seelius? Awhy would I amove?"

"You're a *pure* Seeliot, aren't you?"

"Yeah, we a-proved it at Rep-assembly."

"You agot ascended, right?"

"Yep."

Jowda raised up and leaned over to look his friend in the face. "Then aren't *you* th'new *governor?*"

*   *   *

Once the meeting started to wind down, Shar Calvin suggested the group move down to the beach and stretch out for a little relaxation and to toast their new plans with some ice-cold Zhasou-ade. The pharmacist was feeling better than he had in years, embracing his new determination to enjoy every little aspect of life. His friend, the medical researcher, agreed he'd like to see the pink and blue sand up close. Dow Pfivvel and Buchvan both allowed as how it was a fine idea, indeed.

The foursome lounged in the warm, afternoon sunlight, in awe of the beautiful red mountains in the background, watching children splash and play in the water. Little Darla occasionally shouted, "Look, Grandpa!" showing off the back-flips Selta and Yantanna had been teaching her. The Pfivvel grand-nephews played just down the beach with their new 'shuggers, squealing with delight while the little critters crawled and nuzzled them from head to toe, singing happy little songs for their new friends.

"What a bunch of lazy men!" Pirlhoff exclaimed.

All four jumped to their feet in time to see the newlyweds coming down the slope. There were lots of hugs and touches, laughs and congratulations, a sly joke about finally coming up for air.

"If you can spare a few minutes for your friends and business associates," Buchvan interrupted, "we'd like to tell you about some new deals we've hammered out subject to board approval."

Brog and Pirlhoff flopped into the offered loungers; Shar and Buchvan wiggled comfortable depressions in the sand.

"First," Shar started, "we've convinced Dow to expand his pharmaceutical division substantially, including moving its new headquarters to Seelosia!"

"All right!" Pirlhoff offered.

Buchvan grinned. "We intend to make a nice profit leasing him the land. We're looking at some of the flat-lands to the north where we have options."

"And *I* am gonna run it, with Orman here as head of research," Shar added. "It'll be just a few minutes' commute from the houses we're going to build somewhere along the ridge thataway," Shar indicated, waving his arm in the direction Brog and his wife had already selected for their own home.

Buchvan continued, "We've added some wrinkles to that three-year exclusive deal for supplying Zhasou to Pfivvel, Inc., too. We probably won't need it, but Dow has agreed to provide any financing so we can expand as fast as cuttings and Pirlhoff's expertise will allow."

"Y'see," Shar explained, "it turns out Zhasou is even more valuable than we thought. In the simplest terms, it triggers the release of certain enzymes which act together as catalysts for a chain reaction that spreads through the entire body. Consumed over time, it builds up and has a medicinal effect."

Brog sat forward, his eyebrows raised.

Dow explained, "Once Shar and Orman determined that Seeliots are descended from humans, they were curious why Zhasou consumption had become so ingrained in their culture. It was clearly more than just a favored spice; it became a part of every ceremony or ritual, something youngsters were fed from birth and taught to use as soon as they were old enough to understand. Like so many religious and social customs, we suspected there was a survival element to it, too."

Shar asked Pirlhoff, "Did you ever hear of anything like cancer before you left Seelius?"

"Why no, I hadn't."

Brog blurted out, "You mean Zhasou cures *cancer?*"

"Not a cure, Brog," Shar clarified. "It stops it cold. If the damage is not beyond survival, that gives us a chance to rejuvenate or repair."

"You mean, like *you?* And little Greggo?"

Shar beamed. "Yes, little Greggo—and thirty-six other people who've been tested."

"This is great!" Brog practically shouted. Then, more soberly, he added, "People like Ralorna would have been able to recover rather than losing their precious lives so prematurely." He looked down, shaking his head.

"Better than that, Brog," Shar said. "Based on all the tests we've performed so far on organs from stasis, Zhasou is an inoculant. No matter how much cancerous cellular matter we implant, it's immediately rejected and expelled like so much waste. There will be no more people who have to suffer like Ralorna. Zhasou is the perfect cancer *prevention*."

*   *   *

In retrospect, it wasn't much of a honeymoon—or it was the best one ever, depending on one's outlook. Grief over Sullrob's death proved too prevalent. Sometimes they had fun; often they experienced sadness, consolation, sharing. Pirlhoff and Brog were concerned about Stava and Yantanna. At one point, alone in their room, Brog related to Pirlhoff what Jowda had told him about the boys crying together while talking about Sullrob during the night. Pirlhoff felt relieved that the young Seeliot had finally let some of his feelings come to the surface, if only in the privacy of his room with his best friend. She misted up and started to cry, thrilled that the boys had become such deep, life-long friends. The little boy who hated purple-faces had learned to care for them so much that he accepted one as his father's wife—even loved her—and had made best friends of another. Much to Jowda's surprise, she had come to love *him*, too, more than he could ever imagine.

Brog and Pirlhoff had a long, serious discussion, then went out and talked briefly with Selta and Jowda, leaving them beaming conspiratorially, Jowda practically jumping up and down like Jak did when excitement got the best of him. They rounded up Yantanna and Stava, taking them back to their room for a private discussion.

Brog began, "Stava, Yantanna, we want you to know—both of us—we love you, we love you very much."

"I alove you, too," Yantanna said shyly. Stava looked pleased, but waited to hear more.

"We want you," Pirlhoff explained, "we want you both to be part of *our* family from now on."

Brog continued, "We're not trying to *replace* your mom and dad, but we want to help them now that they can't be here anymore. We want to be you *new* mom and dad from now on."

"If that's okay," Pirlhoff added tentatively.

Yantanna misted up but managed a smile; then she crawled into Pirlhoff's lap to be cradled and hugged by her new parents.

Tears formed in Stava's eyes. He tried to speak, but his voice cracked and he seemed somehow out of breath. Finally, he managed to say, "I awant that very much. So awould my dad." He stood up, reaching tentatively as if to touch Brog's forehead, then was snatched and dragged into the mass hug amid tears and tickles and giggles.

Once the tangle of arms had separated and everybody caught their breath, Pirlhoff explained, "As far as Seelius goes, Yantanna will become our child as soon as we declare her, but you, Stava, are already ascended."

Brog joined in, "But in the Consortium, you, Stava, are not an adult until you are sixteen Earth-years old, so we need to do comm-registrations for *both* of you to give us all legal protection. Stava, you'll be *governor* on Seelius, but to the Consortium, you'll be recognized as both a head of state *and* our adopted son."

Pirlhoff finished, "But no matter what world we're on or what the legal definition is, in our hearts you'll be part of our family—and now you've got a new brother and sister, too!"

Yantanna's face lit up. "Selta is my sister?"

"Yeah!"

Stava stifled a laugh. "You mean that 'shugger-eater Jowda is agonna abee my little *brother*? Sheesh!" He rolled his eyes for emphasis.

Brog called out loudly, "Okay, you can come in!"

Jowda and Selta burst into the room, Jak on their heels. All seven wound up jumping up and down in imitation of Jak, laughing and agreeing the adoption was just a darn good idea.

After a few minutes, Stava looked pensive, then quietly asked Brog. "Awhat awas that word you a-used?"

Brog wasn't sure what he meant.

"Awhat kind of son awill I abee?"

"You mean *adopted* son?"

"Yes. Awhat exactly is that?"

"It's a legal term, meaning even though you didn't *used* to be my son, I've changed your legal status so that you are just as much my son as if I'd been your genetic father."

"On Seelius, we just a-declare. I anever aheard that word." Stava thought for a minute, then got excited. Grabbing Brog by the hand, he led him to his own bedroom. He rummaged furiously through the boxes of documents recovered from his mother's family's house. Finally, he found what he wanted, pushing it in front of Brog, asking if it meant what he thought.

It was a signed original of an adoption decree. Sam Fowler had met too much resistance on Seelius for a Seeliot marriage, deciding to wait until he could bring his true love back to his own world before making it official.

But he *had* "adopted" her son, Stava's ancestor on his mother's side.

CHAPTER 19

A team of lawyers landed in the afternoon of the first business day after the long wedding weekend. Dow Pfivvel lent a small team of legal advisors to Seelosia, Inc. to help Brog and Buchvan screen other attorneys. The unimpressive ones were paid for their time and sent on their way. Several got hired short-term to set up the adoptions of Stava and Yantanna. Those that passed muster were offered generous compensation packages to give up their practices and work full-time at Seelosia. When the offers were sweetened to include parcels of land and generous invitations to join the community, a fast tour of the area was all it took to influence their decisions.

The adoption, normally a process requiring months, was accomplished in two days. Documentation of the birth-parents' deaths, affidavits from key people, background checks on Brog, confusion and attention over the other-world legal status of Pirlhoff, consent decrees from the children, legal research on the status of adopting off-worlders and other non-Consortium races—it was a frenzy of activity that culminated in the announcement that final documents would arrive in two hours.

Everybody available gathered to witness the event. Brog led with a traditional Celebration of Life, expanding *family* to include new members, the bonds of love, commitment and trust.

After the ceremony, all six members of Brog's new family took an aircar by themselves into one of Caskentia's grandest cities. Brog had reservations at a nice restaurant and tickets for the galaxy-famous water circus, a thrill and delight for children and adults alike. Arriving home late that night, Selta carried the slumbering Yantanna while Brog aroused and half-walked Stava, Pirlhoff doing the same with Jowda. This time, somehow symbolic of their new family bonds, Stava shared Jowda's room while Yantanna slept with Selta. With all the young'ns packed off to bed, the newlyweds programmed some soft music and danced together in their room until they were too tired to stand. They managed to stay up for a while, though, finding a good old-fashioned fun way to occupy their time.

Brog rose early the next morning to lead the business meeting he'd scheduled as soon as he knew the adoption would be confirmed. He aroused Stava to attend, too. Jowda, not wanting to be excluded, was invited as a guest. Dow Pfivvel also sat in as a distinguished guest.

Brog, flanked by Stava and Buchvan, began, "Ladies, gentlemen—welcome to the team." More than twenty attorneys and business specialists greeted back, responding enthusiastically.

"I know," he continued, "you thought this would be an easy job, but it won't. One of the criteria we considered in selecting you all is that you're fighters—you like a good challenge, you're fast on your feet. In short, you're good partners to have in a scrap. Well, I've got one for you. You'll understand why I had to keep this secret until we concluded other business yesterday."

Everybody sat forward, anticipating. Dow Pfivvel looked *very* curious.

Brog smiled, then announced, "We're going to seize control of TradCo."

Half the group seemed thrilled at the thought of taking on one of the biggest adversaries in the galaxy. The others looked disappointed that the big surprise was so obviously a pipe dream.

"But, Mr. Pawligan," started one of the nay-sayers, "*nobody* in the galaxy has *that* kind of money."

"Don't need the money. I've found and can document proof of the missing heirs—the rightful claimants to SFP Trust." Looking around the group and smiling broadly, he added, "And yesterday I adopted them both."

Everybody grew *very* intrigued. All eyes drifted to Stava.

Feeling the curious gaze, he perked up and announced, "At least he asked to adopt us *before* he knew we were so rich!"

Laughter broke the tension. Finally, somebody asked, "So what do we have?"

Brog signaled for the secretary to bring in copied files for everyone. After they were distributed, he sat back and enjoyed watching the show. Some raced through their files again and again. Others plodded through slowly, examining each document meticulously. There were whistles, sighs, barely audible murmurs, laughs, and lots of shaking heads. Finally, somebody spoke up, announcing, "Is this great—or what?"

Another added, "I'm going to enjoy this."

A third put in, "This is going to turn the Consortium business community upside down."

"I went to law school *dreaming* about a gig like this someday."

"Do you realize that when we take on Bozathorne, we'll be up against the likes of Heath and Allen?"

"And Siglar!"

"Jodis and Bennett—and Chavez!"

Brog interrupted the lawyerly reverie. "Can we do it?"

Everybody nodded. One spoke up, "It'll be a helluva fight."

"But we're gonna win."

"God, *this is great!*"

*   *   *

What a beautiful ship, sleek and silver, bigger than any the locals had ever seen.

Painted along the side, it said simply, "Pfivvel, Inc." It came down fast, landing to the surprise of the loaders lounging around with nothing to do. After a moment, a portal opened, lowering a platform with Buchvan on it. One of the loaders recognized him.

"Buchvan! How are ya? What is *this?*"

"Damoor! Good to see you! The *governor* is aboard."

"Sullrob? He *is* overdue. He was expected back several days ago."

The other loaders gathered around to hear Buchvan. "Some important developments have happened." Buchvan led the group into the terminal. "We need to call an emergency Rep-assembly for tomorrow."

Buchvan contacted the capital and informed the necessary people. As word spread throughout the three continents, conversation was rife with rumors and speculation, but Buchvan refused to confirm anything. He ordered a groundcar entourage to be at the terminal first thing in the morning, bid his friend good-night, and retired to the ship for the evening.

By the next morning, while the Reps and the Panel elders assembled in the great hall, a crowd of several hundred gathered around the terminal to see the governor, to learn first-hand what was so mysterious. At the last minute, the platform lowered with two people, Buchvan and young Stava, the former carrying a wooden, Zhasou-style chest.

"It's Stava!"

"It's the governor's son!"

"The governor must be dead!"

"His son has come to claim the chair!"

They boarded the groundcar and proceeded to the capital, then entered the great hall. Word spread so fast that everyone had heard by the time Buchvan and Stava moved to the front. The crowd fell silent.

Stava stepped onto the dais, Buchvan beside and slightly behind him. The boyman announced, "The governor is dead, killed in an explosion aboard his ship."

There were gasps, a few loud cries. "No! It can't be!"

Stava continued, "I have come to claim my father's chair—I, Stava of Seelius, to be your new governor!"

The crowd erupted in a buzz of conversation, steadily growing louder and more raucous. Some arguments could be heard, plus chants of support. Finally, the sound of one small cluster of chanters started to spread, growing louder and louder, filling the great hall until every person shouted in harmony.

"Gover-nor! Stava! Gover-nor! Stava!"

Stava watched complacently for several minutes before raising his arms to quiet the crowd. "We will begin with a Celebration of Life!" The crowd cheered wildly.

The young Seeliot led the group through the traditional ceremony, adding to the end, "We will Celebrate our *memories* of Governor Sullrob, all he did for us, the legacy he leaves our peoples—" Stava's voice cracked. He looked at his feet for a second, then, quieter, finished, "We will Celebrate my dad."

"Sullrob! Sullrob! Sullrob!" they chanted, pinching and drinking to his *memory*.

Once they settled down, Stava raised his arms again, then methodically removed all of his clothing. He stood there naked, arms in the air, and waited. Several women, dressed in ceremonial garb, came from the wings reverently carrying the governor's robe. Though it proved way too big for a little guy who weighed barely thirty-five kilos, they lifted it carefully and pulled it down over him. Once he was dressed, the crowd erupted again.

"Gover-nor! Stava! Gover-nor! Stava!"

Stava let them chant for a few minutes, then raised his arms again.

"We will hold Rep-assembly in a half tenth-turn, at regular schedule!"

The crowd murmured approval. The young governor apparently intended to get right down to business.

"Later today, one hour before dinner, we will have a dedication ceremony at the terminal—to welcome our new friends at Pfivvel, to begin again the shipments of Jurnama that saves lives and cures people throughout the galaxy!"

There were more murmurs, mostly approval, not quite as enthusiastic. Buchvan stepped to the side and returned with the wooden case he had brought.

"You have much work to do before next Rep-assembly. We have our first payment from Pfivvel. We must decide how best to spend it!" Buchvan opened the chest. Stava reached in and pulled out handfuls of sparkling metal wafers. The crowd started to cheer again.

"I will give *every* district *ten million units* to spend—just from this first payment alone! Bring me your proposals!"

The crowd went wild. That kind of money was more than any district had seen in a decade of turns. It would build schools and hospitals and roads and upgrade water facilities . . .

Stava let them cheer for a few minutes before raising his arms again. "I will be off-world taking care of business for a quarter tenth-turn. I will return to work in my office for the quarter tenth-turn before the next Rep-assembly. I will have many announcements to amake—to *make* at that time!"

He beckoned the women who had berobed him, closing the chest so Buchvan could hand it to them. Raising his arms one last time, he announced, "I Celebrate Seelius!"

Rather than leaving through the back, as was tradition, Stava stepped down among the Reps, spending more than two hours moving through the crowd, Buchvan right behind him, touching shoulders, accepting praise and support. The entire time, the crowd never stopped chanting.

"Gover-nor! Stava! Gover-nor! Stava!"

By the time he worked his way outside, there were just as many more people gathered around the great hall. Business in the capital city had come to a stand-still. Stava stood before the crowd listening to similar chants. Finally, he and Buchvan entered the official groundcar and made their way slowly back to the terminal. Crowds lined the streets the entire route, all chanting support.

They arrived at the ship with little more than a half-hour to spare before the Pfivvel-welcoming ceremony would begin. They went inside the ship to freshen up and unwind, assuring Dow Pfivvel that all had gone well. By the time they emerged with their human friend, several thousand Seeliots had gathered around the terminal, filling the streets as far as could be seen every direction. Word had spread about the generous payment; Dow was a hero before he ever spoke. There sounded many gasps—none had ever seen a light-skinned human before.

During the ceremony, Stava, overhearing some of the comments, smiled and agreed Dow *did* look like everybody else except for the colors of his skin and hair. "We are more the same than we are different. I have learned this in my travels. I have learned much more, which I will share for the good of all Seelius." Of course, that brought more cheers. He realized that Plekwag had handled the public-relations aspect of trading with other-worlders rather badly, indeed.

Later, aboard Dow's private ship, as they lifted off and slowly climbed toward the atmosphere, Stava yawned, stretching out on a low couch. Buchvan and Dow chattered about how well it had all gone, the Seeliot relating the details of what had happened in the great hall. Finally, Dow begged off and retired to his private suite. Buchvan roused Stava and led him into the quarters they shared.

"Thanks for your help, Buchvan. I awas ascared, you know," Stava offered bleary-eyed, shedding his robe and climbing into his bed.

Buchvan knelt beside him, touching his forehead. Stava reached out and touched Buchvan's. "I would do anything to help you, Stava, especially when it's for our people."

"Hmmm . . ."

Buchvan smiled, whispering, "How does it feel to be the governor?"

Stava smiled back, nuzzling his pillow seductively. "Tiring, Buchvan. Very tiring . . ."

*   *   *

They argued over who would deliver the news but, unable to agree, all three suits went in together. They stood nervously in front of Ling Bozathorne's massive desk, stammering through background information, taking turns speaking but avoiding the bottom line, each playing musical chairs in the desperate hope it would be one of the others' turn to speak when Ling finally demanded to know just what-the-hell they were talking about. The suit in the middle wound up blurting it out.

"What?!" the chairman demanded, but he'd heard.

Nobody offered to repeat the bad news. They were too busy trying to figure out how to beat a hasty retreat.

Ling's face flushed red. He tugged at his collar, then opened his mouth to speak. Instead, he narrowed his eyes, emitting a low growl that caused his chins to quiver. Spittle from his still-gaping maw drooled down to be shunted by the first crevice.

"No way! I'll not let 'em! Not *my* company!" Then, noticing the lawyers again, he screamed, "Stop 'em! Go on! Get moving! Do whatever it takes! If they think they can take *my* company, it'll be over my dead body!"

Bozathorne slammed his fists on the desk, struggling to his feet and glaring every direction to find a suitable target for his tantrum. He kicked the open desk drawer. "Daddy was right!" He booted the side of his desk. "It *was* the goddam purple-faces!" He knocked over his chair. "I won't take this lying down!" Then he punted his waste-basket, losing his balance and winding up flat on his back, writhing in a pile of debris.

"Help! Somebody, help!" He flailed, trying to sit up, growling, "Goddam Seel-iots!"

Several aides peered cautiously into the office.

"Goddammit! *Get me up!*"

*   *   *

"I'm negotiating to buy out the resort," Dow announced.

"That's an interesting thought," Brog responded. "We considered it ourselves, but decided to develop our own in the Jowda Falls valley and out into the plains below it. A lot of it would be very upscale—and hopefully very profitable—but we want to have lots of space for families and others looking for affordable vacations. With your new research center and our expanding operations, there will be a growing influx of employees and other people coming to this area. We think word will spread and this might become a prime vacation destination."

"What a great idea!" Dow complimented.

Lival Hewed added, "I'm acosting out asetting up reg-lar shuttle to Orbiters-one and -two so *aworking* families acan afford some quality time ground-side."

"What's *your* motive?" Buchvan wondered. "Surely it's more than the profit potential."

"I was thinking corporate retreat. A lot of my people will be transferring here—especially in a few months when we get the pharmaceutical division's new head-quarters set up. I want a place to house those people until they settle in and buy or rent on their own. In the meantime, I want to start bringing their families here for short visits to help, um, *facilitate* their decisions on whether or not to stay with the company and accept the transfer." Dow offered a sneaky grin, rubbing his hands together. "I figure a few days here and their families won't *let* them say no."

Pirlhoff, usually not one to speak up very much during business meetings, interjected, "There's a reason *I* voted in favor of building a resort," she started, glancing beyond Dow, out the window-wall, across the valley lake framed by red mountains pointing toward the sky. "It's my dream that someday Seeliots will start to travel beyond my home-world. This is where they should come first. It's much more spectacular than anywhere on our planet; it's the next closest ground-side destination; it's already got a thriving community of purple-faces that can help strangers feel more comfortable in a strange land." She shook off the reverie and smiled. "Plus, attracting people from all over the galaxy, it would be quite the cosmopolitan experience in family vacations."

"She wants a nice place for a second shot at that honeymoon," Brog interpreted, nudging Buchvan in the ribs.

Dow was watching Pirlhoff, entranced by her heartfelt wish. "I hope that happens," he told her. "I'm privileged to have been the first non-Seeliot to visit your world in centuries. I could barely contain my excitement. Even though I was an outsider tentatively hoping to have my business accepted, I never felt more welcome in all the worlds I've visited. The Seeliots are a warm and remarkable people. I would like to see them someday become a part of the Consortium."

"Whew!" Buchvan reacted. "One step at a time. *That* may take a while."

"But it needs to happen," Pirlhoff asserted. "I just hope I get to see it. I want to be here to welcome the first arrivals."

"With a pinch of Zhasou!" Brog laughed.

"And a tab to run—we accept credit from every planet!" Buchvan joked.

They all sipped for a moment before Dow got around to the main topic. "You know, I'm worried about you being able to keep up with demand. My marketing people and Shar's—" He nodded toward Shar Calvin, reclined and sipping his mug, watching the meeting good-naturedly. "—And Shar's research team has started to lay out a strategy. I dare say, no matter how we approach this thing, it's going to explode."

"How's it playing out?" Brog wondered.

Dow nodded toward Shar, who sat forward and explained, "Zhasou is kinda unique far as a medicine goes. It's also a food with a long, proven history of consumption safety. So as word spreads about its effect on cancer, people will want it—fiercely demand it—regardless of whether it's been through the Consortium drug-certification trials or not."

"It'll be like one of those benign health-supplements," Dow added, "that suddenly turns out to be extremely beneficial. People won't want to wait for proof—what would they have to lose?"

"We applied for a license to conduct sanctioned trials—about a six-month process overall," Shar continued, "and discovered we weren't the first."

Brog's eyebrows shot up. "You mean somebody else wants to conduct Zhasou-medicine approval trials, too?"

"Somebody?" Shar reacted. "Hell, we're talking about more than *forty* somebodies!"

"But they can't get the spice from any other source," Buchvan pointed out.

"No they can't," Dow agreed. "We followed up with some of our retail customers and found that it's virtually off the *food* market. Rumors have spread about its effect on cancer, so supplies are being bought up at ten and twenty times regular cost by parties interested in its drug effects. It's a bidding war for the small amount of stock available."

"Who else?" Brog wondered.

"A dozen of our competitors, just as many universities, two large health-consorts, the biggest health-info news service in the galaxy, a large church based on Earth, and two inter-planetary cancer treatment centers who apparently want to stay on top of offering their huge client base the very latest."

"I can *see* that," Brog admitted, "and even see why the info service would want to stay on top of the story, offering its own independent results, but what about the others?"

"Well, the universities are easy to understand—they've been doing cancer research for millennia. They have whole departments—entire campuses—devoted to the subject. What better way to use their labs and resources and trained experts than to study and teach their students about this development? As far as the competitors go, if Zhasou is a scam that needs exposing, they'll want to knock us out as fast as possible. If it's what it's purported to be, they need to see if it can be synthesized—it can't by the way, but they'll try—and they'll want to find ancillary business that might spin off from it."

"You lost me," Pirlhoff said.

"Well, say one can develop a better way to administer the drug—they could make a fortune just supplying kits. Or say there's a buffer or catalyst or something that increases its speed or effectiveness, then maybe they could supply that. Everybody knows this is going to be big—better to scramble for pieces even if you know you can't get the whole pie."

"Well," Brog wondered, "is this good or bad?"

Dow smiled. "It can't be anything but good. It'll replicate our research many times over—at no additional cost to Pfivvel, Inc.—and spread word throughout the galaxy. It'll give us legitimacy faster than I ever dreamed and even help us possibly break into markets in the non-Consortium worlds."

Shar smiled, pointing out, "And Pfivvel here is like an *honest* version of Boza-thorne—he can *smell* business opportunities that come from having the ultimate culture-barrier breaker. Ling figured it out first—if you want to get into a planet's economy, come with an offer they desperately need. Only, Ling had to *create* the need with his deadly virus. With cancer, the need is already there."

"Touché!" Dow agreed, holding up his mug and downing a long draft.

"I see why you're worried about supply," Brog said. He knitted his fingers and contemplated for a moment. "When all of a sudden *billions* of people demand Zhasou, it could get ugly deciding how to distribute it and to whom."

"Now you see our problem," Dow agreed. "It's not just figuring out how to make the most money as fast as possible. In fact, it's the opposite. I don't want it to start out as an *elite* drug where if you can afford to outbid your neighbors, then your family member doesn't have to die."

Pirlhoff put her hand to her mouth. Lival shook her head and looked at her lap. Almost at once, both said, "It aneeds to be fair!"

"That's going to be tricky," Dow pointed out. "That's why I've decided to give up the food portion of the business until supplies exceed the medical demand. We've diverted our stock, for now, to only those who've received approval for research. In fact, we're *giving* them as much as they need. Oh, it's a small loss of income, but it's a great public relations move and it helps us promote and legitimize it in the long-run. Once we have approval, we'll make it available only through physicians. That way, it'll go first to those who most need it for treatment. Then as supplies increase, we'll hit the market over-the-counter. Hopefully, someday, we'll be able to start up the food biz again so all the little kiddies can have Zhasou-ade with their Zhasou cookies—*and* live long, productive, cancer-free lives as part of the bargain."

"How is your supply for research?" Pirlhoff asked.

"Right now, we have plenty. That's why I want to encourage you—surprise surprise surprise!—*not* to sell me any more for a while. Squeeze every little cutting you can out of those plants and expand as fast as possible."

"Well, we've already contracted to have more than two-hundred transparents—greenhouses—built. Forty of them will be started tomorrow. Some of the original plants are no longer suitable for cuttings, so we'll be harvesting some anyway, but we'll push the limits. Jak's been getting favorable results with one-node cuttings—back on Seelius we need to take three or more nodes to give the cutting a good chance at survival. Conditions here, as long as we control the climate, seem to be even better than on Seelius."

"Good! Good then!" Dow asserted. "I don't want to put *too* much pressure on you, but the harsh fact is that the faster you build up your stock, the more lives you will save."

Buchvan seemed lost in thought. He perked up and wondered aloud, "You know, Dow, right now you have a three-year exclusive from us—something we *all* hope will extend indefinitely."

Dow nodded, listening attentively.

"What we *don't* have is an exclusive for *us*—for Seelosia, Inc."

"What do you mean?"

"Well, there's nothing stopping you from buying your Zhasou supplies elsewhere."

"Sure there is," Dow contradicted. "You only sell me harvested stock, so I *can't* start to grow it myself. If I *stole* some of your live plants, you could sue me from one end of the galaxy to the other. The only other source is Seelius itself, which won't deal with outsiders unless it's sanctioned by the governor." Dow smiled, adding, "And last I heard, you guys had the *inside* track with the governor."

"It's that inside track I'm thinking of," Buchvan said mysteriously. He thought for a minute, then tossed out his idea. "Obviously this would need some private discussion with our own board—and it would have to be ratified—but what do you think of this? We extend your exclusive for a fourth year—"

Dow sat forward. Buchvan was singing his favorite song.

"—And you give *us* the exclusive option as your supplier—all at the same prices we've already negotiated."

"But you already have that by default," Dow pointed out. "Sure, I'd jump on that. We all know I need to worry about what happens with TradCo. If Brog's family, on behalf of the Sull children, settles for even a small piece of that company, there would be strong motivation to switch customers and help make TradCo more profitable. So, yes, it sounds good to me—but why would *you* want that?"

"To save more lives throughout the galaxy," Buchvan offered sagely.

"I'm lost again," Pirlhoff interrupted.

"Let's say the deal specifies that Pfivvel, Inc. is barred from owning or cultivating Zhasou plants. If Pfivvel were to acquire any, Dow would be required to turn them over to us—for free, no matter what they may have cost him."

Dow smiled. He was first to see the angle. "Even if I paid a lot of money for them, I'd still be motivated to get as much as I could for *you* to increase the supply so I can make money on the other end—and to save more lives, too," he added as a true businessman's afterthought.

Brog figured it out, grinning his approval expansively. "It would be unethical for the Governor of Seelius to arrange sales of cuttings to a company in which he was a principal."

Pirlhoff started to laugh, finishing, "But if he could get Assembly to agree to sell cuttings to Pfivvel—already a customer of the planet—then Dow would have to *give* us all he could buy!"

"You's a sneaky bunch o' y'alls!" Lival laughed. "I *alike* that!"

"As you said," Buchvan jabbed at Dow, "we *do* have the governor's ear."

Everybody chuckled and sipped for a moment. Then Pirlhoff added more soberly, "And Stava's a good young man, too. He'll want to save lives."

Dow held up his mug again as if to toast. "People, I don't know how long it will take us to infiltrate and saturate all the markets, but someday, *every* sentient being in the galaxy will be our customer!"

"Just think," Brog added, "medicine that even *tastes* good!"

*   *   *

Heilen circled the area directly over Seelosia, just beyond the atmosphere, checking his read-outs for activity. It was fairly routine—a shuttle from the Orbiter-two heading ground-side, two cargo carriers closing in after a long trek from the Beltway Sector, a small private craft whose owner Heilen knew well, and the usual space debris, some floating geostatically while the rest slowly orbited. Heilen had spent the last few hours tracking and intercepting odd pieces—some smaller than a Dilltom-pea—both for practice and because he hated the disorder of space litter. It was a typical day.

Heilen would have stretched out and relaxed, relying on his instruments, except that the *Seelosia-one* was about due to launch. After a few minutes, he received the signal. He did a fast sweep of the area, confirming with his read-outs, then signaled back that Brog was clear to lift off. Heilen would provide surveillance, defense if necessary, and act as escort for the direct flight from Caskentia to Seelius.

Brog was excited to be the pilot for Stava's and Buchvan's return trip to their homeworld. Throughout the time he shared a friendship with Sullrob, he'd never been down to the planet. Now that he was married to a Seeliot, he had a burning desire to see his wife's roots, her village, her people. Stava had insisted that Brog disembark and travel to the capital with him, but Brog convinced him not to push too much too fast. Sullrob's governorship assumption, Stava's immediately thereafter, and the changes both had ordered must have left a very traditional, conservative people reeling from change. Brog argued that Stava needed to solidify his base of power just a bit more—or longer—and get his people used to the idea of their governor having another life and family off-world before parading into the capital with more members of a foreign species.

Brog opened comm with Heilen once he was past the atmosphere. In a chatty mood, he was disappointed that Heilen cut him short to concentrate on surveillance. Sometimes it seemed the dark-skinned neo-Seelosian was overly concerned with security—until Brog remembered the image of his friend's ship exploding. If the likes of Ling Bozathorne would do something like that over lost Jurnama business, surely he would connive as deviously against the family that not only stopped his deal, but threatened to take control of his company away.

Heilen followed them to the Seelius terminal, then signaled his withdrawal and disappeared into the sky while Brog landed. Stava and Buchvan crowded around the controls to look at the external-view screens, both gratified and worried that a large crowd was again awaiting their arrival. As the ship touched down, they could see—then hear when the engine noise was cut—that the people were cheering the return of their governor. Brog wished them both luck, insisting he would wait until they reached the capital and had sent, through hand-comm, a signal that he was free to leave. Either he or Lafave, or maybe Heilen, would return in a quarter tenth-turn to pick them up—if the big Rep-assembly went well and no new crises delayed their departure.

The crowd erupted as the platform lowered. Stava whispered to Buchvan, "You're not acarrying a chestful of precious metals and still they acheer." He smiled, adding, "They must alike *us*!"

"Whatta ya mean *us?*"

They were amazed to see the streets again lined with people as they made their way to the capital. Stava's reputation had quickly attained legendary proportions. Though Seeliots were wary of change, they were starting to understand that sometimes it was necessary. They saw Stava as the man to lead them, somehow trusting his innocence and optimism. Their world had been wounded badly, loved ones lost, fear spreading across the continents. They needed to heal; Stava symbolized the beginning of that process.

Governor Stava spent his quarter tenth-turn ground-side working closely with Buchvan. He read and learned all of the parliamentary procedures and practices, met with key people from the various departments to hear their suggestions and ideas and accept their gestures of support. His demeanor with visitors was somewhat vague and non-committal, indicating only that he trusted the judgments of good, experienced people. Though he planned many changes and wasn't reluctant to speak against ideas he thought were not best for Seelius, he assured people he would always seek their wise counsel. By the time he stepped to the front of the great hall for his first official Rep-assembly, he already had the political reputation as a consensus builder who, nevertheless, had the strength of conviction to stand up to pressure and make the right choices.

During the morning committee meetings, rather than following Plekwag's example of hiding out until time for Assembly, he moved around with Buchvan, making suggestions and lending encouragement, giving strong hints about what his official reaction might be to various petitions with suggestions for how they might be amended to win approval. Throughout it all, he kept drawing on what he had learned watching Brog and Dow Pfivvel. His mentors were men who preferred to roll up their sleeves and talk things through *before* holding official meetings. Stava thought Seeliots could learn a lot from people like them—from citizens of the Consortium. Finding better ways to work together would be a good way to start.

Stava entered from the back of the great hall, bedecked in his custom-tailored ceremonial robe (thanks, Pirlhoff!), walking slowly up the center aisle, pausing to greet surprised Reps, touching shoulders, using all the names he could remember while learning many new ones. He wound his way to the front and stood before the crowd. By then, they had worked themselves into a frenzy again, chanting, "Gover-nor! Stava! Gover-nor! Stava!"

He opened with a traditional Celebration of Life, this time adding the *diversity* portion Heilen had first used at the wedding. He also surprised the crowd when, during the section about *memories*, after he covered his father, he added Plekwag. He explained that he had been studying the records and believed that, except for corruption with TradCo, Plekwag had accomplished much for the people.

Rather than listening to all of the committee's petitions and putting off his responses until the next Rep-assembly, he answered every request right there on the spot. Of almost a hundred, he approved all but two, making suggestions for how those could be resubmitted the next time. He was pleased to see how much effort had gone into finding the best ways to use Pfivvel's generous payment for the betterment of communities all across the continents. With that dispatched, he addressed the issue everybody was most eager to hear—what kind of changes did the new governor plan?

"I want to change how we accomplish our goals!" he announced, offering a wry smile. "I'll bet *that's* a surprise!" The crowd's tension broke with a hearty laugh.

It asure wasn't that *funny*, Stava thought. *They must have needed to laugh at their fears.*

Buchvan chuckled, too, likely not at the joke, but at how good the little Seeliot was becoming at working a crowd.

"Well, I *don't* have a lot to announce today because I want to involve all of you more in the process of making those decisions." There was a buzz of approval. "I have only one small request today and a proposal to consider for next time, but foremost I want to announce two changes."

He waited patiently for the murmurs to quiet, looking confident and relaxed as he took a pinch of Zhasou, sprinkled it into his mug, and took a long drink, wiping his mouth with the back of his hand. Almost as if cued, everybody in the hall took a pinch and drank.

"First, I will follow the tradition of assembling a cabinet of advisors to help navigate me through the many difficult decisions that must be made. But rather than choosing them myself, I want all of *you* to achoose—to choose whom you want. Every region's committee will elect, with every Rep voting, one advisor to the governor's cabinet."

There were more murmurs, then increasing vocal approval, and finally cheers of support. Stava raised his arms to quiet the crowd.

"Second, independent of the petitions from each committee, the cabinet and I will develop proposals for the benefit of the entire planet. I will bring these to you distinguished Reps and ask for *your* votes of approval!"

The crowd burst into spontaneous applause and cheers. Full voting power! Their jobs had just increased dramatically in influence and stature.

"Are there any who would speak against these changes?" He waited patiently, amused at everybody looking furtively around to gauge their colleagues' reactions. There was no dissent.

"Most proposals will be presented for your consideration. You will be able to go back to your regions to discuss them with the people you represent. Then at the next Rep-assembly, we will *vote* on them."

"Aye!" somebody shouted. Everybody else joined in the humor, shouting "aye" as if voting their approval. Though it was a joke, they already liked the feeling.

"Today, I will ask you to vote on a proposal to allow Pfivvel, Inc. to take twenty shipments of Zhasou cuttings in addition to his regular Jurnama cargo. We have learned that there is a dreadful disease that plagues people across the galaxy—but not us on Seelius because Zhasou prevents it. This is a horrible fatal disease that often kills children as well as adults. Pfivvel, Inc. will begin distribution of Zhasou medicine to save countless lives. Today, I will ask *you* to approve this sale. At the next Rep-assembly, I will ask you to approve the proposed method of payment for these extra shipments. All Reps who approve this sale, please raise one hand."

Everybody shouted the traditional "aye" as they raised their hands. It appeared to be unanimous. When he called for dissent, the unanimity was confirmed.

"We learned during the plague that the Consortium is very much more advanced than we are in medicine. I have since learned there are many ways we could help our friends and families, sickness we could cure, ways to enhance our health and longevity—" He suppressed a grin when he used the last word. He'd learned it from Brog during the flight down. "Pfivvel, Inc. is prepared to build a small medical university in the capital city for us, providing teachers from other worlds who can train us. We would expand this university ourselves over time—hopefully building more colleges in other regions—so we can share this knowledge throughout the continents and build upon it with advances of our own." The crowd started shouting more impromptu "ayes"—and it wasn't even time to vote.

Stava left by going through the crowd again, then retired with Buchvan for his final night of this trip in the governor's mansion. By the time they had managed to clear out supporters and staff, it was late and both were tired. They sipped some mugs of Zhasou tea, reviewing what had happened during the day. Finally, Buchvan set down his empty mug and stood up to stretch. "So is this governor thing harder than you expected?"

Stava smiled. "It's abeen easy so far. The hardest thing I've adone the last half tenth-turn was atry to abeat Jowda at centrifi-snag."

Buchvan laughed. "Well, this is only the beginning. You have a *lot* of work ahead of you."

"No akidding. He aplays *real* good."

*   *   *

A Mr. Heilen Hewed signaled that he was tracking the small, decrepit personal shuttle en route from Dilltomarius. Offering a friendly greeting, he appeared on his commuter craft's view-screen and smiled at the visitor. The gaunt, older woman who was piloting made friendly small-talk, saying she and her husband had retired and were considering moving to Caskentia. They would dock at Orbiter-two for a few days to meet with a Tijartian sales rep who promised to show some nice parcels of land. They chattered for a while about what a nice planet it was, then closed the comm before docking.

"Who was that, Ms. Clayjams?" Ling Bozathorne asked.

"Just a local commuter; nothing to worry about. Don't worry, nobody knows you're here."

CHAPTER 20

Heilen followed *Seelosia-one* back toward the terminal on Caskentia, vowing that he would personally supervise construction of a private launch-pad in the flatlands just north of habitat valley someday. The commutes were growing tiresome, but more so, the delays just to land or launch were getting longer and longer. This time, they had to wait for the retirees' decrepit vessel to launch, then for two shuttles from Orbiter-two to land.

They finally received clearance, so Heilen took his ship in first, securing it before wandering into the terminal to wait for *Seelosia-one* to come in. He watched the crowd disembarking from the shuttles, noting that most of the passengers were boarding an airbus with "Seelosia" on its display. It must have been another wave of applicants seeking jobs related to the massive expansion of greenhouse production. Heilen grinned at the sight. Seeing the name on a public bus made the existence of his family's ground-side dream seem all-the-more real.

Hovering by the group was a young Tijartian, maybe about fifteen years old, near as Heilen could guess. The spike-headed lad kept studying the rate-display and carefully counting the hard-wafs in his hand. He looked distraught, obviously not able to afford the fare. Apparently, he was traveling to Seelosia in search of a job, but his funds weren't enough to take him to his final destination. Heilen wondered how he would get back home—wherever that was—now that he'd used up most of his money.

Heilen continued to watch curiously as the young man looked around shyly. Whether he was too bashful or too proud to solicit from the other travelers, Heilen couldn't decide. He felt sorry for him, noting that he seemed almost on the verge of tears as he helplessly watched his employment competition board the airbus and depart without him. Looking around, the lad noticed an attendant who didn't seem busy, so he approached him to ask if there were any jobs at the terminal or nearby, even short-term, just so he could earn enough to move on. Apparently there was nothing else available; Seelosia was the only recommendation.

Heilen checked to see that *Seelosia-one* was still making its descent, so he wandered over to the young guy standing by looking perplexed and disappointed.

"Ha-low there! My name abeein' Heilen. I abet you abee havin' a name, too!"

The Tijartian backed away from the big man, looking somewhat scared. "Um, I um, I'm Tocso."

"Abee alookin' afore a job at Seelosia y'be?"

"Um, yes sir."

"Y'be *oooold* enough?" Heilen wondered, looking suspicious, but smiling.

"Yes, sir. I turned sixteen two days ago."

Heilen threw his arms wide. "Agood then! I abee agoin' to Seelosia. Y'can aride wit' me!"

The young guy looked cautious, backing away another half-step. He was torn between accepting the offer and being too scared of the big stranger. He started to stammer, still not sure how he would answer, when his eyes went big at the sight of two *purple* people walking up behind Heilen.

"Heilen!" Stava called. "Help, they're akidnapping me!"

Heilen turned to see Buchvan and the governor walking up. He laughed, "They acan ahave *you*. It abee only the *ship* ol' Heilen abee aprotectin'!"

"Who's your friend?" Buchvan asked.

"This abee Tocso, a fine young feller t'lookin' fer jobs at Seelosia!"

"Oh, well, pleased to meet you," Buchvan offered, reaching out and touching the lad's shoulder.

"He's Buchvan. I'm Stava," offered the younger Seeliot, repeating the shoulder touch.

"He abee aneedin' a ride," Heilen explained.

"Oh, well, acome with us, then," Stava offered. The threesome turned and started walking toward the private garage where they kept their vehicles. The Tijartian, still too nervous, watched them, unsure if he would follow or not.

Stava quietly said, "A-go on ahead," then turned and went back to Tocso. "Adon't aworry. We adon't alet him eat people anymore." Then he smiled his disarming grin and got the Tijartian to smile back. "Alet's a-go or they amight aleave us!"

They both hurried to catch up.

Noting the combination of purple faces and private garage with expensive vehicles, Tocso no doubt quickly figured out these must be important people at Seelosia. Maybe it would be his lucky day after all.

During the flight out to the valley, Stava befriended the timid foreigner, getting him to talk about his plans. It seemed he was an orphan who waited until achieving legal age before leaving a harsh group-home situation on his home-world to strike out on his own. Short of money, he desperately needed any kind of job so he could save up to pay for his dream of going to college and becoming a veterinarian. Stava enjoyed seeing the sparkle in Tocso's obsidian eyes as he talked about his apprenticeship taking care of animals back home before his mentor had died. His trip to Caskentia to seek employment had cost much more than he expected, leaving him badly in need of any kind of job, desperately hoping the greenhouses at Seelosia would be his opportunity. He either hadn't thought about where he would live or, without an obvious solution, was just hoping for the best. Heilen and Buchvan kept trying to listen in on the conversation between the two, wondering what common interest they'd found that made them giggle so much. Heilen smiled, at one point throwing his arms wide for no apparent reason and laughing out loud.

Once they landed, Stava quietly asked Heilen if he'd take Tocso to get something to eat while he went and talked to Pirlhoff and Selta about a job for his new friend. A few minutes later, Stava joined the threesome in the dining area for a snack. Tocso was being very polite, but obviously hadn't eaten in several days. Stava nodded knowingly to the other two.

Heilen responded with his Cheshire grin.

*   *   *

Time for his interview, Tocso was ushered into a small conference room. Pirlhoff sat at the front. Selta, several meters away, was playfully scratching a ween-shugger as it hummed and nuzzled her. Tocso's eyes went wide; he was fascinated by the sight. Later, there would be much good-natured conjecture whether it was the animal or the pretty young lady that most interested him.

Pirlhoff looked up from some papers, apologizing, "I'm sorry, I'll be busy a few more minutes. Relax and make yourself at home."

Pirlhoff watched out the corner of her eye as the Tijartian shyly approached Selta. "Um, what is *that?*"

"It's a Seelius weenshugger. You a-like animals?" she asked, offering to let him hold the little hummer.

He cradled it delicately, fascinated by the strange new critter, trying to contain his excitement. Selta got him to talk about his experiences with animals as an apprentice, impressed and pleased to hear that they both shared the goal of becoming veterinarians someday.

Pirlhoff was amused at Selta's infatuation with the newcomer. *Better not let her be the one to make the hiring decision*, she thought good-naturedly. *I don't think she'd be objective.* Satisfied that she had heard enough, Pirlhoff invited Tocso to sit across from her, noting that Selta watched with eager anticipation.

He answered her questions earnestly, assuring her that he would work *very* hard at any job opening if she would just allow him to prove himself.

"I understand you have no place to live," Pirlhoff pointed out.

Tocso looked both embarrassed and abashed. He probably didn't care if he had to sleep in the woods as long as he could have a job—but must be afraid his lack of stability and reliable housing would discourage Pirlhoff from hiring him. "No, ma'am," he answered, looking at his lap.

"Well," Pirlhoff started gently, "I don't think you're quite appropriate for our greenhouse jobs—"

He looked like he was on the verge of tears. Pirlhoff half expected Selta to shout, "Wait! Keep listening! It's okay!" But she kept quiet.

Pirlhoff continued, "But we have an operation here for raising and exporting those weenshuggers, and I would like to give you a chance to work with animals."

He lit up, filled with excitement and incredulity over the offer. He grinned at Selta, blushing as she smiled back assuringly.

Pirlhoff slid a sheet of hard-copy in front of him, indicating, "This is the salary and these are the benefits. Because you have valuable experience as an apprentice, I'll also offer housing and meals under one condition—"

He wouldn't care what the condition was, but he listened attentively, barely able to control his enthusiasm. After all, this was a job interview; one had to maintain a certain amount of decorum.

"You must enroll in a veterinary program right away—and do well, mind you—so you can repay our investment in you with important skills and knowledge that will help our weenshugger business."

He didn't have to think it over.

*   *   *

Later, out in the 'shugger building, Selta gave him a tour, then offered to sit and talk about their plans for the business.

"We aneuter them b'fore we aship them. That way, we adon't atake a chance on wild 'shugger populations accidentally astarting on other worlds." She smiled, adding, "And we acan ahave a monopoly on the business, too."

"Are they expensive to buy?"

"We amake a nice profit, but most of the cost is th'shipping."

He thought about it for a moment, gently stroking one of the little furballs, then suggested, "You know, we sure could sell a lots of 'em on Tijartia if people could afford 'em. Maybe someday we could set up a breeding place right on my old planet—or on *lots* of different planets."

"Yes, maybe we could," she said softly. Together, maybe they could . . .

*   *   *

Later that evening, Jowda walked down the ridge to where Stava and Yantanna played with Shuggy on the beach.

"Awho's th'young guy who amoved into the habitat?" he wondered. "I aheard he's a Tijartian."

Stava related how Tocso had come about landing his job.

"But awhy adid she alet him amove in?" he asked.

"She understands abein' young and ascared and not ahavin' family or even friends t'help. You're alucky with your dad and now all us Seeliots who would ahelp you out. Pirlhoff's just abein' a good person."

Jowda was satisfied. "Hey, y'think Selta will alike him?"

Stava grinned knowingly. "She's abeen with him all afternoon."

Yantanna spoke up. "Um, don't atell a'cause this is 'posed to be secret, but Selta tol' me she's in *love!*"

*   *   *

Heilen knew he should give up his shift and start relying on his staff to conduct all the patrols, but the novelty of having a security ship, especially one so state-of-the-art, was still too exciting. Besides, he didn't want to relax his guard until the legal battle for control of TradCo was over.

Might as well pick up another piece of debris—a wrench! How did that get out here? Monitor the flight paths of two freight-ships. Another commuter shuttle was coming up from Caskentia. That decrepit private vessel with the retirees was leaving the orbiter on a trajectory that would take them ground-side for more Caskentian real-estate shopping. Two Pfivvel Jurnama shippers were just launching from Seelius. He'd wait until the pilots were past the atmosphere and could relax a little before hailing them to chat.

His communicator chirped for attention. The read-out indicated it was from a private comm on the Orbiter-two.

Heilen activated the channel, automatically sending the required vessel identification code. "Heilen b'here!"

"Heilen! This abee Tarmin."

"Ha-low, Tarmin."

"Alisten here, Heilen. Abee asomethin' suspicious 'bout that private jus' aleft." The only private vessel that had left the orbiter all day was the one carrying the retirees.

"Ahow be?"

"'Posed t'be amarried, but she abee acallin' him *sir.* Athought not right. Aheard him acall her a name y'put on that list y'wanted me t'listen for."

"Awhat name?"

"Ms. Clayjams."

"A bitty thin ol' light-skinner?"

"At abee."

"Awhat's *he* alook like?"

"Abee a big big *big* beige-face—real fat fat."

"Bozathorne!" Heilen exclaimed under his breath. "Athank you, Tarmin!"

Heilen immediately alerted a private security firm he'd contracted on Caskentia. Several aircars deployed to provide extra patrols over the Seelosian region. He contacted the Pfivvel shippers and asked for their assistance. The big freighters wouldn't be worth much in a cat-fight, but they could provide rescue if necessary, and they sure could follow a small craft like Ling's no matter how far it tried to run.

He tracked the suspect shuttle as it dropped through the Caskentian atmosphere and set up a counter-spiral descent pattern. Though not an uncommon flight style, it bothered Heilen because each swing north took it directly over the Seelosian region. He dropped his own ship through the atmosphere and set up a similar spiral in the opposite direction, carefully calculating to pass over Seelosia during each loop at about the same time as Ling's ship. He registered his pattern with the terminal, set auto-pilot, and activated his weapons and back-up surveillance consoles. There were a lot of possible ways Ling might try to attack the colony—or he might wait for another day—but Heilen figured it would somehow involve subterfuge. It was Ling's style to wreak havoc, then go on merrily about his business, leaving only a cold trail.

Heilen continued to monitor his instruments, trying to anticipate every possibility. Glad he had bribed the appropriate controller for unauthorized access in advance, he tapped into the terminal's tracker system and copied the flight plan of Ling's ship, transmitting the data to the security aircars criss-crossing their way over the Seelosian valleys and flatlands. They also adjusted their patterns to coincide with Ling's passes closest to the habitat valley.

Heilen's trajectory was intentionally steeper—not suspiciously so for the new, faster craft—allowing him to close the gap as they neared the ground. He enhanced his external view to watch Ling's ship. It was obvious to his trained eye, on closer inspection, that the decrepit appearance was mocked up for effect. Ling's vessel was obviously outfitted with the latest and best.

Two more spirals to go. What could they be up to? Was Heilen just being overly cautious? Should he signal them for a friendly chat? That would tip them off that he was on to them, but what was better: averting what they might be about to do, or taking the chance they would try again another day—wiser for the tip?

Nothing happened. Only one spiral to go. No outward signs of intent. No weapon systems were being deployed. Heilen trained all weapons on the craft, tracking aim . . .   Too close to Seelosia to use burst fire, he would have to rely on beams.

Closer . . . closer . . . almost there . . . Now!

Nothing. They passed right over the habitat valley. Heilen realized he had a death grip on the control panel. Relax, big man, it was a false—

A cargo panel started to open—

Psssst! Boom! Psssst! Boom! A direct hit—not enough to destroy the ship, but it fused the sliding panel, disabling any weapon that might be secreted behind it.

Ling's ship was knocked out of its trajectory, yawing south on a wobbly course, descending in a low arc toward the hills. The aircars shifted their flight patterns to follow. Heilen came in low.

It was obvious the ship would have to land. It followed an irregular path just across the tops of the hills, then dropped into the next valley over one of the biggest lakes in the area.

A "Mayday" signal went out on the emergency channel just as the ship skipped like a schoolboy's flat stone across the surface of the water. Its angle slowed it without any noticeable damage. Never making it to the shore, it seemed to float for a few seconds before the aft engine core dipped down into the water, pulling the rest of the ship slowly under.

"Help! Help me!" screamed a deep-bass man's voice. A picture appeared on the view-screen. A fat man and skinny woman were strapped into the pilot's seats. He was frantically trying to claw his way loose. She was methodically operating controls, shutting down systems, activating emergency life-support. "Help! Send a rescue team!" To Clayjams: "Are we sinking?" To the screen: "We're sinking! Help! A reward for whomever saves—"

Clayjams suddenly vomited, then started to shake. "Ling," she cried between heaves. "It went off— went off inside—"

"No! It couldn't! Help! Get us out of here—" He started to shake, immediately followed by a violent spell of vomiting.

The aircars landed on the shore, standing by for instructions. There was no way they could mount an underwater rescue. The Caskentian authorities had already been notified; the transmission was being monitored at all critical stations. Heilen lowered his craft over the lake and hovered, watching his screen in fascination.

Ms. Clayjams regained her composure enough to speak. Her skin was turning ashy gray; rivulets of sweat streamed down her face. "Don't," she said weakly. "We're sealed in here— the virus— thirty days— leave us for—"

"Help me!" Bozathorne was crying now, blubbering like a baby, clawing at his face, shuddering violently.

"I'm sorry," Ms. Clayjams cried. "Virus gone in thirty— don't unseal—" She looked around as if for a comfortable place to rest, then shuddered again and slumped in her harness, gasping for breath, starting to bleed from her eyes and nose.

"Help . . ." he cried weakly, rubbing frantically at his eyes, trying to see through blood and sweat. "Big— reward— for . . .   Please help—"

Heilen tried to watch as exposure to virus six hundred-thousand times fatal levels caused their bodies to start breaking down. He had to look away.

It would be forty days before the Consortium government would raise the ship, encasing it in a quarantine shroud before it reached the surface, transporting it off-world for forensic study. An activated bio-capsule would be found aboard, designed to spew infected bio-pods for several kilometers every direction before self-destructing. The transmitter would keep working until the ship was salvaged, sending out the image of bodies shattering at the most basic cellular level, the murderous chairman and the woman whose last words were a warning.

After a young girl from a nearby town, randomly scanning for signals, discovered the grisly sight, local authorities decided to scramble the entire frequency. Nobody should see something like that.

Heilen wished he'd looked away sooner.

*   *   *

The death of Ling Bozathorne set off a vicious battle to seize the chairmanship of TradCo. There were several insider front-runners, heavily favored by certain blocks of shareholders, plus a niece of Ling's whose only support was to vote for herself with her own massive portfolio of inherited stock. Given the fragmented support for the others, it was looking like she would emerge victorious.

Except that the battle over SFP Trust still raged on. Without a chairman in control, those votes would have to remain uncast. The lawsuit for claiming SFP on behalf of Stava and Yantanna was contested by both TradCo, Inc. and the ancient Earth banking institution that acted as conservator of the account.

Brog's adoption of the Sull children was challenged; simultaneously, several dozen claims were filed for their custody. These came from private individuals and the government's social-services arm on Dilltomarius. The latter was unsuccessful, ruled out of their jurisdiction. The private claims fell one at a time under the juggernaut of Brog's attorney challenges. The adoption, handled meticulously from the beginning, was too airtight. It seemed nobody but Brog and Pirlhoff would take control of any spoils that might be awarded to the minor Seeliot children.

Citizenship challenges were mounted. While there was *some* precedent for non-Consortium citizens making successful financial claims against C-corporations, there were just as many examples of failed attempts. Brog's attorneys established that adoption by naturalized Consortium citizens automatically conferred citizenship on the children, regardless of their origin. However, since the claim was for birthright inheritance, a motion was filed by TradCo to declare birth as the point in time of considered eligibility. It was argued that neither Stava nor Yantanna were C-citizens when they were born. While the hearings about non-C beings' eligibility were going badly, the ruling on point-in-time came down in the Seeliots' favor. It was decided that a claim is official at the time it is filed. The converse argument was that people are free not to claim inheritances—birth or eligibility does not automatically make the claim for them. Stava and Yantanna made their claim *after* they became citizens—*after* Brog became their legal parent. A last-ditch attempt to confer special—and therefore exempt—status on Stava as a head of state fell flat, dismissed with only one hearing, appeal refused within a day.

The authenticity of the adoption documents was challenged. The SFP Trust archive provided ample evidence, including original thumb imprints, that Sam Fowler himself had executed the documents. Sam also had been smart about making sure his legal team had meticulously put together the package. Brog was impressed by the man's understanding of how his heir might have to battle to win the inheritance, admiring Fowler's commitment to his son. It was saddening to think that had never happened; the people Fowler trusted in the Consortium had destroyed all evidence of his intent soon after he died. The only people who felt sure, who believed the growing legend and dedicated themselves to destroying the last possible evidence, were generations of Bozathornes—the people who stood to lose the most if their ancestor's partner's progeny ever came back to claim their legal due.

During a hearing in which Stava's and Yantanna's identities were challenged, Seeliots including Buchvan and Pirlhoff testified to the authenticity of Sullruff's family Chronicles. Ultimately, they were accepted at prima facie value, accurate for their content but not proving of possible omission. It was ruled that the standard twenty-one days' notice would have to be published on Seelius, giving any other people who claimed to be related to Sullruff the opportunity to come forward. Brog's legal team surprised the court—and their adversaries—by showing that notices had already been published the same day the claim was filed. Only three days remained. Unless other Seeliots came forward, SFP Trust would be turned over to the claimants, to be held in trust and controlled by their legal guardians, Brog and Pirlhoff Pawligan. The value of TradCo stock skyrocketed amid speculation of big changes.

In the end, the actual awarding was anti-climactic. Brog most enjoyed the reaction of the banking officials, suddenly his best best friends in the world in spite of that pesky, unsuccessful legal challenge. They suddenly learned that their biggest competitor had already been awarded the contract to administer SFP—renamed "SullTrust." Brog thought the raft of VPs would literally break down and cry.

Though control of Stava and Yantanna's stock was awarded the day before the big board election, most shareholders assumed Brog would allow the principals of TradCo to go about business as normal, content to sit back in his ignorance and collect dividends for his children. Nobody noticed that he'd purchased several thousand shares for himself, making his voting block fifty and one-millionth's percent.

They were all surprised to see Brog appear at the shareholder's convention on Earth, leading in Stava and Yantanna, numerous other purple-faced citizens, and his own children. Naturally, *everybody* at Seelosia wanted in on the long, expensive trip to Earth!

Five grueling hours later, Brog Pawligan was named chairman of TradCo. Some shareholders were intrigued and excited, but most were upset, concerned about their investment being in the hands of a mere novice.

"As your new chairman," he announced, "I want to assure you that I intend only two significant changes in how we do business." Brog looked out into the auditorium, straining to see through the bright lights in his eyes. He was flanked by his family sitting patiently on the dais. Dow Pfivvel stood off to the side with Buchvan. "First, we are going to make an acquisition. TradCo will buy Pfivvel, Inc.—a very successful company with which most of you are familiar—and make it a division of our company. Once the transaction is complete and there is no longer any conflict of interest, I intend to resign and elect, with my majority votes, Dow Pfivvel to assume the chairmanship of TradCo!"

What started as a dull roar grew to a crescendo of cheers. The more the shareholders thought about it, the more they liked it. They had more confidence in Pfivvel and his impeccable reputation and track record than they ever had in the Bozathorne family. The latter had obtained power through inheritance, but Dow Pfivvel played an integral part of his own family's rise to success. The addition of the Pfivvel brand-name would add a high-profile image to the company, too, something Dow would be sure to preserve.

Brog continued, quieter, more serious. "The other change is that TradCo is going to start caring about its customers, its employees, its local communities. We'll rely on Mr. Pfivvel to show us how to do this. Someday, TradCo will be a company my children can be proud of."

Over the next few days, Brog let the lawyers do most of the work. He and Dow had to stay close by to advise and sign and meet and discuss, plus there were lots of public-relations meetings for winning support from key shareholders. Buchvan used the opportunity to learn as much as he could about how Consortium business is transacted. Stava insisted on participating, too, until Brog sent him away to go on some of the Earth tours with Pirlhoff and the other youngsters. It wasn't *every* day a young Seeliot would get to see the Grand Canyon.

And when Jowda described Niagara Falls, well, that certainly was a must-see!

*   *   *

"Gover-nor! Stava! Gover-nor! Stava!" The crowd in the great hall was chanting their approval of the new cabinet. After covering regular business, Stava had one-at-a-time introduced the key advisors sent by each region. Every Rep in the room knew—had a hand in choosing—at least one official flanking the young governor. The concept of replacing Plekwag's hand-picked cronies with elected advocates had proven enormously popular in villages and towns around the planet.

At a gesture from Stava, the cabinet members retook their seats at the back and sides of the dais. Stava held his arms up for quiet. "I have important knowledge to share about our history!" He paused for effect. "All across the galaxy, there are planets colonized and populated by humans. Over time, through natural or controlled selection, many have acome to have unique features or distinctive appearances, but one important fact remains. They are all human; they are people. We are *all* just *people*."

He paused again to give what he'd said time to sink in. Most people caught the reference; some were stunned, others started to shout. Mostly, they were surprised and curious. Finally, they quieted down to hear more.

"The medical researchers who helped us learn about the plague and its cure determined that, genetically, even we Sellosians are just as human as my friends from other worlds!"

"How can that be?" someone shouted.

"We are *Seeliots!*" yelled another.

"It has been a mystery until now. After searching the old records, we finally understand. It was more than a thousand turns ago—more then thirteen-hundred turns—that colony ships were sent to a nearby planet called Dilltomarius. Sixteen ships were sent over a period of several turns. All sixteen reported back that they had arrived. But we checked the early records on Dilltomarius and can only find references to fourteen of those ships. We checked the logs and track-files of the other two and learned they had been launched together. Their transmissions reported difficulty during the trip with bursts of radiation storms, sustaining some damage to their ships, almost not reaching their destination. Each of these ships acarried more than three-hundred settlers."

Stava looked around. The audience was rapt with attention. "I have listened to the final contacts from those two ships—more than a dozen messages sent after they landed. Both had sustained substantial drains on their power sources because of the radiation, reporting that their transmissions would have to end until repairs could be made. They said damage to their navigation systems had forced them to land using only visual contact, and that they had not yet located the colony. These mostly contained routine information, but the final communication included some personal comments. I want you to hear what she said." He nodded toward Buchvan, who activated an audio-broadcast playback.

A soft, pretty voice filled the great hall. She recited a date and log time, then went on to say, "Captain wants me to alert you that power is failing. We will have to shut down the cell today while we continue to make repairs. We'll transmit again *if* we can fix the damage, but if we don't this may be our last communication until we find the colony."

The audience was silent, listening intently, a sense of history, a defining moment filling the room. The young woman's voice continued to speak. "We still have no contact from the others. If we cannot repair the cells, we will have no way to travel in search—no way to scan for the ships that landed before us. We may have to rely on them to find us. In the meantime, if we are stranded, we will begin our own community right here. Everybody is so excited about this wonderful place— so anxious to set up habitats and start planting crops, building our future, I think most don't even care if we find the colony or not. I guess I feel sorta the same way. This is a very pretty place. The pink light from the moons at night is beautiful reflecting in the water. There are so many gorgeous flowers and native animals—" The woman's voice laughed, adding, "I even have a new pet! It's the sweetest little purple furball—and he sings! Uh oh, I see the systems are shutting down, so I'll sign off for now. Don't worry about us. Even if we can't repair the ships, we have a good group of people. We'll survive. We'll build our own world and prosper—" The transmission ended mid-sentence.

Stava looked across the crowd. There were some murmurs, but most seemed too stunned to comment. Stava spoke again.

"We have so much we can alearn from our family throughout the galaxy. And we have so much to share, to be proud of, to show people everywhere who the people of Seelius are!"

The Reps started shouting approval, some chanting Stava's name, others buzzing with excitement, anxious to tell the story at home in every region.

Stava smiled, raising his arms again. "I have two more things before I let you go to share this knowledge with friends and family. First, we will set up a program to recognize student achievement. Outstanding boys and girls all over Seelius will be able to receive an award—a trip with their families to visit a resort on Caskentia—to see another world and ameet people from across the galaxy!"

Yow! The crowd *loved* that idea. Every parent in the hall suddenly had big plans for his children's spare time.

"We will also allow travel to every free citizen of Seelius. It will not be inexpensive, but you may vacation to worlds of the Consortium. You may choose to *live* on another world—to study or enjoy—and return if you want, to share with us all what you have seen and experienced."

It was another hit! Suddenly, everybody in the room was reprioritizing their plans for the family savings.

"Now, before you go, I have one last thing. I awant you to ameet my *brother* and my best friends!"

A door opened off to his side. Through it nervously filed three boys. Jowda led, followed by Tocso and Jak. The boys stood on either side of the governor, looking around, intimidated by the crowd, but excited and thrilled to be there.

The stunned crowd stared open-mouthed. One of those boys had beige skin and *brown* hair. Another had grayish skin and odd-looking spike-like appendages where his hair would be. The third was so dark as to be the cream from bar-choc beans, with jet-black hair wound in tiny, tight curls! And they were just boys! Nervous, fidgety boys. Jak was so excited, he inadvertently jumped up and down several times.

Stava touched his friends on their foreheads, accepting return gestures from each. Then he hugged them one at a time. The buzz in the crowd grew steadily louder, indicating approval.

Stava whispered something in Jowda's ear, then raised his arms to quiet the Assembly. Jowda stepped forward, still nervous, and said, "I have always awanted to asee Seelius, ever since—" He looked at Stava, affection softening his face. "—Ever since I got my best friend and new brother from here. Athank you for awelcoming me!"

The crowd erupted with cheers. Jowda and the others were *very* welcome. Very welcome, indeed.

A lot of aspects of Seeliot life started to change that day. People had a new way to see themselves, a new understanding of who they were, their place in the galaxy. For many turns, for many generations to come, little boys were named after a true Seeliot hero. In homes all over the planet, parents hovering over their children struggling with schoolwork would be heard encouraging, "Now study hard, Stava, and someday you, too, might change our world."

CHAPTER 21

The aircar lowered gently onto the side of the slope, careful not to touch any of the majestic trees lining the ridge. Stava Sull Pawligan was just where they expected, sitting under the biggest tree of all, his back to the trunk, the Sull Chronicle on his lap, gazing absently across the lake-filled valley. Brog and Jowda stepped out and wandered over, sitting down on either side of the young governor.

"Whatcha doin', son?" Brog asked quietly.

Stava just shrugged.

"Hidin' from Pirlhoff, I bet," Jowda offered good-naturedly. "He aworks hard as governor all week and soon's he agets here, Pirlhoff agives him his schoolwork t'do, too."

Stava smiled. "Naw, I'm anot ahidin'. Sometimes I'd a*rather* do school than all that governor stuff."

"You been workin' on the Chronicle?" Brog asked quietly.

"Yeah. I afinished th'part 'bout my dad."

Brog reached over and gingerly opened the last part of the book, quickly reading the final entry. "This is wonderful, son. Sullrob and Sullruff would have been very proud of this."

Stava nodded, then looked across the lake again while Jowda read it. "Y'know, Stava. Y'can't acall Sullrob the greatest governor of Seelius, a'cause that's *you*."

"Not me," Stava corrected. "Sullrob astarted the changes."

"Yeah," Brog interrupted, "but you're the one leading the difficult struggle, the one making a *real* difference. I don't think your dad would've minded," Brog offered with a wry smile, "maybe *sharing* that accolade with you. He would be very proud of what you're doing."

Stava shook his head. "Sometimes it adon't aseem alike I'm adoing *anything*. I acan't ever get everybody t'agree on *anything!*"

Jowda grinned. "Pirlhoff always asays *that's politics!*"

Stava chuckled. "Yeah, she keeps asayin' it t'me, too."

Changing the subject, Brog said, "Stava, everybody's waiting for us back at the house. There's something we want to do and—well, we need your help."

They all stood and started toward the aircar before Stava hesitated. "One more minute," he said quietly. Jowda watched, nodding approval. Stava fished in his pocket for the laser, began to carve under the four names already on the tree. He started with "Brog Pawligan," then added, "Pirlhoff Pawligan, Selta Pawligan, Stava Pawligan, Jowda Pawligan, and Yantanna Sull Pawligan." He hesitated for a moment, then added the date and trotted over to board the aircar.

Back at the beautiful home they'd moved into only months before, built right into the side of the hill, a view toward the waterfall framed by majestic red mountains, surrounded by lush flowers from many worlds, they found the girls fussing around Pirlhoff. Everybody went into the dining room where Brog gestured for them to take seats. He stood awkwardly at the head, trying to find the words, Pirlhoff at his side.

"Well, I wanted us all here at once to get this thing started."

Pirlhoff was crying! Why was that? Then she smiled through her tears and reached up to squeeze Brog's hand.

He smiled down at her and continued, "I figure the little one's gonna have *lots* of questions about who he is." He reached down and gently stroked Pirlhoff's slightly swollen abdomen. The baby was just starting to show. "We need to write down the answer," he finished, turning to pick up a large, bound volume from the counter. He set it in the middle of the table. Carved into the cover, it said "Pawligan Family Chronicle."

Jowda noticed the girls were starting to cry, too. Why do girls get like that anyway? Then he noticed Stava was, too, and, well, in spite of himself . . .

"But first," Brog added, "I think it's time for a Celebration of Life."

*   *   *

Brog just laughed, exclaiming, "Well, I'll be damned."

Shar Calvin laughed, too, shaking his head. "I noticed it last week, but wasn't sure 'til I talked to Orman about it."

The medical researcher confirmed, "There's no doubt, it's the Zhasou."

"And the younger they are," Shar added, "the faster it happens."

But little Greggo was simply delighted. He jumped out of his bed and ran into his mother's room to utter the immortal words that would be echoed by billions of children all across the galaxy.

"Look, Mama! I'm turning purple!"

The Fresh Ink Group

Publishing
Memberships
Share & Read Free Stories, Essays, Articles
Free-Story Newsletter
Writing Contests

Books
E-books
Amazon Bookstore

Authors
Editors
Artists
Professionals
Publishing Services
Publisher Resources

Members' Websites
Members' Blogs
Social Media

www.FreshInkGroup.com

Email: info@FreshInkGroup.com

Twitter: @FreshInkGroup

Google+: Fresh Ink Group

Facebook.com/FreshInkGroup

LinkedIn: Fresh Ink Group

About.me/FreshInkGroup